PLAYING DAD

Chals Wontewe

authorHOUSE®

AuthorHouse™
1663 Liberty Drive, Suite 200
Bloomington, IN 47403
www.authorhouse.com
Phone: 1-800-839-8640

First published by AuthorHouse   2/19/2009

ISBN: 978-1-4389-4945-1 (sc)
ISBN: 978-1-4389-4946-8 (hc)

Printed in the United States of America
Bloomington, Indiana

This book is printed on acid-free paper.

To the memory of Charles Paul Wontewe, my father, a highly disciplined man who taught me self-discipline. And to the memory of Hannah Tigidichira Makwo, my mother, the very epitome of love, who taught me love. If I fail the test of discipline and love for others, it is not because my parents were bad teachers but because I was a poor student.

Chapter One

He came out of the office humming Chris De Burgh's *You Look Beautiful*. He even sang the chorus:

> *You look beautiful*
> *You look wonderful*
> *You're like an angel heaven sent to me*
> *You look beautiful*
> *You look wonderful*
> *I've got a feeling this was meant to be*

A born again bachelor, as he called himself, it was surprising that most of the songs he sang were love songs. "They are tiny windows that let us into the inner you. What your blank face masks so well the songs reveal." That was what Brenda had told him.

"Meaning?" he had asked her.

"Everything about you paints the picture of a man to whom romance and women have no place. The songs suggest an inner yearning for love."

"Really? Amusing theory, I would say."

"The truth," she insisted, ignoring the dismissive implication in his tone.

"There are thousands of women out there who will be willing to be my girlfriends. Why would I have a yearning for love and not go out and have a friend?"

"Because you are trying your damned best to shut out the feeling of love."

He looked at her and she looked defiantly back as she held his gaze. If it was a test of stamina or determination she won as he shrugged his shoulders and turned away. He did not agree with Brenda that singing love songs meant suppressed love. He was certain he did not know how love felt anymore. Then why the love songs? Because, he told himself, musicians composed more love songs than any other songs. You only have to check the collections. *Sonia Spence Sings Love. Love Ballads. Romantic Love Songs.* One day he checked the titles on the Old Blues and Forever Oldies collections with her and she was forced to agree that most of the songs were love songs. He emphasized the point by leaving a *Power of Love* collection on her desk one day. Not that any of those arguments shifted her position on his emotions.

"If you take out songs like *The Gambler, Coward of the County* and *Reuben James,*" he told her as part of his defence, "most of Kenny Rogers' hits are love songs. *Lucille, You Decorated by Life, Islands in the Stream, Daytime Friends, The Long Arm of the Law, We Got Tonight...* I can go on. They are all love songs. You can even say *Coward of the County* is a love song because the man in Tommy came out only when his Becky was raped. It's the same with Don Williams. *Some Broken Hearts Never Mend, It Must Be Love, You're My Best Friend, Say it Again, In the Shelter of Your Eyes...* Again the list is endless. Ginger Williams, Sonya Spence, Thelma Houston, Johnny Nash, Elton John all sang love songs. Bryan Adams, Phil Collins and Michael Bolton all sing mostly love songs. Mariah Carey, Celine Dion, Cyndi Lauper all sing love songs.

"When I sing Jim Reeves you accuse me of thinking of dying young. When I sing love songs you don't see me loving life but nurse unexpressed love in my heart. If I love I will go out and express it."

"I will not argue with you but I know what I see," she said in her usual defiant and definitive mood.

Brenda was his Administrative Officer. She was young, in her early thirties. She had a Bachelors degree in Secretaryship and worked for three years elsewhere before Dan poached her with a challenging JD and a generous salary. Among all the staff in the organisation Brenda was the one who most understood him and responded positively to his invitation to the staff to treat him as an equal. In the culture in which they were brought up, and in the culture of the organisations they had worked in before joining Horizon Leadership, you were not equal to your boss. Another term Dan did not like and had to keep explaining why he was not a boss. In the case of Horizon Leadership Dan was not just their senior but their employer as well. Treat your employer as an equal? Most staff just chuckled at the thought that they and Dan were equal. But they often enjoyed the games played between Dan and Brenda. They admired Brenda's courage and respected Dan for the level of tolerance of the way she related with him, really almost like an equal. She would hold a position if she disagreed with him and if she ran out of ammunition to continue the fight but did not agree with Dan she would announce that she could not go on but she did not accept his views.

"*Donner est un mot pour qu'il a tant d'aversion qu'il ne dit jamais je te donne, mais je te prête, le bonjour.*"

"What was that you said?" Brenda asked.

"One of the most philosophical sayings any man ever made."

"And I am sure the one who made this so called philosophical saying is a crank, like you."

"One of the worst. And therefore one of the people most worth listening to."

"Who is he and can you translate what he said into easy to understand language?"

"Sure," Dan said with all the charm he could muster. " 'To give is a word for which he has so much dislike that he never says I give you, but I lend you, a good day.' You want the name of the crank who said that? He is a character in a play called *The Miser,* written by one of the best creators of comedy, Molière."

"And can you tell me how that quote is related to our discussion?"

"I thought the relationship was as clear as daylight."

"But Dan, you know me. I am a dunderhead and always the last to see the obvious."

"Instead of what Molière said about the miser it can be said of you that concede is a word for which you have so much dislike that even when you see that you are wrong and the other person is right, you would never utter the word concede. The way out for you is to say I cannot go on but never I concede."

This Saturday he had spent the whole day in the office preparing his material for a training coming up in Kenya. It had been quiet, as only Saturdays can be, and as with most weekend work, he had been surprised with the volume of work done in just one day. It seemed more than he ever could do in a week. But he knew it only seemed as he

3

actually would normally do the same amount of work in a day even on a weekday. The difference was that on a weekday he would not be able to do one piece of work continuously. He would be interrupted with a lot of other work – visits, phone conversations, email correspondence and even meetings. Unfortunately at the end of the day the tendency is normally to focus on the main piece of work and to let the work that was expected to have been done but which was not done to influence one's feeling. But he knew that on the normal weekdays if he added the work he really planned and did to the unplanned or 'unseen' work he had done, the total would equal what he normally did on a weekday. Or almost equal it. He said almost because he knew that if you have to move between jobs you lose time.

He whistled, hummed or sang whenever he felt happy with his work, either the quality or the quantity. In today's case it was both. So song naturally sprang like a geyser in his heart. He told himself that the presence of song in his heart signified he was still young, at least at heart, and that he was human. That latter feeling, that he was human, was important to him as he had heard comments about him that suggested the opposite.

When he was done whistling, humming and singing *You Look Beautiful* he found himself singing Crystal Gayle's *Sound of Goodbye*. *... And it ticks and it ticks and it ticks and it ticks, And it ticks with the sound of goodbye...*

After locking the office he went round the block inspecting doors and lights even though nobody else had come to the office that day and he had not opened any other office. The check was just a mechanical attitude, part of his general attitude to risk management. He looked at the imposing Training Centre buildings but did not go over there. He had nothing doing there. There had been three different training sessions going on there over the week. But they all ended the previous day, Friday, and this morning all the participants had left. In fact, a good number had left the previous evening. He smiled. Most workshops ended that way. If they ended early enough on the last day and there was transport, you could be sure some participants would leave, always eager to be back to their homes. He did not blame them because even though he had no home as such, he felt relieved each time he found himself returning to Tamale. And sometimes the journey would seem very long, longer than it really was.

When he arrived at about 9:10 this morning the last person among the participants at that week's three training sessions had left. The staff of the Training Centre were busily cleaning and arranging the various rooms used for training. They were also busy cleaning the bedrooms, checking faults and changing sheets. Now he did not have to check anything at all. He had cultivated in the Training Centre team something that had become their culture so that even when he was away you could be sure that the staff would give all facilities under the Centre all due attention. A veteran of workshops and training sessions himself, Dan listened to participants' comments about little things that irritated them or distracted their attention from the main purpose of their stay in facilities – to learn. He observed what made participants happy. He drilled all that into the staff of the Training Centre. Initially they did not appreciate his concerns and thought he was unduly fussy about nothing. But he kept checking and brought staff back to do things they had intentionally ignored or overlooked. Doing those small things became a religion among the staff over time. When he shared with the staff some of the summaries of evaluations of training that had taken place there the staff began to see the real importance of those seemingly unimportant things and gave them attention not because Dan insisted on them but because they saw how they linked with the fortune of the Centre.

There were two separate entities in the same yard and they had their separate premises. There was the Horizon Leadership Development Service. He did not call it an NGO as many people were wont to do in order not to pay tax. He registered it as it was, a consultancy. Then there was the Horizon Training Centre. This was a facility that provided rooms for training and accommodation for participants. Both were owned by Dan but he kept them separate. Each had its own structure and its own staff and its own account. Both were doing well but the consultancy was doing better as it had very few fixed assets whose depreciated value had to be treated as cost each year. The capital investment in the Training Centre was huge.

He was now again whistling, humming and singing *You're Only Lonely*. He opened the Toyota Landcruiser and put the laptop in the passenger seat when he noticed the school girl approaching. When he was moving to the car he had noticed her talking to the security at the gate but had not paid any attention because he thought she might be asking for directions to a house in the neighbourhood. He did not pay her that much attention either when she came towards him. She must be looking for one of the staff of the Training Centre. But he politely waited for her.

"Good afternoon, Sir," she greeted and curtsied as female students were taught to do.

"Good afternoon, young woman," he responded, equally politely. "Who do you want?"

She twirled the belt of her dress, made from dress material, in her fingers as she spoke. "I came to see you, Sir."

He was surprised and did not hide it. Maybe she was the daughter of one of his staff or a relative of one of them who was bringing a complaint. Or maybe she was a distant relation whose parents had schooled her how closely she was related to him and had strongly encouraged her to visit him and introduce herself. And after that all her financial problems would be taken over by him. Even as he thought about this he admitted they would be right. He supported education and would provide support for the education of any relation, no matter how distant, provided the student was serious with their studies.

"You came to see me? Who am I?"

She did not look away even though she went on twirling the belt. "You are Mr Dan Apeatu."

He blinked. Yes, it was him alright. And very soon he would know who had sent her and why.

"Who sent you?" he asked as he walked round the vehicle and came over to her side. The driver side of the vehicle was away from the entrance. The girl had stopped on the other side, on the passenger side. It did not occur to Dan that by the way the girl had stopped she put the vehicle between them. Besides the nervousness as suggested by how she treated, or maltreated, the belt, was she also afraid? Afraid of him?

"Who sent you?" he asked again as he came to stand by the girl.

"Who sent me?" she in turn asked as she lowered her head, tilted it to one side but raised her eyes to look at him.

"Yes. Who sent you? We have never met before. Yet you say you came to see me. Did someone send you to me?"

"No, Sir." She dropped the belt and put her hands on the bonnet of the vehicle and looked at him.

"Nobody sent you?"

"No, Sir."

"You came to see me yourself?"

She had lowered her head again but she now raised it again. And held his searching look. "Yes, Sir."

He relaxed and softened his look. "Okay now, young woman, you have found me. What did you come to see me about?"

Silence. He also kept quiet. And she did same. And he also did same. It was obvious if he did not break the silence the girl would not break it. He was not experienced in this type of confrontation. Dan lived a regulated life, with little contact with other people other than in professional contexts. He lived alone in his house. He left the house in the hands of private security guards everyday when he came to work. The guard on duty and the night watchman were his only companions in the evenings when he returned home. But they kept to themselves in the security room by the gate while Dan stayed indoors. He rarely left home when he came home from work.

In the mornings he drove to work. Alone, most often. Sometimes he would see someone he knew either going into town or going in the direction of his office. He would give such people a lift and they would probably have a lively conversation in the vehicle. He spent most Saturdays, if he was in Tamale, in the office. Sundays he went to the first mass at Holy Cross Parish. Even though the Cathedral Parish was nearer his house he went to Holy Cross. Matilda attended church service in the Cathedral Parish.

The first mass was known informally as the religious mass. It was the mass for those who really went to worship. They were mostly elderly people and Dan was one of the few younger ones who attended regularly.

From church he would normally drive right back home, into his fortified castle. He would visit families that had something to celebrate, like a wedding, a birth and families that had suffered some misfortune or the other, like a death, ill health, accident or theft. Otherwise he crawled back into the shell of a hermit. He had very little social life and he was not sure how to deal with the young lady. If she went on refusing to answer his questions what did he do? Just get into the vehicle and drive off? What if she created a scene?

In an even more gentle tone he said, "Young woman, please tell me what you came to see me about.'

She raised her head and looked him directly in the eye and told him, "Sir, I came to ask you for my school fees."

He started to smile but it did not grow as the girl's face darkened with seriousness. He examined her closely now. She would be in her teens. Mid teens? He could tell she was in Tamale Secondary School because her dress was made of the school's cloth. Slim. She brought her hands together and her fingers were playing a meaningless game with each other.

Eventually he smiled but the girl refused to raise her head to look at him again. After making the announcement she had held his look for many seconds before she lowered her head. It stayed lowered.

"You came to ask me for your school fees?" he asked, more restating her statement than asking a question.

She raised her head and said, "Yes, Sir."

"Why are you coming to me for your school fees?" he asked.

She did not answer. So he said, "Young woman, there are a lot of men in Tamale. And there are a lot of women as well. Why choose me to come and ask for your fees?"

She again raised her face to look at him before she answered. "Because you are my father, Sir."

He put his elbows on the bonnet of the vehicle and actually rested his weight on it. He felt his knees folding and he had to make a conscious effort to keep them firm to support his weight. He did not take his eyes off her, wondering if this was a joke. But he wondered why this strange girl would come and play a costly game with him. Or was she related to one of the staff who probably was standing somewhere laughing at his discomfiture?

This time the girl did not lower her head. She looked back for as long as Dan looked at her. As if daring him to challenge that.

After an uncomfortably long time he asked, in disbelief, "I am your father?"

This time she lowered her head. "Yes, Sir." But she raised her head almost immediately.

"Young woman, are you playing a game?"

"What sort of game, Sir? That you are my father?"

"Are you serious? Am I your father?"

She shrugged but her tone was severe when she spoke. The initial signs of nervousness and the impression of fear were completely gone. She looked straight into his face. "That is what my mother told me. Why should I just walk up to any man and not beg him but tell him I am coming to him for my school fees?"

It seemed to make sense but ... "What is your name?

"I am Marian."

"Marian what? What is your second name?"

"I am Marian Wepia."

He felt relieved. She was not Marian Apeatu so she could not be his daughter. "Then how am I your father? Who is your mother?"

"My mother is Kadua. She is Matilda Kadua. She said you are my father."

His legs really felt like folding and he had to lean forward to put his weight on the vehicle. He did not trust his legs to support him.

The girl did not notice the effect of her answer on him because she was too engaged in her own worry. She either tortured the belt or kept doing various things with her fingers. She looked down, too self-conscious now that she had told the man who she was and exactly why she had come to him. She had never imagined that her task was going to be easy and that she would walk up to him, tell him who she was and why she had come to him and he would say hallelujah, welcome, I confess my sins and I now take up my responsibilities. Her mother had told her that the man was their father. Her mother's friends had said the same. And she had seen their birth certificates which had his name as their father. But their mother had also said he was a bad man, an irresponsible man who caused the break up of the marriage and shirked all his responsibilities thereafter. In that case he was likely to insult her or, at best, invent a reason to be rid of her without helping her.

No, she had not thought it would be easy. She had considered approaching him several times in the past but the stories her mother told put her off each time she thought of making contact. The idea had been introduced to her by Rosa, her mother's friend, who one day caught her weeping because her mother could not pay her fees. Rosa had asked Marian why she did not contact her father to ask for help. Rosa had made it seem like the father was well to do and helpful to people. She had said that she was sure he would help Marian if only Marian contacted him. But her mother screamed at her and told her to let the thought perish in her mind. She forbade Marian from making any contact with him.

"Why should you contact him now?" she had screamed. "For how many years has he abandoned you? Why didn't he ask about you all these years and you now want to contact him? Why do you think he will now accept you after turning his back on you all these years? If you are a fool, contact him and give him the chance to make your life even more miserable. Foolish girl! Contact your father? Who told you that you have a father? Who put that stupid idea into your naughty head? I want you to get rid of the thought the same way you put it in your head."

That had been last year and as her mother could not pay the fees and her misery in school kept growing and it affected her ability to study, thought of contacting the man her mother said was her father kept growing. There was nobody else she could contact who could help her. Her mother's company was all single mothers who were mostly drunkards as well.

For as long as she could avoid him, she took her mother's advice. Till this week when they were told all those who did not pay up all outstanding fees by the end of the next week would be sent home. She knew the headmaster meant what his said. If she did not pay she would be sent home. So she had the unpleasant alternatives of being sent home and meeting the lion. She considered the first option. One, she was certain she would be sent home if she did not settle up. Two, she was sure if she was sent home, nobody on her mother's side could pay the fees for her to go back to school. She did not know of anybody outside her mother's circle of friends and relations who could help. She did not know anybody who was related to or was a friend of the man said to be her father. Even if she did, it would be even harder to approach such a person. And say what if she approached him or her? If she could not establish her relationship with the man himself, could she establish her relationship with him if she approached his friend instead?

Her choices were narrowed down to one; contact Mr Dan Apeatu. In the case of not contacting him the consequences were certain, dismissal from school. In the case of contacting Mr Apeatu, the possibilities were many. He may turn out as her mother described him, harsh and not wanting to have anything to do with her. It may be the case that he was not her father at all as her mother and her friends claimed and he would be angry with her for her mother's lie. But it could also be the case that he would help her. Nothing was certain.

When Dan felt sufficiently steady to move he stood up and used the remote control to open the locks of the car's doors. The doors locked automatically when closed for five minutes. He asked Marian to get in the vehicle while he walked to the driver's side and got in. Marian was confused and looked at him for a clue about his behaviour. Was he driving her to Matilda to confront her about the stories she had been telling Marian? She searched his face but it was inscrutable – she tried hard but she could not read anything in it. It took her about two minutes to give up and then give her attention to the interior of the vehicle. Very beautiful and very comfortable if she had felt relaxed enough to enjoy her seat. But she was tense and did not notice those things. She however noticed the music. It was beautiful, the sound was very good, and it was soft music. It told her a bit about Dan and she looked at him once again. And once again, she read nothing from the look on his face.

She was relieved however when he took roads that did not lead to their house. It occurred to her that Dan may not even know where they lived. When he took the road leading to their school she initially felt relieved but then became anxious again. He had not told her anything but was just driving her back to school. What next? Was the school where he was going to give her a verbal lashing and tell her in no uncertain terms to get rid of the idiotic idea that he was her father? Then what? If Dan did not help her, what would her future be? Suddenly at this critical point where what Dan said might mean the end of her dream of getting an education, getting a job and moving out of that unhealthy, unhappy state of poverty in which she was growing up, she became afraid. Even panicked. Her thoughts ran riot. What if he said with finality that he was not her father? Beads of perspiration formed on her brow even though the evening was cool and the A/C of the vehicle was on. In a moment of wild inspiration – or call it desperation – she hit on the idea of pleading with him for help even if he denied a relationship with her. The relationship was not as important to her now as the payment of her fees. She would kneel and plead, if need be. She would beg for her fees. She would not make an issue of their supposed relationship. She did not know it to be true, that he was her father. But she needed money for her fees and right now he was her only hope.

Except that where he was sending her to would make pleading very difficult. If he parked anywhere in the school campus there would be students passing by at all times. And kneeling and pleading, with so many students passing by, who would all stop passing by and actually watch her, was not going to be an appealing spectacle.

"How old are you?"

The question was unexpected. It came during one of the few moments in the last minutes when she took her eyes off him. She had spent the last five minutes or so scrutinizing his face for any sign of what was going on in his mind.

"I am sixteen years, Sir" she said, the Sir being said stronger than she had intended to.

His thoughts raced back in time. Sixteen. It could be her. "Do you know your exact date of birth?"

"Yes, Sir." She told him.

He had named the daughter Marian. The date of birth was same as the date of birth of his daughter. He would find out details later but right now, his lawyer friends would say that the girl had established *prima facie* evidence that she was the daughter he and Kadua gave birth to sixteen years back.

He brought the vehicle to a stop by the former junior classroom block, which was also close to the dormitories. And asked Marian, "How much are your school fees?"

For answer she pulled out a sheet of paper and gave it to him. She had come prepared, he could see. The bill. He read it quietly. Before handing it back to her he checked the name on the bill, Marian Wepia. It was only now that he recalled that Matilda's surname was Wepia.

12

"The bill is for last year. Are the fees for this year the same?" he asked the girl

For answer she simply brought out another sheet of paper. After reading it he raised the seat control lever and pushed his seat back and groped for his briefcase in the backseat just behind his seat. He opened it and brought out his cheque book. The girl watched all this initially with anxiety, then wondering. He did some additions on a sheet of post-it note – Marian did not know what that yellow pad was – and wrote out a cheque which he handed over to Marian.

"I don't have money for the fees. I mean cash of that amount. But you cash this cheque during the course of the week and take out the money for the two years' fees. The rest is your pocket money.

"I am travelling tomorrow and will be away for two weeks." He brought out a card holder from his brief case and took a business card out for her. He underlined two numbers, the office phone number and his house phone number. "Buy a GT phone card and call me when I return so that we set up a meeting. You either come to my office or I come here and meet you. We will discuss a number of things."

"You said I come to your office or meet you here in the school?" she said more than asked.

He was putting away the cheque book, the post-it note pad and the pen. He paused and looked at Marian before replying, "Yes, I said that."

"I can't come to your house?" Her mother had said he was alone. He had not married, like her mother. *I was the only one who was stupid enough to marry him. Which worthy woman will marry him?* But the man she had been with so far did seem like one many women would like to marry. But if her mother was to be believed, he did not have a wife. So she could go to his house as well.

"Do you have any problem with coming to my office or my coming here?"

"Oh no!" she said rather quickly. After what he had just done, until she got to know him well she did not want to push her luck. But if she were his daughter, as his attitude – the questions about her age and exact date of birth, and his not arguing about paying the fees and his paying the two years' fees – would seem to confirm, then she should be able to visit him at home. That would come later. But even when it did come up later it was not an issue she would push.

"Call me three weeks from now and we will arrange a meeting. It will either be here or in my office."

The voice told her it was final and she did not make any effort to argue.

"Mr Apeatu."

He had just put back the briefcase. He turned and looked at her. "Yes, Marian."

"I want to say thank you very much. I am very grateful, Sir."

For a brief moment something close to a smile lightened the face of Dan. It impressed Marian.

"That is okay, Marian. When next we meet I will want to find out more about your studies, what course you are offering, if you are serious with studies, your exam reports, your brother and many more. But I will like to find out more about you and your mother, why you are using Wepia. Be a good girl and take your studies seriously now that your fees have been paid."

She had opened the door and come down from the car. She curtsied as she said, "Thank you, Sir. I am serious with my studies. Only my fees were worrying me but now that you have paid them, I will be even more serious. Have a safe journey, Sir."

A group of students was passing by and some softly hissed, "COSD!"

Marian turned and rebuked them but they only kept repeating it. She ordered them, rather loudly, to shut up when they persisted. When they passed Dan asked what they said.

"They were teasing me."

"I heard them say something but I did not hear exactly what they said," Dan said leaning towards her.

She looked embarrassed. "They said COSD."

"And what does that stand for?"

She was shy as she said this. "They thought you were my boyfriend. It means Car Owner Sugar Daddy."

He smiled. Students are inventive. But naughty as well. On the other hand he did not think in this case they were really naughty. They must have observed older men come to the school in cars after the young girls, teenagers, like Marian. So they were not being naughty if they called him a car owning sugar dad. That did not stop him feeling slightly irritated that they should think he would be chasing a student. He was forced to look at the face of Marian for the first time. He had to admit that she had a beautiful face. She needed more flesh on her but if she built it she would be a lovely lady who could attract car owning older men wanting to be sugar daddies.

He said thanks and drove off, the previously serene look in his face replaced with a cloud of one million questions. They would even multiply later that evening, he knew. When he went to bed.

As for Marian, she waved and watched the car pull into the road and drive off. Her heart was in song mode but her mind was in turmoil. Her mother had said of the man said to be her father that … None of that seemed to have fitted the man who just drove off. He had not denied being her father. In fact, by asking about the change of the surname he implied acceptance of her. He spoke about her brother whom she did not mention throughout the brief chat with him. He had paid the fees for two years and not just for one year. And without her asking he had given her a generous amount of money as pocket money. Who was he?

But when she took the road to the dorm the turmoil was gone and it was the song in her heart that filled her whole being.

Chapter Two

S he lay in her bed and looked up at the ceiling, not seeing it. The noise in the dormitory did not reach her. Some hours ago she had set out to seek assistance from a man alleged to be her father. She did not know what the encounter would be like. All she wanted was money to pay her fees so that her education would not have to come to an end. She would not have looked for him or in anyway come near him. But the certainty of her dismissal from school if she did not do something radical made her look for him and to ask for the fees.

She was happy. She had got the fees. She had got pocket money, more money for her pocket than she had ever had in her life. And he even asked about her studies. He said she should be serious. Since her admission at Tamale Secondary nobody had been interested in her education. If she told her mother she was dropping out of school, Marian was sure, her mother would not bat an eyelid. This man cared. Or seemed to care. He did not argue about the fees. He just gave her a cheque when he saw the bills. She was expecting to plead for the fees for the past year and he paid for the two years. She still could not tell what it was that made her take both bills with her.

For the first time in her life she had a man in her life. Father.

She turned and lay face down. Father. How did it feel to have a father? She did not know. As the tears rolled down her face and were absorbed by the pillow she turned her face to face the wall so that a curious student looking at her would not know she was crying.

She recalled their time together. Most of the time he had worn a face one could not decipher. There had been moments when Marian had felt afraid of the look in his face. She also remembered the one moment he smiled and how he looked a kind person then.

Who was he? *Look at you miserable things! You are lucky I saved you from that your worthless father. I should have left you with him. And*

*he would have roasted both of you by now. Why has he never asked about
you? Why has he never come to see you? Why has he never sent you people
any money? I should have left you with him for him to starve you people to
death. That is, if he did not beat you to death first...*

*You! You are a monster. Just like your father. You are a monster like
your bad father...*

*Sometimes I curse God for bringing me into contact with such a useless,
completely irresponsible man. Now he has left me with two miserable
children who are so naughty...*

A father. In her case, what did it mean? She knew what it meant
to have a mother. At least in her case, it meant hell. In other homes
a mother was a comforting figure. Not in their home. Was this man
really their father or did he give the money because he was a kind man
who knew the condition of their mother and knew that if he did not
help she may really drop out of school?

But he asked about her age and date of birth. Oh yes, and even
about the change of surname. He *was* her father. She had found her
father and he did not eat her. He did not roast her. He did not indicate
he would be happy to starve her. But she also admitted that his looks
most of the time had suggested he could be a hard man.

She had a cheque for a handsome amount in her box. She would
cash it on Monday and, for the first time since she came to this school,
not feel the pressure of unpaid fees. She would pay the fees on Monday
and walk out of the bursar's office a proud student. She would still
have some money in her pocket, the largest amount she had ever held
in her hand. Thanks to this man who was her father.

She daydreamed through the night's entertainment programme and
spent a restless night. She wished the night would fly into the next day
for Monday to come very quickly. She kept imagining herself holding
the wad of money in her hand. Then a fear set in. She had never been
inside a bank before and she did not know how money is cashed. What
if there was a problem with the cheque and she was arrested by the
police? Dan would have travelled by then and there was no way she
could prove he gave her the cheque. But, even more alarming to her,
assuming he had given her a bad cheque! The fear of having problems
in the bank made her no more wish for time to fly. She was happy for
it to crawl.

On the Sunday she begged a colleague for her Ghana Telecom phone card and called Dan in the morning. Her heart thumped as the bass drum of an army band as she dialled the number. She was considering cutting the call when she heard the first sound of ringing at the other end. She was wondering if Dan would not be angry with her. What was she going to tell him?

But she did not have the opportunity to cut the call as Dan responded with the very first ring. "Hello, Dan Apeatu here."

"Good morning, Sir," she said in an unsteady voice.

"Good morning. Who is on the line?"

"It's me, Sir."

"Who is me? Don't you have a name?" He could hardly keep the irritation from his voice.

"Please, it is me Marian. I am the girl who came to your office yesterday and you gave me the cheque to pay my school fees."

"Hello Marian. What do you want again? There is no problem with the cheque, is there?"

She almost stammered, this girl who ordinarily described herself as a 'hard girl.' "I don't know if there is a problem with the cheque, Sir…"

"Then why are you calling?"

She resented the impatience in his voice.

"Please, Sir, I wanted to find out if there is anything I need to do before sending the cheque to the bank."

She listened as Dan hesitated at the other end. Finally he said, "Yes, you have to write your name and address at the back of the cheque. You will also have to sign it. It is an open cheque which means you don't have to pay it into your account…"

"I don't have an account, Sir."

"I didn't expect you would have." Surprisingly to the ears of Marian, he had lost his impatience. "As I said, it is not a crossed cheque so they will give you cash when you present it at the bank. But I have written your name on it so it can't be cashed by any other person unless you endorse it. That is, unless you write your name and address at the back and sign it. But you go to the bank tomorrow and ask for Veronica Baah. She is a staff of the bank. Explain to her that you are … That I gave you the cheque and asked you to contact her for help to cash it.

She will help you. She will show you where to write your name and what to do and she will cash it for you."

"Thank you, Sir." Her sigh must have been very audible at the other end, she was sure. But she was surely relieved.

"Marian."

"Sir."

"Is there anything else you want to know?"

"No, Sir," she said hurriedly.

"When you make a call and the person you are calling answers, Marian, identify yourself. Say something like this is Marian Wepia speaking. Don't say it is me. Only someone you have been speaking frequently with on the phone will recognise you by your voice."

"Thank you, Sir."

"Have a nice week, young woman and remember to study hard."

"Thank you, Sir. You are very kind, Sir."

And she meant it. She had been terrified to call him but had been even more terrified to go to the bank on Monday without knowing what her fate would be. The initial reaction of her ... at the last minute she changed from thinking of him as her father to Dan. She remembered that at a point during their conversation Dan had changed what he was saying midstream. He had said "explain to her that you are ... That I gave you the cheque." Had he meant to say that she was his daughter? Would they ever connect as a father and daughter? Would she ever 'own' him as a father? After this vacuum in her life for this length of time, would she have a father?

Anyway, back to her review of the conversation. Yes, it had not started well but it sure did end well. His asking her to contact Veronica was helpful. Who was she, his girlfriend? Maybe that was why he would not ask her to introduce herself as his daughter. Whatever she was to him did not matter to her. *Is there anything else you want to know?* From the impatience at the start of the conversation he ended up offering to give assistance in any other way she wanted.

She looked into the skies and smiled. *When you make a call and the person you are calling answers, Marian, identify yourself. Say something like this is Marian Wepia speaking. Don't say it is me.* Learning. The next time she made a call she would be prepared. Thanks, Dad. Or thanks, Dan.

The monster who would beat his children and if they did not die starve them and if they did not die roast them. Up to this point in their relationship Marian noted that he did not fit the picture their mother painted of him. It would be interesting to listen to him tell his side of the story one day. It would be interesting to know who he was.

She got an exeat on the Monday to go home for her fees. The school was only too glad to grant her the exeat. "But come back with the fees," the Housemistress had warned. "Don't use the school fees as excuse to go and loiter in town."

Marian did not let her impatience show. Some people just don't observe, she told herself. She had been in this school for one year and one term now. She had gone only once to take an exeat. The Housemistress taught them Core English and should have noticed she was a serious student and not one of those who would ask for an exeat to go into town and loiter. The Housemistress had met her on a number of occasions on campus when the students were granted open exeat. And she had explained to the Housemistress that she did not go out of the campus because she had nothing to do in town.

She borrowed money for her taxi into town. She knew she could now afford to pay any money she borrowed. Her courage failed her when she got to the bank. The number of vehicles parked in front of the bank made her afraid again. The crowd inside the banking hall made her even more afraid. She stood for several minutes to observe things before making any move. She walked timidly to one of the counters to ask about Veronica Baah. The man she approached mechanically called Veronica for her.

"Oh, you are Marian," Veronica said when she introduced herself. "Dan called me yesterday and told me you would be coming. Have you endorsed the cheque?"

Instead of answering she gave the cheque to her. Veronica examined it and showed her what to do. She was afraid about signing her signature on an important document like that. It was the first time she had to sign her signature on so important a document. She was not sure her signature was good. She was not sure her signature was consistent and if they would accept it. With her heart beating quite fast, she carefully signed her name.

Veronica took the cheque away and Marian waited behind the counter. As she waited she noticed that the people were in a queue. The person at the head of the queue would move to one of three cashiers anytime one was free. While majority withdrew money a few brought large sums of money to be deposited. She noticed someone tried joining the queue in the middle by pretending to be talking to a friend who was in the middle of the queue but other customers shouted at him to go to the end of the queue. His friend tried explaining that they came together but the other customers just shouted him down.

The queue went as far back as the entrance of the banking hall. So she would have to go behind the last person. Just then Veronica returned with the money for her. She had cashed it and put it in a polythene bag.

"Take it out and count it," Veronica advised but Marian was nervous about displaying that amount of money in public and so she said it was alright.

"What is Dan to you?'

Marian was not expecting that question and it heightened her feeling that Dan would be her boyfriend. As she thought earlier, not that it mattered to her. "He is my uncle," she lied. If they were lovers she did not want to destroy the relationship.

"Your uncle is a good man," Veronica told her. "Study very hard and make your uncle proud. He is a break, you know, and if you pass your exams very well you will make him proud."

"Yes, Madam. I will study hard."

Of course Marian did not know that Dan was a break. She knew nothing about him. And she was serious about her studies not because it would make anybody proud but because she did not like the condition in which they lived. And she knew that if she could become a doctor she would not have to live like her mother. It was the threat of the death of her dream to become a doctor that had generated the desperation that gave her the strength to contact Dan despite the monster image of him painted by her mother. Study hard. For Dan's sake. Of course, she realised she now had a second reason to study hard. Someone was paying her fees and had told her to study hard. Another person, not even related to her, had given her the same advice. People were taking an interest in her studies – and paying for them. She would work even harder, she resolved.

She wanted to buy some provisions before going back to school but she was afraid to go shopping holding so much money. So she went to the taxi rank and joined a taxi to school. She went straight to the dormitory where she sorted out the fees and locked away the rest of the money that belonged to her. From there she went to the bursar's office and paid the fees. She made the cashier and the bursar happy. She looked for the Housemistress and showed her the receipt and received a good girl remark from her.

Marian should have been a happy girl. She should have been a very happy girl. But she was more a confused girl. She was not unhappy. She was simply confused and terribly so. All her life in her mother's hands she had known nothing but insults for even things she did right. Let her mother come near her doing anything and it was all 'Stupid girl! Stupid girl!" At a point in time Marian thought her mother should have named her Stupid Girl instead of Marian. She called her stupid girl more frequently than she called her Marian. But this man who was her father, or was said to be her father, gently taught her when she did not know.

Marian and her brother's upbringing had been a difficult one in many respects. Since she began thinking about searching for her father to ask him for her fees, she had tried recalling memories of him, in vain. She must have been four years old when he left them. She thought that at that age she would have stored some memories, some events, something about his face, but despite the hard work she put into the exercise she recalled nothing. When eventually she was going to meet him she had hoped that seeing his face would bring back some lurking memories but it hadn't.

After the separation of her parents, her mother had a number of boyfriends, drunkards they too, like her mother. When their mother came home to her alcohol induced world, nobody else existed. She and the children lived in a single room which served both as sitting and bedroom. Her mother would come home with one of her men friends, both of them highly tipsy, and sit in the room and engage in romantic acts that should not be engaged in in the presence of children who are so young. Men fondled her mother's sagged breasts, caressed her thighs and almost undressed her in the presence of the children. Some of the men spent the night with their mother in the bed and had sex with her while the children lay on the floor, experiencing the act.

There were a few embarrassing occasions. One night Marian heard a slap on the bed followed by, "Stupid man! Why do you insert your hands in my vagina? Why can't you use your penis?"

Marian had coughed but it did not change the conversation. The man had asked, "Have you ever heard of fingering?"

To which her mother had replied, "Dirty man! Fingering! Am I a small girl? If you will fuck me go ahead and fuck me and don't' finger me."

Her brother could sleep through all those annoying acts, but not Marian. Sometimes her brother slept very early, most often before the acts started. Many times they not only made loud love, they also engaged in disturbing conversation. One night, besides the obvious sound of love making coming from the bed Matilda told the man, "I don't like having sex with you when you drink."

The man had asked, "Why?"

"You take such a long time to discharge. My vagina is all sore."

The man had laughed and said, "It is not me. It is your fault. Your vagina is no more as tight as a young girl's. It is difficult to discharge with you."

Sometimes they moaned and talked loudly as they had sex. *Slow down, you are hurting me. When they were circumcising where were you and you refused to circumcise? I don't want an uncircumcised penis in my vagina. Open your legs, woman. Thrust harder, and faster!*

On another occasion Marian and Daniel – her younger brother who had been named after their father, according to their mother – had gone into the room together in the afternoon only to find their mother and one of her men naked, and having sex, not on the bed, but on the bare floor. They hadn't stopped and before the children could beat a retreat both of them reached their orgasm with loud cries followed by sighs.

Marian had had to complain to one of her aunts, Auntie Gina, an aunt who could tell Matilda the truth and who Matilda detested.

"Why don't you have the least sense of decency, Matilda?" the aunt had asked. "The brain in your head has been replaced by *akpeteshie* so that you don't know what is wrong? How can you bring your men home and have sex with them in the room in which the children are lying? What are you teaching Marian? To be a prostitute?"

Matilda had been unrepentant. "So I should not live if I have children?"

"Listen to the idiotic things she says! Is having sex in the presence of the children the only way to live. What will you do if you came in one day and found your daughter and a boy having sex the way you and your drunken men have sex in her presence?"

Marian was about ten at the time.

"Let me ask you this," the aunt had said. "Don't your men have homes to which they can take you? Are they so useless that they don't even have homes and they must follow you home and sleep with you in the presence of your children, one of whom is a growing girl?"

Even though Matilda had argued with her sister, in the end she stopped bringing men home. But used it against the children as often as she could. "You idiots say I should not bring my friends home because I have children. Who told you fools and your foolish aunt that women who have children must kill their feelings?"

Matilda completed ten years of basic education. At the time she was in school basic education was six years of primary school and four years middle school. After that she had admission at the Nurses' Training College in Tamale and trained as an Enrolled Nurse. Those who completed secondary school and did nursing did a three year course leading to the award of the State Registered Nurse certificate. The Enrolled Nursing course was eighteen months.

Initially, State Registered Nurses, called SRNs, worked for one year after completion and went on automatically to do a one year midwifery course. It was not so for the Enrolled Nurses. Enrolled Nurses had to work for about ten years to qualify to go for the midwifery training. But even then, admission was not automatic. Candidates had to sit an entrance exam, an exam which Matilda failed year after year till she stopped trying. She complained loudly that she was not taken because she refused to bribe the Principal of the College. Her mates were surprised at the change in the Matilda who had topped their class. Drink and the loss of interest in any form of studies had replaced the once bright student in NTC with an out of date nurse who could not even pass her exams into midwifery college.

"I don't even have enough to feed my children," she complained. "Where will I get money to give to someone whose salary is far higher than mine? If he gives me money I will be happy."

But her daughter believed that her mother did not really pass the exam. Could never pass. Marian did not ever see her mother reading, either text book or a newspaper. She did not study and would hardly know what is current trend in nursing. She also knew that her mother spent most of her money drinking and it was drink and not the children who made her unable to raise money to offer a bribe. Marian's aunt once explained to Marian, "If you write the midwifery school entrance exam and you pass well, you will be taken. Matilda will never pass. If you don't pass and you still want to become a midwife, there is a small backdoor through which you can go in. You offer a bribe. But your mother doesn't save even a pesewa. How can she buy her way through?"

So her juniors in the service went on to become midwives and became her seniors. But Matilda did not worry. She did not envy those who came from behind her to be ahead of her. She had only one concern in the world, her drink. The world became a bad place if she could not afford to buy drink and there was nobody to offer to buy it for her. If she had her glass of spirits and her colleagues bought flashy cars and built storey buildings, Matilda would not feel envious of them.

Her own children called her The Wailing Mama. They had heard that the late reggae star, Robert Nestor Marley, had a band called The Wailers. Some children said the band was called the Wailing Wailers. Marian did not know if it was true or not but they started calling their mother The Wailing Mama. Initially they called it behind her but later they realised she did not care what they called her.

"Eh, Wailing Mama!" Marian would exclaim. Daniel did not call her that to her face.

Others in the neighbourhood called her various names. Some called her the TWN, the Wailing Nurse. Others called her DJ of the Year, conferring on her a greater ability to talk more than those presenters who hosted radio programmes and talked more than presented the programmes. Matilda hardly stopped talking. One day Marian told her that she believed her mother's lips would swell if she stopped talking for just thirty minutes, if she was not asleep. In their dorm, one day when Marian was lying in bed and struggling with a Maths problem she overheard her mates sharing jokes. She went on working and did not mind them till one started a joke about children who boasted about the talking prowess of their respective mothers. According to the one telling the joke, two boys were arguing about their respective mothers' talking abilities. One claimed his mother was the most talkative woman on earth but the other contested that claim, claiming instead that his mother was the most talkative. To convince the second boy how talkative his mother was, the first boy claimed that his mother could talk for three hours on any topic. The second boy had retorted that that was nothing compared to his mother's ability. He said his mother could talk for three hours on *no topic.* Marian wished she could meet those boys to tell them how what their mothers could do was nothing compared to what her mother could do.

Chapter Three

When Dan went home the afternoon Marian came to see him he spent the whole evening recalling the events of the afternoon. One thought that came up initially was con. He had been conned by someone who may not have been who she claimed she was. He felt he had not been critical enough of the young woman and that he had given out a cheque to someone who may have been a con woman. He did not even know if she was a student of Tamasco as Tamale Secondary School was popularly called.

But he dismissed that feeling. She was a student of the school. If she wasn't she would have been alarmed when he drove towards the school. Besides, the students who teased her must have known her.

He forgot of her as he went about packing things for his travel the next day. He spent part of the evening in the study going over the information he had obtained about each participant including their work experience and what they wanted out of the training. He checked the slides he had prepared and went through the sessions for each day, taking note of when he expected to bring in other activities. He went over his notes, the guide he had prepared, for the five days training. Satisfied, he went to the bedroom and checked what he had packed. He took the post-it note on which he had listed things he must do in preparation for the trip and found he had done all of them.

Even though he travelled frequently he did not like travelling. For several reasons. One, he did not like the packing prior to the travelling. He always had a feeling that he would leave something crucial behind. The fact that it had not happened trip after trip did not reduce his apprehension each time he had to pack. For each trip he had the feeling that was the trip on which he was sure to leave something behind that would affect the training. He felt that even though that sad event had a very low probability of happening, each time he packed successfully increased the probability of the next trip being the fatal trip.

To reduce this risk, he kept certain items constantly packed in his two travelling bags. He used two bags for travelling. For domestic travel of short duration he had a smaller bag. For domestic travel that would take him away for weeks and international travels he used a bigger travelling bag. In each bag he kept a number of pants, about five in the smaller bag and about seven in the bigger bag. He also had a towel, sponge, soap, toothbrush and toothpaste, slippers, comb and toilet soap in each bag. He even kept condoms in the bags even though he had not needed condoms in the past twelve years. Sometimes when he was packing the bags or checking their contents he would notice that the condoms had expired, or had become soft from being rubbed during his travels. He would then throw out that batch of condoms and put in fresh condoms.

To ensure successful packing he would normally start packing for a trip about a week before the trip. A whole week before the trip he would spend one day over the weekend listing what he needed to take along and start putting them in the bag. Over the next week up to the day of departure, he would keep checking for things to put in the bag and throw them inside the bag. He would have a post-it note on which he would constantly be adding things he needed to carry and cross out items on the list as he put them in the bag.

A meticulous man? But he still worried stiff that he would, on each trip, leave behind something that would spoil the event he was going for. Each time he left home convinced that he had packed everything he jokingly asked if he would not get to the airport and check in his luggage and forget to check in himself. These thoughts started when he remembered the joke about the man who was so forgetful that when he got home one evening wet, cold and tired, he put his umbrella to bed while he himself leaned against the wall and went to sleep.

He went a couple of times between the master bedroom and the sitting room checking things. As he moved between the two rooms and kept up his packing, he consulted the post-it note occasionally, sometimes crossing out some entries and adding new ones at other times.

Dan was a meticulous person, something his Maths masters in secondary school and his lecturers in the university had commented on. That nature had served him well as an accountant but when he moved on to become a leadership development consultant, he had to make radical changes to that nature. His experience in doing that had also helped to inform his facilitation of leadership development. His message to the participants was always clear and strong, you can make yourself a leader. You can always develop a strong secondary nature. You can change yourself.

And he was right. When he did his first personality test, the DISC test, his highest scores were in S and C. He scored virtually nothing on I and D. The facilitator of the session explained the score to him. He was a good systems person. He worked best where there were clear rules and strategies. He liked the known and not the unknown. He was strict about how things were done. He was uncomfortable working in contexts where there were no clear systems and he was irritated by people who did not respect procedures.

He found the results of the test accurate and the description of him true of him. Sadly true of him. Sadly because at that time he had embarked on his journey to become a leader himself and to train others to become leaders. One of the courses he attended explained in its own terms that a leader was one who continued the journey where the track ended. A leader beat a track for others to follow. And he did it not by deciding irrationally which direction to go but in a visionary way hitting on the right direction. His nature, being comfortable only in known territory, following well beaten tracks, did not cast him in the mould of a leader. When he enrolled to study Creative and Collaborative Leadership he was not so sure it would change him that much. He knew it would change him. It would provide him some ideas to allow him to work on changing himself. He knew he would use the ideas and would make the effort to change himself. How much the change would be was what he was not sure of.

But he tried the recipes in the book like a devout Catholic from confession praying his rosary. He found the book *Color Outside the Line* revolutionary and he followed its suggestions. He read a number of other books on developing creativity and found in each doable things which he followed like a novice in a monastery. Among some of the things he had suggested to himself, and the lecturer, to practise was taking on new hobbies and these included drawing. In secondary school he had not liked Art and was glad when he entered Form Four and could and did drop Art. Now he had committed himself to take it up even though not in a context in which someone supervised him.

Surprisingly this was one of his huge successes. As an accountant he did not need diagrams. As a facilitator and trainer he thought he needed to be able to capture some of the issues and ideas in graphic form. He admired those who could translate their thoughts into pictures, summarizing hundreds of words into a simple, descriptive visual object. Initially he made the conscious effort to capture his ideas in diagrams. Over time he found himself impulsively doodling as he chatted with people. And found himself capturing not just what he was saying but what he heard as well.

Over time he agreed that the original Dan Apeatu had radically changed and he was quite comfortable with the unknown and did not fear challenges as he did previously. In training sessions he enjoyed the questions that followed his presentations as much as he enjoyed the prepared presentations. Participants gave him feedback how much they were impressed with his answers to questions he may not have prepared for and therefore how much he knew his subject.

Even then, Dan still prepared for each of his training sessions with the same meticulousness as he did his first training session. Even though he did change originally prepared outlines as the training got underway, he did not stop preparing for each new training by thinking through his sessions from the beginning to the end. And he never stopped putting in several hours to packing, ensuring he put in every tiny aid needed for his training.

Later that evening when he had bathed and put off the lights and dropped into bed he was sure he was going to have a deep sleep. Several hours later he was still tossing and turning. He was very far from sleeping. Dan had never learnt why things he thought he had got over came back in those vulnerable moments in bed to haunt him. As he fought for sleep it was scenes from the afternoon's encounter with Marian that kept coming back. He saw her walking up to him when he first raised his eyes and caught sight of her. He recalled his initial thoughts that she was looking for someone else. How wrong.

He recalled how she said she had come to see him. *You are Mr Dan Apeatu.* And that had been alright. *Sir, I came to ask you for my school fees.* He still felt the surprise he felt at the time. *Go and see Dan. He is great at helping people in need. He will help you.* Others may even state uncharitably. *He is fucking rich and he has nobody to spend the money for him. If he doesn't help people like you what will he do with the money? Go to him. He will help you.* And thought of that had caused him to smile. Now in bed he did not smile recalling that part of the conversation.

What followed had hit him hard, really hard. *Because you are my father… What sort of game, Sir? That you are my father?… That is what my mother told me. Why should I just walk up to any man and not beg him but tell him I am coming to him for my school fees?… My mother is Kadua. She is Matilda Kadua. She said you are my father.*

Each pronouncement by the young woman had built on what she said previously. *I came to ask you for my school fees. And I came because you are my father. I am serious about it. Why should I walk to you, and not to any of the many men you yourself said are in Tamale, and ask for my fees? And why am I not saying I came to beg you but to ask you if you are not my father? You have to take me seriously. My mother is Matilda Kadua. And you know her father is Wepia so if I am Marian Wepia and not Marian Apeatu I am Matilda's daughter. And her daughter by you …*

He tossed again and changed positions but that did not seem to help. He felt physically uncomfortable immediately and he knew that, somehow, for him, on this night as on many nights in the past, sleep had been murdered.

His agony would be made worse over the coming days by the fact that he had not prepared himself for this confrontation with his past. He had never made any plans for engagement with the children if it was necessary. After a while they and their mother had simply ceased to exist in his life. He had never again thought of how he would react to them if they had to reconcile.

The events of many years ago came flooding back and he gave up any attempt to sleep. Instead he got out of bed, went to the bathroom for a pee and then went to the sitting-room where he sat in the darkness and let his past flood over him.

His most vivid memory was not a pleasant one. He was standing outside the door of the room he and Matilda shared. It had been her room. She rented it and he moved in. As her husband he paid the rent but the landlord knew Matilda as his tenant. So she had the right to throw him out and she felt no mercy at all when she did. He still could not tell what the cause of her decision was. They had been married for five years and had two children, the younger one only a few months old. They had not quarrelled even though their five years together, living in a cloud of alcohol, had not been very harmonious. It had not been a bitter five year period either. It had just been as one would expect of any two alcoholics trying to create a family.

Dan was a very bright student, right from primary school to the university. He came from a small community in the Navrongo district, Saboro. In primary school he had skipped the next class on two occasions. From Primary Class Two he had been sent straight to Primary Class Four, skipping Class Three. At the end of that year he had been promoted straight to Class Six. When he arrived in Form One, the headteacher had called him and asked him what he wanted in that school. He was so small, the youngest in Form One and in the whole school. When Dan had explained in very good English who he was he instantly became a pet of the headteacher. In Form Two, he was one of a few pupils in that class allowed to sit the Common Entrance Examination, the exam that allowed entrance into any of the government secondary schools in the country. Each of the private secondary schools conducted their own entrance examination even though most would take pupils who passed for admission to the government secondary schools but were not taken in the schools they chose.

The Common Entrance Examination was conducted by the West Africa Examinations Council which organised exams for Ghana, Nigeria, Sierra Leone, Liberia and The Gambia. The Council set a minimum mark required to be obtained by pupils to qualify them for consideration for admission to secondary schools. But the pass mark did not automatically assure admission. Some of the top schools like Accra Academy which had produced some of the country's Chief Justices and Speakers of Parliament, crack lawyers and other academics, for instance, would have a long list of qualified pupils to choose from. The mark required for even consideration by the school would be far higher than the WAEC determined pass mark. The same was true for schools like Mfantsipim Secondary in Cape Coast, Prempeh College in Kumasi, St John's School in Sekondi and Achimota School in Accra.

Dan chose Navrongo Secondary School as his first choice and was invited to the next stage of the selection process, the interview. He chose Navrongo Secondary because he came from Navrongo, lived there and did not know enough about any other school. He made a Division One Distinction in the GCE Ordinary Level exams and was admitted in Sixth Form in the same school.

He was introduced to drinking sprees in Sixth Form. He drank alcohol, infrequently, in his earlier secondary school days. During the holidays in his junior secondary school days he and his friends would normally come to town on market days, which were every fourth day, stroll around the market, meet other friends, have fun observing how drunks behaved and other young men court girls and end up in houses that sold the locally brewed alcohol called *pito*. This was brewed from malt made from sorghum and could be mild or strong depending on how the brewer treated it. But as students they did not have enough money to drink to the point of getting drunk except at Christmas. Students normally saved towards the Christmas, taxing relations working away from home for money for a new pair of trousers and a shirt and of course the spending money for the day itself. It seemed to be a crime not to get drunk on Christmas and New Year's Day.

He was hardly involved in long drinking sessions. And he hardly took any strong drinks. At Christmas and New Year they would drink beer, the only occasions they were sure to take beer. They did not drink spirits.

In Sixth Form, he found himself in the company of a student from a rich family who did not think he needed to study hard to survive. He seemed to feel set up in life by his father's wealth and thought he should enjoy himself while young. Why work so hard when there was so much around him to make his life easy and comfortable?

Dan began sneaking out with this student, and others who joined the group, to nearby villages to drink, during weekends and on some weekday evenings. They went past drinking *pito* and started drinking *akpeteshie*. This fiery drink, even then, had many nicknames including *kill me quick*. Distilled from sugar solution fermented with the addition of yeast or fermented palm wine, it could have as much as sixty percent alcohol. It burnt the throat and the chest as the drinker swallowed it.

The extraordinary intelligence of Dan showed during this period. While the members of his group, which proudly called itself the Boston Tea Party, fared badly in class, Dan kept topping his class in all the subjects he studied, Economics, French and English. Even in the General Paper he always came tops in Logic. In Sixth Form he earned the nickname the Tanker for his ability to take in so much alcohol and still be able to study. The truth though was that when he drank he hardly studied. He dozed through night studies when he drank but the few hours he spent reading in the afternoon and the evenings he was sober were enough to put him ahead of his mates. And to earn him As in the GCE Advanced level exams.

He studied Administration at the University of Ghana in Legon in Ghana's capital, Accra and he made the time to continue to study French privately. Here he joined the company of students from Navrongo who were on study leave. These were mostly teachers who had been granted leave with pay. Students who came direct from Sixth Form or for any reason were not doing work that qualified them to be granted study leave with pay by their employers were paid a small allowance by the government to meet the cost of meals. Even though students complained about the amount they were grateful for it. Students were paid weekly sums equivalent to the cost of all 21 meals in the week. The money was called PAYE by all, meaning pay as you eat. Those students who depended on only this amount, called Paye-dependent students, except those from better off homes, could not afford to buy drink. Dan could drink and did drink profusely in his university days because of the company he kept. Most evenings they would sneak across the road that ran past the university, to the community where junior university staff lived, mostly to drink *akpeteshie.* Soon after those on study leave received their salaries they would either go to *Hospitality Inn* or the university's Snack Bar for beer. Beer was more costly than the local spirit and their salaries would not go far on beer. So after a day or two drinking beer they would go back to the local gin swearing as drunkards would do that beer was not worth the amount spent on it. When their pockets were healthy however they would feel that beer was worth its price.

Dan staggered back to his room in Commonwealth Hall many times in the evenings and his mates knew him very well for that. When they saw a figure staggering and falling on the stairs leading up to the hall they would stand and watch and count how many times he fell before making it to the hall. Some students would go down and really have fun provoking him and laughing as he clutched the air to pull himself up each stair.

His course mates knew he was super brain and respected him despite his addiction to alcohol. Dan did not buy textbooks or even the handouts that lecturers prepared and sold. He could not afford them and he would tell his colleagues how many bottles of *akpeteshie* that amount could buy. His basic value seemed to have been *akpeteshie* and everything else was measured against it.

He majored in Accounting and collected all the prizes available in the courses he offered. He graduated with a First Class but the Director of the School of Administration said there was no way he was going to select a drunkard to be a teaching assistant in his school. He said the teaching assistant was not a robot explaining things to students but a role model he expected to influence the students in a positive and not a negative way.

Friends who spoke to Dan about the comments of the Director in the hope that he would curse the loss said he asked them who wanted to be the errand boy of lecturers. While other students would have gone to kneel before the Director to assure him they would give up drinking and be model assistants Dan did not see the loss. He would give up many things for the opportunity to drink and not the other way round. Alcohol was his basic value, the value against which he measured all other things. He was out of the university, starting his National Service soon and earning his own money to be able to buy his own alcohol. That was what was important to him.

He was posted to the Ministry of Health in Tamale for the National Service. He worked under the Regional Accountant in the Regional Office of the ministry. Now with his own monthly allowance he allocated generously to the alcohol budget line. In the mornings up to the mid-day break he was not only sober but the finest possible gentleman in the office. A quiet and even reserved person by nature, he commanded a lot of respect in his sober mood. He was very respectful, ceding the right of way to his superiors and offering to help subordinates and junior staff of the ministry. In the company of other staff he listened a lot, hardly saying anything, showing his interest in the discussions only with the changes in his facial expressions.

During the mid-day break he may or may not eat. He would invariably drink and hardly returned from the break on time and hardly sober. He would spend the afternoon dozing behind his desk.

It took about three months for the office to realise an ability he had. On one occasion the Regional Accountant, who everybody simply called Sammy, needed a summary of year to date expenditure on some budget lines to pass on to the Regional Director who was due to make a presentation in about an hour. The Regional Accountant was holding a meeting with District Directors and Accountants discussing their financial returns. Some of them would attend the meeting at which their Regional Director, Dr Amoako-Attah, was going to do the presentation and also return to their districts that day and so their discussions with the Accountant could not be put off. Sammy was therefore not free to prepare the information the Regional Director needed. He was confused knowing he did not have the time to prepare the summary and that Dan would not be sober enough to do it.

He, indeed, did not find him sober but had to shake him awake and ask him if he could prepare something. Even getting the message across was difficult. Dan kept moaning and asking stupid questions. *Why do you want such information now? Why does the director have to go to a meeting now? Can he postpone the meeting? And why only those items? Year to date…*

In exasperation the Accountant went back to the Director who agreed he would do the presentation but explain that the summary of expenditure would be available the next day. Unfortunately, but at the same time fortunately, the Director had to leave the office thirty minutes later than earlier planned. He was held up by a phone call from the Minister of Health in Accra seeking information he needed for a paper he was preparing for a meeting with a visiting WHO representative. This held up the Regional Director in the office for another thirty minutes. Fortunately, as it turned out. A few minutes before he left the Accountant walked in with the summary well done.

Dr Amoako-Attah was surprised. "How did you dodge your directors to prepare this?" he asked, with a pleasant smile on his face.

The Accountant wore an even brighter and more pleasant smile. "You won't believe what happened."

"Try me," Dr Amoako-Attah assured him. "I can believe anything.'

Sammy kept on smiling as he said, "That is good because not many people would believe this. Dan prepared it."

"I thought you said he was drunk?" the Director asked, the promise to believe anything going out the window.

"Yes, I did. And he was really drunk, not even seeming to understand what I was saying let alone show appreciation. I actually walked off and left him with his eyes closed. So I was surprised myself when he came into the office, swaying, with all the District Directors and their Accountants watching us. I told myself that he was going to embarrass himself and embarrass the office as well. Then he put this paper on my desk, still swaying and asked if that was the information I wanted. I said yes without looking at it in order to be rid of him. When he again swayed out I looked at the paper ready to complain to the people in the room the problem I had. They were all looking at me so when I screamed many of them stood up. The information is perfect and neatly done. I don't know how he did it but he did it."

From that day Dan's drinking did not bother his superiors. Instead he became a wonder boy in the block. The Director and his Accountant realised the potential of their new employee and thought they could influence a change in his habits if they talked seriously to him. Both of them took turns having chats with him, in the mornings when he was still sober. They pointed out the potential he had and how far he could go. They encouraged him to take the professional exam, take either the internationally recognised ACCA or the Ghanaian version, the CA Ghana. But they also let him know that his drinking habit would seriously jeopardize the prospects of his developing the potential to the full. Both visited him at home and invited him to their houses in efforts to bring him close to them. Dan would listen with respect and thank them for their concern and their advice. He would stay off drink for two days, at the most, never more than two days. On the third day he would return from his lunch break drunk.

It was Sammy who heard the stories that Dan's drinking problem started in Sixth Form and continued in the university.

"Can you guess what class Dan made?" the Accountant asked the Director one day as they discussed Dan.

"Such students can usually be very brilliant. And in the case of Dan, from his performance here you can tell he is very bright. Despite his attitude to drink I won't be surprised if he made a Second Class Lower or even an Upper. The School of Administration is very strict with their marking and award of degrees."

The Accountant smiled. "Dan made 3 As at the A Level and had a First Class at the university, the only student in his batch who had a First Class. I heard he collected a trunk full of prizes."

The Director who said he could believe anything was genuinely surprised and he showed it. "Really? Waw! Why was he not retained as a Teaching Assistant?" But he laughed at his own question. "You don't need to answer. If I am a head of department bringing up young men and women, Dan is not the person I will want to use to influence them even if he is the morning star."

The Accountant also started using Dan for even more difficult assignments but he seemed to relish challenges and he not only accepted them but provided very high quality output each time.

It was here, in the early months of his posting, that he met Matilda. Matilda Kadua Wepia was a nurse in the Regional Hospital in Tamale.

Matilda lived on alcohol, just like Dan. A very beautiful young woman, when she first arrived at the Nurses Training College in Tamale, men competed for her. Like Dan she was Kassena too and came from Navrongo. She had a very beautiful face that sat well on a well proportioned and beautifully shaped body. Big men in the municipality called daily to take her out, making studies difficult for her. She was hardly in the hostel in the evenings and most often she came back drunk. Her mates expected her to fail her exams but she kept passing. Initially her mates spread the rumour that she was sleeping with the tutors for marks. But when they read assignments she did in class they realised she was a very intelligent girl who would waste herself because of drink. And men.

Some of the men who took Matilda out were not just interested in keeping her as a girlfriend. About three of them were really serious, really loved her and wanted strongly to marry her. But her drink problem made each of them drop the idea. Once she started drinking you could not stop her. And once she was drunk the men realised they could do anything they liked with her. Within a short space of time she had acquired notoriety as a cheap of source of sex, all a man needed to do was to buy her drink and after a few bottles she was available for anything the man wanted to do. That fact scuttled her chances of marrying. And over time, as her drinking only got worse and her reputation with men went down hill, no serious man came to her.

The final nail in the coffin of her doomed reputation was driven in by a very sad event. One evening as Matilda was strolling towards the entrance that led from the main road towards the bungalows of health staff and the Training College, a Benz car pulled up and two young men engaged her in conversation. They ended up inviting her for a drink. Since she never said no to drink she joined the men she was meeting for the first time. Such was her nature. Her mates advised her against being so willing to go drinking with anyone who just said let's go have a drink. The night ended with Matilda as drunk as never before. Before the young men supported her to the car two other young men joined them. Together they drove off to a quiet spot where they took turns having repeated sex with her. They returned her to the hospital after midnight and dumped her on the way to the hostel where any passer-by could easily see her. They removed and took away her pant and hitched up her dress. They wanted the story of what had happened to her to be told loud to anyone passing by.

She did not know the young men and she had not taken the number of the vehicle. She could have made inquiries at the bar where they drank but that would have been selling the story of what happened to her.

The event sobered her up for a short period, but for only a short period. When she came to her senses and discovered what had happened to her, she remained indoors in the hostel for about three months. She kept to herself and sat quietly throughout lectures and night studies. She stayed in her room when they were not attending classes, or in the dining hall and they were not studying on their own in the night. Many of her mates thought the humiliation would affect her performance in class but it seemed to drive her during the period to spend all her time with her books. And so she got even better marks and left the rest of the class even far behind her.

Her refrain from drinking and even going out lasted only three months. In the fourth month she started going out to drink. With men hardly available to take her out and offer her beer, Matilda switched to other drinks. She could not afford beer on her student allowance but needed alcohol. So she took to drinking *akpeteshie.*

As a nurse she was very hard working. And very honest. She endured insults from her colleagues because of her drunkenness but she was proud to point out to them that alcoholism was her only problem. "I don't steal patients' drugs to sell to enable me drink. I use my clean salary and anything that patients or their relatives have given me. No patient will ever die in my hands because I did not administer his or her drugs. No patient's condition will get worse in my hands because I pilfered their drugs. I drink. Yes, so what? Has anybody ever come back with an abscess from an injection I gave to them? I am the one you always call when you have sweated for ten minutes and can't find a patient's vein to insert your needle in. Why is my drinking a problem to you? I have never gone after a colleague's husband or boyfriend. It is only drinking you people see as a wrong but when you chase your mate's husband or her fiancé that is right, is it? When you come on night duty and lock yourself up and go to sleep as if you are in your house and falsify entries in the patients' folders that you administered drugs you did not administer, there is nothing wrong with that, is there?"

They called her *Kanawu* Matilda because she could be forthright about issues her colleagues would either say in whispers or state in a roundabout way.

She was right, though. She was a very upright nurse. She was liked by patients and their relatives. She did not pilfer patients' drugs. She did not drink before and on duty. When she was on night duty, she did not sleep. She would take one wing of the floor she was on and ensure that she administered drugs at the right times throughout the night to the patients in her wing. Sometimes patients or their relatives in the other wing would come calling her for help because they could not find the nurse on duty in that wing. She received gifts from patients and relatives for the attention paid to them when on admission. Despite her drink problem she was popular among patients.

It was that common interest both Dan and Matilda had in drink that brought them together. They had seen each other a number of times when they went out drinking. However their relationship started when Matilda went to the office one day to have her salary corrected. The Regional Accountant had been rude to her, telling to go to the Accounts Office and tell Dan her problems. "He is your brother boozeman, so if you promise to take him out and make him drunk as only you know how, he will be more than happy to help you."

Even though she had felt insulted by the remark she needed to have her salary corrected and she did not want to offend the Accountant. Dan, on the other hand, had listened carefully and respectfully when she approached him and promised to help. It was the third of the month and at the end of that month her salary had been corrected. She really did not notice it till two weeks later because she temporarily lost the pay slip. It was given to her in a drinking bar two weeks later. She looked at it when she was still sober and noticed the changes. The boy Dan was very good, she said aloud but to nobody in particular. She had never known the Accounts Office to take any action after just one complaint. Normally you would go there about five times or more before you got the service you wanted.

By the time she realised what Dan had done for her she had spent all her money, and, as was the case in all previous months, already living on credit. She did invite him out for drinks when she got her salary the next month, and thanked him for his help. It was when they went out together that they realised two common factors. One, they both came from Navrongo. Two, and of even more importance to them, they had a common interest, strong drinks. So they ended up drinking what they liked best, *akpeteshie,* instead of the beer they had set out to drink.

They discovered an area of common interest and that bound them together. They were inseparable outside working hours when they had money. Each saw something bad in the other, though. "It is not good for a woman to drink that way. She drinks too much," Dan complained. "Dan does not have working hours for drink. Every hour, including office hours, is drink time for him," Matilda complained.

"You will never catch me drinking during working hours. When I am off duty and I drink till I become senseless it will not affect my work in anyway. I respect my work. Without it I can't drink."

Their relationship grew, fed and bound tighter by *akpeteshie*. He was a young nice man of twenty-three. He was handsome and quite gentle if not drunk. He was a silent listener in conversations. She was a beautiful young woman of twenty-two. She was a beauty, a very beautiful young woman damaged by drink and the rape in her days as a nurse trainee. Before friends could say hi folks they were living together. Dan moved into the single room in which Matilda lived. The house was the type called a 'compound' house in Ghana. It was rectangular in shape, enclosing a common yard into which the twelve rooms opened. The only entrance into the house had a wooden gate. But three of the rooms, including the one rented by Matilda, in addition to the door that opened into the yard, had a door that opened outside.

Without going through any ceremony, either traditional or official, they started referring to each other as wife and husband. Dan was the worse of the two in how far he drank. He was the worse of the two in the things he did when he was drunk. One day when he came swaying home Matilda had the patience to encourage him to eat. It was not long after they had been paid so they still had money. And she prepared some palm nut soup with *fufu* which she coaxed him to eat. He sat at table with his eyes partly closed and murmuring to himself, incomprehensible things. She immediately became angry when he washed his hands in the soup. With his eyes still partially closed he poured the water meant for washing his hands around the ball of *fufu* and went on to eat it. Matilda was so angry she refused to correct him.

"What sort of woman are you?" he complained, his speech barely understandable. "How can you cook food without meat? I gave you money not long ago. What happened to it? You used it to drink the fucking *akpeteshie* so that you can cook soup without meat for me. Don't worry. I won't complain. I am not a witch; meat doesn't mean anything to me. But a woman who loves her husband will not prepare his soup without meat."

He got up and staggered toward her. "Matilda you should know how much I love you. I really love you. Do you know why? Your soup is always the best even though you have denied me meat." He groped to touch her but she kept moving away and said nothing. "You are moving away from me. Move. We will see where you will sleep tonight. If it is the same bed I am going to sleep on, we will see how you will prevent me from touching you. First you prepare my soup without meat. Then you refuse to let me touch you. And you call yourself my wife."

When they did not go out drinking together and he went out alone, he would return very late and bang on the outside door for Matilda to open for him. Several times he came home too drunk to even knock on the door and just passed out on the step leading to the door.

Dan was the bar keepers' nightmare. He was nice to talk to when he first came in to buy a drink. But after a few tots he would lose all his senses. He would be the last to leave. And for some hours before the bar closed he would not even buy anything. Bar keepers had to force him to leave many times when they had to close the bar. He would resist, saying things nobody understood because his speech would be slurred by drink. A few times sales girls had to drag him out and lock up their bars.

He got home most often. Sometimes he did not. He would pass out either a few metres away from where he was drinking, midway between where he was drinking and home or somewhere near home. On two occasions he came to his senses only after he was drenched by heavy rains. Several times he fell and hurt himself.

Matilda's mother hated him and did so intensely. In Kassena tradition, the bride price is paid in stages, each stage involving different items. In the first stage, Dan's parents sent kola nuts, salt, tobacco and smoked guinea fowls to Matilda's home. Her mother was not at home at the time and the visitors were well received. But when she came and was told who had come, why they had come and what they had brought, it was only the combined effort of the men of the house that had prevented her from sending back the items. She was at home when they came to discuss the performance of the second part of the marriage rites, the offer of a goat and a dog, and she made it impossible for the discussion to take place.

She said openly that Dan was a bad influence on her daughter. She accused him, saying it was because oh him that her daughter was poor and could not remit her. She had a right to decide whether to like him or hate him and she chose to hate him, period. Things got worse and she stopped visiting them when one evening, when she was visiting them, they both come home highly tipsy and started having sex even before she fell asleep. She left the room, which they did not notice anyway, and spent the night on the veranda. She left for Navrongo the next day.

At the end of his National Service year with the Ministry, the Regional Director and his Accountant were confused what to do. He did very good work and performed any task given him, whether he was sober or 'under the weather,' very well. Nobody liked drunkards and Dan was among the worst type. But he delivered what was expected of him.

He did not make mistakes when he prepared inputs for salaries. He prepared payroll data with accuracy and on time too. He kept accurate records and prepared accurate accounts whenever they were needed. In a few hours he could prepare status reports of donor funded projects.

So they decided to keep him. They again tried to talk to him, fearing that it was going to be wasted effort, which exactly was what it was.

By the end of their first year together, they had a baby, a baby girl. Dan was in a drink induced stupor when labour pains set in shortly after midnight. Matilda tried very hard to get the urgency of her condition across to him in vain.

"Matilda, I say you should sleep," he said in his slurred speech. "Even if you go to the hospital at this time there is no doctor. We will go in the morning when the doctors start work."

When she insisted and tried explaining the pain she was going through and how that meant the child was coming soon he asked her, "Why are you stubborn? Why do you want to give birth in the night? Why don't you just wait till morning? Children born in the night are thieves. Why do you want to give birth to a thief? Labour is not difficult. It is just like going to toilet. Why do you want to make it difficult?"

He tried pressing the tummy resulting in a yelp from his wife.

She ignored him and went out and woke up one of the tenants, a lady, who woke up another and between them, they sent Matilda to the hospital.

Dan was asked to name the child. Even though he was tipsy he was not too drunk to give a name. He named her Mariama and everyone laughed. They were Christians but Mariama was a Moslem name. Matilda hurriedly controlled the damage caused by the blunder by saying they had not heard him well; he had said Marian and not Mariama as they thought. Another three years later they had their second child, a boy. When he was born nurses claimed he resembled his father so much that they called him Junior. And that was the name Matilda gave when she went to register the birth, Junior. The registrar asked for the father's name and when he was told Dan Apeatu, the kid was recorded in the register of births as Daniel Apeatu Junior.

Junior was only a few months old when Matilda asked Dan to pack. There had not been any quarrel. There had not been any argument. Nothing had been simmering, at least as far as Dan could tell. One fine morning when he came back into the room from bathing she told him to pack out of her room. She said she wanted him out of her life. He just laughed.

"You can laugh as much as you like," she told him. "I mean it."

"Mean what?"

"I mean this fooling around with each other pretending to be married is over."

"How?"

"I thought they said you are a graduate?"

"What has being or not being a graduate got to do with this?"

"I expect graduates to understand simple things and not ask stupid questions."

"Woman, don't give me bad luck today. You start the day with insults and everything will go bad for me in the office."

All this while Dan went about combing his hair. Matilda, who was not on duty that morning but was on the afternoon shift which started at 2:00 p.m. lay in bed watching him.

Still taking her talk for a joke or romance, he leaned over to kiss her but she slapped him instead. The girl who was awake at the time, screamed.

"What sort of village romance is this?" he asked. He felt his cheek as he looked at her without understanding her. He decided not to make it an issue but went out briefly and came back.

"Are you going to pack your things and go with them when you leave?" she asked firmly when he was dressing.

"No," he said and started whistling.

When she smiled he thought he was right about her joking about it. He came home at about midnight and, as usual, knocked on the outside door.

"Stand back," she instructed him.

"Why stand back?" he muttered drunkenly. "Stand back where? Why stand back? Open the door for me and you are asking me to stand back."

He went on banging on the door but she just stood by the window looking at him and saying nothing.

"Open up!" he shouted as he banged on the door, staggering and almost falling in the process.

"If you keep making noise you will wake up people who will come out and beat you. I have told you to stand back. If you want me to open the door for you stand back. Otherwise you will spend the whole night out there making noise in vain"

"I don't like your rural romance, woman." He staggered back and came forward, hitting his head against the door. He banged on the door. "I said open up, don't you hear me? You are my wife. I haven't divorced you. You can't lock me out. Open up!" He staggered and fell back, falling on his buttocks. He fell flat on his back when he tried getting up. In that instant the door opened and Matilda flung his suitcase at him and closed the door, locking it.

He made such a din neighbours came up. While some expressed their annoyance others tried to plead with Matilda to open the door and let him in. By the silence she kept inside the room one might think she was not even inside. The scene out there ended when some people led Dan away and gave him a place for the night.

When morning came he did not know where to go with his worn out suitcase. He did not know who he could call a friend. He dragged himself to the office and told Sammy his story. He cried, really cried, his body vibrating sometimes, as he told what had happened. He could not tell what had caused his sacking. He didn't remember doing anything that should have warranted such action by his wife. The Regional Accountant probed. Was he sure he did not beat her, refuse her money for the housekeeping, taken a girlfriend…? The issue of his drinking was not raised. Well, because Matilda drank excessively herself. To all the questions he said no. So Sammy arranged to put Dan in one of the Ministry's guest houses, give him some days' off while they tried to reconcile him with his wife. Each evening for three days Dan went back to the house where Matilda lived to try and see her but she would not receive him. For the three days he did not touch a drop of alcohol.

On the third evening she warned, "If you come here again to harass me I will have you beaten up."

"Have me, your husband, beaten up?"

"No, have you my father and my god beaten up," she said sarcastically. "You thought I was joking when I asked you to pack. If you want to find out whether I am joking or serious about having you beaten, come here again, say tomorrow or the day after."

He stopped trying to see her but he contacted her friends and asked some of his drinking buddies to talk to her. He wanted to know from her friends what it was that she said he had done. Her friends said truthfully that they did not know.

And they said the truth. When her friends asked her what had caused her action she said nothing.

"You can't just get up one day and say he should pack out," Kachana, a not so close friend, told her. "He must have done something."

Matilda patiently told her, "Then you tell me what it is that he has done since you know so much."

"I don't know anything," Kachana said in self-defence. "But the two of you have been living together for five years now and you have two children. You can't just get up and say get out of my life without him doing anything."

Very calmly she said, "Well I just got up and said to him to pack out without him doing anything. And when he refused to pack out I threw him out."

"Matilda, nobody will buy this," said Adisa, a Moslem who joined the group because she defied her family and drank alcohol, and spirits too.

There were a lot of interesting stories about Adisa. She really stopped drinking in the day during the Moslem month of Ramadan. People who knew her distantly wondered if she could fast considering the fact that she was tipsy every day. But she did fast and would give up drinking during the day. Her friends told stories that she kept a small bottle of alcohol in her room during Ramadan and after breaking the fast, the first thing she did was rush to her room and take her life-saving drink. It was not true about her, really. During Ramadan she fasted and would go through the whole of the evening's prayer session without drinking. But before retiring to bed she would gulp down the alcohol she really kept in her room. That she kept a small bottle of alcohol in her room during the Ramadan was true.

Her drinking colleagues called her by various titles, all offensive to serious Moslems. They called her Hajia, a title given only to women who went to Mecca. Going to Mecca was one of five pillars of Islam and she did not seem to have regard for the pillars. They also called her Imam, a highly revered title.

Many years back Adisa prayed with the women in the house she lived in. There was a mosque behind their house. The men and older women went there five times a day to pray. Women in nearby houses would gather on one of the verandas inside their houses and pray together, bending, kneeling and squatting as the men in the mosque did. There was a loudspeaker mounted on top of the mosque so the caller's every word echoed in many houses in the neighbourhood.

In the past Adisa prayed with the women whenever she was at home, especially in the evening which was when they prayed together most. She would join them reeking of *akpeteshie*. The scent of *akpeteshie* was very strong and even though she tried not to open her mouth during the prayers she could not keep a lid on the scent. Some women stopped joining in the group prayers, preferring to pray alone in their rooms arguing that Adisa's drink profaned their prayers and prayer with her was just as bad as not praying at all.

It was not the attitude of the women who stopped praying with her that made her stop praying with them herself. It was an embarrassing incident. One evening when she must have taken in more than her usual amount of alcohol when she bowed to pray she stumbled forward, hitting her head on the floor. Women screamed and ran off in different directions. Some thought she had a seizure of epilepsy. She struggled to get up and some women went to her aid. When she opened her mouth to speak she polluted the air around with the fumes of spirits and the women withdrew. It was so embarrassing a spectacle she stopped joining them for prayers.

"Hajia," Matilda told her, "nobody is asking you to buy anything and you are free to buy whatever you want to buy." She turned to all of them. "Which of you brought Dan and I together? When I met Dan and we became friends and later wife and husband, which of you did I invite to arrange the relationship for me? So today if I say he must pack out and he packs out, why must I justify myself to you? You can believe what you want and don't believe what you choose not to believe. It won't force me to invent a reason for asking him to go. I just asked him to go. I don't want him for a husband anymore. If any of you want him please go for him. If you can't approach him I will talk to him for you."

And with it had been full stop to anything anybody wanted to discuss.

Sammy had a chat with his boss who agreed only reluctantly to be involved in any way with any personal business of Dan. Dr Amoako-Attah was gone and he had been replaced by Dr Antwi. Dr Antwi did not make any effort to hide his dislike for the alcoholic staff. He was told by his predecessor that he was still able to perform his responsibilities quite well. The Regional Accountant, to whom he was accountable, also confirmed it. So long as he delivered Dr Antwi had no problems with him. But he could not be forced to like him, having observed his drinking habits.

So he agreed to discuss Dan with the Accountant only reluctantly and in the end agreed that Sammy should meet Matilda and find out what was behind her action. Dan had been sober since being sacked by Matilda. In confidence both of them agreed that the marriage was not right, right from the beginning. But they also agreed that Dan had the right to decide who he loved, if love was involved in this relationship. They both agreed that if the relationship could actually end to give Dan his freedom from a woman whose reputation they did not like and, particularly, make him stay sober, may the relationship stay broken.

She made it clear to the Accountant he was not welcome when he called at her at home the first Saturday after she packed out her husband.

"What is bringing this big money man to a lowly house like mine this early morning?" she asked when she came to the door after he knocked.

"What is wrong with my coming to your house this early morning?" he in turn asked, seeking to play with her. After all he needed to be in her good books that morning.

"How long have I been living here?" she asked seriously, ignoring his invitation to be playful. "Can you tell me if you ever set foot here?"

Sammy observed quietly that this woman was very intelligent and could have gone very far if she had not spoiled herself with drink and a bad reputation. He knew that she could have studied and sat the General Certificate of Education Ordinary Level exam privately and passed. With that she could have gone on to do the State Registered Nursing course and even gone to the university to do a degree or diploma in Nursing. That would probably never happen thanks to addiction to drink.

"At least, can I come in?" he asked her.

"I hope it is not because of that useless Dan that you are coming," she said, still holding the curtain but blocking his entrance.

"Matilda, this is not the way to receive visitors. Receive me, offer me a chair and then ask me for the purpose of my visit."

"I don't want us to waste our time if it is because of Dan you are coming." She let down the curtain and went back into the room and said carelessly, "Anyway, come in."

He went in feeling he was going to waste his time. He looked round the room. Bare, poor and poorly managed. A room two drunkards kept, he noted mentally. How else did he expect it to look? No pictures of Dan but a few of Matilda, beautiful Matilda. He just could not help relapsing into thought of who else she could have been. And if she thought of this herself and if she missed the opportunity.

He started with greetings as the small girl came into his lap. He stroked her hair and noted how beautiful she too looked. She did not take her mother's face. Nor her father's. But she was beautiful.

He knew Matilda would be impatient if he did not go straight to the purpose of his visit.

"Matilda," he started, "despite your warning that you will not talk about Dan, I am afraid I am here to talk about him. You can't work with someone who goes through the experience Dan has just gone through and you leave him to stew in his juice. So we asked him what was the problem and he said he just did not know. He did not know what he must have done to annoy you so much that you asked him to pack. He said when you told him in the morning to pack his things he believed you were only being romantic. He said he can't guess what it is that caused you to want to end the relationship. I thought I should come and find out. And if it is something he has done that is wrong, I will apologise on his behalf."

She smiled and shook her head. Sammy could not tell what that meant.

"He did not do anything," she said calmly, looking straight at Sammy.

He thought he did not hear right. "Pardon."

This time she laughed aloud. "I am sure you heard me. He did not do anything."

"Matilda, I'm serious. You can trust me and tell me what it is that he did wrong."

She lowered her head, cocked it to one side and with a smile on her lips said, "I trust you. And I tell you; he did not do anything wrong."

"You just decided he should pack out?" he asked, not hiding his disbelief. Actually making it obvious.

Without batting an eyelid or changing expression she replied, "Yes."

He sat for more than a minute unsure what to say. Nor how to proceed. The small girl was playing with a pen in his breast pocket. He searched in his pocket for something for her to play with but found nothing he could give her. Instead he gave her money. She showed it to her mother who asked her to say thank you which she did.

"Matilda, I can't press you to tell me why you asked him to move out," he said trying to find a way to evoke a meaningful discussion. "But whatever it is, the two of you have lived together for five years now. You have two children between you. Nobody will advise breaking up. I am here to apologise on his behalf. I will be happy to see the two of you together."

"Accountant, you are apologizing for what?" She tilted her head and cocked an ear.

"For whatever Dan has done."

She smiled. "But I told you he didn't do anything. So your apology is not necessary. You will be happy to see us together. I won't be happy to see the two of us together. So you won't see us together. Right from the beginning I told you that you will be wasting our time if you came to talk about Dan. Dan is a closed chapter in my life. People who want to re-open that chapter are only boring me. Dan is a closed file."

Sammy knew when he was beaten. There was nothing in Matilda's face to show she would listen to Sammy. He knew that in the next few minutes she would be throwing him out and so decided to throw himself out in a more dignified way than she would do it. He felt strongly tempted to tell her she was lucky to have gotten someone who would marry her despite her history. But he did not come to rake her feelings. Or tell her the truth about her past and her luck. Dan was still very much interested in her and if he burnt Dan's bridges he may never be forgiven.

Dan tried even seeing the children, especially the girl. Matilda really started creating scenes any time he went to the house to see her. He did not like scenes but Matilda seemed to like them. She would raise her voice and shout over things that did not require that. She would be telling her story loudly to people who would be attracted by her raised voice, something that greatly embarrassed Dan.

One day he went to the ward to see her.

"What do you want here?" she started screaming when she saw him. "I am asking you what you want here. Why are you chasing me everywhere?"

"Matilda," Dan said in a lower voice. "I am not chasing you. I came to discuss seeing the children. I need to be seeing them."

"I need to be seeing them," she imitated him. "You can't see them. I don't want to see you. And since the children are with me and you can't see them without me seeing you, you can't see them.'

Try as he would Matilda refused to discuss his seeing the children. He tried going to the house when Matilda was working but when he met Matilda's mother in the house, he stopped trying to see them. Her mother lived with her for one year before she left.

Chapter Four

As Diane Orengo drove through the gates, she observed another car making a turn into her driveway. She became alert and looked in the driving mirror to take a good look at the car. It was a light green Mazda. Then she saw the registration number and relaxed. She parked in the shed built in the yard and left enough space for Harriet to park. She brought out the shopping bag and closed the door of the car and walked towards Harriet's car. She had not seen Harriet for some months even though they spoke to each other many times during that period. As her niece ran up and took the shopping bag and welcomed both Diane and Harriet, Diane walked over to Harriet. They hugged and exchanged kisses on the cheeks. Then they stood apart and each made an open appraisal of the other.

Harriet was a very close friend, a friend from a long time back. They had been intimate, the level of their intimacy reducing only as work separated them. Harriet had moved from Nairobi to Mombassa about four years back with her husband, David, and had set up practice that boomed within a very short time. In that period she had also had her first child, a son, a fact that had made both David and his parents very happy and proud of Harriet.

They walked together into the sitting room and Harriet stood admiring the furniture, the decoration and the general beauty of the room. The decoration was not expensive but quite beautiful.

"No, Diane, show me around the house, starting from the outside," Harriet said as she pulled her friend towards the door. "The house looks great for a devout spinster."

They both laughed. Harriet knew of Diane's misfortunes of not so long ago. She knew it still hurt even though her friend had done well in getting over it. Harriet could not tell how much she had gotten over it but she knew it was far. She also knew that she could call her friend a devout spinster because of the intimate relationship between them. Diane was not a spinster by choice. So to call her a devout spinster could be taken to be insulting by any but very few friends. Harriet was one of those. And Diane's laughter was confirmation of her friend's right to tease her over an issue that could be said to be sensitive.

"It's a small house, quite compact and that is how I like it," Diane said as they walked round the house. "When I saw it I thought that if I had to design my own house I could not have made it different from this in any way, size, layout, colours and all that." They walked past the parked cars beyond which some vegetables were growing.

Harriet suddenly seized Diane's right hand and examined the fingers. Diane looked at her friend, puzzled.

"What is wrong with my fingers?" she asked as she looked closely at them herself.

"They are not green," Harriet explained to a still confused Diane.

"Are they supposed to be green?"

Harriet only looked back at her friend with an amused smile on her lips.

Suddenly understanding dawned on Diane who pulled her hand away from her friend's hold. "They are green. It's just that you are colour blind. I have not only green fingers but green toes as well."

"Really?" Harriet asked in mock surprise. "Green fingers grow vegetables and crops. What do green toes grow?"

"Successful lawyers." They both laughed. Harriet always admired her friend. She knew how much pain Diane had gone through in the past three and half years. They talked about it immediately it happened and Diane had been very stoical about it, taking it all as something that could not be averted, once it had happened. Harriet could feel the pain she knew her friend was experiencing but you did not hear the pain in what she said. Several times during the first time they discussed the events, she had looked very long, very hard, at her friend's face searching for a sign that would tell her that her friend did not truly believe in taking what had happened. Try as she did, what she read in her friend's face was conviction that yes, she had been hurt but she had accepted what had happened and would move on with her life. Harriet had to admit then that she had yet to come across one so practical and so philosophical about life. At the time she had already moved from Nairobi to Mombassa but each time she visited Nairobi she stayed about a day longer in order to spend time with her friend. Sometimes she wondered what would have happened to her sanity if it were her and not Diane who were treated that way.

As they walked round the house and came back inside and went from room to room, only part of her mind was on what her friend was saying. The other part, the bigger part, was thinking how strong her friend was. She had plodded on with her life and now lived in this little dainty house. It was not her own house, she only rented it, Harriet knew, but it exuded everything one could call home and personality. It was Diane, quiet, seemingly unnoticed but there if you cared to look. Harriet admired the very character of the house, which she noticed strongly reflected the character of its tenant. The furniture, the colour of the walls, the curtains and the decorations made such a perfect match Harriet wondered if her friend had someone, an interior decorator, for instance, to help her.

"Who helped you design the inside?" she asked, knowing she would get a true answer.

"What do you mean?" Diane asked.

"Diane, this is one of the most powerful statements in a house about the personality of its owner. The blend between colour and everything in the room is not only perfect but the story of your character. Did you get an interior decorator to design it for you?"

"I've never met an interior decorator all my life. Have you? Do you know if they have four eyes, three hands or they are just normal humans like the two of us but have a sixth sense when it comes to design?"

They both laughed

"You can earn a living doing interior decoration if you designed this yourself." Harriet said truthfully. "Everything is simple. Everything blends into each other very well. And for those who know you, the sum is you. Simple, not loud, serene but beautiful. It is a place I can see you longing to come back to and a place in which you melt into the environment like a chameleon does when it turns green among the leaves of a tree."

Diane smiled. "Thank you. I am glad you like it. I met most of the colours in the rooms, which is why I said there would have been little difference between the house I rented and one I would design myself. I made a few changes, but very few. Once I found I liked the colours I chose the furniture accordingly.

"And you are right. It isn't loud. The room doesn't shout at you when you come in. For me it just whispers a welcome when I walk in tired from the long day. It blows a gentle have a nice day to me when I am leaving in the morning."

"Diane, this is home." Harriet looked round the sitting room once again, admiring all that she saw.

"Really? I thought a home had a man and children."

Harriet slapped her friend jovially in the back. "Naughty thoughts."

They continued the walk around the house, inspecting the kitchen, another simple place but one where Harriet knew she would feel at home spending half of a morning preparing sauces and soups that she would use during busy weekdays. The cabinets and shelves were mahogany, and nicely polished. Everything in the kitchen was where it should be, neat, orderly. The French would say *une place pour chaque chose et chaque chose à sa place*. A place for each thing and each thing in its place.

The bathroom and toilet were neat and well kept. You could lie in them and have a very sound sleep. Harriet exhaled when she entered the main bedroom. It was, like the rest of the house, simple but again beautiful in its simplicity. The walls were bare of sentimental pictures and other mementos. The only exception was the bed, it was a king-size bed. She threw herself on it and found the springs of the mattress cushioned her fall on it and allowed her to bounce up ever so gently. She felt drowsy almost immediately. But the drowsiness disappeared immediately when her eyes fell on the picture on the wall. It was hanging right on the wall to the left of the door as you entered, above the door and facing the bed. So that when you lifted your eyes from the bed they fell on it directly.

She got up and walked up to stand directly under it. When she turned round to look for her friend Diane had gone to sit on the bed and was watching her.

"Can I ask a question?" she asked Diane, with her back to the picture.

Diane laughed. "I can answer your question without you asking it. He is not who you think he is. If your question is who is he, the answer is he is not who you think he is. He is not my boyfriend."

Harriet smiled and turned to look at the picture as she spoke. "Lawyers have been accused of all kinds of things and this reflects sometimes in the stories told about us. One story said a lawyer was cross examining a witness who kept prefacing his answers with I think. The lawyer cut in impatiently to tell him that he wanted the truth and not what he thought. To which the witness told the lawyer that because of the lawyer's great learning he could talk without thinking but for a simple person like him, he needed to think before he spoke."

They both laughed.

"Any other story about lawyers?" Diane asked, knowing her friend would have lots. Telling jokes was a common hobby of the two friends. And as she looked up at the picture her friend was examining so closely that was one thing she remembered about him. He told some of the most interesting jokes and told them with such a straight face you wouldn't know he was joking. And given how calm and apparently disinterested he seemed in the world around him, Diane and most participants of his sessions found his sense of humour at variance with his appearance and demeanour.

"Plenty," Harriet replied. "One David likes to tell is the one about two people in a balloon who were sailing round the world. It says that after many days up in the balloon the two came near the ground to find out where they were. They asked the first person they met where they were and know his reply?"

"No," Diane said with a smile, expecting something funny in the response.

"He told them they were in a balloon a hundred feet above the ground."

This only got a smile from Diane.

"As the two people in the balloon upped and went on their way, one said to the other that the person they spoke to was a lawyer. His colleague was surprised and asked how he could be so sure since that was the first time they were meeting him. The first speaker then said from the answer he gave. 'His answer was one hundred percent right but totally useless. It didn't tell us anything we didn't know.'"

They both roared with laughter.

Harriet walked back and sat by her friend on the bed and looked up at the picture. "Back to my question and your answer. I asked who he was. You told me who he was not. As a lawyer I insist; who is he?"

Harriet continued to look at the picture as she waited for her friend to answer the question. A nice man. Well kept face. Calm disposition. If one could guess the character of a person from a picture, a quiet man who kept a lot to himself. Beyond that, nothing. She turned and faced her friend.

"Nobody you would know," Diane said. "He is not my boyfriend, I already told you that," and held up her hand when her friend was going to speak. "He is not Kenyan. He is someone who, I would say, has had the most influence in my life. My father is great. I drew a lot of strength from him. He moulded me and pointed me to the future. This man is a teacher. A teacher who does not ram knowledge down his students' throats. He has a way of tickling you in a way that is imperceptible but makes you hunger to discover more of yourself and grow to your fullest potential. He wakes up your faith in yourself, and challenges you to do things you had not known you could do.

"I attended two training sessions facilitated by him and he touched me more than anybody has ever done. He gave me tools that are simple to use but extremely effective in building yourself. It was not just me. It is about true of all the participants who attended the two sessions I attended. He has influenced a drastic change in the direction of my life. I would previously have said he changed my life. But he teaches that the role of the external person is to stimulate you to make decisions. So who you become is your responsibility. You take credit for it. He doesn't take credit for it."

When she stopped talking Harriet got up and walked up to look at the picture again and spent time doing so. "He must have had such a tremendous influence on your life for his picture to be placed where it is."

"He does have a strong influence in my life. The most influence on my life"

"You said he is not your boyfriend. But do you love him?" She turned and faced her friend as she asked this.

"I know him as an excellent teacher. Clearly one of the best I have ever met. Outstanding among teachers. And that is saying a lot considering who has taught me. You get the sense that he is a generous spirited person, a missionary out to touch people and change the course of their future and the condition of their families. You can read sincerity in him, that he is genuine and not another of those false prophets taking advantage of their charisma. This man does not even have charisma. You don't even notice him when you come into contact with him. Maybe I am wrong about his charisma and he does have charisma of his own kind because he leaves a lot with you for a long time. Beyond that I don't know him. I have never considered love because I don't know him enough to begin to have a stirring heart. I am sure he is married and has a lovely family he loves. No, I don't love him."

"I will let it pass for now. But as a lawyer there is nothing you have said that says you can't love him. Women have loved married men even though if he is married I would sincerely pray that you don't fall in love with him. You have spoken so positively about him I don't know what you need to know about him to make a woman fall in love with him. Women have fallen deeply in love with men knowing less about them than you know about him. But tell me about how he touched your life."

Diane got up from the bed. "Shall we go back to the sitting room?"

As Diane went to fix something for her friend to drink Harriet sat back in the comfortable sofa and played back the painful events of her friend's past.

They met in secondary school, Alliance Girls Secondary in Nairobi, and even though they came from different backgrounds they developed a friendship that grew with time. Harriet was a Kikuyu and Diane a Luo. Diane's father, Mike Orengo, was a highly educated professional while Harriet's father dropped out of school but did very well in the crafts business. Harriet's mother was illiterate but Diane's mother was a graduate as well. In their first term in secondary school form one, the two girls had bonded as if they had known each other since their infancy. They studied together, and at the beginning of each term they would pool their provisions and use them together.

Diane's father had attended Makerere University in Kampala in Uganda and it was there he had arranged for Diane to have her first degree, in Sociology and Psychology. Harriet read law in Mombassa and moved to Nairobi to start her practice. Diane returned from Uganda on graduation and sought out Harriet and the two musketeers, as they had been called in school, picked up where Diane's travel had made them leave off. Then Diane won a Chevening scholarship to do a Masters in Development studies in Sussex. On her return the two had found each other again and were so intimate people mistook them for sisters.

It was Diane who introduced Harriet to Jane, Jane Austen they called her after the author because of her brilliance in English Literature in secondary school. Jane was a bitch of a girl but Diane had such a high tolerance level she was on good terms with Jane. Despite her bitchiness, Harriet agreed, once you became familiar with Jane you would like her. Her bitch nature came up strongly in their minds only after what happened to Diane.

Jane was a very beautiful woman. She had a very shapely figure. It was as if the one who carved her was determined to enter her in a competition and so made each curve as perfect as a woman's curves are supposed to be. Add to that a strikingly beautiful face that lit up with her smiles and blinded onlookers when she laughed and you had the picture of a heartbreaker. Jane knew about her beauty and showed it off. She wore dresses that accentuated her figure and through which you could feel how tender her flesh was. She enjoyed encouraging men to come after her. She would flirt with them and lure them on only to dump them when they were emotionally attached to her. She was a bitch, they all knew it, Harriet admitted in retrospect.

Diane and Teddy met in the UK and came back the same year. They had been on good terms with each other while in the UK but their friendship really developed and deepened when they returned to Kenya. He preferred to be called Teddy but friends sometimes insisted on calling him Eddie. He was Edward Kioh.

Friends of both Teddy and Diane admired the two and thought they were perfectly matched. Teddy's friends thought he made the right choice in Diane while Diane's friends thought she was headed for a happy, stable marriage. Teddy's friends thought Teddy deserved

Diane. He was so loving, honest and gentle and deserved someone similar. Diane's friends said the same of her; that given her qualities she deserved someone like Teddy. Diane introduced Teddy to her parents as her fiancé and he in turn introduced her to his parents as the fiancée. In fact, Diane started thinking of herself as a wife and thought of and related to Teddy as her husband.

Then, sad to say, Jane struck. All friends close to Diane heard was a sudden announcement that Teddy and Jane were going to be married. Friends heard it at the same time that Teddy told Diane he was terminating his relationship with her to marry Jane. In a very heart wrenching exchange, Teddy had apologised but said his mind was made up about marrying Jane. He realised he loved her more, that was the only reason for the change, he told her. He said he had loved Diane and still did but he loved Jane more. It was unfortunate he met Jane, he told Diane, but that could not be prevented now.

Friends of Jane told how the coup was staged. They said her initial intention was to attract the attention of Teddy, like all the men she attracted and dropped. Her intention was to prove to herself that she was so attractive that even someone said to be as committed as Teddy would not only look twice at her but would actually be tempted by her. When Teddy did not bite she stepped up the temptation, but he refused to show interest. The same friends said she went all out to entrap him because she could not afford the insult that a man would not feel attracted by her. But as she intensified her advances to him she really fell in love with him and decided he was the man for her. Once decided that she wanted him for a husband she changed into full gear to have him and got him.

Harriet remembered how shattered Diane had been. She also remembered how strong she had stood with even the shattered emotions. She still remained practical and philosophical. She remembered commenting several times on Jane's bitchy nature. It was Diane who had drawn attention to the fact that they knew about her bitchy nature and they had accepted her in the group as a friend. And that she did not become a bitch just recently.

Diane had loved Teddy deeply and very sincerely. She had considered the marriage consumed. To her then it was not an end to a love affair but a divorce which was very sudden and came when her love for her 'husband' was still at its peak. It ripped her heart in two and she bled profusely from it. It upset her emotionally and friends feared for her sanity. But throughout the crisis she had kept a very clear mind. Harriet was convinced she must have lost up to ten kilos in weight. That was the most visible sign of the effect of her loss, the weight loss. Another sign was the fact that she stayed indoors, away from the public. People close to her noticed she was very pensive. She felt hurt deep inside her and was undoubtedly grateful to the friends who flocked around to provide her company and support. But she did not spend the time pouring out her woes and complaining about Teddy, Jane and the injustice of it all. Friends offered her all manner of advice including inciting her to disrupt the marriage when it came on. To which she only smiled and they all knew she would do no such thing.

"My mind tells me I could be opening myself to ridicule in addition to the loss of Teddy if I do anything stupid," she told Harriet, the person to whom she opened her heart. The person from whom she kept no secret. "To succeed to ruin the marriage or their relationship would require planning I am not in an emotional state to undertake and on which I have no intentions of spending my energy. If a plan to ruin the marriage or to cause a rift between Teddy and Jane succeeds the only thing that can be derived from it would be sadistic satisfaction. It won't change anything. It won't bring Teddy back to me. If anything should happen independently and Teddy and Jane split, and Teddy comes back to me, I can't take him back. So why should I want them to split? Why should I want the marriage not to come off? Why should I wish the marriage fails? Why should I wish they have a miserable marriage? Because that is what Shylock would have done? Because it is human to want to return ill to people who have treated you badly? How will that benefit me or help me or lessen the pain I have gone through and am still going through? As I said earlier, the only satisfaction anybody can derive if such an event happened is happiness or satisfaction that can only be sadistic in nature. I pray for the strength to be above sadistic joy

"Jane will probably go to extreme lengths to take back a man taken away from her. I am Diane, not Jane. If we wreck their relationship, it won't take away the pain I have felt. It won't heal my wound. I will live with the scar of losing Teddy forever. Nothing will ever take it away. If I meet an angel today and marry him tomorrow and can say whew! I am better off, it won't take away the pain I felt losing Teddy. I will from time to time remember the pang I felt when he broke the news to me. So why should I want to cause unhappiness for Jane if that will not take away the pain I have felt? I think I am better off spending the energy that would go into destroying the joy of Jane and Teddy in rebuilding myself.

"Harriet, I am struggling to get over the pain. When I am alone, the recent past comes back, ugly, unjust, illogical and extremely painful. I am ill, very ill. In my heart. But my mind tells me that let me cut my loss and not multiply pain. Let me try to come to terms with what has happened and not try to harm the relationship between Teddy and Jane or either of them personally. We should learn to take pain and not return it. I don't like the pain I went through. I won't try to wish it on anybody, not even someone I must admit I can't love."

At the time Harriet had thought her friend stupid. It was not Harriet who had been wronged and wronged so painfully. But she was emotionally more worked up than her friend seemed. It was only slowly over the months that she had the emotional stability to reflect on what her friend had decided and the rationale for it and to respect her even more. Sometimes she remembered essays they wrote in the junior forms in secondary school. And thought that if she ever had to write an essay on The Most Wonderful Personality I Have Ever Known Diane would stand out not because she was her best friend but because she was really the most wonderful person, the strongest person she had ever known.

When Diane brought the bottles of Tusker beer and glasses, her friend shared her thoughts of her strength.

Diane smiled. "There are two things you should know, Harriet…"

"Don't lecture me on philosophy again, Diane," Harriet cut in to say. "Sometimes you should accept facts about you and not explain them away as if they don't exist or as if they should be taken for granted."

Again Diane smiled. "I don't take anything for granted, Harriet. I acknowledge one baptism for the forgiveness of sins."

They both laughed, knowing Diane had quoted the Catholic Nicene creed.

Diane became serious. "Seriously now. What I was going to say was there are two things I have to share with you, from my experience. If anyone had told me I would go through such an experience and survive it with my sanity intact, with a heart that still worked, I would have said it was impossible. Things were really, really terrible, at a certain stage, I must confess. I had migraines several times. My mind was constantly in a state of turmoil. And my heart seemed eternally on fire. But the first lesson is that you don't really know the potential you have, the strength hidden in you, until you go through a crisis. You may have more strength than I have, but we will not know until, and God forbid, you have to go through a crisis. You may even find yourself singing through the process and wondering why people pretend it is painful."

"You have a very fertile imagination, don't you?" Harriet told her friend. "You exhibited extraordinary strength, Diane, and I am not sure anyone can exhibit half of the strength you showed in the process. Singing through the process and wondering why people pretend it is painful ... Very poetic but not possible. I can't do that and I don't know who can.

"And the second thing? Let's hope this is something I can accept."

"If you don't accept this we must change your name to Thomasia after the doubting Thomas in the Bible. I had a lot of strength to carry my burden and to ease the pressure on my heart through the strength each of you lent me. I probably did not fully appreciate the gifts of your time, your concern and your very presence at the time I was feeling so down under. And rightly so. I was in no mood to feel and appreciate anything. But later on, in retrospect, I realised how much your presence, your concern, the countless little things each of you did for me, lent me strength, supported me and helped heal me. I don't underestimate the value of friends and their support in such critical times."

Apparently Diane didn't underestimate this as evidenced by the supper she invited all her friends to one year after the loss of Teddy. It was an event she organised, she had told them, in order to express her gratitude to each of them and to all of them collectively for their friendship, for helping her in the most critical way at the worst period in her life.

"You know," Diane continued, "when I reflect on what my friends did for me at the time, some of you virtually stopping work to be with me all the time, many of you doing things I would not have had the presence of mind to do, some just being present and letting me know in the silence that I needed that I had a friend and silently taking away part of the pain, some just slightly touching me and in the process saying a lot in the most appropriate way, I tell myself that the only way I can repay each of is to take death away from you if you are dying. You did a lot for me, individually and collectively."

"You deserve everything we did for you. Two of us would get together at the time and express our worries. We would tell ourselves that if it had been one of us facing such crisis you would take charge and know exactly what to do and how best to do it. You love people so much you give yourself to them. You deserved more than you got from us."

They poured their drinks and as they raised their glasses to clink, they both laughed knowing what each would say and why they had started saying this.

As the rims of the glasses touched with a clink sound Diane said, "Cheers. To blissful married life."

Her friend said, "Cheers too. To the liberated life of spinsterhood."

As usual they rocked with laughter.

Alone, Harriet would normally recall these moments. And each time she would wonder what it was that had brought the two of them together to form such a strong bond. She did not know if any friendship existed anywhere else in Kenya in which one could take liberties with what was a painful status of the other. But with Diane, she could take such liberties. And she took them for two reasons. One, and the more important of the two reasons, was to help her friend confront her painful situation and get used to living with it rather than put a thin sheet over it. Two, to her, joking about it was also an indication of the intimacy between the two. She knew she would never try joking about something as serious as why Diane was still a spinster with anyone other than Diane. But she could joke about it with Diane, that extraordinary woman who happened to be her friend. And she did.

Many times, she would lie on the sofa in their sitting room in Mombassa and recall the happiness Jane was going through with Teddy. And tell herself Diane deserved more than that. She would recall how happy she was with David and the little David Junior. And again tell herself Diane deserved to be happier than that.

Chapter Five

He went to bed every evening now with a radio. He bought a portable Sony radio with many bands. In the evenings after work, he would listen to BBC while he cooked and ate his supper. He would watch TV if there was an interesting programme on. Otherwise he read his books and played music, with the volume turned low. But when he was tired and retired to bed he turned on the radio and listened to news and later just kept changing stations searching for those that played music. In his student days he loved music when he was sober. He lost it completely when he was drinking heavily. Strong drink had crowded out all other interest. And now the love for music had returned.

It was Friday morning and he knew he had a lot of work to do that day in the office. But he was looking forward to the day and the pressure of work. In the dark he groped for the radio and turned it on and began his search for stations. In a minute he got one that played music and he put the set next to him on the bed. The station was playing the type of music his younger days drinking colleagues called expired music; it was music from long ago, when he was younger.

After listening to the first two songs he decided to play a game, guess the title of the song and the artiste who played it before the DJ gave those away. He got the first song right. He remembered how popular the tune was when he first heard it. *Strumming my pain with his fingers … Killing me Softly* by Robert Flack he said to himself. The next one was easy. *Don't leave me this way, I can't survive…* Again he said the title aloud, as if speaking to an unseen judge in the room, *Don't Leave me this way* by Thelma Houston. *Sometimes it's hard, to be woman, giving your love to just one man…* He knew the title, *Stand By Your Man*, but was not sure which version was playing. He knew Tammy Wynette had one version and Margaret Singhana played another version. As

68

the song played on he knew it was Tammy's version. But the song reminded him of Margaret Singhana and her collection. *I Surrender. At The Zoo.*

He got the next one from the initial instrumentals alone – ABBA's *Fernando*. He wondered about the group, why it broke up and why it did not come back together and why he had not heard Benny or Stig Anderson or Bjorn Ulvaeus release their own albums. He remembered a lot about the group because he liked its music and read a lot about it when he was a student. He knew for instance that for many years it was the second highest foreign exchange earner for Sweden, second only to the car manufacturing company, Volvo. He also knew that in the years before the group broke up it earned more foreign exchange for the country than Volvo did. *Où sont-ils? Que font-ils?* As happened sometimes, his mind switched to French. Where are they? What are they doing? He did not know and he would love to know.

As if to add to his wonder about the groups that did so well that broke up and would not come back together, the next song started with organ and drum music. He did not have to wait for the singing to start before he could tell which song it was and who sang it. It was *Love is Strange* by Paul and Linda McCartney. Paul, of the Beatles fame. He remembered the Beatles, John Lennon, Paul McCartney, George Harrison and Ringo Starr. He read a bit about the Beatles, like ABBA. In one book he read about them, John was painted as a fighter as a kid. So once when he moved to a new school, on the first day in school when he looked at how many students there were, his thoughts were 'My gosh, so I have to fight all these students.' Dan loved George the most, among the Beatles. He also remembered that in one of their foreign trips, George had been denied entry into the dance hall because he was under-age. He was the youngest of the Beatles. For some reason Dan loved him a lot.

Why could they not come back together after many people tried to bring them back? He wondered about those groups, Beatles and ABBA. Were they afraid they may not reach the standards they set earlier? Was there some fundamental difference between them that they could not get over?

He waited for the next one. He knew it, but only the title. He did not know who played it. *Wait just a minute more, Before you decide to quit... I Go To Pieces,* he knew the title. He tried very hard to recall the artiste. He did not know who played it. His whole body just went limp when the instrumentals of the next one started, a tune he had loved a long time back. His went back to Richard and his sister Karen Carpenter. *Top of the World* by The Carpenters. His mind began wondering again. The siblings played very good music even though the best known of their songs, to him, was *Top of the World.* But they also had *Yesterday Once More, Jambalaya (On the Bayou)* and *Super Star.* Then Karen was said to have developed some sickness that made her feel funny about herself.

The next song came on. *I can be faced, With troubles as long as I live...* Another of the songs he loved – Shirley Brown's *Long as You Love me.* He remembered Shirley Brown and the album from which this song was taken. The title track was *Woman to Woman.* He loved this song more than the title track but the title track was interesting in its own way. As he lay there listening to Shirley on his radio, he thought of the magic of technology. Shirley would be somewhere at that time, doing something else. But here she was in his room, squeezed into a tiny box, and singing a long time ago hit to him. He also recalled his thoughts about what made Shirley sing *Woman to Woman.* A woman telling another woman that the man she was with belonged to her, the singer, from the top of his hair to the tip of his feet. That the clothes he was in were hers and she made the food he ate possible. Musicians were like poets, weren't they?

The next was all instruments but he knew Grover Washington Jr's *Mr Magic.*

Just then the DJ came in with, "Thanks for inviting me into your life this morning. It has been my pleasure being with you for the last thirty minutes. I hope you enjoyed my company. It is the beginning of yet another day and let us join Jim Reeves to give thanks to God for giving us yet another day, for the birds that sing outside your window and for the fish that swim in the pool you will walk past on your way to the office. Let us thank Him for all the wonderful things in the world around us and that He gave us eyes for us to see all those beautiful things. It is just a minute to six o'clock and at six o'clock Tina will be here with the morning's news. Ask yourself as you leave your bed if you are committed to do good today. I wish you good luck if your answer is yes. Tina is standing by with the news…"

He thanked God that the music had come to an end. Whenever he had a lot of work he would leave home very early and start working before people started arriving in the office. It was amazing how much work he could do without distractions. But if the music played till 9:00 he was sure he would be lying in bed listening to it. He carried the radio to the bathroom and listened to the news as he brushed his teeth and later had his bath.

His breakfast was normally a beverage, preferably coffee, with bread and either groundnut paste or fried egg or beef sausage. Today he fried two eggs. He anticipated a long, hard day.

After staying in the guest house for three months, Sammy had discussed with Dr Antwi the possibility of getting him a bungalow. He explained how he thought Dan would not be allowed to stay in the guest house forever. And, since he was really a senior staff with many years in the ministry he deserved a bungalow. It took a lot of talking to convince Dr Antwi that it was worth it to give Dan a bungalow. In the end they gave him one when one was next vacant. It generated some murmurs but nobody said he did not deserve it. Many junior staff said that but for his drink problem and his own careless attitude in the past, he even deserved a bungalow much earlier than this.

The bungalows owned by the Ministry were behind the hospital. Beyond them were quarters for lower level staff.

He had to walk all the way to the taxi rank outside the fence of the hospital to get a taxi. Taxis would only come into the hospital if someone hired one to bring him inside. Some days he was lucky to get a lift either to the gate or all the way into town. Today was one of the days he was not so lucky. He didn't mind walking. Weekends he walked all the way into town, turning down offers of lift. When the day wasn't hard for him, and when it was not too hot, at the end of the day he walked home. He had very little exercise and even though he promised himself to go jogging and do indoors exercises like press-ups, he had so far not managed to start doing them. So whenever he could he walked. And his choosing to walk seemed strange to a lot of people. Fortunately now he did not drink otherwise this behaviour would definitely have been attributed to alcohol.

He walked up the side road and joined the main road serving the residential area just adjacent the Nurses Training College which his ex-wife had attended. It was easy now to think of their relationship in the past without being hurt about it. And without wondering why it had to end. He never got the answer to that question but accepting the fact that they had separated made the question not strongly relevant. He would be interested, if she would ever tell him, why she decided to throw him out. He would especially want to know what he did wrong. He could not remember all that he did in those days when his life was covered in a fog of alcohol fumes. He had tried many times to penetrate the fog and remember things which might have offended Matilda so much as to make her take that decision. That part of his life remained very hazy.

He walked past the very spot where, many years earlier, the young men had dumped Matilda after the multiple repeated rape. Not that he ever heard the story. So the spot did not mean anything to him.

He was about the first person to arrive in the office. But he met two nurses, one female and one male, at the gate having a chat with the security guard.

"Eh, Mr Dan, you are very early today," the female nurse said.

"Yes, I am. But is that how nurses say good morning?"

The nurse laughed. "No, but I heard that is how accountants say good morning."

"But you are not an accountant and I am not an accountant either. So why say good morning the way accountants would say it?"

"Oh, it's because I heard you are an accountant."

"You heard wrong. I am an errand boy in the Ministry. Anyway, good morning to you all."

The three of them responded.

"But Mr Dan," the female nurse called, "you haven't answered my question. Why are you so early? It is not yet eight o'clock."

"No, it isn't. But I have a lot of work and if I wanted to complete it I had no choice but to come early."

She laughed. "You really like work, don't you?"

"No, I don't."

"But you work hard. Very hard."

"Yes, because I have no choice. When you nurses get promoted and we don't ensure that your salary is corrected as early as possible you won't be happy, will you? We have funds from a number of donors and each of them requires timely reports otherwise we will not receive funds for the next phase. I don't like work. If the Ministry will let me sleep the whole month and still come for my salary, I will be happy. But that is not possible. And sometimes, unfortunately, I have to come early or leave late in order to stay on top of the work I must do.

"I hope you were not waiting to see me." He looked at both nurses as he said this.

"Yes, we came to see you."

He raised his brows and asked, "What did you come to see me for? What can I do for you? I was hoping I could have an early start on my work but let's go in all the same if you came to see me."

The male nurse made to say something but the female nurse beat him to it. "It won't take time. A friend of mine who is Rahim's sister wants to marry you so we came to see you."

The quizzical look on the face of the nurse referred to as Rahim confirmed Dan's belief that she was pulling his leg. "She needs to have her head checked if she wants to marry a divorcee."

"For some reason," the female nurse said with a lot of mischief, "she says she has a strong preference for divorcees."

"Good to know, Habiba. Can you look for another divorcee for her? She missed me. I am going to the seminary next month. I applied to be a Catholic priest and I have been admitted to the seminary."

When he was gone Rahim remarked, "He has changed a lot, hasn't he? He is a gentleman now and quite nice to talk to."

"He was a gentleman even when he was drinking. The only difference is that he was gentle until he hit the bottle. But in the mornings and whenever you met him when he was sober he was quiet but very nice to talk to."

"I don't have a sister who wants a husband, anyway. If you are giving him a scholarship why don't you just tell him so but go about it in a roundabout way?" Rahim teased.

"Because I have a fiancé and so don't intend to marry him. Besides, marrying my co-workers' ex-husbands is not my hobby."

"So what is your hobby, marrying their current husbands?" Rahim went on teasing.

"No, my hobby is marrying my co-workers themselves and not their ex or current husbands."

"Stop looking at me that way," he told her and tilted her head another way. "I'm married."

"I have a fiancé too so we make two of a kind. Besides it is even more fun to marry someone who has a wife and watch the look on the wife's face during the marriage ceremony."

He again turned her head away. "I said stop looking at me. It won't happen with me."

"Unfortunately for you I don't have eyes for anybody else."

Dan worked till late that day, leaving the office after 8:00 p.m. He agreed with Sammy that they would come to the office the next day, even though it was a Saturday. They had work that had to be finished and they were determined to finish it. By 7:46 a.m. the next day Dan was in the office. Sammy came over two hours later. He and Dan sat down and reviewed what Dan had done up to that point and shared the rest of what was left between them. At midday Dr Antwi came in, had a chat with Sammy and later walked to Dan's office and saw him hunched over a pile of paperwork.

It had been eight months since Dan was packed out of Matilda's place and in those eight months he had not touched liquor. Dr Antwi came to respect him tremendously, now seeing the hard worker whom drink had masked. Above all, he saw a gentleman and was happy for Dan that he had been saved from the clutches of alcohol. He was happy with himself that Sammy had persuaded him to do the things that helped to resettle Dan.

The highlight of his respect for Dan came at a regional meeting at which the District Directors and their Accountants mounted an attack on the Regional Directorate for what they described as unfair directives, undue interference in how they used funds and late release of funds to the districts. The attack had been started by Nathaniel Aforo, the Accountant for Salaga. Nathaniel was a dictator who terrorised his subordinate staff, made staff of the Ministry in Salaga afraid of him, including senior health staff. It was even known that he manipulated the District Director but the two were very close too. Nathaniel was the first to be making inquiries about the release of funds and made the most noise if funds were delayed for any reason. He liked to deal directly with Accra, ignoring the Regional Directorate to which he was accountable. He operated with little regard to financial policies of the civil service generally and those of the Ministry. He submitted returns late, they were inaccurate and incomplete sometimes.

The unjustified attack went on for about thirty minutes with Dan looking at the Regional Accountant trying valiantly but without success to defend the Regional Directorate. When Dan asked if he could speak Sammy was relieved. He needed any help he could get. The Regional Director knit his brow, unsure what this reformed alcoholic could say and on whose side he would be. The staff from the districts looked amused as they had never heard Dan speak at their meetings.

For ten minutes he spoke. He started by drawing attention to policies and procedures which all those in the room should know very well. He drew their attention to provisions which should guide the disbursement of funds and accounting for funds. When he started to show how the Regional Directorate had sought to ensure compliance with those provisions Nathaniel sought to silence him, knowing where his speech was leading. Sammy made to support him but they soon found that Dan did not need support. He asked Nathaniel in a calm voice, "Is this a meeting to put the Regional Directorate on the carpet or to agree what is right and what is not right no matter who is right or wrong?"

"Who is talking of right and wrong here? Your question is academic," Nathaniel retorted.

"So far the Regional Directorate, including the Regional Director and the Regional Accountant both of whom are your superiors, listened to the issues you raised about them. Now that you know I am going to raise issues about you, you want to prevent me from doing so."

Nathaniel flared up, "No! No! No! I am not preventing you. How can you say I am preventing you? How can you say I am preventing you? How can you accuse me falsely?"

"If you are not preventing me you will stop shouting and allow me to continue my statement. I have the floor. The chairman gave me the floor. You have hijacked it from me to prevent me from making the points you don't want to hear."

Even though Nathaniel tried to cause more commotion with his rebuttals Dr Antwi was firm and silenced him, telling him he did not have the floor. And that he would walk him out if he did not shut up. It was the excuse he needed, after feeling so hurt by the unjustified attacks.

Having refreshed the meeting on the provisions under which the financial transactions of the Ministry were to be conducted, Dan went on to explain, citing examples, how the Regional Directorate sought to ensure the provisions worked. He recounted how they had been flouted, mentioning several instances when they had not been respected and how accountants had challenged the Directorate for simply trying to enforce what they all should have been respecting. He turned the tables so strongly against the recalcitrant districts which were the same that had been vehement in their attack on the Regional Directorate.

To the surprise of the Regional Accountant he informed the meeting of measures the Regional Accounts team had instituted to ensure increased availability of information among health units in the districts and therefore increase monitoring at the district to ensure compliance. The accountants from the districts were visibly unhappy with the measures.

When Dr Antwi and Sammy walked to their wing of the Ministry after the meeting Dr Antwi said, "I am glad you people had planned those measures before this meeting. If the various units in the districts will be informed how much has been released for activities under their respective units, we will see how the likes of Nathaniel will continue to lord it over them."

Sammy was laughing heartily and Dr Antwi did not see what was funny.

"We have never discussed any measures to provide financial information to anybody in the districts," Sammy said, still laughing.

"But Dan said…"

"My respect for him increases daily. He must have just thought about how to silence people like Nathaniel and mentioned the measures. We will surely now institute such measures and I am sure Dan will come up with very good ones. But we have never discussed any such measures before."

Dr Antwi's respect for Dan grew astronomically. A hard working staff. Very knowledgeable of his field. Hardly complaining. Willing to accept extra responsibility. Proactive in his attitude to work.

That Saturday afternoon as he walked towards Dan's office he approached it with true respect and affection for this innocuous member of his staff. Dan's total absorption in his work when Dr Antwi peeped through the window did not surprise him. If there was a workaholic on his staff, his name was Dan.

He took Dan and Sammy out for lunch. "I am not sure you will even remember that you need food if I don't force you to go and eat."

In the breezy atmosphere of *GiddiPas* the trio relaxed and ate and chatted. Dan ate *fufu* while Sammy and Dr Antwi ate fried rice. "I can always prepare rice on my own but I can't prepare *fufu* on my own," Dan explained.

Dan surprised Dr Antwi that afternoon. They had finished eating and were having drinks. Dan was drinking water while Sammy drank a *Guinness* Stout. Dr Antwi drank red wine. The Regional Director looked at Dan and shook his head. "Dan, now that you have given up alcohol I am sure you have many friends."

"I am not sure," Dan replied. "But at least fewer people dislike me."

"So people didn't like you when you were drinking, is it?"

Dan chuckled and said, "Sure."

"Who didn't like you?' Sammy asked innocently.

Dan chuckled a second time, and cast a tell-it-all look at the Regional Director.

Sammy was amused. Dr Antwi was looking directly at Dan. "You mean Director didn't like you?"

"I know for sure he did not like me," Dan said looking only briefly at Dr Antwi. "But I guess it was justified. It was not personal but principled. I'm different and his feelings about me are different."

Sammy could only look at Dan, a smile dancing on his lips. Dr Antwi, on the contrary, was looking critically at him.

Sammy asked, "How did you know he did not like you?"

"I knew, just as I know now that he likes me."

"How do you know I like you?" Dr Antwi asked.

Dan looked lazily at the Regional Director. "Many small but telling things. This lunch together for instance."

"What of the lunch?"

"The three of us coming for lunch."

"This was your lunch," Dr Antwi said. "Sammy came to the office only because you were there."

"In the past, Doc," Dan said in his usually unhurried manner, "you may just have told Sammy to take me out for lunch. You would not have come with us. As I said there were many tiny things but which told their story when put together. If the three of us found ourselves together at lunch, the most likely scenario would be that I would not be sober. But even if I were sober, the attention you have been giving to me this afternoon, inviting me into conversations you start, consciously seeking my opinion just to make me feel part of the conversation – all these are things you would not have done. The way you respond to my greetings when we meet in the office, the way you ask about personal issues when we greet, the way you receive me in your office and many more tell a story."

The surprise to Dr Antwi was that he noted things so critically in those gone by days when he seemed to live in a fog. He was right about how he felt about him when he was an alcoholic and now. And he was right about his feelings being based on principles. And he was right about those little indicators, now that he thought about them. He had not thought Dan, or anybody, noticed. As Dan had said they were things which put together told the story. And Dan did put them together even when people thought his mind must have been foggy.

Things changed quite rapidly for Dan. They changed for the better, that is. In a way. His marriage was forever dissolved, he had to admit that to himself. After a lot of efforts to see the children he had to accept the fact that he had lost those too.

He did not go back to drinking. Instead he worked hard and became a very respectable member of the Regional Ministry of Health. So much respected that when, two years after he gave up drinking, they had to make HR changes and it was initially proposed for Dan to go to Yendi, the Regional Office opposed it. Both Director and Accountant discussed it many times, each time agreeing that Yendi needed Dan. Well, not exactly Dan, they would say, but someone like him. Unfortunately there were not two of his kind in the region, which would have meant that Dan then should go to Yendi. But the Regional Office did not want to lose him.

In the end they invited Dan himself to discuss the issue with him, hoping his own preference would reinforce their position about his movement.

"It's a difficult choice," he told the two. "I know I am needed here. We need a strong Regional Office Accounts team. But Yendi is our highest expenditure district after Tamale. And it has been giving us problems since last year. For me personally, going there will be challenging since I will be working on my own and have to sort out the mess. Yendi is a quieter town and I can concentrate on my studies without being distracted. You can also call me to help during peak periods if you need more hands."

So he went to Yendi. He continued to study for the ACCA and also enrolled to do an MBA through distance education. For the MBA he chose Human Resource Management since the ACCA would further his knowledge of Accounts. In the second year in Yendi he also registered to do a course, through distance education again, in Leadership. And a whole new world was opened to him.

A year later he approached the Regional Director and offered to run a 3-days training on leadership for the District Directors. Dr Antwi was curious but when Dan discussed the contents with him he seemed convinced it was worth trying. Dan was not asking for any fees. The District Director for Yendi did not turn up, not convinced his Accountant could teach him anything. Some Directors came only because the Regional Director had asked them. Some came because they had other things to do in Tamale and did intend to absent themselves from many of the training sessions.

On the first day of the training they did very simple exercises and had very lively discussions after each exercise. When Dan did PowerPoint presentations they listened with rapt attention and had very animated discussions after the presentations. It was only when they were leaving the MOH conference room that it occurred to them all that nobody had left the sessions and that the day had been very pleasantly but very usefully spent. Telephone calls were made that evening and activities the Directors had planned to carry out over the next two days were rescheduled, reassigned or cancelled.

Since this was going to be Dan's first training in his long term plans, he spent a very long time developing the contents and thinking through the delivery method. He wanted the training to be more than a success. If he could make the Directors see the value of the training, then it would really be valuable. If he could not make them see it as valuable to them, after he had put in so much, then, he told himself, he was not ready to go into consultancy in leadership development.

The Regional Director came in to observe one session in the morning of the second day. At the end of the first day he had asked the Tamale Municipal Director how the day's training had gone and he had been surprised at the strongly positive feedback he got. So he decided to sit in one of the sessions just to get a feel what it was all about. He intended to stay for thirty minutes, one hour at most. It was when his secretary called that he realised he had spent more than one hour and probably intended to stay longer. In fact, he stayed throughout the morning session, leaving only when they took the break for lunch. During the morning's coffee break he had gone round the groups in which people stood to hold informal discussions to find out what they thought about the sessions so far.

"I think all senior staff should go through the training," the District Director for East Mamprusi District said.

"What do you think anybody can gain from this training?" Dr Antwi asked.

"What I like about this training," Mustapha said, "is that it makes you see the connection between your development and the success of the district. It makes you see your relationship with your subordinate staff and what is expected of you in order to influence your staff to go on doing the right things even when you are not there. It makes you appreciate yourself and it makes you see staff as the human beings that they are, intelligent, independent willed and not tools you must command. Do you want results? Even if you didn't so much care about results you change your mind after this training. So you want results. How do you achieve results? The door is open for you to look into a room full of strategies you can use in different contexts to achieve your results.

"But I feel if the rest of my District Health Management Team had the same training, we would work better together and we can achieve more."

Dr Antwi came with Sammy for the last session on the last day and told the Directors that he heard their feedback about the training. He also told them that Dan had not charged the Ministry a single cedi for the training. From what he had observed during the half day he spent with them, Dan must have spent a considerable amount of time designing the sessions, looking for very practical exercises they could relate to their contexts. "So he must have worked very hard to offer you, and us the Ministry as a whole, this gift. I ask myself why someone would work so hard to give us something as valuable as this for free. The answer is not far-fetched. Dan worked under us here in the Regional Office. He has always been a committed staff. He is committed to producing results. He is an observant person, noticing what others gloss over. So he noticed our need to have results oriented leaders. He has designed a package which according to you, addresses this need. He has delivered effectively, according to you the participants. You say you now see the relationship between your personal development and progress in your district. Will it make any difference in the way you work? Will you achieve more success than you have done so far? How will you pay Dan?"

When the Yendi District Director heard from his colleagues how the training had been he just kept following Dan with his eyes wherever he went. The word enigma kept coming to his mind whenever he contemplated Dan. At work he was still the simple Accountant. Of course, he admitted Dan was a very good accountant, very knowledgeable and very hardworking. But the possessor of such knowledge as his colleagues described? It was difficult to reconcile the easy to ignore personality of Dan with the teacher they said had impressed his colleagues so much.

With the success of the first training, there was no stopping him. Many times in the night after he had approached the Regional Director and got his agreement to conduct the training, he had thought of possible excuses to abort the training. He had not been sure it would be successful. He had imagined how he would fare in the Ministry if the training proved disastrous.

The session with the District Directors was a very important first step in the next phase of Dan's life. Dr Amoako-Attah who was now the Brong Ahafo Regional Director of Health heard of Dan's training and offered him his first consultancy. Some of the Directors in Brong Ahafo had heard about the training from their colleagues in Northern Region and so came quite expectant and left completely satisfied.

Then the Northern Regional Directorate arranged with the District Directors for Dan to come round and train their DHMTs. From the Ministry of Health he turned his attention to NGOs. By that time he had began to earn some reputation as a trainer and leadership had began to catch on. Some of the Directors spent time in tennis courts and beer bars with some NGO colleagues and told stories about the training. That you don't even know that you are in a learning session because you are not under pressure. The exercises are simple. The lessons are very easy to draw. It is easy to apply what you learn in your workplace and in your life.

So when he approached some NGOs to send their senior staff to a leadership training session, while some said no, a few agreed. After all, the course was ridiculously cheap. But the impact had been incredible. At the end of the fifth year after the disastrous end of his marriage, Dan resigned from the Ministry and set up Horizon Leadership Development Service. Initially he rented conference rooms in hotels for his training but quickly started building his own premises when he began getting big fishes. He had a contract from Standard Chartered Bank to train its most senior staff. The training had gone down so well with the management of the bank that the next level of senior staff was sent for the training. Then he was contracted to train international staff of the bank in Africa. When he started earning big bucks he started thinking big, including separating the training facilities – conference rooms and accommodation – from the leadership service. So that other people in need of just a venue for training could hire the facilities.

Over the next five years he covered Africa extensively, providing training in different settings and to different clientele. He trained in both Anglophone and Francophone Africa, his being fluent in French serving him well here. He did some training in some European and Asian countries as well.

Chapter Six

In Diane's sitting room, the two friends were still sipping their beer and Harriet was waiting to hear about the man in the picture in her friend's bedroom.

"Now," Harriet said as she sipped her beer and put the glass down, "tell me about the man in the picture and how he touched your life."

It was the turn of Diane to push the rewind button in her mind and relive the series of events in which the course of her life was changed by Daniel Apeatu. And to decide which to share with her friend and how to tell them.

"I repeat that he is not my boyfriend. I know him professionally but not personally and can't answer some of the questions you may have. We met in workshop settings, twice and have maintained email correspondence, mostly with me asking questions and testing ideas. He knows nothing about my personal life and I know nothing about his. Is he married? Most likely but I don't know. How many children does he have? I don't know…"

"A lawyer would have asked if he has children before coming to their number. Pardon my intrusion. I will keep my mouth hereafter forever tightly shut."

When only six months after she lost Teddy Diane was asked if she would be interested in a course on leadership taking place in Zimbabwe her initial thought was no. She did not see that she needed education on leadership to promote her work. She was working on gender and women's rights and doing very well about it, she thought. That was the area she wanted to grow in. She was already learning a lot. She could present gender as a process that was not confrontational and many men had given her feedback that her approach to gender made them appreciate the issue more than they had ever done. Some gender advocates, especially activists, accused her of being too soft and that her approach would not help the cause of women. Any course that would enhance her understanding of the real issues in gender and the most affective approaches to influence both men and women would attract her. She did not think that she had any problems with leadership.

Her supervisor came back to say that a UK foundation was sponsoring the course and they recommended it strongly, saying the facilitator was an excellent facilitator on leadership. This particular workshop would be on women as leaders, particularly in the African context. She needed a holiday and if it would cost the organisation nothing to send her off on a holiday, why not. She would meet women from other countries and she could learn a lot about their approach to gender and women's rights.

So her contact information was passed on and a few days' later she received correspondence welcoming her to the training and expressing the hope that she would find the workshop useful. She had then been asked to fill a questionnaire which she did and returned, providing information about her, her work and her knowledge of certain aspects of leadership.

She arrived in Harare and was met at the airport. It was at the airport that she was told that the training would take place in a town called Kadoma, which was far from Harare. It had irritated her then, even though it was a minor issue. She felt the organisers should have given the participants information about the venue and travel arrangements among others. She joined five other women who were participating in the same workshop. Four were older than her but the fifth one was younger. It was during the drive to Kadoma that she learnt that they had been sent a lot of information, about the venue, the facilities at the hotel they would use for the workshop, about Zimbabwe in general, weather, exchange rate and many more. She had received a pack of information but had thought it was all workshop handouts and she did not read them.

She spent her time during the drive reading the documents that had been sent to the participants which she had not read. She was surprised how much information had been sent. Besides the information about the country they had also been provided some handouts and participants had been encouraged to read them before the workshop. She now spent her time reading them, finding them quite interesting. So interesting she was lost to the chatter of her colleagues some of whom, it was obvious, knew each other from a long way back. Occasionally she stopped and listened to the conversation around her, turned to smile to indicate interest in a point that had been made. And went back to the reading materials.

Her fears about the facilitator were somehow allayed by the information given and the handouts. She had previously wondered if the facilitator was not going to an old firebrand, a fiery activist whose presentations would make the like of Diane seem as guilty as men in the denial of women's rights. She could not tell how old she (the facilitator) would be but she seemed to think that she would not be fiery.

The hotel in Kadoma was called The Ranch. It had no ranch and she never learnt why it was given that name. She met some of the participants that Saturday evening and others on the Sunday. There was one surprise for her. The facilitator was a man, a quiet type who did not smell of leadership.

On the Monday for instance, the session started some minutes late because the participants took some time to settle down, some spending longer than necessary time moving around and greeting and chatting. She had expected the facilitator to stamp his authority on the sessions right from the beginning but he did not seem capable of stamping any authority. He did not even seem to have any authority.

When there was order he welcomed them and introduced himself. He was Ghanaian. Diane had met a few Ghanaians in the UK and she remembered there had been two Ghanaian students in Makerere when she was there but she had not expected that there would be a Ghanaian living and teaching leadership in Zimbabwe.

He asked them to stand up and when they did he made them move round the room, making them change course several times, bumping into each other. He made them stop after they had been going on for about two minutes. He asked each to stand where she was when he asked them to stop. For the next fifteen minutes they did an exercise from which they learnt about each other. It was so interesting they forgot it was an exercise. They found themselves spontaneously clapping when it was over. When they went on the break for their lunch, Diane had a different opinion of the facilitator. They were twenty-five and ranged in age from a twenty-five to thirty-two. They came from all over the continent. There were four women from South Africa, one white, the second coloured and two blacks. There was a Rwandese who spoke perfect English and French and one woman from Namibia as well. There were two from Zimbabwe. There was a second woman from Kenya. There were women from Tanzania, Uganda and Malawi. There was a Senegalese whose English was only marred by her French accent. There were women from The Gambia, Ghana and Nigeria. Diane was surprised that the country she always referred to as Gambia was actually *The* Gambia. There was a Somali woman, very quiet woman. There were women from Ethiopia and Eritrea as well.

The methodology had been very simple, hardly noticed but very effective. They did exercises either in pairs, or small groups and once during the day they split into three groups. After each exercise he asked what they learnt. Diane liked to tell her friends that she was not a participation person. By that, she explained, she meant that she was not one who found participatory sessions fun. She would sit through such sessions and hardly make a contribution, not because she did not know but because she did not like speaking when in a group of more than four. But to her surprise, she had found herself a number of times during the day offering to make a contribution on what she had learnt.

Not for once did he lecture or do any presentation. He would introduce a session, discuss an issue or a situation and ask people to write their thoughts on post-it notes he had given them earlier. At the start of the session he had given each of them a pad of post-it notes, the large size. Diane had wondered what they were each going to do with a whole pad. But he had assured them that they would use the post-it notes a lot. And they had. When they wrote their thoughts on the post-it they collected them and pasted them on the board set up for the purpose. They would then read what had been written and follow with a discussion.

He kept changing their sitting positions and so each time they had to work in pairs or in small groups it was always with someone new.

He connected his laptop computer to an LCD projector. As they shared what each had learnt he typed it on the computer and it was projected unto a screen by the projector.

When he announced that it was fifteen minutes past five in the evening and he wanted them to leave the conference room at five thirty exactly, they were surprised at the time. When they came out at the end of the day's session they found themselves forming small groups and chatting as if they had known each other for ages. Conversation during supper was equally lively and they laughed a lot. Diane was sure she was going to like the rest of the days, she liked the group and she knew that in spite of her initial thoughts about the workshop she would learn a lot. And would find what she learnt useful.

Dan, she noticed, was a quiet person by nature. At supper they did not sit at the same table but she could see him from her table. She noticed that he listened a lot, and did so intently. He hardly spoke and each time he spoke it seemed he asked a question. The intensity with which she listened to others surprised her. She wondered what he was hearing that was new and valuable as to make him give it so much attention.

He did a brief presentation the next morning which generated first questions and then a lively discussion. He used the PowerPoint and spoke clearly. When their questions were exhausted Diane found herself exhaling. She had been holding her breath as the questions came in, some quite difficult, but he gave to each question a very informative answer. In that one short presentation he convinced them he knew his subject.

It was not till the afternoon of the third day, at lunch, that one of them drew their attention to the fact that they had not had to strain themselves to learn anything since the Monday. But she admitted that when she reflected on how much she learnt over the two and half days, she felt she had learnt more than she did in five days in other workshops. They all agreed. They spent the last hour of the Wednesday, the third day of the workshop, in a general discussion, with the facilitator answering questions participants posed. He used the participants a lot in answering their questions but when he made an addition to what had been said, it was a worthy addition.

If they were impressed by the sessions over the first four days, the sessions on the afternoon of the Friday were even more impressive.

"When the director of an organisation takes lessons on financial management, or human resource management, or planning, what will she or he be using the knowledge for?" he asked them.

They listed what the person would use the knowledge for. This time he wrote it on a flip chart.

"When you undertake studies in leadership, where do you want to apply the knowledge?" he asked and wrote down what they said.

"The unfortunate problem with us," he told them, "is how we use knowledge. A company accountant will keep such excellent records it is easy to see with the press of a few keys of the computer what is the financial position of the company. She can tell the director how much they still have as balance on staff salaries and therefore whether or not they can afford a raise for staff and if they can by what percentage. The accountant of an NGO will advise the director that they need to manage their fuel costs better because in the first quarter of the year alone they had spent forty percent of the year's budget for fuel. Yet this same accountant, if he is a man, will have a chain of girlfriends on whom he will be spending more than his income. His personal budget will not require good management. He does not see the relevance of the principles used in managing the finances of the organisation in his personal life, in the management of his personal resources.

"When I asked where a director will apply his or her knowledge of human resource management or financial management, you rightly left out the family. Because what we learn in courses, workshops and other training sessions we think apply only in the workplace. When I asked where you would apply your knowledge of leadership I expected the first to be mentioned to be you yourself. Why do you need to lead your organisation, your women's group, your church society or your village group better than you need to lead yourself?

He asked them, "How many of you, if given the chance to start your university or tertiary education all over again, will study different courses from those you studied?"

A lot of hands went up. "Why did you choose to study the course you chose at the time then? I don't want an answer. Just ask yourself that question and answer it for yourself. Why are you in your current position? Why are you in your current job? Are the reasons any different from the reasons why you did a course you say you will not do if you had to decide what to study today?

"Is the job you are in the one you should be in? Many of us are comfortable in our jobs, having never asked if we should be there. You are an accountant in an organisation and your vision for your future is to become senior accountant, then principal accountant and then head of finance. Must you be an accountant? But, you may argue, that is what you were trained for. A leader won't accept that argument. Can you make a change in direction anywhere in your career? You can. But if you must make that change you must explore yourself and your environment and ask yourself critical questions at the end of the exploration.

"There are simple, basic steps to charting our career path. And we have all the tools needed to make us consciously chart that path. We should start with finding out who we are. What do we find easy to do? What do our colleagues in the workplace and our supervisors praise us for? What do we know to be our strengths and what are our weaknesses? What don't we enjoy doing? What do we struggle to do?

"We should then next turn the spotlight on our environment. What skill areas are beginning to emerge today which will be the key to the development of our countries over the next ten years? What skill areas are more likely to grow? Which will be the areas of high demand by industry, in management, in development and so on? You can find out by pausing and reflecting, by talking to people, by reading reports and searching for sources of information. A leader gathers and uses information, current information, to inform her decisions. A leader has a variety of sources from which they get information. A leader is a friend to information."

He went to the flip chart and drew two boxes. One he labelled *My Knowledge and Skills* and the other *Skills and Knowledge with a Future*. "A lot of times," he told them, "your strengths and knowledge and experience will not fit the knowledge and skills that you have identified will be in great demand over the next ten years or so.

"That brings you to the next set of questions you then need to ask yourself. Given your knowledge of the job market for the future and your knowledge of yourself, are you going to be relevant or irrelevant in the next five years? In the next ten years? What do you need to do to make you relevant? What do you need to do – what skills, knowledge, attitudes do you need to acquire – to make you develop a career in one of the careers of the future? Which do you think your knowledge, experience, personal strengths and weaknesses, best suit you for? What do you need to do to fit you into the career you think suits you? What do you need to learn? What attitudes do you need to acquire? Which do you have to give up? What are you going to do this year, next year, the year after and so on, to grow you?"

Diane sat quietly and swallowed every word she heard. Very simple things she didn't need anybody to have told her but which hit her very hard. She felt as if Dan had taken hold of her and shaken her so hard her brain rattled and the sleep had gone out of her eyes. She looked round and found her colleagues busily writing. Even though she did not write she was sure the essence of his speech had been filed away indelibly in her mind. She would play back this last speech many times in her life, she was sure.

"How many of you have ever developed plans – a strategic plan or even a programme or project proposal?"

Many hands went up.

"Is there anything I have said in the last few minutes which you will say you have not had to do in developing your plans or programmes?"

A silence and shaking of heads.

He smiled. "So again, we have knowledge, skills, tools we have used in the workplace but which we don't think are necessary for our own self development. In Time Management, we learn that you save a lot of time by spending part of it in reflection and planning. So when you pause, take time off and go away somewhere, or in the quiet of your bedroom, and do an introspection and examine your environment in order to find out how you can construct the path to your future, you are not wasting time. It is time well spent…

"How many of you have ever worked with a strategic plan or a multi-year plan like a five year programme?"

Many hands went up.

"Good. Now, let us suppose you develop a five year programme last year. Is the document a sacred document you refer to every year in the five years and from which you must not deviate at all?"

The participants provided information. No, it is a guide but if it was carefully thought through and developed with the participation of those affected by the problem, it would be a strong guide. But you monitor it and may review it if you are convinced about the need to modify.

"Good," he again said. "The strategic plan or the five year programme is a very good guide. Last year when you were developing it, you made some assumptions. As you said yourselves, if the analysis was critically done, most of the assumptions will be true in the second, third and maybe even in the fourth and fifth years. But it is possible a few crucial assumptions can be wrong. Things you did not foresee can come up. Since we are in Zimbabwe, let us use Zimbabwe as an example. Assume you develop a five year programme to help poor rural farmers increase their incomes from agriculture. One of the strategies is to introduce high yielding early maturing maize variety to farmers. The variety will allow for a good harvest before the drought which had destroyed crops in the past set in. It would also allow farmers increase their yield about three times from the same acreage with the same inputs. Two years after the programme has started, rice is the crop that has become more important and attracts a higher price than maize. A new rice variety has come in which is in high demand in neighbouring countries. If the farmers you are supporting switch to it, the expected increase in income you expected to achieve through your programme will be achieved even more easily and even faster. What do you do?"

The discussion was lively.

"We earlier described how you can use simple tools you already use in your work to plot a road map for your development. How do you see the discussion we just had applying to your developing your career map?"

Another round of lively discussion.

"You all know that leadership has to do with finding a path where the manager says the path has ended. It has to do with not accepting the stop sign where it shouldn't be. Being a leader means when you are told something cannot be done, you look very hard for alternatives to known strategies used in the situation. When you apply leadership to yourself, it means you look very critically inside you and find parts of you you did not previously know about. It means you take a second and even third look at things you previously said you could not do. It means you challenge yourself more than you have so far done…"

On and on he took them through simple things they knew and which people hardly thought to apply in their own lives and in the family. It took more than one hour, the longest presentation over the five days and done without notes and without the use of the LCD. The discussions took another hour at the end of which each of them felt they had a lot of useful hints to change their lives drastically with. When one of them told him it is easier for some people to make changes than others he agreed.

"If you are trained to be a lawyer and you have been practising law for say three or four years, you don't want to risk going into a new area and starting all over again," said Sabine, the Senegalese. "Some people are adventurous while, unfortunately, others are not."

"Very sound point, Sabine," Dan agreed. "But a leader does not accept that. When you have looked at who you are and your current job you may find that you are well placed. You may find you are in the right job and you are doing well and you are happy. If you find you are not in your right job, as a leader you should be able to face the difficult task of making a change in your career even though you have been trained for your current job."

It was then he told the little about himself he ever told participants. "I was trained an accountant. I did Business Administration, with Accounting option, at the university. After graduation I took the Chartered Accountants' exam and got chartered. I have ACCA. But I find the work I am doing now fantastic. It has nothing to do with Accounting but it is the job I will do all over again if I had my life to start all over again. Like many of you I was not the adventurous type. I liked the comfort of my job – I knew it and was good at it. I did not like the unknown. But growing people seemed such an exciting job.

"There are three things I like about this job. One, it is challenging. Each time I have to facilitate a session, even with the information I get about each participant, I don't assume the sessions will be easy or interesting. I have to work to make them interesting and to ensure that you each leave here a changed, touched person. Despite having done this many times now, each new set of participants comes with its own challenges and I have never been complacent about any session or had any illusions that the next session will be easy or successful just because I have had successes so far. I prepare for each new session with some fear. And I like it that I prepare for each session with fear. The anxiety, the fear, shows how much I want to make the session successful and it makes me work harder.

"The second thing I like about the job is that it is interesting. I meet each new group of participants with some anxiety, as I said before. But I also come with an expectation that we will have an interesting time together. I am never wrong. The questions you pose, the fresh and different perspectives each of you bring, the information you pour into the discussion, all these make the five or so days very interesting. The debates among you, the points we differ on, all these make each training session very interesting to me.

"The third reason for liking the job? It is rewarding, very rewarding. It is not the monetary rewards I am talking of. On Monday when we were going to begin the introductions I could see the cloud of doubt in many faces. Is it this easy-to-ignore person who is supposed to lead our discussion on women as leaders?" They all laughed and he smiled. "Oh, I know it and expect it each time. So for each group I am meeting for the first time, our first interaction generates scepticism. Then over the next few days, you can see the change in them. Not only in their impressions about me, but especially in their desire to unlock themselves. Over the past three years I have been in constant contact with many of those who have attended my leadership workshops. And you can see the differences developing in them over the years. Many people are looking harder at themselves and finding hidden strengths, finding potential they had allowed to lie dormant, and recreating themselves and redesigning their future. In a positive way, in a way that will make them reach out and influence many others. It is the greatest reward you can ever expect from anyone who attends a leadership course…

"Before we move on let us discuss something essential to leadership. How many of you have read *Dr Jekyll and Mr Hyde*?"

Many hands went up.

"I am glad there are many of you who have read it. Now, just sit back and close your eyes for a few seconds and try to recall the story. I am sure many of you must have read the book several years back. So spend some seconds recalling what the story is about."

After about a minute or so they told what they remembered of the story. Essentially about the man who by day was the respectable doctor Jekyll but at night was transformed into the monster Hyde.

He next asked what they thought the story wanted to convey or portray. The dual nature of our personalities, was the summary of their answers. "You are right. The book brings out the fact that we have more than one nature," Dan admitted. "We all must have heard said that human beings are half human and half beast and that that would explain the part rational and part irrational nature of humanity. When the beast in us takes over, we are irrational.

"It is believed that some people really suffer what is called Multiple Personality Disorders. They really live like the doctor and his hideous other personality. Two different personalities live inside them. They hear voices inside them. They can transform into the other unseen personality and go out and do things which they don't remember afterwards. Don't ask me if it is true but there is a branch of science that says it is true.

"In real life we all live more than two lives really," he went on, "and we live them separately. If we only brought those lives together the quality of our lives would have been better. And to develop the leader in you that is what I want you to do, bring the different aspects of your life into a harmoniously integrated life. For many of us, on Sunday, we are one personality. We remember the principles of virtue and reconciliation. We try to take our lives to a higher spiritual plane, but for only a few hours. During Lent, or Ramadan, we fast, do some acts of charity and again try to take our lives to a higher spiritual level. In the office we use principles of time management; we apply rules on resource management to the resources of the organisations we work for. Unfortunately, when we return from church we hang the lives we lived that morning with the Sunday dresses in our wardrobes. We lock up the good practices of the office in our drawers at the end of the day when we are going home. Our lives would certainly benefit from the combination of the principles of our religious, organisational and private lives. Remember I said the principles, not the bad practices from each of those lives; so that if you are very good at stealing resources from your professional life you fight to become the treasurer of your church association so that you can continue to steal money from that source too. That is not what I meant, please…"

At 3:30 p.m. he asked them to spend the next twenty minutes quietly going over what they had heard from the first day to that Friday. He knew they had been writing notes but now he wanted them to write down in bullet point things they had learnt. At the end of the twenty minutes he asked them to spend the next fifteen minutes starting a table of how they would use their learning first in their own lives and secondly in the organisations they worked for.

"I don't teach people," he told them. "All I want to do in my facilitation sessions, is to tickle you, prick you and prompt you to take control of yourself. All I want to do with you is stimulate your interest in yourself and see if I can interest you in unlocking and growing the talent you have. It is when you have done that, that you will look up studies and experience building opportunities that help you grow the talents you know you have and which you are determined to grow. Workshops that seek to dump information and knowledge passively on you are not helpful. We all have lots of information which we don't use appropriately. Until we are hungry to improve ourselves, unless we consciously develop a map leading to our tomorrow with clear expected results at definite points along the road and we have agreed how to reach each point, a lecturer can hammer into your head all manner of technically sound information but it won't help you."

He told that when they went back they were welcome to bounce off him any ideas they would develop on what they wanted to do. He encouraged them to use him to challenge themselves to do things differently and to try and push the borders of their world outward. Then had followed a very interesting discussion. One of the participants drew his attention to the fact that he was inviting them to engage in a relationship with him that could be very long term, to use him over that long period of time. He said yes. The participant said she asked the question because she knew he would have been paid for this training. Would he be paid for long term support for their development?

"Are you afraid that after a number of exchanges of correspondence between us, you will wake up one fine morning to find a bill from me for services rendered to you?"

They all laughed. "No, I will not be paid for that."

As other participants asked if he would be happy to be bothered by them continuously and if he would have the patience to be used for the bouncing of ideas over a long time without payment he smiled, one of the few times he smiled. He did not keep a face that scared people, Diane admitted, only that he was serious most of the time or kept a bland face. Even when he told a joke he hardly smiled or he would wear just a wee bit of a smile, one that played only at the corners of his lips. "I sure work for fees. I am paid for this workshop. But I see the contracts awarded me to facilitate learning in leadership as opportunities for me to influence leadership development on the continent. The contract ends with the successful delivery of the workshop. Am I a mercenary only interested in selling my knowledge and skills? The continent needs a breed of leaders, self-motivated and committed to influencing others in other to free their locked potential. I have a privilege to facilitate that by the opportunity given to me by those who contract me to facilitate sessions. I accept that privilege, the rare opportunity to support as many people as people to grow as leaders. One day, if I can go to bed in the night with the knowledge that there are one hundred women and men on this continent who are influencing the people around them to be better than they would have been, the value of that fact to me would be more than a million dollars.

"I have had feedback throughout the week that you are taking some useful things away from here. Will you apply them? I will be happy to be available if you need me in any way. If that helps you achieve for yourself a given target, my reward is your success. If you need to consult me, engage me in discussions or let me challenge you over the next ten years, with you getting in touch every fortnight over that period, please do get in touch that frequently and for that long. I will have the patience to respond to each mail you send me, I assure you."

There were many things they were all taking away in addition to the knowledge they had gained on leadership. They all noticed his use of music and its effect on their learning. He brought an Aiwa stereo and played music throughout the sessions. Whenever they went into groups to work, he would play very soft music with the volume tuned very low. The music would float over them, hardly disturbing them but soothing and relaxing them. Whenever they had a break, for snack for instance, he played more danceable music and a lot of people swayed while mixing or sipping their beverage. His taste for music was very wide. He played music from the fifties up to very current music. They enjoyed some of the tunes they heard when growing up but which had long been lost. He played music from France, from Latin America, calypso and what is called Latin American music at home. He played Congo music and had a collection of very good South African music. He introduced some of them to Senegalese and Malian music. He introduced some of them to Nigerian *juju* music even though Ijeoma from Nigeria had explained that *juju* music was very old music.

Another thing they all went away impressed with was the sheer amount of his knowledge; it was vast. During the sessions he encouraged the aggregation of their knowledge which they all shared willingly. So he would let them lead in presenting their ideas on any topic and let them debate whenever there was a clash of ideas. He was never in a hurry to intervene and act as the all-knowing authority on any issue. But when their contributions had ended and he made his addition, they all still sat up and listened. When they strayed into an area he had not prepared for and he had to speak on it they all listened with the same rapt attention given to his presentations on what he had prepared.

At the end of the last session on the last day, he asked all of them to stand shoulder to shoulder in a circle and hold hands.

"How many of you know of a singer called Al Jareau?" Only a few did. "He has a song called *Lean On Me* but the words for that song were written by someone else, called Bill Withers. We are all going to sing it and pledge ourselves to be there for each other." He gave out printed copies of the song and started it on stereo. As they sang along they leaned one way and then the other, leaning one on the other at one time and the next time the other on the one.

"Be there for each other and use each other. You are not in competition with each other. Be supportive of each other. I wish you good luck. May you grow into gentle giants." And with that he brought the five days' journey to a sentimental and memorable end.

Diane had not up to that point had the chance to sit with him at table and get close to him during the tea breaks to talk to him. But that evening when she joined the queue for supper – it was a buffet – it seemed she was the only one in the group who was hungry. There was no other participant.

"I am glad to find you here, Diane."

She knew the voice without turning. "Good evening, Sir. I didn't notice you coming."

"I have told you all I am not Sir, Diane. I am Dan."

"I am only calling you Sir. Do you know what we all call you when we are talking about you?"

"It has to be Dan of course."

"We call you Prof."

"You don't say!"

"But I've said it already."

He laughed aloud, the first time Diane had seen him do that.

"Can we share a table? I want to have a chat with you."

So the two of them sat at a table for two. "I have not had the chance to commend you for the quality of your contributions to the discussions," he told her when they were seated. When she raised her eyebrows he said, "I mean it. You are a critical observer with a strong ability to see relationships, to see connections in issues and to see what does not fit."

"I don't know why you would want to tell me what is not true or to flatter me. But I am pleasantly surprised by your comments."

"You rarely speak," he admitted. "But when you do you compel us all to listen to you. When many people have spoken before you, it is interesting to listen to you pick up what they have all left. It is interesting to listen to you look at things from a different perspective, a different angle. It is not how many times you talk, but what you say when you talk that is important."

She felt flattered by his comments and she told him. They spent more time talking than eating. He wanted to know in detail what she did and what her plans for her career were.

"I am not sure," she told him. "Before I came here I was certain I had a definite career. I knew what I wanted to be doing over the next five years. If you had asked this question about my career this past Sunday I would have given you an answer. You have changed that over five short days."

He bowed and touched his heart. "Touché," he said with a smile.

"Honest, you have stirred my mind and it is now in a kind of turmoil. I am not sure what I want to be doing. I know I am going to spend some time thinking about options and it will take a while before I can say I have even an outline of what my career will be."

He nodded. "That will be you. You won't decide in a hurry. Just one little advice. Don't underestimate yourself. You have a lot of potential. Look critically at yourself and set very challenging targets, set for yourself a high peak. I know you can climb it."

"Waw! You have more faith in me than I have in myself. You have more faith in me than anybody has ever had in me."

"My job is growing people."

"I thought you said that you don't develop people but you only stimulate people to develop themselves?"

"Yes, I said that," he admitted. "I grow people in the same way a farmer grows crops. A farmer will till the land to loosen it and allow for a balanced retention of water and air in it. He does not pull the shoot and roots out of the seed after he puts it in the wet soil. The seed itself shoots out the leaves and roots. When the plant appears above the ground the farmer can continue to support its growth by continuously weeding to keep the soil loose enough and getting rid of weeds which can choke the plant. But he can't pull the plant to hasten its growth. We say a farmer grows crops but he only facilitates the growth of the plants, in real terms. He does not grow the plant. That is what I do with people."

Over the next year she had maintained constant correspondence with him. She had not understood what he meant in Kadoma when he offered to challenge them. She understood it when she started sharing her plans with him. She remembered one mail from him: *It is interesting to note that you think you can do other things and you have a plan to make that possible. I have looked at your targets and how you propose to achieve them. I will say that the strategies will allow you to achieve the given targets. It is just like you – critical, methodological and thorough. Of course you know that there is a but... One can make incremental changes in one's life. That is, instead of aspiring to move from Accountant to Senior Accountant, one expects to compete for the Principal Accountant's position. It is a change but it is not the same as moving out of accounts altogether. The targets you have set enable you go up faster in your current career. Is that where you want to be? If yes, there is nothing wrong with that. You know yourself and you are the one best placed to answer that. But if the answer is no, then your targets are not about changing at all…*

When nine months after the workshop in Kadoma she was informed that there was an opportunity for a follow up workshop on the same theme she did not wonder if she would gain anything from attending it. Instead she sought to know when it would take place so that she could ensure that she was free to attend it. When the date was confirmed and she submitted the completed application form, she began dreaming of another exciting week with her colleagues.

Even though they had been corresponding with each other since they returned from Kadoma, when they knew that the same group was meeting again, this time in Malawi, the mails increased in frequency. It was clear they were all looking forward to the event. Their first day in Salima, where the workshop was taking place, was like a reunion of her secondary school mates. They interacted as if they had known each other over the past ten years. Some of them had been given nicknames during the training in Kadoma and the names echoed whenever their owners appeared. Other lodgers at the hotel would have been wondering who were these lively ladies who kept such titles as President, UN Secretary General, The Coordinator, Role Model and others vibrating in different parts of the hotel, by the pool, at the reception, in the restaurant and on the stairs.

They genuinely asked what each had been doing, how much progress they were making and how much they had changed. Almost everybody had a story to tell, a story of discovering someone different in them. As they shared experiences they came to admire Dan even more. He had maintained constant communication with all those who had corresponded with him. He replied to each promptly and the reply to each showed how much thought he gave to whatever was shared with him.

"He must have been very busy," Anita, from Namibia, said.

"Busier than the busiest bee," Magdalene, from Uganda, added.

The descriptions just went on. Fantastic, incredible, extraordinary stamina, passionate about his job, real practitioner of what he teaches and so on.

When Dan arrived he was welcomed like a favourite former teacher arriving at the reunion of a year group. As usual, he took it all calmly. An incident on the first day of the sessions was etched strongly on Diane's memory. It kept reminding her of two traits of the Dan; his sense of humour and his genuine interest in people.

As he walked round the room distributing post-it notes, he told them, "I have always tried to limit the number of participants to any session to twenty-five. I can have thirty in a session but twenty-five is my preferred limit. I want to be able to relate with each participant, know each of you well and learn how to make the most use of your nature during the sessions. I am comfortable with twenty-five. But now we have twenty-six participants."

They all quickly looked round the room for the new participant. They couldn't find her.

He went on distributing the post-it and talking. "The difficulty I have is, this week we are going to build on what we learnt the last time we were together. One, I have to learn to bring the new person up to the point where they can participate because they were not at the last session. Two, this is a leadership training session for women and I am not sure what is the sex of our twenty-sixth participant."

Apparently some of her colleagues knew the new person and so started laughing. But the whole room burst into laughter only when he walked back to Annabelle from Rwanda and put a second post-it note on her table and said, "Since you are two, have a second post-it."

They all burst into laughter. Annabelle was about six months pregnant.

"I have been told pregnancy can cause hormonal disturbances," he told the whole class, very serious this time. "And I also know it can cause discomfiture and bring on other ailments. Please let us support Annabelle to enjoy her participation in the discussions as much as the rest of us."

Turning to Annabelle he said, "If at any time you think I can carry the burden just so that you can heave a sigh and rest please pass it on to me."

They all, again including Annabelle, laughed.

Diane came with a few issues to discuss personally with him. The correspondence had been very helpful and she had found his questions and suggestions very useful. But there were things you developed better through discussion and Diane hoped to be able to spend an evening or an afternoon discussing some of her ideas with him. Almost all the others came with the same intention so he had someone different with him at lunch each day. The evenings after supper were also given to people who wanted to see him.

On the Wednesday at lunch when Diane picked what she wanted to eat and realised that there was no space on the tables around which her colleagues were sitting she was forced to sit alone. At least, initially. Till Fatou Njie from The Gambia joined her. "Dr Dan is in consultation," Fatou said pointing at Dan and one of their colleagues in conference at a table not far from the one Fatou and Diane sat at.

"Has he been demoted?" Diane asked. "I thought he was a professor."

"Oh, he is still a professor alright. I mean a medical doctor."

"And how is he now a medical doctor?" Diane asked as she sipped her mushroom soup.

Fatou had chicken cream soup and she took a tentative sip before answering. "Come on, Diane. Don't tell me you haven't noticed."

"Noticed what?" Diane asked innocently as she looked around.

"That here in Malawi Dan has been turned into a gynaecologist. The way we have been consulting him these past days makes him seem more like an expert on women's diseases. So you have women consulting him with their candidiases, others painful menstruation while yet others see him about the odd vaginal discharge. I know you have lower abdominal pains; my problem is a lump in the breast."

"Dan really is a very good teacher," Diane said with a smile. "He is passing on his sense of humour to all of us."

Fatou shook her head. "I wish I had half his sense of humour. He knows just when to bring in a joke. Just when we need it. And each joke just fits what he was saying at the time he took the break to tell the joke. And he tells them with such a straight face you don't know till he ends that he is telling a joke. You initially think it is part of what he is explaining."

Fortunately for Diane, she was not leaving on the Saturday, unlike most of her colleagues. Dan was not leaving till the Monday so she hoped to meet him on the Saturday. And that was what they did, they met on the Saturday. They agreed to come for lunch at 1:00 p.m. and start the discussions over lunch. Dan had some work he wanted to spend the morning doing but would be free from lunch.

They spent more than four hours together. After the meal they found a table and ordered drinks. Diane wanted to take fruit juice too, which was what he asked for, but he insisted she went ahead and had her beer. She was surprised he did not take alcohol and he laughed.

"At an earlier stage in my life, I drunk alcohol but am glad I gave it up."

"So are you a born again Christian or do you belong to one of the charismatic churches?"

"Why do you ask? Because I now don't drink?" She nodded. "I am orthodox Christian. I am Catholic. Somehow I don't think drink is good for me."

They talked about the ideas she had been tossing over in her mind. They talked about her work and some things Diane planned to do. When they exhausted that they went on to talk about women's rights, African culture, economic and political issues in Africa and in the world. They parted at close to 6:00 p.m. only to meet again over supper at about 7:30 p.m. But this time they sat together for only an hour and half as Dan had work and Diane had to pack her bag for her travel the next day.

Chapter Seven

D an was about to set off from the house to pick the driver for the journey to Accra when Marian called. The call seemed to remind him of the encounter with his past the previous day, in case he was forgetting. When he put down the receiver after talking to her he sat by the phone for almost two minutes. This was his daughter. She did not know how to cash a cheque. This was her first cheque and she was not confident about going to cash it. *It's me, Sir.* That was his daughter. Or maybe Marian was not his daughter. It did not take away his worries. If Marian was not his daughter his children with Matilda were somewhere. How were they faring? Any better than Marian? And he was a sophisticated jet age international consultant. Whose children were faring how?

He had promised to meet Marian when he came back from this trip. What would he find when he met her? His daughter? Assuming yes, then what?

This journey was not going to be pleasant. Dauda was driving. He liked Dauda. Dauda had been working for Horizon Leadership for four years now. When on the road he concentrated on his job, driving and only talked when he had information to give. Which was hardly.

Dan was not in the mood for conversation and was grateful to be driven by someone who was not chatty. Or would it have been better to be driven by someone who was chatty and who would drown him in so much talk that he would lose his worry? He did not know. And now it did not matter anyway as they had two ladies as passengers. He did not know them and so could not tell if they were the chatty type. But what he knew was that he could not ignore them and on this trip he would have preferred total silence.

His fears were baseless as he did not have to talk to the ladies. One of them talked endlessly on, and her companion offered an ear into which the first lady poured everything. Dan was grateful not to be included in the conversation and did not try to listen. So he did not know what it was that the lady called Mina spent the whole ten hours talking about and which the lady called Khadija had the patience to listen to for that long.

So he spent the time on the road agonising over his neglect of the children, the pain he felt each time he remembered the face of the young woman as she confronted him for her fees. Assuming she was the Marian he had named as a baby. Was it right for her to have been forced to come as she did, furtively, uncertainly, with fear written on her face, to her own father to ask for her fees? Was it right for him to have abandoned the children to grow up little knowing the world around them? That was one set of thoughts that tortured him throughout the journey.

There was another set. So he meets the children. Even if this Marian was not his daughter, he should establish contact with his two children with Matilda, and support them. How? What exactly should he do for them? How could he atone for the neglect of these many years? And how would he relate with them? Questions, questions and yet more questions but no answers.

When they stopped in Kumasi for lunch he could tell that Khadija was not happy that they had just carried on their conversation and seemed to ignore him. After all they were travelling in his vehicle. She consciously turned off the conversations Mina started and ensured that they had topics on which all of them could talk. They all sat together at table, with Dauda sitting with them. Khadija observed that the driver did not feel uncomfortable sitting at the same table or joining in the same conversation with Dan. Dan paid for all of them and they thanked him.

After the meal he took over and drove to Nkawkaw from where Dauda took over again and drove the rest of the way. When he handed over at Nkawkaw Khadija commented on his taking over the driving. And he explained. You make mistakes more easily when you have been driving for a long time and are tired. In case a driver made a mistake everybody inside the vehicle were at risk. It was not only the driver who risked injury or death. So their policy was for senior staff travelling with drivers to drive part of the way to allow the driver to rest. It fitted everything she had heard about Dan. Mina was impatient about the temporary break in her story telling and was not paying attention to why someone had to take over from the driver part of the way.

Khadija was a friend of Mercy, the Matron of the Horizon Training Centre and it was Mercy who had begged the lift for Khadija. Khadija in turn had said thank you but she was going with a friend. Mercy had gone back to ask Dan if he had space for another person.

"They are both ladies," Mercy had said with mischief. "And both are spinsters."

"Thanks," Dan had said. "It is good to know but I am also very sure they will not tempt me."

"Why?" Brenda who had been present asked.

"Why?"

"Yes, why?"

"Oh it is easy to see why. If they are the attractive type they would have been married or they would have had rich boyfriends who would be falling over each other to drive them to Accra."

Mercy had laughed but Brenda had puffed jokingly. "I am not sure you will even notice the difference between Miss Ghana and a walking stick if you saw the two side by side."

"Without even seeing them side by side I can tell some differences between them. One is alive while the other is not living. One can move by itself while the other cannot do that. I will be surprised if a Miss Ghana is as short as a walking stick. Or as slim."

Mercy had laughed and walked away when Dan told her there was space for her second passenger. She always enjoyed the sparring sessions between her employer and Brenda. She had teased him a number of times herself and she had been happy with his response. She wished that she could arrange a marriage for him. But she also realised that he did not need anybody to arrange a girlfriend or a wife for him.

Dan became a topic between Mercy and Khadija when the latter returned from Accra. "Your boss is a wonderful person," Khadija told Mercy.

"What did he do now? Is he wonderful because he said he loved you?"

Khadija was alarmed. "Who lied to you that he said he loved me? How many times did he even speak to me? Who told you he said he loved me? Who?"

Mercy laughed. "Is it a crime for him to say he loves you if he is such a wonderful person as you say?"

"The fact that he is a wonderful person does not mean he said he loved me. But who told you he said he loved me?" Khadija was sure it was the lying driver.

"Nobody told me, so relax. I was just pulling your legs."

Khadija's sigh was not a full one because she took the pulling of leg with a pinch of salt. She still wondered if the driver had come back to tell tales after all that his boss had done for him.

They were sitting on the wall of the veranda in Mercy's house. Mercy moved closer to her friend. "Now tell me. What did Dan do to make you convinced he is a wonderful person?"

Her friend told her about his driving part of the way. "You know, in Kumasi we all sat together at table, with the driver. Mr Dan paid for all of us. He told us to ask for them to stop for us if we needed them to stop for us to do anything. I wanted to buy some plantain for Hajia Kawala and they stopped. There is this place before Nkawkaw where the fingers of plantain are so big. They look very healthy. He was then driving and I was afraid to ask him to stop. But when I asked him he stopped and said we should take all our time. He overheard Mina saying she wanted to buy some foodstuffs for the friend she was going to stay with but she did not have enough money. Then your boss does the extra wonderful thing and gives each of us a bundle of money. Even Mina was embarrassed.

"When we got to Accra we thought he would have let us get off at Achimota to look for a taxi to Madina. They drove us all the way to Madina."

"Was that where he proposed to one of you?" Mercy asked, the mischief not hidden at all by the smile.

"Oh no," Khadija said. "That is where he put the wedding ring on my finger."

They both laughed.

"It is an invisible ring," Mercy observed.

"No, it isn't. I took it off this morning. I put it at the bottom of my trunk. It is too valuable to be carried around."

They both laughed again.

"Seriously," Khadija said, "he did not even ask us for our names. I am sure he won't recognise us when we next meet. It is not because he showed interest in us that I think he is wonderful. It is because he was very helpful, willing to go out of his way to do things for others you don't expect."

"Well, that is Dan. That is how he is at work. When he is passing by the training centre and we are carting say crates of soft drinks into the stores he will join us. We have learnt not to say no because he doesn't stop just because you say no. If he is busy he will walk past. If he is not busy he will stop and share in the work. No work is below him. Yet he is the boss."

Khadija shook her head.

The subject of their conversation spent the Monday at Volta Hotel in Akosombo. He spent the afternoon going over the notes and reviewing the outline for the Kenya training. He spent the evening going over the preparations for the Akosombo training. He inspected the training room and checked that things worked. The participants arrived that evening but it was not till breakfast the next morning that he met the majority of them. This was his first encounter with this team and they were not known to each other.

They spent three great days together. To Dan each training session he conducted was an adventure. He compared his experience with what must be the experience of a mountain climber each time he was climbing a different mountain. The fact that he had climbed other mountains so successfully would not make him expect automatic success with the next mountain. Whenever he set out to climb a mountain he would study the mountain and devise the best way to climb it because each mountain was different in structure. He would probably slip some times and the whole process would be challenging. In the end he would climb it, just as he had done other mountains. But he would not take his success for granted. He would know he earned it because he worked for it. And he would celebrate it just as he did when he got to the summit of the other mountains.

He felt the same. He never assumed he was just going to walk into the sessions and wave a magic wand and attain success. He knew he would always plan each session with the same care he had been doing so far. He knew each group of participants would throw up their own challenges but he also had enough confidence in his skills to know he would always overcome the challenges.

The venue was very good, as he found out from the participants. It was serene and conducive for concentration. The rooms and services were excellent. According to the participants the beauty of the surroundings, hills, greenery and dam gave the place an added romantic feel. In the evenings as they walked from their rooms to the restaurant for supper or as they loitered between the restaurant and their rooms in groups of twos and threes they were encouraged to linger awhile by the sweet scent of the lavender trees whose flowers chose the early night hours to exude their scent. Dan admitted to himself that sometimes he wanted to hang around under the trees and just breathe in the lovely scent. But he was a duty conscious person and he did not let enjoyment get in the way of work. So he would go to his room and prepare for the next day's work.

When they left on the Friday morning he knew he had made another set of friends. He knew some among the group, as with all the groups whose learning on leadership he had facilitated so far, would grow and would become leaders and influence others positively. The lives of some would change in very dramatic ways, the way his had changed.

As Dauda drove him to Accra he felt a warm glow in his heart. He loved his job. It was not the money. It paid him really well but he hardly thought about the money. He was certainly glad to be paid that much because he could do a lot with it. He knew how much that money had transformed his home – his parents and the family. He supported an uncountable number of cousins and nephews and nieces in school, in secondary and tertiary institutions. It assured that the family, the extended family of his paternal uncles and their families, did not ever go to bed on unfilled tummies. It assured that many children he was only distantly related to had education. It allowed for the payment of good salaries to his colleagues in both the Leadership Development Service and the Training Centre. And they in turn could support their families and some extended family members.

He did not disregard the money. But the warm glow he constantly felt in his heart was from the changes he brought to people. The emails he received were full of positive experiences, people who discovered more of themselves and took action that they did not have the courage to take earlier. Stories of people who now lived on dreams and ever shifting visions. His heart was always warmed by the unfailing change in people attending his training sessions for the first time. It never failed to happen, the halo in people's faces at the end of the last day and the excitement in their faces as they contemplated the changes they would make, to themselves and to their careers.

Dauda loved attending the training sessions with Dan. He loved Dan. He did not treat him the way other drivers said their bosses treated him. Sometimes during training sessions Dauda would come into the training room and find a quiet corner from where he could listen to the discussions and observe the participants. During the breaks he would stand near different groups and listen to their comments both about the training and the person who facilitated the training. His admiration for Dan increased as he listened. If these big people could be impressed by him, if they said they learnt a lot from him, then he had to be a very, very learned man. But you did not see the learned man in him. Sometimes Dauda was uneasy when he asked him, "Dauda, what do you think?" Over time he noticed that Dan did not ridicule his thoughts, his ideas.

As they headed towards Shai Hills and Accra, Dauda stole glances at Dan. His seat was tilted backwards and he reclined in it. His eyes were not closed but you could see he was thinking. This was his most usual mood when they travelled. Dauda wondered what it was that he ceaselessly kept thinking about. During one of the short periods he looked at face of Dan he almost hit a baboon. He remembered that on that stretch of the road one needed to be vigilant because baboons would suddenly run across the road or sit on the edge of the road unmindful of oncoming vehicles.

They spent the night in Accra and on Saturday Dauda drove him to the airport to catch his flight to Kenya. Another thing for which Dauda admired him. He was always travelling to different countries. According to staff of Horizon Leadership he went there to train people. This also showed the greatness of this man who insisted Dauda should call him Dan and sit at the same table with him when they stopped to eat in restaurants.

Dan spent the Friday afternoon buying gifts for the participants. He always did this. Each training session was, to him, an opportunity for mutual learning. He strongly believed in the invaluable contribution participants made to the success of the learning process. And this was not just by listening, being attentive and creating a conducive atmosphere for learning, but by their contributions. He always sought, as early as possible in his sessions, to arrive at what Jane Vella called the 'death of the professor.' This was necessary because he greatly valued the rich knowledge and practical experience of the participants, which combined, often constituted his greatest source of most appropriate information. He did not believe in academic theories far removed from the lives of learners. He wanted people to identify with issues and the best issues they could identify with were those from their lives – the challenges they faced, the successes they experienced. He believed that once the professor died, then he could form what the revered Parker Palmer called a community of truth. He wanted his learning sessions to be as Palmer saw real learning; a group of peers exploring the truth, each, like each of the blind men who experienced the elephant, holding up and describing the truth as seen from their perspective. And by putting together the different perspectives they formed the holistic view of the truth.

He recognised the contribution of the participants to the learning process and thought he should acknowledge it in very practical terms. So he spent part of his fee on gifts for each of the participants.

He told Dauda when he expected to be back and said if the date changed he would inform Brenda and she would inform him. They said goodbye because only passengers were allowed beyond a certain point. But Dauda sat in the car in the car park and waited till he saw the plane in the air before he drove off. This was another sign of his reverence for Dan. He could always leave. And, in fact, if Dan knew he was waiting in the car park he would ask him to leave. But he always waited. Ostensibly so that if anything happened to the flight and Dan had to return he would be there to pick him. But his staying meant more than that even though he could not tell, or really admit, what it meant.

Chapter Eight

Marian decided to go home during the general exeat. This was her fifth term in school, the three terms of Form One and now the second term of Form Two. And this was the first time she was going home during a general exeat. She had three reasons for going. She expected people to say she was going because she now had money and going to town had meaning. Previously with no money and no expectation of getting any money if she went home there was no point bothering. She wanted to buy provisions. She needed some milk, sugar, *Milo*, and soap, both toilet and laundry soap.

She also wanted to take her birth certificate and even Junior's certificate if she could find it. Because Dan had asked for the birth certificate when they next met as proof that she was who she said she was, Matilda's and his daughter. And finally she wanted to tell her mother she had met her father and he had paid her fees. She did not stop to think of the storm her telling her mother would evoke. After living through so many storms she just seemed to stop thinking about them.

"What do you want at home? What do you want here?" her mother screamed several times when Marian entered the room. Her mother was inside the room with one of the people she called her friends and her children called her drinking companions, Auntie Alice.

"Mama, why can't I come home? What is wrong with my coming home? Have you now sacked me from this house?" she found herself shouting back, the first time she had had the courage go shout back even though she had been tempted several times before.

Junior was outside but when he heard his sister shouting he came running in, expecting his mother to be beating his sister. When he discovered what was going on, his sister shouting back at his mother, he smiled. He had wanted to do that to his mother several times himself.

Her mother recoiled and actually took a step back. Her voice was lower when she spoke. "Am I the one you are shouting at? Are you shouting at me, your mother?"

"Who started the shouting, Mother?" Marian also lowered her voice. "How did you welcome me? How do you usually talk to us if not by shouting? And if you shout at us why don't you expect us to speak to you that way?"

Matilda held her jaw and looked surprisingly at her daughter. "Don't tell me that you came here looking to fight me."

"Mama, I came in and greeted the two of you the way I normally do. I didn't start shouting at you. You started it."

"It is rude to shout at your mother," the woman the children called Auntie Alice rebuked Marian.

Marian turned furiously on her. "You can tell me that it is rude to shout at my mother but all the time that you have been coming here and have witnessed our mother shouting at us you never for once advised our mother to talk to us like human beings."

"Don't they shout on human beings?"

"Is that how you talk to your children?"

Junior actually laughed and banged on the door. The woman wanted to say something but thought it wise not to.

"Okay, tell me what you want. Why did you come home?" Matilda asked her in a more human voice.

"I came to tell you that they have paid my school fees."

"Heh? So you now have a boyfriend who pays your school fees?"

"Yes, Mama, I now have a rich sugar daddy who paid my school fees."

"Are you being cheeky to your mother?" Auntie Alice asked.

"When she cheeked me by saying I now have a boyfriend who pays my fees why did you not advise her against that? You support everything our mother does whether it is right or wrong."

"So you admit that you cheeked me?" Matilda asked, very surprised at her daughter's challenging attitude.

By the door Junior's eyes lit with delight. He was having fun listening to his sister take on the women he did not like. He did not like his mother but he hated her friends when they encouraged their mother against the children. Today Marian was putting one of them in her place and Junior was happy.

"Mama, you started the cheek by telling me I have a boy who pays my fees. You know I don't have any such boy but you must say it. That is not cheek. When I admit it you call it cheek."

She was, as usual, twirling the belt of her dress.

"Okay," Matilda said in a very low, mother-like voice as she walked to stand by Matilda, "so tell me. Who paid the fees for you?"

"My father did," Marian said very calmly looking up from her belt to her mother.

Matilda cocked an ear. "Eh, eh, eh! Repeat that. Who did you say paid your fees?"

Even Junior came farther into the room and close to Marian.

"Mama, I'm sure you heard me. You just want to hear me repeat that name, that's all."

Matilda tilted her head, came even closer and used two fingers to widen the ear. "No, Marian, I did not hear you. Who did you say paid your school fees?"

"I said my father."

Auntie Alice clapped her hands and exclaimed and Junior's eyes widened even further.

Matilda was unperturbed. "When you say your father who exactly do you mean? Who is your father?"

"Mr Dan Apeatu."

Matilda screamed and Alice shot up. Junior retreated to the door and looked on apprehensively at the charged atmosphere in the room. Matilda grabbed Marian's dress by the neck and squeezed it and shook her but Marian wringed the hands free of her dress.

"Did I not tell you never to contact that man?" Matilda screamed.

Marian shouted back. "You can't pay my school fees. They were going to sack me. What did you expect me to do? Mama, tell me. What did you expect me to do? Did you expect me to pack my things and come home? For two years now I have been asking you for my fees and all you tell me is you don't have money. What did you expect me to do? They were going to sack me. Did you expect me to pack my things and come home or what did you want me to do?"

"Look at her shouting at her mother." Alice said as she stood up. "How can you shout at your mother?"

"Why is it any business of yours?" Marian turned with fury on Alice. She clenched both fists and shook them with rage before Alice. "Leave me and my mother alone!"

"If you shout at me I will bash your face." Alice threatened.

Marian was unfazed. She screamed at her, "You are telling lies! You dare not! Touch me and you will see."

"See what?" Alice retorted, moving threateningly towards Marian.

"I will report you to my father. My mother can allow you people to treat us like garbage. If you touch me I will report you to my father. You know that he is not like mother and he won't allow you to treat us like we are a dustbin and anybody can dump their refuse on us"

Alice stopped her move towards the girl. "Who said I am afraid of your father? Is he a police man?" Even the soft tone in which she said this confirmed she was afraid of him.

Even Matilda seemed jolted.

Marian went on telling Alice, "When I come to your house and provoke you and you beat me I will not complain. But you can't come to my house and beat me when I have not done anything to you"

"Who told you this is your house?"

"Is it your house? My mother is not your wife. My mother is not your sister. Is this your house? It is my mother's house."

"And who told you that you have not done anything to me?"

"If you beat me and I report you to my father and he takes you on you can then tell what I did to you."

"You don't scare me with your father."

Marian laughed – the scare in Alice's face was obvious. The initial fury with which she had taken on Marian was gone and she was only engaged in a face saving act, Marian knew. Alice saved herself by going out to the veranda. Junior held the door open for her and laughed as she walked out. On the veranda other tenants asked Alice what was happening inside the room. "Her daughter has come from school threatening all of us because she said she met her father."

"And what did the father do to her to make her mad?" someone asked.

Alice only shrugged

"So you contacted your father," Matilda asked in a calm voice.

Marian was not sure whether it was a question or a statement.

"Yes Mama."

"Did I not tell you never to contact him?"

"Mama, I asked you some questions and you did not answer me. You have not been able to pay my fees for two years. I don't know any of your friends or relatives who could pay my fees. I was going to be sacked. Did you want me to be sacked from school?"

"I didn't go to secondary school. Am I not a human being for that?"

"Mama, if you did not go to secondary school, does it mean you don't want any of your children to go to secondary school? Will you be happy if I leave secondary school and come home? You keep saying yourself that without a secondary school certificate nobody can be a nurse now. Do you want us to leave school so that we can't even be nurses? You are a nurse; why won't you be proud if your daughter or your son becomes a doctor? You did not go to secondary school so you can't even pay the fees for your children to go to secondary school. Is that what you want to see happen to us one day?"

"Is that what your fucking father lectured you?"

Marian did not reply. She could see that Matilda was not sure about her father. She would have hit her if not for her uncertainty what their father would do.

She eyed her daughter with many questions in that look. "So you have become a lawyer and you now pose so many questions expecting me to answer them. I won't answer any questions from you. I forbid you to contact that man again."

"Mama, he is not that man. He is our father. And I need help which you can't offer me. If I don't contact him I will not complete my secondary school."

"I will rub pepper into your vagina if you dare see him again," she threatened, knowing even as she said so that her threat was without weight and that Marian would not be scared by it.

"Mama, if you do that our father will simply come and take us away.'

Matilda again screamed. "You have gone to meet this stupid man and because he drives a big car you are now thinking of packing to him.

Over my dead body! Did you hear that? I said over my dead body. You will need a grader or a caterpillar to run over me to move you to that man's house."

Marian was calm when she replied her, "Mama, we don't need anything to run over you. Don't you go to work? Will you stop going to work because of us? Are you going to lock us in the room forever? If we go out we don't even need our things to go to our father's house. There is nothing we have here that he can't replace."

This time Matilda put her hands on her head and wailed. Alice came in and held her but Marian simply sat on a chair, defiant. The two adults left the room and went out to the veranda.

Junior came and sat by his sister after their mother left the room and held her. She knew he wanted to talk but she wanted to be silent. She was tired, drained by the shouting match with her mother, drained by the emotions released from her. Tired by the fact that she had talked back, no, shouted back, at her mother.

She had not intended to quarrel with her mother. She came to tell her she had met her father and he paid her fees. She had foolishly expected her mother to feel relieved that the fees had been paid even if by the man she hated. But the very reception had irked her. She guessed her patience had been wearing very thin over the years as her mother talked to her friends and only communicated with her children through shouts. She guessed she felt the pain of the neglect they felt in the hands of her mother and both the fact that her mother welcomed her with queries why she came home and shouting just made something inside her snap. That something had been wearing thin and was strained to the point of snapping.

She did not regret what had happened or the way she had stood her ground or the things she had told her mother. She felt glad that she had the strength to match her mother.

As for Alice she hoped she would tell all her mother's friends what had happened between them and they would let her and her brother alone. Alice had two daughters and the older one was very rude to her mother and very rude to everyone else. Her mother feared her and worshipped her. So it was hypocritical on her part to treat other people's children like dirt. But all that was because their mother treated them like dirt.

She felt no elation, no reason for jubilation. In fact, she felt wretched. Here was she, daughter of a mother who demanded to know why her daughter should come home on exeat. Who said she had not gone to secondary school and so implied she would not be bothered if her children dropped out of school. Who would not let her children contact their father for fees but would prefer that they left school instead. And whose friends helped insult her children rather than correct the mother. Then on the other hand, despite all her boasting about her packing to her father and reporting people to her father, she did not even know the man. She could not say she had a father. She had a mother who seemed to take delight in bullying them and a father she could not claim any relationship with. Except that she hoped … And that hope gave her something positive to hang on to.

The encounter made her anxious and yet afraid to meet their father. She noticed how Alice had found a way to back out of the confrontation with her when she threatened to report her to her father. She struck Junior once and Marian was sure she would have struck her too the way she rose to her friend's aid. That Auntie Alice had backed down from an encounter with her and left the room instead of shouting her down and giving her a knock on the head spoke volumes. What did they fear about the man? Her mother feared him too, didn't she?

She had been to the man's office and knew it was a big place. She had seen his car. It was big and she had sat inside it and known it was not like the vehicles used for taxis they were used to. He had given her a cheque for two years' fees and some money in addition. He was not poor. Was it what his money could do that made Alice afraid of him? Or was he a bully who should not be crossed? Was he a physically aggressive person? He did not seem so from the meeting with him she recalled and the way he spoke to her on the phone the next day did not suggest an aggressive person. The lady at the bank had said her uncle was a break but had not said anything about his being aggressive or gentle or firm or a no-nonsense brooked person.

"Are we going to pack to Dad?" Junior asked in a low voice so that those on the veranda would not hear him.

She had forgotten about Junior sitting by her. She looked down at him. In her mind she said she did not even know if their father wanted them. "Junior, no," she answered in the same conspiratorial low voice.

"But why? You told Mama we will pack to his house."

"No, I didn't. I only said if Mama rubs pepper in my vagina Dad will come for us."

"Then I wish Mama will do that so that Dad will come for us."

She looked down at him and smiled. "Maybe she should cut your penis instead so that Dad will come for us."

He held her arm and leaned against her. "If she rubs pepper into your vagina you will still have your vagina. You will only feel small pain for say one minute or so. If she cuts my penis it will be funny to urinate and it will be for life, see? And it will be so painful I will have to be admitted at the hospital."

They were silent. It looked like they had tacitly agreed to share the places, Matilda and Auntie Alice had the veranda and the children had the room. The children did not want to go out and the adults did not want to come into the room.

Marian leaned and whispered in Junior's ears, "We've staged a coup. We sacked Mama and her friend from the room."

They both laughed and Junior whispered, "Let's go and sack them from the veranda too."

Marian shook her head and pinched her brother on the shoulder and they again laughed.

"What are the two of you laughing about in that room?" That came from their mother on the veranda.

"So Mama, we can't even laugh now, is that the case?" Marian asked.

"You know Marian has become a lawyer after meeting her father and you invite her to practise her law on you," Alice said.

"Laugh. Laugh all you can. You now even own the room," their mother told them.

"The lawyer even told me this is her house," Alice said.

Marian ignored her and replied her mother. "Mama, if there is something to laugh about we will laugh. But if there is nothing funny we will not laugh."

"I told you she is a lawyer," Alice complained. "You just give her the chance to practise her law on you. Leave her alone."

There was silence, an uncomfortable silence, for a few minutes.

Then, "Junior, come out." That was Auntie Alice. "Come out unto the veranda."

Inside the room the two children exchanged conspiratorial looks and smiles and clamped their hands on their mouths to keep them from laughing. Marian motioned for her brother to go and he shook his shoulders, no.

"Auntie, what do you want me to come out for?"

Matilda clapped her hands and looked into the sky.

"Hey! Junior, you too? Eh, Junior. You too?" Alice wailed.

Inside the two children exchanged glances and smiles. "Auntie, I too have done what?"

Matilda exclaimed and Alice said, "So your sister has rubbed her law on you, has she?"

A silence that lasted about ten minutes. While the adults outside sat stiffly on the wall of the veranda, the children were communicating in whispers and sign language. They giggled and suppressed laughter.

"Are you not going back to school?" That was their mother.

"Mama, why is my coming home such a bother to you?"

"Listen to how a child answers her mother. You will think she is talking to her equal," Alice said from the veranda, adjusting herself on the wall.

"Auntie, I am not talking to you," Marian replied from the room. "You can take offence by the way I talk to my mother. I have never commanded my mother to shut up. Bernice tells you to shut up and you just clam up. Is she your equal?"

Matilda clapped again and said, "Hey ya!"

"When did Bernice ever tell me to shut up? And you were present and you heard and saw it?"

Marian chose to ignore her. "Mama, today is an open exeat. Many students have gone to their homes. In their homes their parents will prepare food different from what they have been eating in the school for them. They will give them money and some provisions to go back. You did not welcome me when I came. You started shouting at me, asking me what I want. I have to be queried when I come to my own mother. It is like you are happy to be rid of me and it irritates you to see me around. And you say why should I contact my father. You say it is over your dead body that I will pack to my father. But if I am not welcome here what do you want me to do? Sleep in the bus stops in town?"

Matilda came into the room. "Listen, both of you. When your father walked out on both of you, you," she pointed at Junior, "were not even walking yet." She found a place and sat down. "If I did not want you, it was easy to kill you at the time. You," she pointed at Marian, "were just this high." She held up her hand to indicate how high. "And I took care of you till you are this big. But now just because your father is rich and has a big car and a big house you want to pack and go to him. Because he can pay your fees and I can't pay your fees."

"Mama, it is not just because he can pay our fees and you can't pay our fees," Marian said, her voice low and soft. "Mama, can we talk? You have always shouted at us and ordered us to shut up. Can we talk? You need to listen to us sometimes."

From the veranda Alice said her good-bye and Marian was tempted, but only tempted, to say good riddance.

Matilda eyed her daughter suspiciously. She looked at Junior and was surprised that Junior seemed amused by what Marian was saying. She said, "Okay I am listening to you. Talk."

Marian looked at her mother a few seconds wondering what the command meant. Would she listen? She decided to talk even if she would not listen. "Mama, today is a general exeat. Students who have relatives in Tamale all went home…"

"You told me that earlier," Matilda cut in.

"I can see you are not even going to listen," Marian complained.

"If I were not listening I would not know that you already told me that. You go on."

"Okay, I will cut out what you already heard. Mama, we were given a deadline to either pay our fees or be dismissed. I had two years' fees unpaid. You could not pay even one year's fees. I needed two years' fees. Next year in addition to the fees for the year I will have to pay the examination fees as well. It is a lot of money. I can't even fuck to raise that amount. I won't attract the people who can pay my fees. Our father can pay the fees. No matter what you say about you and secondary school Junior and I need not only secondary education.

We need university education as well. I don't know anybody who can support us to get it if we don't go to our father.

"I came home to inform you that I met him. I had to meet him because if I did not contact him I was going to be sacked from school." She did not notice it but Junior had become keener in listening and looked up straight into her eyes. "Fortunately when I met him he agreed to pay my fees, the fees for the two years. I need a lot of other things. I will need the fees for next year and the exam fees. If I qualify to go to a tertiary institution I will need him to bear the cost. You say you forbid us from seeing him. But we need him. You won't tell us why we should not see him."

"So if I tell you why you should not see him, will you stop seeing him?"

"Mama, if I think the reason is good I will stop seeing him."

"So if I tell you the reason you will now judge me and decide whether my reason is good or not before you do what I tell you?"

"Mama please! You can't pay my school fees. Assuming you tell me the reason you don't want me to see him is that you don't like him. And I need my school fees which you can't pay. And if I don't pay the fees I won't write my final exam. What will you expect me to do? Say yes I will no more see my father because you don't like him? That I won't go to him for fees because you don't like him? Mama, tell me, then what happens to me? I'm sure you don't care so long as I don't see him."

"So you are bothered about your precious education so much so that you will defy me?"

Marian shook her head. But so far so good. Their mother was not shouting at her. She would not have thought it possible that her mother would one day let them talk for even ten minutes within which period she would say the things she just said without her mother screaming at her.

"So Mama, what kind of future do you want for your children? We should not be bothered about education. Then what should we do? If we should not be bothered about our precious education what do you want us to do? You can't pay our fees. Can you give us money to become businesspeople?"

It was the kind of conversation you feel can go on endlessly and never come to a conclusion. Marian felt she had told her mother sorry but she had to see her father. She needed him because her education depended on him and she was not going to sacrifice her education. Her mother kept pointing out she was defying her because Dan was rich. One thing though. After the initial violent reaction she had stopped screaming about Marian referring to Dan as her father. In the past she would scream at her shouting, "Who told you he is your father?" She even did the first time they started talking.

As expected she got nothing from her mother when she was going to school. She gave the usual excuse, that she was broke. And Marian knew she really did not have money. Drink had taken most of it.

Junior walked with her to the road from where she took a taxi into town. He tugged at her hand and pleaded, "Tell me about Dad. How is he like?"

She looked down at his eager face and snorted. "He doesn't resemble you and they called you Junior."

"No, I was told they called me Junior because *I* resembled him. It was not the other way round."

She hit him jokingly. And told him a little about the meeting with him. "He said I should call him for us to meet when he comes back."

"Where did he go to?"

"Junior, I was scared of the man I could not ask him the questions you are asking me."

"Why were you scared of him? Does he frighten people the way Mama says he is?"

"Junior I don't know. He was quiet. And he hardly smiled. But when I told him who I was and told him my mother's name and my date of birth he agreed to pay my fees." She told him about the cheque and what a cheque was and how you could get money from it. "He did not argue. He did not tell me I was not his daughter and he did not tell me he did not have money or he won't pay my fees. He even said that we will discuss why I changed my surname, meaning we are Apeatu, don't you see? That is even what is written on the birth certificates. But imagine going to someone who doesn't know you to tell him you are his daughter and you need money for your fees. That was what made me scared of him."

She gave Junior two thousand cedis and warned him not to let their mother know.

"Will you take me with you when you are next going to see him? As for me I want to go and stay with him."

"Junior, maybe after he left our mother he went and married another woman and has children with that woman. Mama says he did not marry but I don't know. He may not want us to come and stay with him because of that woman and her children. The wife may not like us and may maltreat us. Let me meet him first."

They walked on in silence. At the roadside Marian told Junior, "I have learnt a few things. One, mother will not be happy for us to leave her and go and live with Dad."

Her brother looked surprised. "But why? She doesn't like us."

"I don't know. But you could see she agreed to talk with me for the first time when she knew I met Dad and that we can walk off to Dad if she maltreats us." She brushed her younger brother's face because he was staring at her, unblinking. "It doesn't mean we can use that to threaten her frequently, mind you."

"What are the other things you have learnt?" her brother asked.

"I don't know Dad. But whatever he is, if he does not reject us as his children, mother's friends will lay off us. I have a strong feeling he will not reject us. He already admitted, as it were, that we are his children. I am not sure they will want to treat us like dirt if they know we go to him and can report them to him. Mention of Dad sure got Alice to back down from her threat to beat me."

"I hate her and I hate Mama's friends," Junior said vehemently.

"You can't blame them for treating us the way they treat us. It is Mama who makes them treat us that way. They see how Mama treats us and they support her. Mama cannot go to Auntie Alice's house and say anything to Bernice. She will wash Mama and Auntie Alice will not go to Mama's aid. She fears Bernice. Bernice is a terror."

They were silent till a taxi came and Marian joined it. When they set off she turned to look and Junior was still standing by the road. She sat back. The two of them were different. She wondered if at sixteen Junior would be challenging his mother the way she had done that morning. Maybe. Maybe not. Junior was not like her. It was true that what happened this morning had not been intended. And she was surprised at herself that she had found the courage to shout back at her mother, say the things she had said to her and finally had the showdown she had thought of several times with one of her mother's friends. The opportunity just offered itself. And her contact with their father helped. Even though she was not sure how their relationship would be he had paid her fees, given her extra money and showed some interest in her studies. It was enough, so far, to make him a pillar on which to lean and look at her mother and her friends. She did not know how he would react, or what he would even do, if she ever reported an abuse on them by any of her mother's friends. Would he take it up and address it? Or would he...?

Her mind went back to Junior. He was not like her, challenging. Today's had been the first major open challenge she had yet made but she had protested things her mother did and said through murmurs, stamping her feet, shaking her shoulders, looks and other body gestures. Junior would just shut off. He could be there and yet be completely absent. So that he did not hear what you said. He could just switch himself off.

Their father was due back the next weekend. She would call him and they would arrange a meeting. At that meeting she would know where they stood with their father. She had taken on her mother. Assuming the meeting with her father did not go well and he told her he would only pay her fees but she should keep her distance. Assuming he said that. Then what?

Chapter Nine

This was Dan's third visit to Nairobi but he did not know the city. He knew that the airport, like Addis airport, was huge by African standards but he did not know Nairobi. He could not say that he knew any of the cities he visited and held trainings in.

He found the airport quite orderly despite its size and the checking out was very fast. He went through Immigration in a short orderly queue. He did not have to take a visa from Ghana for a visit to Kenya. He was surprised the number of countries he, as a Ghanaian, did not need a visa for. He had needed a visa for Zimbabwe but it was given at the airport in Harare and he paid for it there. He had not needed visas to Tanzania, Uganda and Malawi. In Tanzania people who went to Zanzibar told of a strange arrangement in moving from mainland Tanzania to the island of Zanzibar; they stamped on your passport to indicate both arrival to and departure from the island. He had heard that Zanzibar was beautiful. Exotic was the word a Dutch lady staying in the same hotel with him in Dar es Salaam had used on her return from the island. He had been told earlier about the beauty of the island and that a trip to the country was incomplete without a trip to the island. The boat ride cost about one hundred dollars or so. Small amount he could easily afford but sightseeing had not been part of his life at all. He was not curious and even though he had decided some years ago to cultivate an appreciation for nature, he had yet to start doing so.

He found his suitcases, one big and one small, on the conveyor belt and went through Immigration and Customs with very little trouble. When he told Customs Officers he was visiting a country for only a week or two for a training but carried two suitcases, one heavy, some rightly felt suspicious about him. Something about him always made them to let him pass. He never carried anything illegal so he was prepared to open the suitcases and explain the gifts he had for the participants and to pay duty if they said he carried things in commercial quantities and they were dutiable.

He hired a taxi to the hotel, *Silver Springs*. The driver spoke little so he learnt nothing about the city besides what he knew already. This was his second time staying at the *Silver Springs Hotel* and he knew they would be in the hotel in a minute when he saw the teaching hospital. The mortuary was not far from the hotel and he joked, the last time he was there, that if a guest died at the hotel, including him, the hotel authorities would incur very little cost in sending him to the morgue.

He was given a room on the first floor. He knew the conference room already so he did not need to check it to decide how to arrange it. He knew already. He felt relaxed and he spent the time before supper reading and moving from one TV channel to the other. Sometimes he left the dial on a channel where they spoke Swahili. He listened with amusement, trying to guess what whey would be saying. He never succeeded.

At 7:30 p.m. he went to the restaurant for supper. It was buffet and he knew what he wanted. A man was playing the organ near the buffet table while a woman with a very beautiful voice sang. Their rendition of the songs they chose were very close to the original, Dan noted.

He had just fetched his soup and was about to go to a table when Diane joined him.

"Look at this," he said in mock shock. "How did you know I like food so much the best place to find me is here?"

She laughed. "When will you ever be serious?"

"Me? Serious? Never. I will always be Dan."

She fetched some soup too and they sat together at a table.

"Tell me everything you have been doing since the last time we met," Dan said when they started eating their soup.

"You don't mean it, do you?"

He looked at her suspiciously. "Why do you say I don't mean it?"

"Because I know you can't mean it," she said rather seriously. "Dan, assuming we met only three days ago. It will take me three days to tell you everything I did in those three days. When was the last time we met? Years ago? It will take me that length of time to tell you everything I did over that period."

"Very intelligent woman," he said blowing on the spoon of soup he was ready to shovel into his mouth. "The machine inside here," he tapped his head, "doesn't work very well these days. It may even give up the ghost one of these days, if I don't have it checked."

They talked about many different things, what they had been doing and many others before they mentioned the training they were going to facilitate together. This was the first time they were going to facilitate training together and Diane was both excited and apprehensive.

"I didn't expect you today," Dan told her. "I thought we could spend the afternoon of tomorrow, maybe an hour or two, to share ideas and agree how to manage the first day."

"I'm so anxious this being my first time training alongside you." But her anxiety did not show in her face when Dan looked at it.

"I am sure you will be alright, Diane. This is not your first time facilitating and this time won't be different."

"I'm not sure. The people I have trained so far have been different."

"It's the same approach. I am confident you can handle the discussion sessions as well and answer the questions they will pose to us directly. Have more faith in yourself."

She was partly but only partly convinced.

"I have a parcel for you," Dan said as they got up. "Let me run up and bring it."

"Can I come along?" she asked. "I don't know how the rooms look like."

He wasn't sure she should come but he could not say why not. She saw the puzzle in his face but because he did not say no she went up with him.

The rooms were okay, she noticed. Not too big, no wasted space. The bed looked comfortable and the furniture was made of very good quality wood.

"Please pardon my invasion of your privacy but can I look in the ladies?"

"Sorry there is no ladies here," he said with the usual mischief. She could read the mischief in his voice and face. "This is a men's room so there is only a gents."

"May I look? I don't mind if it is a gents."

The bathroom and toilet were neat and the towels were white. When she came back into the main room Dan was rummaging in his suitcase. There were materials on the desk so she sat on the bed. The mattress was firm enough to make your sleep sound, she thought. She leaned back and rested on her left elbow and put the left leg on the bed. He saw her sitting that way on the bed when he brought out the package he had for her. He stiffened momentarily but recovered fast. She sat up and took the parcel. It was heavy. Typical of him, she thought. She remembered the first gift from him in Kadoma. It had been a very beautiful dress material. And she remembered the second gift at Salima. It was not her alone. He always brought gifts to all to the participants, quite costly gifts. Things typically Ghanaian.

"Dan," the surprise showed in how wide her eyes opened. Dan feared they might pop and the eyeballs fly out. Her mouth opened. "This is fantastic! For me alone?" She looked up shaking her head. "No, Dan, you should not have gone to that length."

"Come on, woman. You don't even know what is in the wrappers. It might well be pieces of wood or something worthless."

Her thanks were effusive. "The parcel is so big. I know how valuable each of the first two gifts is." She had stood up reflexively. So she looked straight at his face.

He smiled and shook his head. He closed his eyes and touched his heart. "Touché, *comme dit-on en français*. But please remember we are partners. I am really touched by your effusive thanks. It makes me feel I have given you the world. I am touched by your appreciation."

She wanted to take a step forward and kiss him on the cheek but she checked herself. He had never suggested he welcomed intimacy with anyone and he might misconstrue the gesture. She strongly wanted to do it, though.

Her trousers were made of a material that reminded him of the crimplene material that was popular in his student days. The material made the trousers hug her hips and buttocks. The blouse also hugged her upper body and her outline stood out very strongly when she turned and he saw her in profile. For the first time since he knew her he realised she was shapely and beautiful.

They walked down the stairs, instead of taking the lift, Dan holding the parcel. Dan would walk whenever he could and did not take the lift even once when his room was on the third floor the last time he stayed here. Diane had agreed they should walk. He passed the beautifully wrapped parcel through the window of the passenger side to Diane when she got into the car. She admired the wrapping.

"I am not responsible for the wrapping," he told her as he watched her look at the wrapping. "The Administrative Officer did the wrapping. Trust her for her sense of finesse. I would probably have put the contents in a brown paper and tied it up with twine."

"Once again, thanks very much," she said as she put the parcel on the front passenger seat. She again felt the urge to lean over the seat and plant a kiss on his cheek as he leaned against the window. Again she restrained her urge and did not do it.

They agreed to go to church in the morning and meet at lunch.

It was a long drive home for Diane. She wished she could fly home to open the parcel and look at what it contained. She was anxious to examine its contents and she became irritated whenever traffic was halted. When she did get home and opened the parcel in the security of her bedroom, she was not disappointed. She had good cause for her anxiety. There were three dresses, the material of each one very beautiful and each so beautifully embroidered when she put on one and looked at herself in the dressing mirror she felt like standing before it forever. And it fitted her so well she wondered how he got her size right. She kept asking herself if he made them sew the dresses or he bought them already made. She did not know but she would ask him. She held up each of the other two dresses in turn in front of her and looked at herself in the mirror. Each looked very beautiful. She could not make up her mind which was the most beautiful.

Diane knew about the beautifully designed dresses of West Africa. Now she had three of them, all at one time. She slumped on the bed and held the dresses clasped to her chest. She looked at his unsmiling face in the picture on the wall. She picked the phone from the bedside table and called the hotel and asked to speak to Dan.

"What are you doing?" she asked when he came on the line.

"Me? Putting names on the gifts for the participants."

"Well, I called to tell you I will spend the rest of the evening admiring the dresses. Dan," almost a whisper, "I can't say thanks enough."

"So don't bother to even try. Honest, I think you have said thanks enough. Diane," she noticed the drop in voice, and thought maybe he even sat on the bed, "we communicate through a variety of mediums. For me your face, the whole of your body and your physical reaction when I gave you the parcel said such a thank you that came straight from your heart it was more than enough to me. Your calling me again is more than enough."

"Well, to me, I will never feel convinced I have said thanks enough. One dress alone would have required more than the thanks I have been able to convey to you so far. Three dresses, Dan! It's so wonderful a gift I will be saying thanks for many months to come."

"By saying that you have said your thank you for all those months to come. You needn't be saying any more."

They played ping-pong with the thanks. Till she said, "One serious question. The dresses fitted as a fiddle, as the English would say…"

"But I thought you were Kenyan."

She started to respond but stopped, recognising he was pulling her leg. "I won't mind you. I am English."

"Thanks for letting me know. I'd always thought you were Kenyan."

"To the question. How did you know my size? How were the dresses made? Did you buy them already made …?

"No, they were sewn. I went with a lady I felt was your height and size and the seamstress measured her. And these are really loose fitting dresses so they don't have to have the exact measurement of the wearer."

She chuckled and he knew she was going to pull something. "Does that mean you had been secretly observing or even admiring my shape?"

He remembered taking note of her shape in his room less than an hour earlier. "Not at all. I got your shape from the night you came to bed with me naked."

"Several nights. Not one night. Why did you cut out the other nights?"

"To the best of my memory – and I have not reached senility yet – it was just that one night."

"Be consistent, Dan. You told me only this evening that the machine inside your head is not working well these days. That is senility."

They both laughed. When Diane put down the phone she smiled and shook her head. He did have a sense of humour and could stand having his leg pulled.

He was standing on the stairs leading to the reception when she pulled into the car park at 1.40 on the Sunday afternoon. And he immediately understood why the emotions she conveyed the previous night when she opened her gifts at home. She was in one of the dresses and it was very beautiful on her.

"I could not answer all the questions they put to me in church today. All my friends wanted me to get them dresses similar to what I wore. Where did I get it? How much did it cost? It is so beautiful. It is so exquisite. As if I did not know that. Even ladies who have never spoken to me before spoke to me today and they all wanted me to help them buy something similar."

He listened to all this and while looking at her calmly he said, "I don't know much about Kenya but I am not sure that is how you say good afternoon in Kenya."

"You are right," she admitted with a smile that suggested mischief, "but in Kenya we get the heaviest things off our chests first before we greet. Good afternoon."

He smiled, very broadly.

Impulsively she said, "I wish you will smile and laugh more often."

"Why?" The smile was gone and seriousness had taken over the face.

"We all look nicer when we smile. We are more easily approached if we smile often."

"It's true. But we all have certain fixed biological natures which we can alter only slightly."

They had lunch together and then got the key for the conference room and spent about an hour discussing the arrangements and the sessions. Even though they had discussed each session over the phone and through email, Diane still went over how she intended to lead and facilitate her sessions. As Dan listened he thought training was her area and he was right to have influenced her to step into that arena.

He would have done a few things differently but he knew that was more because their styles were different and that her approach would be equally effective. Or even more effective.

So he told her, "Excellent."

She looked up into his face searching for the signs that he did not mean what he said. She said, "You flatter me. I am sure you have your criticisms but you just want to make me feel good."

He took a deep breath first and she noted it. "Diane, I am certainly doing what I can to put you on the road to independent training. And I am doing that because I think you are an excellent trainer. What I observed when I just listened to you was an excellent approach, some very original ways of doing things. I would have done some differently because as a person my style of doing certain things will be different from yours but it would not necessarily be superior to your style.

"Understand this. I will encourage you and not say things that will deflate your ego and make you turn around on the road of your career. But I am equally committed to ensuring that those coming for the training go away with the maximum they can get out of the five days. I will not tell you your approach is excellent if it were not so. I will not promote you to the detriment of the interest of the participants. I have no good reason to be more interested in you alone than in the twenty-five participants. So if I found flaws in your approach or had my doubts about any of your proposed facilitation methods I would have voiced out the concern for us to discuss them and agree on the best thing to do. The best I can do for you is support you to come out at the end of these five days convinced you are a good facilitator. How the participants feel about your facilitation will make or break your confidence. I will not encourage you to use an unworkable approach that will only expose you to ridicule."

Her hand impulsively sought his and took it and squeezed it. "I believe you. And thanks. I will do my best and I am sure your faith in me will be justified. I won't disappoint you. I will not disappoint the participants and above all I won't disappoint myself." She again squeezed his hand. She did not even know she was doing that.

It was past 4.00 p.m. when they came out. "Shall I buy you a beer?" he offered.

"You make me feel embarrassed drinking because you don't take alcohol. The natural order of things is for the man to drink beer and the woman to have a soft drink. When we drink together it is the woman having alcohol and the man rather having something soft."

"You are a leader. Leaders are supposed to be prophets and not priests, remember that. You are supposed to challenge wrong 'natural' things and not amplify them. So reverse the expectation and let the man have the women's drink and the woman have the men's drink. Besides, in my case I am taking the right drink for my sex. I am female."

"So will you encourage me to drink?"

They were standing near the reception with Dan facing the street. He could see inside the gifts shop from where he last bought some Kenyan T-shirts for his staff. It was closed and he did not know why. It also stocked magazines and he bought *Newsweek* from there as well.

"Will I encourage you to drink? Sure. I will even suggest gin and whisky. The beer is mild. Especially for a woman who is going to lead learning sessions gin will be excellent. Have you ever heard the term 'Dutch courage'?" She nodded. "You know how women are easily frightened if they have to stand before people and drum real sense into their heads. You will need gin for your sessions tomorrow. Otherwise we should expect disaster of the highest magnitude."

He led the way to one of the tables where a waiter promptly met them.

"I thought what you just said of courage was rather true of men." She moved away from the table he originally chose to one where they would have less disturbances.

"No, it's rather true of women."

Dan kept checking to see if he could make out which of the arriving guests and those already in the hotel were coming for their training. He had interacted with each of them. He sent each of them questionnaires and got their completed questionnaires which gave him some information about them. He had spoken to some on the phone and knew a bit about them. In the past he had tried to create a face and a structure from the tone of the people over the phone but never got it right. He did not now try to see if he could guess who Annette was, who Jerome was and so on. While they chatted and sipped their drinks, he kept looking at the people who moved around. All of the participants were young so he discounted the older looking type.

It was past 6.00 p.m. when Diane got up to go. He walked her to her car and said good night.

He joined some of the participants at table that evening when he came down at 7.47. The tables were tagged so he could tell who were those he would be meeting the next day. He had told himself some years back to normally use the lunch and supper of the day before the start of the training to get familiar with the participants and let them get to know him so that it would make the icebreaking sessions of the next day easier. But he never could get himself to do that. This evening he knew the best would have been to move from table to table but he did not do that. He was happy to sit with a group of three of the participants to whom he introduced himself. After that he just listened to two of them dominate the conversation.

There were twenty-five of them, fourteen men and eleven women. He enjoyed the mixed groups. Even though most participants, both women and men, came professing gender sensitivity, it was common practice for (some of) the women to cede leadership to the men in very subtle ways. It was equally very common for (almost all) the men to expect to assume leadership.

He and Diane had to do the introductions the next morning. "This lady here," he showed Diane, "is not just one of the best leaders on this continent but also an authority on leadership. She is going to engage you in such a way that by the time you leave here on Friday evening you are going to be well versed in what individually you would do to develop the leadership potential each of us has. And I am very honoured to be carrying her papers and running her errands for her in order to make it possible for her to do what she is best known for."

Some participants were not sure if he was serious or not. Others looked at the smile on Diane's lips and knew he was joking. They later introduced themselves properly with Diane telling them, "Dan introduced me to leadership. And I really feel honoured to be sharing this training session with him. If you ever doubt that you can be completely different from whom you are right now, I am the evidence that yes, you can."

On the Wednesday they were joined by a woman whom Diane told Dan she would introduce during the coffee break. She was not introduced during the break but just before the break for lunch she asked Dan if they could share a table and have some discussions during lunch.

"I'm not sure," he told her. "Some of the participants normally want to have discussions with me during lunch. If any of them asks for a chat, they have first claim to my time."

"I am a potential employer," she said without sounding arrogant. "And the discussions may have to do with a contract for you."

He shook his head. "I appreciate that, but I will never short change a current employer in order to win a future contract. It is unethical. My current employer has paid for my time to train these people and make my time and my services totally available to the participants. They come first."

She nodded without telling him she admired his ethics.

When they were going for lunch he told her, "Sorry we can't sit together for lunch. But we can have fifteen minutes before the afternoon session begins. I am afraid if that is not enough you will have to wait till the end of the day or come tomorrow morning."

She was non-committal. "Let's see what happens in the fifteen minutes."

At lunch he and Diane sat with different groups of people and he was glad to note that over the three days Diane had been as engaged as he had. People did not seem to prefer talking to him and they accepted the equality between him and Diane. It made him happy.

He met Mrs Mary Magdalene Murungi before the start of the afternoon session. "Diane has told me a lot about this training and the tremendous change it has had on her. And on other women who attended the two training sessions with her. She asked me to sit in for just one hour and I ended up spending the whole morning because I loved what I was learning. It was interesting listening to and looking at the participants and how they were learning from each session. My compliments. Very sincere compliments."

"Thank you."

She produced a gold rimmed card holder and took out a card from it for Dan. She was the HR Manager of National Trust Bank (NTB).

"Diane told me about the leadership course. I have read some literature on leadership and how that differs from management but I have never really asked if our senior staff needed leadership skills. From talking to Diane and from discussions with others who know about leadership I realised a training in leadership may be useful to the bank. I have discussed the issue with Management and the reception was very good. Apparently some members have come into contact with some of the people you trained and they know about your training programme for Standard Chartered Bank staff. So we agreed that I contact you during your visit to discuss your training our staff, very senior management staff. We will see what happens later.

"What I want from you now is if you have the time to stay on after this training and spend next week holding a series of discussions with us. First with management to discuss their thoughts and for them to hear about your training – what has been your experience so far in terms of your observation of changes for the individuals and their organisations. We need to agree clear objectives and then we, Management that is, can weigh the cost against the possible benefits.

"Personally I will want you to spend some time on the ground talking to some of the possible candidates for the training, looking at their responsibilities, their role in the bank, having a personal chat with them about their views about their personal development especially as it relates to the bank's mission and so on. By then we will have some TOR for you. Then you can submit a proposal for our discussion."

"You assume I am not committed next week?"

Mrs Murungi nodded. She should have expected that. "Well, I am hoping you don't have a commitment you can't postpone. Once you are here it is reasonable for us to have the discussion in a face to face. And I will like to have you see our vision and mission and strategic plan in general. And also meet some of the people. As an HR person I prefer that you have some deeper knowledge of the bank and staff before you propose any training."

Dan agreed to call Brenda and find out about commitments. If he could afford it, he would spend the next week meeting with Mrs Murungi and the management of the bank. He invited her to come the next day. "You can drop in at 10.30 when we will be having our coffee break. Then you can sit in till lunch. I am sure you will find the sessions interesting and I will later tell you why it is important for you to sit in."

"I'm not sure about being able to come tomorrow. They rang for me from the office twice. I had not expected to stay for more than an hour and so the Secretary kept some people waiting for me. I am not sure I can afford to come tomorrow. But we will see. You won't tell me what it is that you expect me to see when I come tomorrow?"

"No, but I will strongly encourage you to come if you can afford the time. I will want it to be a surprise. If you can't come I will tell you what it is later. I will give you feedback what is the outcome of my phone call this evening if you come tomorrow. If you are not able to come," he held out her card, "since I have your card I will call you."

When Mrs Murungi left he called Brenda. The advantage of travelling east, he told himself, was that, he could call the office at what was the end of the day where he was. Josephine's professional voice came on the line with, "Horizon Leadership, may I help you?"

He answered, "Yes, you may," and just listened. At the other end he was sure Josephine was waiting for him to say in what way Horizon Leadership may help him. He was about to say hello again, afraid Josephine may think it was a crank calling and cut him off, when her voice came on, "Yes, how may I help you, please?"

Very professional, he admitted. Someone less professional would have been impatient and rude. Not Josephine. In her and Brenda he had a good team for Horizon's administration. Josephine was the front desk officer.

"May I speak to Miss Josephine Damba, please?" he asked, putting as much change as possible into his voice.

"Josephine speaking."

"Hello Joe. Brenda would have recognised me at once." He reverted to his normal voice.

She started with "Who is on the …." She then screamed, "Oh Mr Apeatu. How are you and how is the training going on?"

They chatted for about two minutes and he asked to speak to Brenda. When she came on, like Josephine, she asked how he was faring in Kenya and how the training was going on.

"I am fine, just great," he told her. "To me the training has been good so far. I can't tell from the perspective of those attending the training."

"Don't you use the daily mood barometer?" she asked. "I thought the daily mood barometer is intended to tell on a daily basis how people feel about the training."

"I think so too," he said knowing it would only irritate Brenda.

"Oh, you think so. I am glad at least you are thinking. So how come you can't tell from the perspective of the other side?"

"Sometimes I forget I am talking to an experienced detective. From the feedback so far, everybody feels the training is going well. How is the office? How badly are the rest of the staff suffering in your hands?"

"The office is fine. As for how much staff are suffering in my hands you will have to ask them. The one inflicting the pain often doesn't know how the sufferers feel."

"That is very true. And it is even worse for an insensitive person like you. And how is your family?"

"My family is fine. When will I be able to ask you about *your* family?"

"Oh, right now. You can ask me now about my family."

"And what will your family mean?"

He did not know what he would have thought of this question some three weeks back. But it was not three weeks back. And Marian had come into his life to remind him strongly that he had an unclaimed family. But it was too early to tell Brenda that. "Brenda, I do have a family. My father and my mother are still alive. They are my family."

"When you asked how my family was who did you have in mind?'

"I had in mind whoever you considered as your family. Including adopted children and so on."

After the playful chat he asked about commitments in the office. "Brenda, do we have any commitments next week that I can't wriggle out of?"

"Dan, how will I know? I don't know how you can contort yourself so how can I tell which commitment you can wriggle out of and which requires more contortion than you are capable of?"

They sparred a while.

Then Dan asked, "Brenda, do I or don't I have commitments I can postpone?"

"Why, aren't you coming this weekend any more?"

"You know what I don't like about you Ghanaians?"

She imitated his fake seriousness. "No, please my Kenyan friend, tell me what you don't like about us Ghanaians."

"It is your tendency to answer questions with your own questions. Someone should educate you that we reply to questions with answers and not more questions."

"Very educative, I will write that in my diary and also type it out and paste it on the notice board for those thick skulled Ghanaians to read and hope that some of them will be educated by it. But tell me, are you thinking of extending your stay or travelling somewhere else. Tell me while I consult the calendar of activities for next week."

"I am planning to extend my stay here, by maybe up to five or six days," he told her.

He could hear her flicking through paper. Maybe her diary. "And why are you extending? A woman?"

"Yes, a woman."

She laughed. "Miracle of the century."

"What is the miracle of the century?"

"A woman making you to extend your stay in a country. That you even saw her is very, very surprising. That you took enough interest in her to extend your stay for her sake happens in this world only once every hundred years. You have a meeting with an official of the Shippers' Council who is visiting the region. But we are to confirm your availability tomorrow. You also wanted to meet with the Christian Council; another proposed but not firmed up meeting. So nothing to which you are so chained you can't break from it."

"And the week after that? Oh yes, I know. That is when we have the youth leadership training. It starts from Wednesday, not so? Not bad. It is likely I will now return to Accra on Friday next week. I will confirm tomorrow."

He enjoyed the false sparring sessions he had constantly with Brenda. She had a very good sense of humour and he liked it. Otherwise it was always tense work and work and work.

Diane brought him a rose the next morning, a fresh pink one which smelt sweet. He put it in his buttonhole and had it there the whole day. Diane was facilitating all the sessions that morning so Dan just sat back and helped when she needed him to do anything.

When they went out for the tea break at 10.30 Mrs Murungi was just arriving with a man. She did the introductions. "Mr Matthew Koech is the Director of Corporate Affairs. I managed to convince him to take a rest while letting knowledge infuse itself into him and he agreed. This is Dan. I am afraid he will have to tell you the second name himself. He makes learning so easy and so interesting. It's like watching an interesting comedy. You just relax, observe and don't exert yourself and at the end of the day you are wiser."

Dan bowed slightly. And shook hands with Mr Koech. "I am Dan Apeatu." Turning to Mrs Murungi he said, "Thanks for your compliment."

"What compliment? I just told the truth."

"That makes the compliment even more valuable," Dan told her.

"I won't say anything because you will find something to counter all I say."

Diane came along and Dan introduced her to Mr Koech. "Diane, my wonderful boss. She is really the wonderful facilitator. My role is just to fetch her laptop, prepare her cup of tea, fetch her tissue paper if she must sneeze and hold her handbag to the car when she is leaving." Looking at Diane he said, "Mr Matthew Koech, Director of Corporate Affairs of NTB. If you will excuse me I must get her a cup right now. As usual I am sure," he said supposedly to Diane. "Two cubes sugar and one teaspoon of milk."

They all laughed and he stayed.

"Nice to meet you, Diane," Mr Koech said as they shook hands.

"It was Diane who told me about the training," Mrs Murungi said. "She is co-facilitator with Dan."

"So must you be a Dan or a Diane to be a good facilitator?" Mr Koech asked.

Dan jerked. The closeness of the names did not occur to him. "Maybe a Diane. Dans make lousy facilitators."

They all had their snacks and went back for the next session at 11.00 a.m. Dan sat by the door and slipped out after only thirty minutes.

When they came out at 1.00 p.m. he was sitting near the reception reading a *Newsweek* magazine.

"You ran out and left me alone," Diane accused.

"You did not need me. That was why I left."

It shocked her. It was intentional. And she had two people observing her all that while.

"You said you would tell me what was special about the session if I came today," Mrs Murungi reminded him when she and Mrs Koech joined the two facilitators.

"Yes, yesterday you watched me facilitate. If we agree I train your staff, it will be Diane and I. You saw me yesterday. You know Diane but don't know her as a trainer. I left you alone with her so that you would appreciate the quality of the second trainer. You won't be needing me for future training sessions. I thought you should see Diane leading sessions all by herself so that if you need to use her alone you know you can rely on her to take up the job alone."

Diane put her hand to her mouth.

Mrs Murungi smiled. "She was fantastic. She was not the Diane I have known. But if we ever use her it means you lose a contract."

"Yes, I am hoping that many more people will come into the field and we can reach many more people. The continent needs many leaders. And I am glad for Diane to project herself into the world of training and consultancy as the expert that she now is. She needs that recognition."

Diane did not hear the rest of the discussion because she hurriedly thrust her bag into Dan's hands and made for the ladies. She thought she would vomit. In the toilet she had to squat next to the bowl but she did not vomit. She sat on the bowl and rested her head on her hands. She felt better by and by.

Behind her Dan held her bag and said, "This the best part of my job I like, holding her bag." They laughed.

She found Dan and the two bank staff engrossed in conversation at one table. She joined them and they showed concern about her health. "I suddenly felt some rumbling in my tummy."

"Have you ever eaten lion meat?" Dan asked.

The other three were all amused and it was Mrs Murungi who asked, "What has lion meat got to do with rumbling tummies."

"I heard that if you eat lion meat anytime one roars your tummy rumbles. But please don't ask me where I heard it from."

They are laughed.

Dan told them he was available to do their work the next week. He then asked if Diane was free. She said no but she would rearrange what she had to do the next week. So it was agreed that they would do the assessment and have the discussions with NTB the following week. Mrs Murungi then said the bank would have to take the bill for his accommodation from the Saturday. It would pay him per diem and the three of them would arrange to go to the three sites she had chosen to meet the staff. They developed a programme from Monday till Thursday. Fortunately there was an outbound flight on the Friday so he would leave on the Friday. Mrs Murungi would take his ticket and let the bank reschedule the flight and pay the penalty for the change of date. Dan said he would foot the accommodation bill and rather include it in the invoice for his work.

Mr Koech shook hands with Diane and told her, "Keep up the good work, lady. I was really impressed sitting inside that room and listening to you." He turned to Dan. "I heard you trained Diane. I am eager to work with you in our effort to improve the quality of leadership of the bank. I am glad you are available to work with us."

"It has always been an honour for me to be given the opportunity to influence people and stimulate their interest in developing the latent leadership qualities each of us has. We still have a lot of discussions to make."

All four walked to the car park and the two bank staff drove off. Diane turned and faced Dan, "You played a game on me. You did not tell me you invited Mary to watch me facilitate."

"What good would telling you have done? It would have put you under some pressure and you may not have been your calm best."

She went on looking at him. She did not know whether to be angry or not.

"You know, in my middle school days we had these books called the Red Book and the Blue Book. They had stories from the *Readers' Digest.* One of them had this story of a girl who was in a swimming competition and got to the final which was between two of them. She was afraid she was not good enough to win and that the other competitor was superior to her. When the strap of her swimsuit came off when she went up to dive she got the excuse she wanted to back out of the competition. I learnt one thing from that story, what the girl's mother told her. She said winners don't quit and quitters don't win.

"I am not a good swimmer. I can't even remember when was the last time I swam. But I have loved swimming since reading that story. And so I have used swimming as the area in which I explain how some people can have their talents freed to grow. You know, it is like a good diver who is not sure of herself. But you know she is a good diver and can make perfect dives if only she got over her fear. So you coax her up the spring board and push her. She screams all the way down, cursing you as she goes into the water. And comes up and finds that she survived. And she tells herself she made it and that she can dive.

"I am glad Mrs Murungi came with someone else. They are both experienced in observing training and both gave you high grades for what they saw. And both saw you leading sessions without me. If I had told you about the arrangement with Mrs Murungi you would have insisted on my being present, and my presence would have been absolutely redundant. If I insisted and left you, you may have been highly self-conscious and it may have affected your concentration and therefore what you did. Now you have two people who will be needing someone to train their staff in future appraising and passing you. Now you can look at yourself and say within you that you are ready to be on your own. You don't need me to tell you this anymore."

This time she had to admit to herself that if they were not standing outside in public, she would definitely have given him a peck on his cheek.

When they finished packing up for the evening and the two of them were coming out together she stopped and looked at him straight in the face and said, "The best gift anybody has ever given me was the confidence vote in me this afternoon. I can't ever forget it. You have always spoken of intangible things being more valuable than money and other tangible things. Today I agree entirely with you."

A tear trickled down her face and he blocked its flow with his right thumb and then flicked it off her face. "I can only say you deserve it. And it is true." He made to remove his hand but she held it there for a few seconds.

"Thanks." She smiled through the wet face.

"You know the best way to thank me?"

She shook her head, not trusting her voice.

"Go ahead and surpass me as a leader. I will watch your growth with pride, the way you will watch the development of your very bright child."

He accompanied her to her car. "Sorry to be telling you this too late. I am taking you home to have dinner with me and my family tomorrow evening."

"You and your family? Wow! My hands will be trembling so bad I will drop all the food from the fork and I will be putting what is left on the fork in my nose instead of my mouth. I will lose all my manners as well."

"Your hands can develop St Vitus' dance. And you can even put lumps of meat in your nostrils, I am afraid this is not a negotiable thing. You are coming."

"Isn't that dictatorial?"

"Sure it is. That is what I am this evening, dictatorial."

He gave a mock sigh of resignation. "I give up. But let me know, how many other people will be there?"

"Oh, only two. My parents."

"Only two? Your parents? What about your husband and children?"

She put the bag in the car and leaned against its door. "They won't be coming." She saw his arched brow and knew he was going to ask a question so he added, "They won't be coming because I don't have them."

A cloud came over his face but she could not tell what emotion that was.

"I am sorry," he said in a very low voice.

She laughed. "You haven't done anything wrong."

It was true. He was just being African. His European friends did not understand that African trait that made people apologise for things they had not done. Like saying sorry when someone struck a foot and fell or almost fell. But he realised the sorry was not used in the same apologetic way the English used it. The local expressions in such circumstance meant have my sympathy. So saying sorry meant I am sorry for you that you struck your foot. It was not that I am sorry I caused you to strike your foot.

"Do you stay with your parents?" he asked more to get over the awkward silence than really probing about her.

"No, but we get together once in a while and have supper together. I either go to their place or I invite them. I invited them this time."

"It is going to be intimately family affair. I will look out of place," he protested.

"My parents know I am doing this training led by a Ghanaian. And they asked me why not invite him to join us. They both think it will be nice to meet you. I was already going to invite you, anyway."

"I feel honoured by the invitation but I have this strong feeling I am intruding on a very private family affair."

"Well, you have up to tomorrow evening to get rid of that feeling so that you can be one of us when we sit together at table."

When they met the next morning the first thing he said was, "Diane, I am being Kenyan now. About yesterday. I am sorry about asking about your husband and children."

She shook her head. "Do you think that is a very sore topic with me and that your bringing it up hurt me? I think we will one day tell each other more about ourselves. I don't have children yet and I don't have a husband. It is a fact about me same as I am a woman or a Kenyan. And what is it about being Kenyan? What makes you Kenyan?"

"You told me that Kenyans replace greetings with what weighs most on their hearts. Was that not what you said?"

"And your asking about my husband and children weighed on your heart? And now to what was heaviest in my heart before we greet. Thanks ever so much for the gift of yesterday. I called my parents and told them about it. I called my best friend who is now in Mombassa and told her about it. Thanks."

Her hand was lying on the hood of the car and he put out his hand to pat it. "You deserve everything I did for you. I am looking for people who have leadership potential and can be committed to helping others develop the leadership in them. You are one of the very good leaders I have come across. I see a lot of me in you. With some differences of course but I think you can beat your own path and win souls in your own territory as I win souls in mine. Between us and others who are starting their own careers not only as leaders but nurturing others we will have a sizeable flock. I need people like you."

The evaluation that evening was an interesting event. Mrs Murungi came for the last sessions and listened with interest to the free expression of feelings about the course. There was the written evaluation, on a form people were not required to put their names on. Both Diane and Dan had thanked them for their participation, for their contributions and for the rich experience they had brought to the sessions which they hoped would help all of them build a good foundation as leaders. The participants then insisted on saying a few words themselves and it turned out that almost everybody wanted to say something. Dan kept a bright face and thanked each of them for the gift in their compliments while Diane was visibly overwhelmed with emotions. In the past she had been one of those making those comments but today some of the comments were directed at her. She had come far and stole furtive looks at the man who had pushed her on so hard on this road. He did not seem conscious of his achievement, Diane noted, or he just took it for granted.

Mrs Murungi's mind raced to the last day of their own training and what the staff of NTB would be saying. She was very happy for Diane whom she had known for many years but had not known she was such a powerful trainer. Quiet, virtually unnoticed but very effective. Like her boss. Or like her bag carrier as Dan chose to describe himself. She looked at each in turn and observed the intoxication in Diane's face and the quiet acceptance in Dan's. She remarked to herself that they had an excellent relationship and Dan was the most extraordinary man she had ever met.

Would they marry; the question crossed her mind as she looked from one to the other and listened to people share their impressions. One of the participants did make the comment that, "If we did not know that Diane was Kenyan and Dan Ghanaian, we would have thought them siblings. But they sure would make good Mr and Mrs." The others clapped and laughed. Dan only smiled, the kind of half smile that showed amusement but did not go all the way to light up his face. And he looked round the room at the participants and not at Diane and Mrs Murungi. Diane on the other hand would have been said to have blushed if her skin were light. But her face went through many changes, capturing the emotions that changed rapidly inside her.

Mrs Murungi smiled at herself. She knew Diane was not married but she knew nothing of Dan. He must be married even though she did not see a ring on his ring finger. But then she did not wear her ring all the time too, like now, but she was married.

It was bound to be a climactic ending for Diane. After they saw Mrs Murungi off, they met with some of the participants who asked to discuss things with them. But before Dan went up to his room to change for the supper with Diane and her parents, the two of them went back to the conference room where Dan gave Diane an envelope and asked her to count its contents. There were 60 one hundred dollar bills inside it. He gave her a receipt to sign for him. It said that Diane had received the amount of six thousand dollars being her fees for twelve days of services to Horizon Leadership.

She coughed and almost choked. She held her chest first and then put her hand to her mouth and sat there looking at Dan.

"In the discussions both on the phone and in the emails we agreed your fees would be five hundred dollars a day and that I had agreed with the organisation that each of us would be putting in twelve days of work. Five days were for the training, two days for reflection and report writing and five days for interviewing the participants and developing the contents of the training. So what you received is what the organisation paid for your role in this training."

"I know that consultants would charge a client for say a second person's role and agree a fee for that person with the client," Diane said, putting the envelope down. "But the consultant would then negotiate a lower fee with the second person. You are giving me the whole amount you charged the organisation for my services. Secondly, you did most of the assessment of the participants and developed most of the contents of the training. I did not do twelve days of work and you know that. I can't take six thousand dollars because I didn't earn that much."

"How much do you think you earned?" Dan asked with that small indecipherable smile on his lips.

"About half of that, I would say," she replied seriously.

"Of course, please say it," he told her, looking back at her. It was like some sort of looking match. "But I am not going to take back what I negotiated for your services. If I don't give it to you then I should return it to the organisation that contracted us to provide this training. I was paid my fees and all other costs related to this training, like accommodation, my travel cost, material production and so on. So if I don't pay you how much the organisation agreed to and did pay for your services then I should be returning the amount to the funder and explain that I over-charged it. I charge for services I provide and don't trade with people."

While Diane sat at the reception Dan went up and took a quick shower and changed into something quite respectable but casual. He was not appearing before a committee that was going to vet him so he did not seek to impress with his appearance. Downstairs Diane wondered about him. He may be married but other men she knew would have taken advantage of the open admiration shown by the female members he trained to have affairs, even if illicit ones, with them. She had met Dan three times now and having an affair with women seemed far from his thoughts. She was not sure he even noticed the open admiration and, sometimes open invitation, in the faces of some of the women. His wife was lucky, she told herself. It made her respect him all the more.

Dan was surprised when Diane admired his casual wear. It was a long dress, caftan style, covering his ankles and made from fine cotton material. The embroidery around the neck was a very simple pattern, but a pattern he had thought beautiful when he bought it.

They drove past what Diane described as one of the largest shanty towns in Africa. "It is called Mathare and has a population of more than half a million," Diane told him. "It is a sad place," she went on. "The structures are mostly improvised and made of highly inflammable material. If fire should ever break out there the casualty rate would be fantastic. It won't be possible for fire tenders to go into the town easily because of the way the structures have been constructed, making no provision for access by vehicles. And the number of people in a single room in that town is so high if there were pandemonium their own confusion will cause many deaths.

"The town is right next to rich settlements so those who live there have the misfortune of contrasting their lot with what is attainable just next door. Most of the people who live there work away from there but are so poor they can't afford the cost of buses and taxis. So they leave home before daybreak and begin walking in order to arrive at their workplaces in time.

"These are people who come from rural areas, know nobody in Nairobi or the only people they know are living in that town and they have nowhere else to go to."

He looked out of the window, through the rolled up glass. He did not say anything. Quite a familiar story but he was surprised at how she told it. She lived their lives with them. She shared the reality, the vulnerability of their lives with them. But she was not one of them. There was silence in the car for a long time. Even though he said nothing Diane was sure his mind was on the plight of those poor fellow human beings imprisoned in this open prison.

"The only difference between me and the people living there is the circumstance of birth," she said at length and Dan turned to look at her and to listen to her. "I did nothing to make me stay out of that town. I was just fortunate to have been born into a family that had resources to give me a good education and support. If I contrast the security of my life with the precarious lives lived in this town, I don't feel sorry that I don't have a husband or that I don't yet have children. There are a lot of people living here, and in many places in the country, who should not be having children but who have children. I'm not sure what sort of life awaits those children in future." She sighed.

Dan continued to look at her. But he did not see her because his physical eyes were turned off. Instead the eyes in his mind were turned on. And through them he could see Diane more clearly, a caring person with very strong capabilities for empathy. She was a missionary and therefore would make a very good leader. She would support others to grow and she would find joy in her work and not in the money she would make. He turned away. They were again silent for a long time. As he sat there looking at her and not seeing her he reminded her of Silas Marner in one of his trances.

"I won't go back to those people living in the town or their colleagues living elsewhere," he told her after a while. "My respect for you has gone up very high listening to you recognise your luck in birth. We often take that for granted. My respect for you has grown listening to you share the pain of the lives of people you are not connected to. It is a strong virtue you have. But let me ask you a question on something different. Something personal. For the second time I heard you say you don't have a husband and you don't yet have children."

He turned and looked at her. She did same too, wondering what in that statement he was picking out.

"Does it mean you give having children a high probability of happening but marrying a lower probability? Does it mean you are saying to yourself you will have children but you may not marry?"

She thought a while before saying, "Is there anything wrong with that?"

"Don't act Ghanaian."

It amused her, his saying she should not act Ghanaian. "How do Ghanaians act?"

"They answer questions with questions."

She laughed. "I haven't noticed that in you."

"No, I don't have that bad habit. My parents are Kenyan, only living in Ghana."

When she looked at him she smiled. He had this capability of keeping a very straight face even when he told the most ridiculous story.

"Apeatu is no Kenyan name," she reminded him.

He sighed, one of his famous sighs of false resignation.

"The answer to your question could be yes, Dan," she said. "I will like to marry. But each time I celebrate a birthday the probability of marriage moves one rung down the ladder. Each time I achieve success the probability of marriage reduces because few men want to marry a successful woman, an established woman. I want children. First because society frowns upon unproductive people, especially women. But I want children more because I love them and will want to have my own, and be responsible for them and give them love. So yes, having children has a higher probability of happening than my marrying because even if I don't marry I will like to have children. I know it is going to be difficult and messy. If I don't marry who do I get pregnant with? It isn't as simple as it sounds, mind. Most men my age are married. So if

151

I am going to get pregnant, do I go for someone younger than me or do I go for someone's husband? And what do I tell him, just impregnate me but don't worry about the child? I am Catholic. How do I face the church and society with a pregnancy? What do I tell the child, or children, about their father?"

He reached out and put a hand on her shoulder, held the shoulder and squeezed it. It was the only thing he could do to let her know he was sorry for her but he could not help her.

Diane's parents were younger than Dan had expected. She left Dan with them and went into the kitchen immediately. Her mum had been running the kitchen with her niece till Diane arrived. She had spent the past two evenings in the kitchen till late, preparing various sauces and dishes. So her mum and the niece only had to heat them.

From the kitchen she could hear her father's unrestrained laughter. She also heard her mother's more subdued but equally happy laughter. They were getting on very well with Dan. She had expected it but was not sure. They used the round dining table and Dan sat between her parents. Her mother kept explaining the various dishes and insisted on helping Dan to more. Diane knew how little he ate and she left the worrying and pressurising to eat more to her mother. She definitely had more success than Diane could have expected to have.

After the meal, they cleared the table with Dan insisting on helping in clearing. Despite the protests of her mother he worked with Diane and her niece to clear the table. They sat in the sitting room and chatted till almost midnight, drinking beer. Dan drank lemon grass tea.

"What are your plans for tomorrow?" Mr Orengo asked, looking at his daughter.

"We will spend part of the morning reviewing the training and summarising the evaluation sheets and agreeing recommendations." That was what the programme said. "After lunch I expect to take him to the National Park and later show him round Nairobi. We may visit the Maasai market."

"Please show him round the city," her father said. Turning to Dan he said, "She knows every corner of the city, including the not so respectable corners as well. She has been concerned for disadvantaged people. She is not like me. I spent my life chasing money and not worrying about others, I am afraid. I am glad she is different though."

Turning to Diane she said, "Let us drop him at his hotel. We can all go out together in the evening tomorrow? We can go to Carnivores."

They all agreed it was a good plan for the next day.

"Dad can I show you and Mum something?"

"So late in the night?" her father asked.

"It won't take a minute," Diane told them. She brought out the envelope and gave it to her mother and asked her to count the money. She explained what Dan had done and what other consultants would have done. Her father was impressed and her mother was even more impressed. She had worried about her daughter leaving a paid job to be on her own, seeking contracts. Six thousand dollars for twelve days work was fantastic.

They listened to Dan explain the future ahead of Diane, how training came naturally to her. He explained what he had learnt about her on the way and how that fitted what her father had said about her concern for others and said she would go very far in her career. He told them the money he paid her was what she deserved to be paid, what he had charged the client for Diane's services.

That was how the evening ended for the group. The parents drove Dan to the hotel, talking and laughing as if they were peers and had known each other for many years.

The next day went very fast as well. Dan and Diane had a successful meeting during which they aggregated comments from the evaluation sheets, tabulated issues and agreed recommendations to the organisers of the training. They still had time to kill before they could go for lunch.

It was one of those impulsive things people did. Turning to Dan she said, "You asked me yesterday about the probability of marriage and having children. I told you why the low probability of marriage. Many people would be asking themselves why I had not married up to this time. You may have asked yourself that question but thought you could not put it to me. I want to tell you why."

He shifted, feeling very uncomfortable, unsure he should listen to something so personal about her. But he had no good reason to say she should not tell him, especially as she chose to voluntarily tell him.

He listened to a moving story but told in a flat voice, a voice in which all emotions had been killed. There was no accusation and no bitterness. Her message was clear; this is a part of me, just like all the other parts of me that you have seen, that I want to show to you. It was such a very private part of her life and he did not know what to say to someone who had considered him friend enough to let him have a look at her painful past.

Unable to think of what is the right thing to say in the circumstance he asked her, "So do you meet Teddy and Jane sometimes? If they are still in Nairobi you must have met them occasionally."

"I have met them a number of times since then," she admitted. "Jane has called me a number of times since they married."

"She has the nerve to call you?"

She looked at him. Someone would have been greatly surprised. He did not seem so surprised. "Yes. Jane would argue that she did nothing wrong. She only fell in love with Teddy and proposed and Teddy accepted. She did not put a gun on his head to take him away."

They went on talking about how she felt and how she had felt about receiving calls from Jane. By the time they were going for lunch his admiration for Diane had increased.

They had lunch with the few participants whose flight was the next day or even Monday and had not gone out looking at Nairobi. Diane then drove Dan to the National Park. She knew the animals and told which was the wildebeest, which were impala and the rest. He knew the zebra, the giraffe, the baboon and the ostrich. She told him stories about the cheetah and the tiger and the lion, things he did not know.

She later took him round the city, such a developed city he thought. At the Maasai market he loved the stone crafts but was not sure they would survive the journey back home. He bought things for his staff mostly. It was only when Diane asked about the family that he remembered to buy items for Marian and Junior. He had difficulty guessing how big Junior would be.

Diane filed away the information but asked no questions; two children, a girl aged sixteen and a boy aged twelve. Nothing for a wife.

"If you are here in April, May or June or around October and November, you can view the migration of animals at the Serengeti. It is one of the most interesting things to see in Kenya. Over a million animals moving together. It is just spectacular."

Her father took over in the evening. He knew the Carnivore Restaurant and ran a commentary. From him Dan learnt that the restaurant was opened in 1980 and had a branch in Johannesburg in South Africa. The open air restaurant was very impressive. It was vast and there was a crowd eating there when they arrived. The game was strung on what he learnt were Maasai spears and then roasted over coal. They took their seats and servers came round with the spears offering different meat – crocodile, wildebeest, zebra, ostrich, impala, buffalo, gazelle and others. Dan asked if they were allowed to hunt those animals and learnt from Diane's father that the animals served here were raised in a ranch and not in the wild. He had to take very small pieces of each as he wanted to taste as many different species as possible. Diane watched and smiled as her mother forced more meat into his plate each time the servers came round.

She occasionally looked at this strange man who was liked very easily but who, it seemed, preferred a quiet life alone. Even in company he hardly talked but he could make people laugh when he wanted to. He and her father took turns telling jokes. Her father's laughter filled the whole restaurant sometimes. Her father told more stories, with Dan telling them only when he was asked to. But they laughed more at his stories. She didn't know where he got them from.

Chapter Ten

She spent the next week observing her friends and recalling what they said about their fathers. She recalled as much as she could all that her friends and mates ever said about their relationship with that parent called father. She didn't want to know how they related with their mothers. She had a relationship with her mother that could not be changed. So if some girls had excellent, friend-like relationships with their mothers it would not change how their mother treated them. But she was going to establish a relationship with her father. Yes, establish, not re-establish. She was anxious to know what sort of relationship they would have. If beneath her father's seeming concern for her he turned out to be worse than their mother in the way he shouted at them, in the way he insulted them and the only good thing about him was that he would give them money, how would their lives be like?

Starting from the families in the house they rented, she recalled what sort of fathers the children had. Iddris lived next to them. He was the one who led the prayers in the mosque behind their house. He was very quiet and very strict. Too strict. Even to his wives. He had two wives. He hardly spoke. In the evening, after the prayer, one of the children would bring his chair out and put it in the veranda in front of their room. From prayers he would come straight to that chair. And woe betided them if the chair was not out and ready by the time he came back from the mosque.

He would sit in his chair and recline in it. He expected his meals within minutes of returning. One of the wives would bring his food, kneel and put it on a table in front of him. One of the children, most often the older girl, Zelia, would bring his water. She would also kneel and put the bowl containing the water on the table. One of the boys would bring the water for washing his hands and put it on the floor by him. Like the others, he must also kneel before performing his chore.

He hardly talked to anyone in the family but when he joined his fellow men on the bench under the *dawadawa* tree behind the house he would be animated, talking, arguing and laughing. His children feared him and whenever he was coming home from outside they ran back into their room or sat on the wall of the veranda.

Abu, who was next, was a bachelor who brought girls as young as Marian to bed. She skipped him and went round. The one whose relationship with his children she loved was Mustapha. He had two children, one boy aged ten and a girl aged four. He bought a bike for the boy to ride to school but carried the girl on his bike daily to her kindergarten. He called her his wife and played with her whenever he was at home. He had someone teaching the boy privately at home. He had a very good relationship with the children. His son would run and meet him whenever he saw the father coming home.

Her friends and school mates? The stories varied. She chose to focus on the stories as she recalled them and not who said them. *My father is hardly at home. Which is good for all of us. He is pain in the arse when he is at home. He is a womaniser and spends all his time outside with women. He complains about money whenever I need money for my fees, or school uniform or provisions. But I hear he is very lavish with his girlfriends…*

Another had an even more interesting story. *My father even has a girlfriend here. She is swimming in provisions and he pays her fees. They have never bothered her about fees because she pays promptly. But I have to follow him and plead and plead till he reluctantly gives me part of the fees. The last time he paid was when we were threatened with dismissal. If I ever ask him how come he pays the fees of his girlfriend so promptly he will skin me alive…*

My father is my best friend. We can sit together for hours and chat and play. He played with us when we were kids. He would carry us around the neighbourhood and later go for strolls with us, telling about the things we saw on the way. Today he is the one I enjoy spending my time with. I can tell him my secrets, including dirty things I have done. He will listen. The way he will talk will make me so bad I will never do them again. But he will never share my secrets with anyone, not even mother…

My father is there and I am also there. What is there between us? He gives our mother the housekeeping money. He pays our fees when we are retuning to school. He buys us provisions. Whenever we need anything we let him know. He buys some of the things we need for us, he doesn't buy others. If we have a problem we can talk to him. He prefers talking to mother and his friends and not his children...

So Dad was a different thing to different children. Maybe like the elephant to the blind men. He was a rope you could twist and turn and skip with, to some. He was as flat, and high and hard as a wall to others. He was useful, like a fan, to some children, but he was dangerous, like a spear in some other homes.

Who was their father? She did not think she could answer the question from just the brief meeting with him that once. The events of that evening gave her high expectations. Some of them, like his bland face, also gave her some fear.

It was this fear that made her keep pushing back her decision to ring him. She had promised to do it the Monday of the week he had asked her to call. She pushed it back till she was forced to ring on Thursday, feeling that if she waited till too late they might not even meet. Afraid or not, she needed to meet him.

She rang the office, her heart pumping but she was prepared to show better ability in the use of the phone than she did the last time she spoke with him.

"Hello, Leadership Horizon, may I help you?"

"Good afternoon, Madam. My name is Marian Wepia. Can I speak to Mr Dan Apeatu please?"

"Mr Apeatu has travelled."

"He told me he was coming back last weekend and that I should call him this week."

"He extended his stay. He will come to Accra tomorrow and come to Tamale on Saturday. Who did you say you are?"

"My name is Marian. I am his daughter."

"His daughter? Mr Apeatu's daughter?"

She beat a quick retreat. "I am his sister's daughter but I call him my father instead of uncle."

"You can call him again on Monday. He has not come back yet."

"Thank you, Madam."

She heaved a sigh. The 'I am his daughter' had come so naturally she had not stopped to think of how the person at the other side would take it. In the office they may not know he had children. They would not take anyone claiming to be his child seriously. She was glad she could think of something to say so quickly.

She called the house Sunday morning and got him just before he left for church. This time she was sure she did the right thing on the phone. "I called the office on Thursday and was told you had not yet come back."

"Yes, I came back yesterday."

"Dad, you asked me to call you when you come back for us to agree when to meet."

"Look, I am going to church and I am almost late. When are visiting hours on Saturday? Are you engaged in any activity on Saturday? Is it okay if I come on Saturday?"

"Yes Dad. I will be there on Saturday."

"When is visiting time?"

"People visit throughout the day, Dad. You can come at any time."

"The fact that people come throughout the day doesn't make it right to come outside visiting hours. I will come at two o'clock. I am sure visiting hours for most schools start at that time. Is two o'clock okay with you?"

"Yes, Sir. Two is okay, Sir."

"Okay, see you at two o'clock on Saturday. I will come to where I last dropped you off."

"Okay, Sir. I will be waiting there."

As was the case with the first meeting with Dan, Marian spent many hours going over the short conversation, feeling at one time elated and expectant of the coming meeting and at another time afraid it would bring her pain, it would bring her dream world crashing to over one million pieces. He had been so brusque she had not even thought of asking if she could come to the house. He had seemed impatient with her. *Look, I'm going to church and I am almost late.* It was like, *Will you hurry up with what you have to say and let me go?* The church first. She was a distraction. He had not asked about her studies. He had not said good bye, he just hanged up.

But what could she say? Assume they met and he told her, *Look, I am doing you a favour. You are not my daughter. Your mother got pregnant with someone and only chose to put the responsibility on me. I am doing you a favour by paying your fees.* Then what? She had told her mother if they felt badly treated their father would come for them. She had threatened her mother's friend on the strength of a relationship with this man, that he was her father. If he wasn't?

Tears streamed down her face, warm and even pleasant. She felt self-pity. Poor girl, she told herself. She had a mother but could not expect motherly care, the love and protection mothers gave to their children, from this woman. She did not know if she had a father. She could have. It may be Dan. But she may not get the protection and care that a child needed from a father either. The examples of irresponsibility were too many. And in his case... He had left them for about twelve years and not bothered to support them. He would not invite her home. He had been abrupt with her, his church being more important to him. She remembered the story of the bat, neither a bird because it had teeth, gave birth to its young alive and had mammary glands with which it fed its young milk, nor a mammal because it flew in the skies like birds. Why me, she asked several times. Why her and her unfortunate young brother?

Sometimes she would look cheerful and see a rainbow in the sky. She would reason that she called at the wrong time, when he was late for church. He offered to come on Saturday. He proposed it, she had not made him do it. He kept his word of meeting her on his return by agreeing to come the next weekend. And he had tried to be nice, hadn't he? *Is two o'clock okay with you?* He could have said he was coming at two o'clock and simply ordered her to meet him. He talked to her like a human being.

The way she ironed her dress on the Saturday morning one would think she was going to meet her boyfriend. She shrugged to herself. She was at the appointed place some thirty minutes before the appointed time. At a minute past two o'clock his ash coloured car was pulling up. He got down as she approached and they shook hands.

He looked at his watch and said, "I hope you have not been waiting for long. We agreed two o'clock."

"No, Sir," she lied. "I just came."

He looked at her, appraised her. "How are you, Marian?"

She looked the respectful student with her hands held in front of her. "I am fine, Sir. How was your journey, Sir?"

"It was great. Longer than I expected because I got some other assignment. But it was great. How is your brother? How big is he? Show me with your hands how tall he is." He wore a friendly look and that put Marian at ease.

Holding up her right hand to demonstrate, she said, "He is this tall."

He looked pleased. A question occurred to her, why he should look pleased to know her brother was this tall when he had abandoned them. Why did he do it?

He looked round. "Is there somewhere we can sit and talk?"

She was not sure. In the end they agreed on the Assembly Hall. They drove there. Inside the car Marian took a good look at the inside this time. She also searched for the shopping bag for her and found none.

"Tell me, how is your mother? Still drinking?" he asked when they were seated in the Assembly Hall.

"Yes, Sir."

"Did you bring the birth certificates?"

She offered them, hers and her brother's. He looked at them and returned them to her. Marian's certificate said she was Marian Apeatu born on the date he knew. It said her father was Daniel Apeatu of Navrongo in Ghana and that her mother was Matilda Kadua Wepia also of Navrongo in Ghana. Marian Wepia was her mother's way of denying him any title to her as she had sought to do since the separation. It was not surprising. "Why did you change your name from Apeatu to Wepia? You can see it says Marian Apeatu in the certificate."

"Sir, can I ask you a question?"

"The typical Ghanaian attitude, isn't it? Go ahead and ask."

"What is the typical Ghanaian attitude, Sir?"

"Oh, answering questions with questions. Is this Tamale? Why do you want to know? Ask me your question."

She laughed at his answer. So Ghanaians answer questions with questions? How old are you? Why? She laughed. It seemed true. "Sir, why did you leave us for these twelve years? You never asked about us your children."

He was not prepared for this. He had not anticipated this. It hit him and hit him hard. He raised his head and tilted it backwards, not to ease the nerves but to find something doing. He looked at her and she was watching him. The girl had shown a very strong character when they met the first time. She had asked him why she should choose to come to him to ask and not beg for her fees if he were not her father. She had shown an ability to match him. He should have anticipated this question, that she would want to know why he had abandoned them. This was not what he had come for. He was not prepared for this question and it threw into disarray all that he had planned. He was not meeting a six year old girl to whom he could dictate what to do. Her first question would help them establish the kind of relationship they must have. He should recognise a young adult, quite bold and unafraid to hold him to task. He looked at her unblinking eyes.

It was a legitimate question and she and her brother deserved to know. He looked at her and decided he would tell her. But it was not now. They would one day have a discussion but now was not the time.

She was still looking at him when he said, "Marian, you have a right to know why I have been absent from your life for this long. You have a right to an apology from me. You will get both one day. But I am afraid it is not now."

"May I ask another question, Sir? Why not now, Sir?"

"Marian we will talk about this. We can't come back together and not discuss why for twelve years you did not see me. We will talk about it. But not now. Why not now? You are young. We will talk about it when you grow older. When you hear our story – my and your mother's story – you should be in a position to decide who is to blame for what. I don't think now is the time, that is my conviction. So I won't talk about it."

She seemed undeterred. "Mother has been accusing you."

Dan felt being under critical scrutiny in the eyes of this young woman whom he had expected to just tell how he was going to support her, how he could support her studies and help bring her and her brother up. "Let her say them. I am not going to sit here today and ask you to repeat all that your mother said and offer defences of them or say which is not true. I am not going to tell you my side of the story today. I will tell it but I will tell it when *I* feel convinced you are ready for it."

It sounded so final she knew nothing she did would make him answer her question. It surprised her that she even asked that question. Even though it had been strong in her mind at no time before the meeting did she think she should put it. It surprised her therefore that she put it and it surprised her even more that he did not react angrily. She leaned forward and rested her head on his shoulder. When he put his arm on her shoulder she felt a sensation she had never known since her childhood, being in kinship with someone.

She sat up suddenly and said with the same suddenness, "Dad, you don't know how to be a dad." She took his hands. He looked down at their interlocked hands but did not take away his hands.

It surprised her yet again that she called him dad. It was unplanned. And even though she had been thinking of him as her dad she had never decided to call him dad.

He wondered if this was going to be a grilling session. But he reasoned that if it were going to be a grilling session it would be one he deserved. Her question had been unexpected and difficult to answer but it had not been unreasonable.

"What do you mean I don't know how to be a dad? What have I done?"

"It is what you have not done. You are coming to visit your daughter in school and you did not buy anything for her. I checked when I got into the car. There is nothing."

Another blow to his forehead. He should have done it. He should have bought her some provisions. He even forgot to bring the items he bought for them in Nairobi. He even bought those items because Diane had asked him. As a father he had not thought of his children. But how could he explain to this girl who had just found her father that he had not been a father before and that she should not expect him to play his role right immediately?

Instead he said, "I was not sure what you would need. So instead of buy you something I brought you money."

She laughed. "I am sure you always carry money with you. So even if you had not intended to give me money now that we talked about it you can give me money and say that is the money you brought to give to me."

He smiled, but his smile was for a different reason from the reason why she laughed. This girl was very intelligent and he should learn to expect challenges from her.

He decided to take over the discussions. "Now tell me about your studies. What subjects are you reading?"

She was doing Science and it surprised him, very pleasantly. She wanted to be a doctor and it seemed she was doing well enough to be able to make it to the university. "I could not concentrate on my studies and that sometimes affected my performance. I didn't know who would pay my fees. Sometimes the way mother or her friends treat us upsets us so much that I can't read. Then I kept asking myself why you would not help us; why you would not one day seek to find out whether there is anything you can do for us. I didn't know who to turn to for all the things for which I and my brother needed help. I wanted to enrol in the extra classes offered by the Chemistry, Physics and Maths masters but when I could not even pay my fees how could I be thinking of extra classes?"

He sat in silence and listened to her story of their life at home.

Suddenly she said, "Dad, we missed you. Did you ever miss us?"

He was beginning to shake his head in awe at the type of questions she could ask and how they just popped up, very difficult questions. But he stopped because shaking his head would have been taken to mean no, he did not miss them. Well, it was true he did not miss them but that was not what she wanted to hear.

"No, you didn't miss us. Maybe you never even thought of us."

He sighed and looked away. How true. And this young girl whom he had abandoned and so now did not know had picked it up by looking at him.

She went on, "You wouldn't miss us, would you? We needed you but you did not need us."

He did not know whether to take it that it was good justification for his not missing them or that she was being sarcastic.

She picked his hands again. "Dad, are you married? Did you marry again after you and mother were divorced?"

"Why do you ask?"

She raised his hands and dropped them and laughed.

"What is funny?"

"The Ghanaian attitude, Dad."

It hit him, a question for a question. He laughed too. He kept looking at this young woman and his respect for her intelligence went up by the minute. But at the same time it made him worried about the relationship they were going to establish. Could he manage this young woman? Would he know what was the right thing to do with her or would he be found fumbling every time?

She said, "You are my father. I don't know you. If I don't ask questions, how will I know you?"

He sighed at the rightness of her answer. "Like your mother I did not marry. I don't have a wife."

"Then why didn't you want me to come to your house?"

It surely wasn't what he had expected this meeting to be like. The young woman was leading it and leading it so painfully, springing surprise after surprise. He could not reconcile this heavy punch throwing woman with the shy girl whom he met about four weeks back.

"At the risk of indulging in the Ghanaian attitude, let me ask why you say I didn't want you to come to the house."

"If you don't ask a question when questions are put to you that won't make you Ghanaian, will it?" They both laughed. Sometimes a question would call for another question and not an answer. "When I met you the first time and you said we should meet when you came back from your journey you said we would either meet here or in your office. When I asked if we could not meet in your house you asked if I had problems meeting you here or in your office. And you told me firmly that it would either be here or in the office."

He looked at her, shaking his head. Intelligent. He felt like agreeing on how he would support her and then get up and leave but he dismissed it knowing that he could not dictate things if they were not right. This was not your usual sixteen year old. But then, he checked himself, what did he even know about children to be able to say this is what is right for a ten year old or not to be expected of a twelve year old?

"Why did you want us to meet in my house and not here or in the office?" He expected another very intelligent answer, a very strong and very convincing one but one so obvious he would have known it if he were not so stupid.

She did not fail him. "Dad, I thought that was obvious. You are my father. Your home is my home. Why should I want to know my home? And if I don't come there how will I know it? If you are sick and don't go to work how can I come and visit you if I don't know where your house is? If I need to see you urgently and you are not in the office how can I find you?"

This time he was prepared for her even though her answer was, as usual, brilliance itself. "Marian, a girl walks up to me and says she is my daughter and that the reason I should believe her is that she would not choose me from many men in Tamale to ask me for her fees if I were not her father. I agree to pay the fees because even if she were not my daughter she would be hard pressed and maybe did not have anybody she could turn to if I did not help. Helping her pay the fees is one thing. Accepting her as my daughter is another thing. If I wasn't sure you were my daughter I could not be expected to be inviting you to my house." He was astonished that he was defensive before so young a woman. "You will come to my house.

"Why did your mother change your surnames? I guess she did same with Junior too."

"Yes, he is also Daniel Wepia. She said you went off and left us and that since then you did not even care about us. So we had stopped being your children because you had denied us yourself."

He listened to her tell about Junior. "He is not like me. He is a gentleman."

"But you are not a lady, are you?"

"Me? I am not like Daniel Junior. I can be rough. I can ask when I don't agree. Junior will keep quiet and just know in his mind that you are wrong. He may even stop listening to you, but he won't challenge. He is not a fighter like me."

"So you know you are a fighter?"

"But Dad, I have not been fighting you."

"Marian, you have kept me under heavy gunfire since I came here. I came for a simple discussion on how I can support you. Instead

I have to be defending myself and answering difficult questions, questions I must admit I had not expected to be put by a sixteen year old woman."

She looked at him intensely. He knew even though she was looking at him she was not seeing him. In that respect he recognised himself in her. In the end she said, "Dad, I came looking for my father. Being dad is more than paying my fees, providing me pocket money and buying me clothes. I can ring your office and ask you for money for my fees, or to buy soap and provisions and you can let someone bring it to me. That is not being dad. How do I know who you are and if when I am upset and I put my head on your shoulders to cry you will put your hands around me or push me away? How will I know if I don't ask you questions? When I put my head on your shoulder and you put your hand around me, did you know how it felt? Nobody had ever done that to me."

Tears stood in her eyes and they rolled down, two streams that started slowly but soon swelled and flowed rapidly downhill. He pulled her to him and she lay on his chest and wept. He fought to keep his own tears, tears of pain for this woman and tears of his guilt. The guilt of the past when he denied this woman and her brother his presence and his responsibility to them. Guilt of the present, that he did not really understand the need of this woman and what she needed from a father, him. Her throbbing body pinched his heart sore. Her sobs, very soft sobs, pricked his heart to bleed. God, how could he have been so wicked to his children? How could he have been so insensitive all these years?

When she stopped weeping she dried her eyes and sat up. "Dad, I hear your father is still alive."

He did not want to answer. She had been setting traps into which he had been falling so badly. He looked down at her searching eyes, a girl less than half his age, his own daughter, yet he was afraid of her.

"You grew up in the comfort of family," she went on without his answer. "You don't know how it is like not to be an ordinary child. Junior and I grew up differently. We were not ordinary children. We were worse than that. What does it mean not to have the privilege to grow up as ordinary children? It means you cannot ever speak about your father because you don't know him and you don't know if he will even say yes he is your father. Dad, you don't know the pain I felt as my colleagues kept saying their father did this or was this and I could not, even once, say anything about mine because he did not exist. If he were dead and I said my father died I would receive sympathy. But I just didn't know him and could not say anything at all about him. I dreaded the day someone would say tell us something about your father.

"We had mother all right, but what sort of mother? And all we ever had from her were shouts and negative things. So we went through life like orphans when our parents were still alive. There was nobody I could think of approaching if I needed say five thousand cedis and be sure I could tell the person I needed this money and that the person would get it for me even if he did not have it. I could not think of anybody who would ever stand by me if I needed help. If another student accused me of something I did not do and they took me to the police station do you know what would happen? Her mother or her father or both of them will come and stand by her and support her to accuse me. My mother would come and not even listen to me but rain insults at me and make the police believe I am a very bad girl who had always been disobedient even to her mother. I will not have a father who will give me an ear and after listening say he believes me and will fight for me. The police will brutalise me because I have nobody behind me. How does it feel to keep thinking of yourself that way? If a careless driver ever hit me or my brother and we were taken to the hospital our mother would come screaming at how she had been warning us about using the road. She has never even sat down with us to talk to us about anything but if we ever got involved in an accident she would be the one to let the world believe that it was our fault that we got hit. You will not be there to find out exactly what happened and to defend us if you realise we are right. So we get hit by someone who acts carelessly and, in addition to the pain of being hurt through someone's carelessness, we will be branded careless and inviting the harm on ourselves.

"How would you feel if at my age you know that there is nobody in the world who cares for you, but your two parents aren't dead?

"Our grandmother hates us. All we get from her are insults, how we are as bad as our father. Our mother and her friends insult us all the time. You have a home you go to. You can always say you are a member of this family in this village. Maybe it doesn't mean anything to you because you take it for granted. We don't have a home. We can't claim our mother's home to be our home because grandma hates us and will tell us we don't belong there. But where do we belong? Nowhere. We are you and mother's unwanted children. Who else will want us? What did we do?

"In the mind of a girl in such a situation a father is bigger than he is in the life of other children who grew up with their dads. You said I have kept you under gunfire. I just want to know who my father is. I had to find out if you are who I fantasise my father to be. I had to know why you aban … Why you left us and did not miss us."

Her head was down. When, in one of those swift moves, she lifted it she said, "Dad, you are weeping." His eyes were wet and when she said this it was as if the words ordered the tear down and it rolled down, a single line of water. She brought her hands together and leaned heavily against him. "Dad, I am sorry." He hugged her and in the apology of his daughter, beautiful word, daughter, he found strength for the moment. But he knew he would need a lot more strength to play his role in the life of this girl and her brother. To be not just a provider of their monetary needs, but to be their father.

He also knew he needed more than strength to do this. He didn't know what being dad was. He had never been one, really. And no book would ever teach him what each of those children needed and what was the best way to relate with each. The only person who could write that book was him. He was going to face the most important exam of his life without any previous lessons and without a syllabus from which to expect the questions. He looked down at the girl who nestled in his bosom and looked up, clear eyed, at him and knew that failure in this exam would be disastrous for the children and also for him.

He could not adequately respond to the girl. He knew he should not try responding that day. It was a day for reconciliation – meeting, pouring out feelings, acknowledging guilt and expressing remorse in order to let the healing process start. But in the anguish of the young woman the image of a father began to take shape. A friend. An older brother. A loving uncle. A confidant. A pillar of support. The one at whose door the children should expect to be able to knock after midnight and be received with love. A refuge they can run to. A warm bosom in which they would be cradled if they must cry. A sounding board.

As the enormity of the role of a dad in the children's lives became clearer he admitted that was not how he had expected it to be. He did not ever reject the children. But he had seen his duties simply in terms of providing them with money for their needs – food, health, clothing, education, leisure and so on. He had been convinced once he did that he had discharged his duty to them. Now he knew that was not true. They were not going to be a secondary or tertiary responsibility. They were going to be his main responsibility. So he did not give them time only if he could afford it. They should have priority over anything else in the demand on his time. He should not give them his surplus time. He should be there for them. It may not even be enough for him to budget his time for them even though he should do that. If she should be accused falsely by someone else he should drop everything he was doing to go to her aid. And such an event cannot be foreseen and so you cannot budget time for that.

He pulled her up and they walked out to the car. It was only then they noticed students had been passing by the Assembly Hall. Dan wondered if some peeped in and saw him and Marian in what they would describe as a compromising posture.

He asked her when their next general exeat would be and she told him they had one only the past week. He told her he planned going home the next weekend but would be in Tamale the weekend after that. Could she take an exeat and come with Junior to the house? She said she could.

When they got into the car she said, "Can I ask you a question, Dad?"

"Marian, you have asked me so many questions already."

"And I have even many more."

He shook his head and laughed. "Go on and ask."

"When you travelled the last time, where did you go to?"

"Akosombo, Accra and Kenya."

She sat in the front seat looking at him with an open mouth and a half smile. He wondered what was wrong. But he waited for her to tell him. "Dad, am I supposed to ask you what you did in those places? You won't be telling me anything about yourself unless I ask."

He adjusted himself in the seat and faced her. "I am a trainer. I train people in an area called Leadership. It is like management but it is not the same as management. I trained staff of partners of an American organisation in Akosombo. I trained people when I went to Kenya."

"So what do you people do in Horizon Leadership?"

"Horizon has two parts. One part provides training. That is what we do. We develop some courses and run them. We invite organisations to send their staff to attend those courses for a fee. At other times, an organisation may contact us, like the American organisation did, and ask that we train its staff. They pay us for doing that. So Horizon Leadership Development Services trains people in various aspects of leadership. Then there is the Horizon Training Centre. The Centre provides venue for people and organisations that want to hold meetings, or conduct trainings. There are rooms with chairs and tables that organisations can hire for their meetings or workshops. We have two rooms that can each take up to 20 people. We have two rooms that can take up to 40 people each and we have a large hall. We have projectors and other equipment that any organisation using our place can also ask for. The Training Centre also has guest house facilities. So that if any organisation wants to organise a meeting or a workshop in the Centre and the people attending are not from Tamale, they can stay in the guest house. The guest house can accommodate up to 80 people."

"Is Horizon Leadership for government?"

"No, it is private."

"Really? Who owns it?"

He said nothing for a long time. He looked at her and she looked back. "Dad, you own it." It was more a statement than a question.

"Yes, Marian, I own it."

"S-w-e-l-l!" she shouted. "Dad, you are a big man oh!"

He started the engine.

"Dad, your parents are both still alive."

Another of those more statements than questions but he said yes. "They are my grandparents. But I don't know them. I don't even know Navrongo but that is my home town."

He turned and looked at her but she was looking out of the window. He was not sure if it was a matter of fact statement or an accusation. He did not probe. He wanted to ask if their mother did not ever take them there but he thought it wise not to ask.

To talk about something he could interpret he asked if she thought Junior would be happy to see him.

"Yes, he will be very happy to see you. Dad, which child do you know who will not be happy to meet their father? He will be happy to see you. But he is not like me. He is very quiet. Maybe like you." She laughed.

"Who said I am quiet?"

"Then why don't you want to talk to me? I even have to ask you for specific information before you give it to me. Junior is like you. You have to ask him for information he should be giving. Like you. I am like mother. I talk too much, don't I? I ask too many questions." She laughed. The sad emotions of a few minutes ago seemed to have gone. The accusatory looks seemed replaced with a warmth of friendship.

Back at the place where she had to get down he asked her, "Do you remember you told me I did not know how to be dad?"

"Yes. I am sorry I said that, Dad."

"No, don't be. You were right. I bought some items for you and Junior when I was in Kenya. I forgot to bring them."

She smiled. "That is all right. At least you remembered us when you were in Kenya."

But he shook his head. "No, Marian, someone even had to ask me about family, if I was not going to buy anything for my family. That was when I remembered."

"Dad," it was a reproach, "you should not have told me this. You should have let me believe that you thought about us when you were in Kenya."

He remembered *Who Moved My Cheese*. He thought Hem's idea of writing down the lessons he learnt was great. So lesson number one in relating with your children would be what? *A little lie, especially one told to protect their emotions or build your relationship with them, does not kill.* He knew he would struggle in developing his relationship with the children. He did not know what he should do and how he should do it.

Chapter Eleven

She half floated like a nymph all the way back to the dormitory. She was so happy she did not notice that the looks on the faces of her dormitory mates were curious and cold. She walked to her bed and lay on it and when she closed her eyes some of the girls laughed. Her mind was far away from the dormitory and she did not hear the laughter.

The first sign of trouble was when her friends came back to the dorm. They called her out and told her. "Marian, do you know the story going round the campus?" That was Leila, the more talkative of her two closest friends. "They said your COSD came to visit you and you people went into the assembly hall and smooched and kissed, moaning and moaning. Then you went into his big posh car and continued to smooch and do all kinds of romantic acts."

The two friends, like Marian, were sixteen and both were Science students. There was no good reason for their friendship. They were all Science students, in the same year and in the same house. But they were not the only female Science students in that year in that house. But right from the first few weeks of the first term in their first year the three had been inseparable. They did not know each other before meeting in secondary school and they had very little in common in background. Leila Mahama was Gonja. Her father was a building contractor who had been very rich in the past but whose company was now struggling. But the Mahamas lived in their own house and Leila's father drove a BMW which he bought second hand. It was old and now broke down frequently but it gave him the false status that all people who had come down the social ladder still craved. Her mother was a teacher and was headteacher of her school. She was a Principal Superintendent in rank and so fairly senior in the Ghana Education Service. She rode a Yamaha 50 motorbike. Also bought second hand but quite strong and better maintained than the BMW.

Leila attended Presbyterian Junior Secondary in Tamale before coming to Tamale Secondary School.

Caroline Tigase, like Marian, was Kassena. She went to Junior Secondary School in their village, Nayagenia, in Navrongo. She was orphaned in her final year in Junior Secondary School. Her aunt, on her father's side, worked for an NGO in Tamale. It was the aunt who went for Carol, as she was called by her mates, and brought her to Tamale Secondary. She did not even choose Tamale Secondary as her first choice but her grades were very good and her aunt did not have trouble getting admission for her. Her aunt was a very quiet woman who went on trek a lot but spent a lot of her time indoors when she was not at work. According to Caroline she read a lot and loved music.

Despite their varied backgrounds the three girls developed one of the strongest friendships in the school. They were separable. They left together in the morning for their classes, went to the dining hall together and even though they sat at different tables in the dining hall they left the hall together. They went together to the library and studied together in the afternoons.

The three students were hard working and liked studies. They were nicknamed the Three Musketeers and given numbers, Leila was Number One, Marian Number Two and Caroline, the quietest of the three, was Number Three. Initially they protested against the names but came to accept them and even called each other by the numbers.

Whatever force it was that made the three girls come together must have known something about them which others did not know. The three competed with four boys in the Science class for the top position in the class. Leila had an advantage as her parents paid for her to attend extra classes provided by the teachers. Caroline's aunt was kind to her and wanted the best for her. But Caroline got closer to her only when her father died. She had known her aunt but from a distance. So in their first year she had been afraid to ask her aunt for money to enrol in the extra classes after all that she was doing for her. However the aunt, Aunt Polly, for Paulina, looked at Carol's terminal examination reports with her every term and discussed her performance. It was the aunt who suggested enrolling in the extra classes.

Now Number One and Number Three confronted Number Two and told her what they had heard. "They said he was smooching and you were smooching and smooching even harder and the old man almost had a heart attack."

Marian did not take them seriously. "Didn't they describe the part where we fucked?"

Leila hit her jokingly. "Bad girl. You're spoilt. How can you say such a thing?"

"Let me say it oh, Number One. If they saw the smooching then they should have seen the …"

Leila clamped her mouth shut with his palm. "The two of us are under-aged girls. Don't spoil us."

"You Leila are more rotten than the two of us combined."

Carol was the interesting member of the group. She enjoyed their company and followed their conversations with her smiles and grunts and laughs. But she hardly spoke. It was Marian and Leila who were always at each other's throat. Sometimes other students would ask Carol why she went everywhere with those two girls and she would say she loved their company. "It is the most interesting company in the school. I will be sick if I miss them for a day."

That seemed to be true because during the holidays the three girls were together. Initially Marian felt extremely reluctant to take them to her house. They went to the Mahamas' house first. Leila and her younger sister, Memuna, called Mouna by the family, had a room to themselves. There were shady trees behind the house where the girls could sit and chat and play games of their choice.

Carol had been unsure how her aunt would feel about her bringing friends home. So it took her a while to invite her companion Musketeers home. But hers was the next house they went to. Her aunt was at home most weekends and stayed indoors. She would sometimes move to her bedroom when the girls came visiting. At other times they sat outside. They played ludo, Scrabble, Monopoly or just chatted.

"Number Two, please tell us about the man who came visiting you in the big car everyone is talking about," Leila pleaded.

Marian had kept the issue of her parentage a secret from even her friends. Not a secret as such. All she told them was that her mother was not with her father. She evaded all questions about her father such as where he was, what he did and if he was in touch with the children.

"Please girls!" she pleaded, "I will tell you all about him one day very soon. It is a long story. He is not a Car Owning Sugar Daddy. He is not my boyfriend. He can't be my boyfriend and we did not smooch. We did not romance. Believe me. One day I will tell you all about him and one day you will meet him."

Leila was insistent. "Is he your uncle?"

"Number One! *Wo nti gyae.*" Meaning you're deaf to the order to stop.

"Why tell us tomorrow? Why not today? That is me, Number One."

They laughed without knowing how serious the rumour was and how high the alleged misconduct had been reported. On the Sunday after church service Marian was told that the Housemistress wanted to see her. She was not afraid but kept searching for a good reason why the Housemistress would send for her.

"Marian, you have been a good girl so far. In fact, you have been one of the girls in my house who I don't worry about. But what is this story I hear of you and an older man shamelessly kissing and romancing in the open and in his car?"

Marian was not prepared for this and opened her mouth in genuine shock. Her widened eyes spoke volumes of her disbelief. She wanted to speak but looked at the other lady sitting with the Housemistress. The lady was not a staff and Marian was therefore uncomfortable to explain something as personal as her father in her presence. The number of times she made to speak but stopped and looked at the lady made the Housemistress and the lady know that she did not want to speak before the lady.

She got up and said, "Hajia, let me go. I have been long and I can see your student will feel easy speaking to you alone." Hajia Rukaya Iddris led her friend some distance from the house and came back to listen to Marian.

"You had better tell me something reasonable and not spin a yarn I cannot accept," she warned as she joined Marian on the veranda and took her seat. "Who was the man and why didn't you people even have the courtesy to act with any decency?"

"Please, Madam, it was my father who came to visit me."

"What? Marian, what do you take me for? I know the man they said came to visit you. You are not related to him. Don't annoy me with some childish lies. You had better come clean if you want to reduce the punishment waiting for you."

Marian opened her mouth to speak but shut it in order to keep down her emotions. She tried again but shut it again. She looked down and this time the dam burst and the tears flowed down her cheeks freely.

"Crying won't help you," said the Housemistress who was used to the variety of tricks used by students to get out of jams, including crying. But Marian went on crying softly till she cried enough and the crying ended in sobs. She kept her head lowered for whole minutes after which she dried her tears and cleaned her face. She looked up at the Housemistress, noting that her hard looks had softened somehow.

She made two attempts to speak before she was successful. "It is the truth, Madam. It was my father who visited me."

The Housemistress shook her head to express her disbelief. "Who is your father?" she asked.

Marian dared look her in the face as she answered, "Mr Daniel Apeatu."

"Mr Apeatu is your father?"

"Yes, Madam."

The Housemistress grunted more than laughed. "Marian, tell me a story I can believe. Since when has Mr Apeatu been your father?"

"Since I was born, Madam."

With tears threatening to spill, Marian told her story. "He and my mother were divorced when I was only four years old. I lived with my mother alone. Last year my mother could not pay my school fees."

The Housemistress said nothing but they all knew the story of Marian's mother. They all knew she was a drunkard and that because she spent all her money drinking she could not provide the children what they needed. The only positive thing they all said of her was that whenever a staff or student of Tamale Secondary went to the hospital and she saw the person, she helped them. If any student or staff was admitted in her ward she gave the person very good attention. Patients admitted in her ward and their relatives agreed she was a hardworking nurse committed to the interest of patients.

"She could not pay my fees this year too. When the headmaster announced that he had given us a deadline to pay up or face expulsion I had to trace my father. I did not know him before then. But when I found him he agreed to come and meet me in the school. He was the one who came. He is my father. He is not my boyfriend and he is not my sugar daddy."

"Is he Wepia?"

"No, Madam. Wepia is my mother's father. Apeatu is on my birth certificate but our mother changed our surname after she left our father."

Marian did not look away when the woman looked at her for a long time. She looked back, swallowing repeatedly but saying nothing.

"Marian, I know Mr Apeatu very well. I will find out. And your story had better be true."

"Please, Madam, it is true."

"If it is true I am sorry for recalling your pain. But I will find out."

"Yes, please, Madam. You can find out."

The other Two Musketeers were waiting anxiously under a tree and looking in the direction of the Housemistress's bungalow from time to time. As the minutes dragged on they stopped talking and each kept her worried thoughts to herself. They ran to meet her when finally they saw her coming. They pestered her with questions initially, anxious to know why she had been called and what happened in the bungalow. Then they saw that her eyes were wet.

"You've been crying!" Carol observed, looking into her friend's eyes with concern.

For answer Marian just nodded and the effort opened the floodgates and tears gushed down her cheeks. Her friends led her to the tree under which they had been standing and they all sat down. She wiped her face and looked brave.

She told them why she was called. That the Housemistress called her because she had heard that Marian and a sugar daddy had been engaged in kissing and romancing. "I know I have never mentioned my father to you people. But he was my father. He and my mother divorced when I was four years and I had never seen him till just a few weeks back." She told them the story of her life. And her two friends sat silently listening to her.

She leaned back against the tree and just let the tears flow down her cheeks when she was done telling the story. When the flow stopped Carol took out her handkerchief and dried her friend's eyes. Leila, who was sitting on the right hand side of Marian, leaned closer, giving Marian her left shoulder. She gently pulled her towards her making her lean on her shoulder. She tilted her head and rubbed her palm against her left cheek, the cheek away from her.

"A sad story, Marian," Carol, the one who hardly spoke, said. "You have a right to weep. But do you remember the story of the man who was sad that he had no shoes? I'm sure you remember the story. He went on feeling sad for himself till he met someone with no feet. He must have been saying to himself how unfortunate that everyone has shoes while I don't have. And when he met the man without feet he must have said at least I have feet so I am not so unfortunate after all.

"At least you have now found your father, after all these years. I hope he is a good father to you and Junior. But it is not the worse condition. Look at me. I will never see my parents again no matter how long I live. But I don't complain. Why? I am not the first orphan. I am not the only orphan. I will not be the last orphan. I have my aunt who has filled the space created by the death of my parents. There are many children my age and younger whose parents are dead and who don't have anyone like my aunt to love them and take care of them. I cry because I miss my parents sometimes. But I know I am lucky.

"You have found your father. You are lucky. Look at things that way."

Marian found it unbelievable. Carol hardly spoke. And as she listened to her she wondered if this was the same sixteen year old friend. Such wisdom.

Leila sighed. "I am the luckiest among you, the odd one out, am I not? I have both parents and they have taken good care of me, I must admit." She sighed again.

"Yes, Number One," Marian said, "and God gave you a heart of gold. You are different from us. But you made yourself one of us. There was no difference between us. You are a true friend."

They walked leisurely back towards the dormitories.

"Tell us, how is he like?"

"How is who like?"

"Your father, of course?"

She pretended to think. "Hmm! Let me see. He is tall. He has two legs, two hands, one head on which I saw two ears, two eyes…"

Leila hit her. "Sometimes I forget that your head is not sitting on your shoulders."

"You're right. My head is sitting on my neck. It is my neck that is sitting on my shoulders."

They walked in silence.

"Let me ask again," Leila said. "How is he? Is he nice? Harsh?"

"It is too early for me to say. He looked very strict and acted so when I met him the first time. But I can talk to him and he seems to listen."

Dan spent the Tuesday morning in a session with female staff of NGOs in Tamale. They were attending a training session at the Training Centre. The training was not provided by Horizon Leadership but he was asked to present a paper on women as leaders. He had been given the whole of the time before the first break of the day, the morning break. His presentation generated so many issues that the women insisted on his being given one hour after the morning break to continue the discussions. It was almost midday when he returned to his office. Five minutes later he was told on the phone that one Hajia Rukaya wanted to see him.

He did not know who she was but he met her at the door as he did to all visitors to his office. Her face was familiar but he could not immediately place it. He offered her a seat and asked if she would want tea, coffee or a soft drink.

"Do you offer these to any visitor to your office?" she asked.

"Yes, we do," he answered, still trying to place her.

"What if someone chose to come here every day just to get the cup of tea or coffee?"

He smiled. "Then he will need more than just a cup of tea or coffee. If someone will come from wherever all the way here just to get a cup of beverage he must really be needy. We can't begrudge such a person their drink."

"I am not sure how many organisations offer drinks to just any visitor."

"Everybody who walks into our office is our guest. We can't offer them lunch or anything more expensive. But we can show we sincerely welcome the person with an offer of a beverage."

"How will you receive someone you know is coming to complain about you or take you to task?" the Hajia asked.

"We must have done something to warrant the person coming," he said, "even if what we did may not have been wrong. We will still want to start the discussion of the issue on a friendly relationship, if that is possible."

"I am not sure you remember me because you Kassenas have a memory that is not bigger than the full stop at the end of a sentence."

That gave him a clue about her, but not enough to remind him who she was or where he had met her. Kassenas were playmates with Gonjas and Sissalas. They teased each other and made jokes about each other. She looked like Gonja but he could not be sure. He pushed his memory to its most extensible limit but could not remember a Gonja acquaintance by that face.

He was going to admit defeat when things clicked. She was the mistress in charge of library in Tamale Secondary School. She had been there the three times he presented books to the school and on one of the occasions she expressed the school's gratitude. He smiled. "I thought this was rather true of Gonjas and not Kassenas. Our memory chips are the biggest you can find among that species of animals called humans. You have the unenviable task of encouraging students in Tamasco to use the library and not steal the books."

She said she would have a cup of coffee and he offered to prepare a cup for her. "It is an honour to serve someone who is naturally my slave."

Now that she had come she found it difficult to ask the questions she had come to ask.

"Do you mind if I ask you some questions?" she asked as she took a sip.

"Will you ask me if I said no?"

"Why should you say no?"

He smiled at the question for question.

"Because it is my constitutional right to say no if I feel like saying so. I don't have to have a reason. I just have to feel like saying no. But you have already started asking me questions, anyway."

"Will I ask the questions if you said no? Yes, I will still ask."

"No, please don't ask me any question."

She again picked the cup and took a sip. "Good. Do you have a girlfriend in our school?"

"Do I have a girlfriend in your school?"

"Yes." And another sip.

"Student or staff?"

"Student."

He eyed her suspiciously. He knew there was something serious behind the question but he decided not to ask what it was. It would come when it would come, he told himself. "I am forty years old. Most students in your school would be teenagers, mid teens mostly. Do you see someone my age having a girlfriend that age?"

She smiled and put down the cup. "I see people twenty years older than you having girlfriends that young."

"I have a daughter that young. How will I feel if someone my age had an affair with her?"

"I don't know but I know men who have daughters older than the female students in our school but who have even younger girlfriends."

He again considered her as she lifted the cup from the saucer and took another sip. "I have a daughter in your school. Do you know that?"

"There is no girl called Apeatu in our school."

He smiled. And she asked why. "You did not say yes, you knew her or no, you did not know her."

"Marian?"

"Is she in trouble?"

"They said she received a boyfriend on Saturday and they engaged in indecent romance."

She was relieved how the discussion had gone so far, she admitted to herself.

"I visited her on Saturday. And I know in our chat she cried at a certain point and I embraced her." He stopped and looked at her. She said nothing.

He got up and walked to one of the windows and pulled aside the curtains and looked out. There was not much to see but he stood there looking out for a few minutes while his guest sat quietly. When he turned round he walked back to his seat.

"Have you spoken to her?" he asked.

She put the cup in the saucer and used the tissue paper he had provided to wipe her lips. "To be honest with you, Mr Apeatu, we received a complaint that she received and entertained a sugar daddy in an inappropriate manner. I talked to her and she said it was you that visited and that you were her father. If I reported back to the headmaster he would naturally ask me if I had found out from you if it were true."

"She must have told you why our relationship is the way it is. You said there is no student in the school bearing the name Apeatu. She must have told you why she is not Apeatu."

"Yes, she did."

"A sad story. But true. I was absent in their lives – hers and her brother's – for twelve years. It was a very sad period for the children. It is a very shameful period for me, now in retrospect. Marian found me some weeks back and I went to the school on Saturday to meet her as part of our return to each other. We sat in the assembly hall. There were very moving times and times when she wept." He looked at her for a few moments and then added, "I also wept."

Another moment of silence. "I apologise if we created an indecent scene. Maybe I should have met her in my home and not in the school. But I could not have foreseen how emotional the meeting was going to be." He confirmed much of what Marian had already told the housemistress.

He drove her back to the school. As they drove back her mind kept turning over the fact that this stranger had shared with her a very private part of his life and had taken her into his confidence.

Turning to Dan she said, "I am glad for Marian for many reasons. One, I am glad she is reunited with her father. I imagine it will be painful for anyone her age to go through life without a father, especially if the father is still alive. Two, she is a very bright student but her inability to pay her fees would ultimately have resulted in her expulsion from school. I am sure she will now have all the support she needs to

183

develop her intellect. She is a very intelligent girl. Three, Marian has been a very good girl and hearing that she had indulged in a public engagement that is indecent in nature was worrying. There are some students who don't surprise you when you hear they have indulged in something outrageous. With others your faith in people is shaken if you hear they have done something terribly wrong. Marian was one of the latter group of students."

"Can I leave her in your hands? She will need a mother figure, someone to correct her and help her stay in the right path. Can I ask that favour of you?"

"I will cane her every day," she said with a smile.

"Please cane her three times a day." With that they signed the agreement for her to support Marian even though no yes was said.

They drove to the classroom block where Hajia Rukaya sent for Marian. Her heart leapt when she came out of the class and saw the Housemistress. But she told Marian that her father wanted to see her and when she looked up the road and saw her father smiling she put her hand on her heart and sighed, a deep, deep sigh of big relief. The three of them went to the Headmaster's office but Marian remained outside by the vehicle.

Dan was well known in the school. He donated various books to the school on three occasions in the past. Unlike other donations, the books were novels by well known writers and textbooks relevant to the subjects on offer in the school. Some of the books were meant for the staff, books on various topics, including leading oneself, making one's finances grow, working with young people and many others. In the office Hajia Rukaya informed the Headmaster of her findings. And added that Dan offered to come and meet him and inform him of his relationship with Marian himself.

"We all have skeletons in our wardrobes," Dan said when the Housemistress had narrated the story. "You just found mine."

The Headmaster took a deep breath and looked out of the window for a few seconds before turning to look at Dan. "We all do have our skeletons. Some are more serious than others. I am not sure I will say you have rotten skeletons."

He scratched his head. Turning to look through the window at the girl he said, "You have a daughter you should be proud of. Marian is a very bright girl and works very hard. She is one of the best in their class." Pointing to Hajia Rukaya he said, "This is her housemistress. She will tell you more about her character but she seems a very respectful student."

They spent some time discussing Marian agreeing that if she were able to attend the extra classes she would do even better than she had been doing so far. Dan committed her to the care of the head and the housemistress. They promised to take care of her not only as a student but as a daughter. Dan also promised to play his part, monitoring her performance and procuring all study materials she would need to make her study better.

Marian was waiting by the vehicle for her father. She put a hand on his shoulder and whispered, "Thanks Dad."

"I would invite her to the house from time to time," the Housemistress said when they left the headmaster's office, "but there are three of them. They move together. Whenever you see one, be sure that the other two are right next to her. Having all three of them in the house will crowd the house and they will eat up all my provisions."

Dan promised to help her stock her house so that they did not empty her store when she invited them to her house.

That evening he could do nothing but recall and live in the sad world of the events of the afternoon. It made him ask himself even more serious questions about fatherhood. He had gone to the school intending to reconcile with his daughter but very worried about how he would fare in the process. How *he* would fare in the process. He ended up giving the girl an image that was false. He blamed his inexperience as a father. He was convinced an experienced father would have been able to tell the risks his student daughter would be exposed to by their uncontrolled expression of emotions. He may even have thought about it long in advance, seeing the potentially emotional moments. If only he had thought objectively about the whole process, and not selfishly subjectively, he would have met the girl in his house and not in the public in the school. He asked himself how many more times he would create problems for the children before they settled to a healthy relationship.

Just before he fell asleep however, a part of him reminded him of the apparent good that was coming out of the unfortunate process. He hoped Marian would have the attention and support of the Headmaster and the Housemistress. He thought about what to do to support the Housemistress to support his daughter without offending her.

So he turned up the next evening at Hajia Rukaya's with a bag of polished rice, a four gallon container of oil, packets of tinned soft drinks and biscuits. She screamed when he made her children start to offload the items. And protested, refusing to let them offload the items. Dan encouraged the children, two girls in their teens and a younger boy. He joked with them and had them laughing before long. He helped them to take the items into the house despite the protests of their mother.

"I didn't tell you to come and feed me and my family."

"I don't intend to feed you and the family. I am just showing appreciation for all that you will do for my daughter. I have been an errant father and I don't even know what much support I am going to be able to give. You are not her relation. We can't ever say thank you enough for whatever you do for her. I appreciate your agreement to support her not only as a student but as a daughter. And your offer to invite her to your house from time to time. If you ever try to cost the gesture to support a girl not related to you in anyway, do you know how much that will come to? You can't cost it. A gift, an invaluable gift, is not only something tangible. Some intangible gifts defy money value."

They discussed the cost of extra classes and with the recommendations of the Housemistress they agreed which subjects she would need the extra classes in. Dan left her with enough money but with the understanding that the Housemistress would discuss with Marian in which subjects she needed extra classes.

Chapter Twelve

Since he was not making a return trip Dan woke up quite late. Quite late by his own standard. Weekdays he woke up before 6:00 a.m. On Saturdays he would normally wake up around 8:00 a.m. He now woke up at that time without being disturbed. He had some rather irritating experiences in the past but that was history. He was sure he would not be irritated anymore.

He worked late most days. On Fridays he sometimes worked till 2:00 a.m. He would go to bed comfortable in the knowledge that he did not have to go the office and did not have early morning meetings and so did not need to wake up early. Even when he went to bed at 2:00 a.m. he would still feel awake around 8:00 a.m. He would normally wake up between 7:40 and 8:30. Never later unless he really felt the need to sleep long hours and so took sleeping tablets. When he did not have to go to the office, which happened only rarely, he would sleep some time in the afternoon.

But at a point in time people took to disturbing his Saturday morning sleep. There were times when his doorbell would ring just around six o'clock. There were two sets of doorbells. There were doorbells at the two gates, the side gate and the main gate through which vehicles passed. These doorbells sounded in the security room. A private security company provided security. He paid for and had one security guard in the day and one in the night. He also had a night watchman.

The knobs at the gates would sound the bell in the security room. The security would then open the gate and let in whoever rang the bell. They would open the gate to find someone wanting to see Dan. They would explain that he was still in bed. Some would ask when he normally woke up and they would go away and return later since there were two whole hours between six o'clock and eight o'clock. Some others would come into the yard and wait till he woke up and opened the door. Yet others would insist the security woke him up.

On about three occasions he had woken up to be met with accusations by people who had been waiting for an hour or more. "You have punished me," one accused. "I have been waiting for almost two hours. They told me you were sleeping. Two hours."

He did not notice the offensive nature of the remark till a similar remark was made when another person came and waited. "How can a man be sleeping at 8:00? My buttocks are sore from sitting and waiting for you to wake up. You must give me what I came for. You can't say no."

On the third occasion he was told, "I came here before 6:00. It is now almost 8:30. I have been part of your security for over two hours. Are you going to pay me for that?"

He was blunt. "Did I invite you? Today is Saturday. Why should you expect me to wake up even before ten o'clock? Is it reasonable for you to even expect to go to someone's house over the weekend before six o'clock?"

He was also brusque with him. "Now tell me what it is that you want to do for me that made you decide to come so early because it could not have been done at any time later in the day."

The man was apologetic. "Please, don't be angry. I am not saying that I came to do anything for you or that you should have woken up early. Today is Saturday. If you don't have anything doing early in the morning why should you wake up early? Your work is very tiring and I know that you can be so tired you need to rest. And Saturday is the only day you can rest. I didn't expect you to wake up that is why I waited when I was told you had not yet got out of bed."

The first time it happened he felt irritated later because it was when he was seated across the man in the sitting room after a breakfast of bread, egg and beverage that he learnt the man had come to ask for help. Someone in need of help from him who was aggressive. He regretted giving the man the breakfast because after he ate the meal he made a remark Dan did not like. "If I am sure of waking up to eggs and coffee to start my day with, why should I wake up at six o'clock?"

The third group of people would tell the security to wake him up. In fact, the first time he was woken up because the security guards did not know the relationship between the caller and Dan. If an uncle calls to see his nephew and you prevent him from seeing him with the excuse that he was still in bed, he could be angry with the nephew and the nephew could in turn be angry with you. But Dan had told them to let anyone who came when he was not awake wait for him. They should ask the person what he wanted Dan for and if it was not an emergency to let the person wait. A distant cousin came visiting and when he was asked what he wanted Dan for he told them they were too small to be asking him what he needed Dan for. He told them it was a family issue and they should not be asking him to tell them what family issue he had come discuss with his 'small brother.'

They woke him up. "So you have asked strangers to be asking me for my mission when I come to see you?"

"I did not ask them to ask anybody for their mission when they come to see me. But I asked that if anybody comes when I am still asleep they should find out if the reason for the visit is urgent to warrant my sleep being cut short."

"So you are now setting strangers to judge me and decide whether I should see you or not?"

He knew Kaba and he decided he was not going to give him a long rope. "Kaba, you don't live in my house with me. You don't know when I go to bed. So you can't come and decide when I should wake up in my house which you will like to do. So, yes, I have given authority to strangers to prevent you from waking me up if the reason for your wanting to wake me up is a frivolous one."

"What reason is a frivolous one?"

Instead of answering Dan queried him, "Tell me. What brought you here? What do you want?"

"So that you decide whether it is important or not?"

"Listen, Kaba. If you came with anything serious, I am listening. It is only 6:21. I don't get out of bed at this hour on Saturday. If you won't tell me what brought you here and made you cut my sleep short I am walking back to my room to sleep."

"You are such a big man your sleep is more important to you than the reason I came here. Can you go back to bed and leave me sitting here?"

He got up and walked to the door. "You are right, I can't." He called the security. "Please see him to the gate."

He walked back to the bedroom while his cousin protested, insulted and shouted. The security firmly led him out.

Such people told their stories and everybody knew that if you were visiting Dan over the weekend you should either go when he was awake or you should be prepared to wait for him to wake up.

He could tell that he had grown over the years. He had changed a lot. In the first few years after he gave up drinking and started to improve on his economic situation he also started receiving a lot of attention. People came to him with all kinds of pathetic stories. Someone had a hernia that had been causing him unbearable pain but he had no money for the operation. A woman told of a daughter who had passed to go to secondary school but could not go because she had lost her husband five years previously and earned little from the petty trading she was engaged in. An elderly man came almost crying because he was being thrown out of the room he and his wife and four children lived in because he could not pay the rent.

He would sometimes even borrow to be able to support those people. He had had so much trust in humanity until he began to hear stories about some of the people who had come to him for help. He also started growing because he noted that the number of people coming was growing. Some of the stories he heard made him feel pained, pained that he had been cheated. The man who claimed he was being thrown out of his room, he learnt, had no family. He was a labourer but with nobody to support he could afford to pay his rent. The woman who said that her daughter had passed to go to secondary had told a lie. Her children were all still in primary school. He was generous at heart but he disliked being taken advantage of. It hurt him that people thought he could be had and he resolved to stop that.

Over the years he also learnt to give consideration to himself. He continued to love people. He knew he would always love people, and he would always be sympathetic to the disadvantaged but he told himself that he should love himself equally. He should therefore expect to be treated the same way people expected him to treat them. So when people came with aggression he would listen quietly and either tell them a no and walk off or he would return their aggression. He told himself that if he would not go out to offend anyone but the person came to him and was insensitive to whether he hurt him or not, he should not be worried about telling that person things which, provided they were not lies, the person may find offensive. He told himself that he had a right, in fact, a duty, to protect himself.

In the past five years the once soft, easy to push around, can-never-say-no gentleman had become a man of steel among the Kassena community. He could watch a person he knew to be telling lies shed crocodile tears and present himself in all pathetic manners and not show the least bit of emotion for the person. He would not have thought himself capable of being so callous, as he had been described by some of the people who had failed to get money from him by false pretence, if he had been asked five years back. But in the last five years he had grown to understand humanity better and he had his way of finding the truth about people's stories. For people he did not know who told a probable story but he was not sure of the truth, he told them to give him time. The fake ones almost invariably tried to convince him their situation was so dire it could not wait. He was not afraid to tell them that if they needed the help from him at that moment his answer was that he could not help them. He no longer felt bad asking such people why they considered that the thousands of people living in Tamale could not help them but that he *must be able* to help them.

Another irritating attitude he had stopped was people lurking in the house in wait for him on the day of return when he had been away for say two weeks or more. On one occasion, for instance, he spent three weeks in Ethiopia and Eritrea and came back to Accra on a Sunday. He came to Tamale on the Tuesday having spent Monday in Accra on business. He had worked throughout the weekends while in Ethiopia and Eritrea and he was tired so he had even told his office not to expect him in the office on the Wednesday. He and Brenda had engaged in their usual sparring sessions when she insisted he took the rest of the week off.

They left Accra after ten in the morning because he had to see someone at 9:00 on the Tuesday morning. They arrived in Tamale shortly after 8:00 p.m. The security guard and the watchman were still helping him to carry his suitcase and foodstuffs he had bought on the way out of the vehicle when he had a visitor. The security guard told him that the man had come three times earlier that evening.

Dan did not hide his impatience when he met him in the sitting room. He cut short the man's intention to engage in long exchange of greetings, informing him, "Let's get over the purpose of your visit because after this length of time away from home and this length of time on the road all I want is the comfort of my bed."

"I am very sorry to be bothering you when you must be very tired."

Dan said nothing. In the past he would have pretended he was not too tired to be bothered. Now he chose not to tell lies to please others.

"I should have waited for you to rest today and come tomorrow and not be bothering you so soon after you arrived…"

"I heard you came here three times this evening. Did they tell you I had been away for three weeks? At least the security would have told you, I am sure."

"Yes, they told me. I came last week. It was the security who told me you were coming back today. Initially they said yesterday but when I came yesterday they told me you were coming today instead."

"So you knew I had been away working for three weeks. And you also knew I was coming in today from Accra?"

"Yes, when I came yesterday they told me you were in Accra and would be leaving Accra today."

"Well, you know that Accra is more than four hundred miles from here and that it takes a whole day to travel from Accra to Tamale. So if you could not wait for me to even rest this evening and you must catch me despite the fact that I must be tired, you must have a terribly serious problem which needs to be solved today and which nobody else in Tamale can solve. I am listening to you."

The man began to stammer. Dan did not know a lot of those people who came to him for help. Some he knew by face, having met them in funerals, or seen them in church or met them once or so somewhere. Some he knew who they were, having had some interaction with them. Others, like the man that evening, he did not know at all.

"It is a serious problem, yes. Well, to me it is a serious problem. But it is not that it must be solved today. As I said earlier I should have waited for you to rest, and then come tomorrow…"

"Well, you were thinking only of yourself. You were not concerned about me to consider the fact that I am human. And that as a human being after being away for three weeks and after travelling the whole day I would need rest. Please tell me what brought you so that I can go in and have a bath and begin to rest."

"I can come tomorrow."

"It is something that you can bring tomorrow that you chose to come this evening?" He got up and the man got up too. "You know, you are going to someone to ask for help. You don't show any consideration for the person. Assuming it is money you need. I am arriving in the night. Banks don't work in the night. So even if I can help you it has to be tomorrow. But you will come and make my already long day longer by another one hour, making me even more tired. Sometimes we act in a certain way to some people and when they react in what is the most appropriate way we then go round and give them a bad name. Back in my village, when a man returns from his farm in the evening, if there is an important issue to discuss with him, they wait for him to have his bath. Then he takes his supper before they bring up the issue. In our culture we recognise that if a person is tired he must be allowed to rest before taxing him with anything serious. You know I have been travelling since morning. It is past eight now. You don't even know if I have had my supper. But you must come ask me to give you one hour of my time. Are you being considerate to me?"

So this Saturday morning he woke up and came to open the door of the main entrance of the house without feeling any worry at all that he would have an irritating visitor. The sun was very bright on this late February morning. He went out and exchanged greetings with the security man and went back into the house and prepared his breakfast. When he left home it was almost 11:00.

He loved the drive home. Whenever he was going home for leisure, and not because someone had died or to visit a relation who was sick, he wished he were driving a vehicle whose top he could roll down. He hardly used the air-conditioner on the drive home. He preferred to roll down the glasses and let the air blow his face. It was already beginning to be very warm. In December and January, and even early February, temperatures were normally lower and the breeze would be very cool. But he did not mind the warm air. He loved the sound of the air as it whistled through the window.

The grass had already been burnt and he could see far on both sides of the road. Overhead various birds were flying, slowly circling and looking down for prey like grasshoppers and other insects. An early morning vehicle had run over a small animal after Diare and hawks were engaged in a tug of war with the asphalt to get the flesh off the road. He slowed down and let the birds fly off before he passed. They were heavy birds and if they crashed into your windscreen it was sure to be shattered.

When he descended the Karamenga hill and headed towards Balungu he parked off the road and took the toilet roll out of the glove compartment and headed for the teak trees. It was a ritual he performed each time he was on the highway. He grew up in the village going to toilet in the open. Free range, they called it in his secondary school days. In his adult life he still recalled the joy of sitting in the shade of a tree and feeling the relief of the faeces easing out of his anus as the breeze caressed his exposed buttocks and back. In June of the previous year, during one of his trips home, he stopped to use the bushes as his wc, as usual. He could not remember what prompted him to turn round. Somehow he did and nearly froze as he saw a snake gliding towards him. But he froze only temporarily because within seconds he had shot up and tried pulling his trousers up. But the snake also took fright and slithered back. It only gave him time to pull down his trousers and wipe his anus and pull the trousers up but he did not squat again. He had gone home three times since then and each time he had gone to toilet in the open despite the experience with the snake.

It was not just during the drive home. Each time they drove either from Tamale towards Kumasi or Kumasi towards Tamale he was sure to make Dauda to stop for him to use the bushes. Despite his education, exposure and what he himself called his sophistication he felt a rural boy at heart. His upbringing in the village left an indelible imprint in his heart so that the signs of his boyhood kept living with him even now in adulthood and living in an urban area.

During the trips home he was always reminded of the Economics concept of alternative cost. He loved to have the wind blow in through the open windows, even if it wasn't the very cool breeze. But he also loved music. With the glasses rolled down and the wind roaring in through the open windows, music from the stereo was swept out through the other window. So when he wanted to play music as he did now he would roll up the windows half-way and have half of each, the breeze and the music.

The first cassette he put in was music by Silver Convention and he relived his childhood days with *Fly Robin Fly.* He did not know what had happened to the group. They had been popular and he remembered that they made what his colleagues called the synthesizer very popular.

He drove on to Bolga and went looking for Ntim. Ntim was the Branch Manager of Ghana Commercial Bank in Bolga. They had been mates in the university. Both read Business Administration. Ntim's wife, Gloria, was fascinated by the stories her husband told of his quiet friend. She would look at him searching for evidence of the past that her husband described. He continued to puzzle her. She could never imagine this gentle, soft spoken man a drunkard. But he himself admitted he was a drunkard once. When they were together Ntim would remember some of the episodes on campus involving Dan and recount them. While he and Gloria laughed Dan would only smile.

She complained a lot to her husband about Dan. When he stopped in front of their bungalow Ntim's children all came running to welcome him. Even little Akos, who was only two years old, ran excitedly to meet him. He picked her and threw her in the air and caught her. She screamed excitedly and asked to be thrown again and again. He had a bag of yams for them and the children removed it and took it inside. He had a gift for each child. While he carried Akos the other three children hanged to various parts of his body and escorted him inside.

He always brought them very good tasting yam. For a man he knew very good yam. They knew such yam would be expensive and that was the type he always bought for them, good quality expensive yam. And he also brought gifts for the children. He played with them, teasing them and playing games with them if he stayed for long. He told them jokes and invented some of the jokes around the children. If any of the children were playing anywhere and suddenly saw Dan's vehicle parked in front of the house they would stop whatever they were doing and run over to the house.

Sometimes he brought gifts for Ntim and Gloria too, from this travels outside the country. She complained to her husband because she did not feel she was able to adequately return the good he did for them. He would come unannounced, making it difficult for her to prepare his favourite *fufu* and groundnut soup. When they managed to trap him to stay for her to prepare food for him he ate so little it did not please her.

"That is how much he can eat," her husband would explain. "He doesn't feel a stranger in this house and so will not stop eating if he can still eat more. He has a small stomach. It is not everybody who is like me."

"I don't feel he is entertained enough," she said.

"He eats to his fill anyway. And he always eats more of the soup, you know that."

She dismissed that. It was true he would take more of the soup after eating a small lump of *fufu*. But the lump was normally so small one would think it was meant to feed a child. He did take more soup but she felt that with the small amount of *fufu* he ate he could take four times the amount of extra soup he took.

"And he doesn't drink," she went on complaining. "Soft drinks are nothing so far as I am concerned. And he won't take more than one bottle of soft drink at a time. He doesn't make me feel that I have received him properly."

'You never inform us that you are coming. You just come," Ntim complained when he came out to meet him after hearing all the noise made by the children.

"Why do you want to reduce the size of the dictionary?" Dan asked.

"What is the relationship between your informing us you are coming and reducing the size of the dictionary?"

"If I inform you I am coming we will be making the word surprise redundant. If we continue to make words redundant we will be shrinking our vocabulary. And over the next twenty years we will find it hard to express ourselves because we have such a limited amount of words."

"Each time you speak you only confirm my conviction that you belong to a psychiatric hospital and not the sane world outside. Anyway welcome."

He stayed for Gloria to prepare rice balls and groundnut soup. She pulled her chair very close to his and said she was going to supervise his eating. "Dan, I put so much into preparing food for you so I am not in the least amused when you put so little in your plate. Even Akos competes with you in the amount of rice she eats. Today you won't leave this table if you nibble at the edge of a ball and pretend you are full." She drew her chair closer to him to let him know she meant what she said.

He turned to her and said, "Ntim complained that I never inform you in advance when I am coming. You know, I see this place as home to me. I feel in my heart that if I drop in at midnight you will still want to prepare food for me. You inform friends you are coming. You just go home."

When he got up to leave, Akos, as usual, clung to him and insisted on going with him. The older children had stopped pleading to go with him because their mother had said no each time they brought it up in the past. He was grateful to her. He loved children but was sure he did not know how to handle them. If he ever took any of those children to Navrongo he was not sure he could manage them.

This encounter with Ntim's children brought back his fears about how he would relate with his children. It had been easy to tell Marian that they should come home the next weekend. Remembering that fact would make this coming week one of the most haunting as he would constantly be fighting horror scenes of his impending encounter with his children. As he drove out of Bolga he recalled the painful scenes in the Assembly Hall in Tamale Secondary. He felt the pain of Marian's tears and her painful tale of what life without a parent had been to them. But what he recalled most painfully were the difficult questions she posed. How long would it take for them to exhaust those questions?

He seemed to have handled the difficult encounter with Marian the previous week relatively well. They were going to have a relationship which was not going to be the same as a one-off encounter. How would he manage that? When he drove out of Bolga worry about his impending meeting with his children and how he would relate with them, came very strongly over him. He could see in his mind's eye that he would be inadequate as a father and that they would have a very trying time together.

The sun was setting when he drove into Navrongo. He put in an *Osibisa* collection and listened to the deep rich voice sing *Welcome Home*. The member of the now defunct group he loved most had been Jamaican born Wendell Richardson. He loved his voice in *Flying Bird*. *Osibisa* brought back to mind his lucky escape from alcohol. Kiki Gyan was the organist of the group and one of the best in the world at the time. One of the youngest too. He made millions of dollars in those days in the seventies and acquired property even in New York. Dan remembered the album he released when he broke away from *Osibisa*. *Keep Me For A Night* and *I'm Doing My Thing* had been very popular.

Then Kiki Gyan found drugs and his life was ruined. In his heart he thanked God that he was able to give up alcohol.

He drove slowly from Nayagenia into the town. He looked for the smoke escaping over the walls of houses spiralling towards the blue sky overhead. He could not hear it but he knew that the smoke was accompanied by pestle in mortar as women pounded either groundnuts or fish or *dawadawa* or smoked guinea fowl. He caught the sound of pounding when he left the main Paga road and hugged houses as he drove past the borehole on his way home.

He felt relaxed and even happy at the familiar scenes on the way to the house. He did not stop at the borehole but waved at the people fetching water. He saw his aunts Kada, Nuwe and Kadiga. He saw his cousins' children and women and children from neighbouring houses. He drove past goats and sheep that had come to drink water from the cemented trough that collected waste water from the borehole. He slowed down as he came across a flock of guinea fowls which were chasing each other playfully and making loud noises as they prepared to go home to roost.

When he stopped at home, the smell of smoke, the various foods on fire and fresh cow dung hanged in the air. He took a deep breath to assure himself that he was back home. He heard the rhythm of pestles in different mortars. And from one of the rooms came the ring of laughter, that real laughter of happiness that came right from the heart. He looked up the big neem tree in front of the house as guinea fowls flew up to their bed for the night. About twelve sheep came trooping in, walking majestically. As he watched the sheep he had the feeling that the sheep felt like coming to their *home* and that the human beings who were standing outside were only having a chat and would move on to their own homes. The goats came bounding in. Goats liked running.

Coming home was not without its cost. But between him and the family they had come to an understanding over certain issues.

He was still standing outside by the car when his aunt Kada came home with her container of water. "I knew you would be coming today," she said.

He smiled. "Is that welcome?"

"The welcome is after this statement," she told him.

"Okay welcome me so that I can ask you a question."

"What question?"

"Auntie, in Kassena culture the first thing we say to people we receive in our homes is welcome. Without that I don't feel I am welcomed to the house so I can't engage you in conversation."

She laughed. "Okay welcome. Now ask your question."

"Thank you. How did you know I would come home today?"

"I knew you would come because I wanted you to come."

He called the children who took his bag inside the house and asked them to bring it back. "I am going back to Tamale," he announced.

"Why are you going back?" someone asked.

"Because Kada wanted me to come. It means she needs me for something but I just want to come home for a quiet time."

He went inside after greeting those outside. He made for his rooms, switched on the light in the sitting room and lay on the sofa. He was lying on his back in the sofa when the door opened and he raised his head. He had been in that state of being eighty percent asleep and only twenty percent awake. Kada walked in with a woman of between the ages of 28 and 30. Dan sat up. Then stood up.

"We knocked but did not get any response," Kada said.

"I was almost asleep," he admitted.

"I want to introduce my daughter to you," Kada said.

Dan looked at the woman for the first time and found her very beautiful. He shook hands with her not sure he had ever heard mention of Kada marrying somewhere else before coming to marry his uncle. "Welcome," he told the woman.

She smiled. "I should be saying welcome. I was here before you came. I have been here for four days now."

"So thank you for welcoming me." He didn't know what else to say.

"My mother has told me a lot about you."

"Oh, that I don't respect my elders. That I am rude and I insult people. That I don't like people and I beat children. Are those the things she has been telling you?"

"If you have been those things, yes, that is what I have been telling her. Why should I tell her that?"

He shrugged. "That is what people have been saying about me."

The woman looked at Kada and then at Dan. "Maybe she will tell me those things later but the things she has so far told me about you did not include that."

Looking at the woman Kada said, "Don't mind him. I will tell you all the worse things about him this evening."

"You said your daughter," Dan said, unable to put the question as he would have liked to.

"Yes, she is my daughter."

The woman sensed Dan's confusion and explained, "In English she is my aunt. My father is the first of their mother's children. Kada is the third. My name is Rosemary."

"You people like your English names," Kada said. "Her name is Agyegekwaga. What is wrong with that? She completed the big school in Kumasi." Looking at Rosemary she told her, "You tell him the name of the school."

"UST. I did Pharmacy at UST. I am a pharmacist at the Komfo Anokye Teaching Hospital."

"You did Science in secondary school. You must be a break."

"If I were a break I would have read Medicine."

"Which secondary school did you attend?"

"St Francis in Jirapa."

"You were a break. For a girl to do Science in a Northern secondary school and still make it to Pharmacy school at the time you went to varsity, she must have been a break."

"I will leave you people alone and go back to my cooking," Kada said and headed for the door, leaving them alone.

Dan was not sure if to invite her to sit down. He did not know if she wanted to stay. She did. She stayed when he offered her the seat. He recalled his aunt saying she was sure he would come because she wanted him to come. It was because of Rosemary. His thoughts left the room and began wandering. She had completed her training and was working as a pharmacist in one of the best hospitals. If she had been a student he would have thought that she needed financial assistance and that was why her aunt wanted him to meet her, to support her. But if she had completed her studies she would not be needing sponsorship.

Another area extended relations made demands he could not meet was employment. *Can you find a job for your brother?* This would be from a woman who called herself his mother's sister because the two of them came from the same village. With her being his mother's 'sister' her son was his brother.

Dan, these are your son's papers. He has completed university but he says he does not want to teach. Which is where majority of graduates doing their national service were posted to. *He says teaching has no benefits so he wants a job with an NGO or somewhere where it is good.* For someone just starting life to discriminate between jobs, describing teaching as useless when he would not have come this far without teachers, was interesting.

"And why do you say teaching has no benefits?" he asked the young man.

"In teaching you don't get any side benefits. It is only your salary," the young man said without shame.

"During the one year national service everybody is supposed to take the same allowance. It is supposed to be a year spent giving back to your country for all the investment in you as an individual. Why are you already looking for where you can make money quickly?"

"Look at this nonsense," the man's mother said. "Are you not making money? Why don't you want my son to make money?"

"Do you know how long it took me to start making money?" he asked knowing very well that whatever he was going to say would be lost on mother and son. "I did my national service where they posted me. I worked for many years in that place before leaving to begin making money."

"That is you. Don't expect everyone to be like you," the man's mother said.

"Thanks. Don't expect me to also be like you. I can only be myself. I believe we should all give ourselves for one year to the country and we those who have had the state spending so much money to educate us should go where the government wants us to. If the government wants him to teach I will say go and teach. I won't be looking for any place for him."

"You are just wicked," the mother said strongly. "You could even have taken him in your own organisation if you want."

"Of course, I don't want. The organisation would have been like a market if I were to employ every relative of mine who completes school. You said you want your son to make money."

"Why not?" she retorted. "What is wrong with that? Are you not making money?"

"Oh I am making money. Like you and your son I also want to make money. But in order to make money I must keep my organisation small, just as big as it needs to be. I won't stop you from making money. But don't ask me to support you to take a path I don't believe in, and did not use, to make money."

His mother felt uncomfortable with his strong, frank talk. But his father was amused about it. His mother knew she could not stop him anyway. He once told her if she could stop relations from making unreasonable demands on him and tightening the screws on him in the process he would not be telling them what they did not want to hear.

My son is completing in three months. Get ready to take him in your organisation.

My organisation is full. We don't have space for additional staff.

Well, create one for my son.

I can only tell you the truth. I won't promise you something I can't do. If you promise yourself and I don't deliver it you won't blame me, will you?

Sometimes they did not just ask Dan for help; they accused him.

You don't like helping the family.

Oh really? I thought I helped Grace a lot when she was in secondary school and at the university.

Yes, but you are not helping her to find the job she wants. And now you say you won't help my son.

She is very determined to work in only a bank. I don't own any bank. At the time I completed university if I got a bank I would have been happy to work there. I am not working in a bank because I did not have any influence over anybody in any bank.

She says she wants to work in only a bank.

I wish her good luck.

Is that all you will do?

It is the only thing I can do.

You discriminate among your relatives.

Really? Now what have I done to one person and refused to do it to another relative?

You helped Abuga's son to get a job but you won't help Grace.

I did help John. But not to get a job in a bank, if you remember. He wanted a job, any job. You and your Grace want a job in only a bank.

She will work in a bank even without you.

I wish her good luck

You already wished her that.

I know. But making the same wish twice does not make them cancel each other. If God did not hear the first wish He is sure to hear the second one.

Rosemary had a job. So what did she need from him to make her aunt want him to come and meet her? Maybe she wanted to go outside for further studies. Or maybe she just wanted to go outside. Say she's won the green card lottery and needed money for her ticket. Or she just wanted to go out because there is money in heaps in Europe and America and one only needed to get there. And the ticket was the only obstacle.

He rejected that as well. As a pharmacist she could save to buy an air ticket.

Maybe she wanted to open her own drug store.

He gave up speculating and they spent the next thirty minutes or so asking and answering questions about each other's work and the town they lived in. At the end of that time he could not guess what she needed. But he thought they had been alone inside for too long so he gave the excuse of going out to greet. She returned to Kada.

He liked evenings at home. They were a part of his past he always recalled with nostalgia and could relive several times. All the men in the house, four brothers, his father and three uncles, and six grown sons who also had families, had their spot of the space in front of the house. His uncle Adi was the oldest of the four brothers and rightly owned the space directly under the neem tree facing the entrance of the house. Some of the men constructed sheds covered with guinea corn stalks.

In each man's space he constructed his own 'seat.' The 'seats' were made from the trunks of young trees. The trunks of two young trees would be cut about five feet in length. The two were placed about six feet apart and the trunks of between 3 and 6 young trees were then placed side by side one end resting on one of the two trunks and the other end resting on the second trunk. These wooden platforms were the seats of the household.

In the evenings the men would be the first to come out and rest on the seats, most often lying down. Some would occasionally sit up either to make a point or to listen better to someone else speaking. Supper would be served out there. Even though they did not eat together, Dan found it interesting when sometimes over thirty people turned the space in front of the house into a dining hall. There would be the grown up men. There would be their wives. And there would be the children he did not try counting. You could tell which children were eating alone. You never heard them talk. Some of the children, from the same parents, ate together. These quarrelled, accusing each other of real and invented crimes. Some of the children were wicked. A child would cut a morsel of the hot *TZ* and intentionally drop it on the back of the palm of one of the children he was eating with. The scream of the hurt child could be heard in neighbouring houses. So could they also sometimes hear the screams of children from other houses.

When the meal was over the women and the children would clear the earthenware bowls and calabashes in which they had eaten while the men just reclined and went back to rest.

It was the period after the meals that Dan liked the most, as a child and even now. This was the time when they told folk stories, or recounted bits of the history of the family or just engaged in general conversation.

Sometimes the moon was so bright you could see almost a mile away. At other times it was so dark if you held your hand about two feet away you could not even make out its shape.

The stories could be frightening. Very interesting but also haunting. They told stories of ghosts. Some ghosts returned to protect their relations. Others returned to exact vengeance for wrongs done to them. Some came to share secrets while others came for things left behind or an uncompleted task. They told stories of wild animals. There were stories of animals assuming the shape of humans to teach boastful people lessons. There was a story of the baby buffalo that turned into a pretty young woman in order to find the hunter who killed her mother and left her orphaned. There was the story of the python that turned into a man with no scar on his skin in order to teach the young woman who set her standard for marriage unreasonably high.

Stories that scared did scare whether it was dark or bright moonlight. When the moon was bright and he could see afar he kept turning expecting to see the ghost on its way to the funeral of its mother, carrying a calabash on its head. When it was dark he could sense the eyes of the young buffalo in human form scanning them for the guilty hunter.

Between the months of November and February when the evenings were cold, they would light a fire to give them some warmth. The children would be asked to take turns going to the farmlands around the house to gather farm waste to keep the fire going. This was not a difficult task and they all went happily to fetch guinea corn and millet stalks. But when a horror story had just been told no child would have the courage to move away from the comfort of the family to gather farm waste. In fact, with some of the stories you could feel the fear creeping into the children, forcing them to move forward towards the older members of the family. Dan could still remember his back tingling not from the cold but from the sensation of fear.

After the meals all the children and even the adults would listen to stories or discussions with active interest. Then eyelids would grow heavy and droop till they forced heads to droop as well. One by one the children and the adults would fall asleep till only a few were left awake. During the hot season few people would be anxious to go inside their rooms. So they would all lie out there sleeping for a while. But when it was cold, once it was confirmed that many members had fallen asleep, the whole assembly of children, women and men would be roused to go in and sleep.

Dan loved sleeping in the family home. Since he started making good money he started converting the mud buildings constructed in traditional architecture into modern concrete block structures. Now there were only three traditional rooms in the whole compound of over twenty rooms. One of them was his mother's room. He remembered the quarrel with his mother when she decided she was keeping that room. She argued that it was there she wanted to be laid for the wake when she died. That was where Dan slept when he came home, not in his own modern room.

His room was roofed with aluminium roofing sheets and ceiled with plywood. His mother's room was built of mud bricks. The roof was a mud platform that was well screeded. In the day the platform became a place for drying foodstuffs. In the night it provided ample space for two traditional mats on which about six adults would sleep comfortably. Dan would bring his fibre mat and small foam mattress and pillow to this platform and pass the night there. He enjoyed lying down and looking up the most wonderful roof over his head, the sky beautifully decorated with countless stars. It was interesting how the sky was so active if only you had the time to look. Many tiny stars moved across the sky but you had to look keenly to find them. It was also surprising how many stars shot themselves across the sky every night.

He could always recognise the constellation Orion. It was the only constellation he made out. The three stars that constituted his belt were easy to make out by their equal distance from each other. Once you saw the stars of the belt it was easy to see the stars said to be his shoulders and those said to be his feet. It was the dog he could hardly make out.

There was a cluster of stars the Kassena called the mother hen. He could recognise that one too easily.

With stars moving slowly across the sky, some shooting themselves out of the sky, with the guinea fowls crying good night up the neem tree, with bats occasionally flying very low over him as if to fan him to sleep and with various night insects copying the example of the guinea fowls and wishing him good night in dialects he did not speak he fell sound asleep.

Chapter Thirteen

She was in one of the dresses Dan gave her when they did the training together at *Silver Springs* Hotel. It was emerald and she loved the colour, the design and the embroidery. She got up from the dressing table and looked at herself one last time in the mirror. The dress sat well on her. She picked her handbag from the bed and made for the door. Just by the door she stopped and looked up at the face in the picture up on the wall. He looked down at her, quiet, as was his nature in real life, and calm. He seemed to wish her well.

She remembered his message about each person having different personalities and how the principles of each personality type, if brought together, would enhance the quality of a person's life. She had reflected on this several times in the past and was convinced he practised what he taught. You could see the Christian in his life. He showed love for people he came into contact with. He gave support to people he did not know. In all the circumstances in which she interacted with him she could say that he exhibited Christian virtue.

She knew nothing of his personal life and so could not tell how much he brought the fine principles of religion and organisational life into his personal life. Live a Christian life not only on Sundays but all week and all month and throughout the year.

I will try, she said as she gave the silent picture a salute with one finger.

She normally went to church early in order to park her car easily. She exchanged greetings with the wardens and the early arrivals. She dipped her hand in the holy water at the entrance of the church and did the sign of the cross with it before going into the church. She kneeled and for a minute emptied her heart of any feeling of hate for anyone. She found doing that very helpful to her. It made her feel light and it seemed to make her heart feel healthy every time. She asked

208

herself many times in the past why we carry grudges and fill our hearts with hate. When you hate, she told herself, you cause so much pain in your own heart but the person you hate does not feel anything. Why punish yourself by hating, she asked. She concluded that hate was an unwise act. She recalled all those acts which she had committed in the past week, which even as a human being, she did not think acceptable. She expressed remorse for all of those. Then she made the sign of the cross and started her prayers.

She thanked God for her life, her health and the many little mercies of the past week. She thought of her life in the past week, and the people she loved and the people who had a space in her life and thanked her maker for the mercies granted those people. She thought of those people she had cause not to like and asked for strength to love them. She prayed for the poor, the homeless, those in need with nobody to help them, the sick and dying and asked for God's mercies for those people. She committed herself to her maker over the coming week and asked that her life over the period should reflect love and neighbourliness with all people.

Whenever she prayed, whether in church or in the privacy of her bedroom, she felt a sense of peacefulness in her that made her value prayer. She said she had no scientific knowledge of the existence of God or any kind of deity that ruled humanity and could intervene in people's lives. But she had faith, call it blind faith she admitted, in such a deity. And that belief influenced her thoughts and her feelings. Even if God did not exist the life she lived as a result of her belief that He existed, the calm and happy feeling in her when she unloaded her heart unto Him, made her faith worth it.

She was reminded of Dan again that morning during the homily. The gospel was on Christian love and the priest explained how different Christian love was. "Our Lord told us in very plain words that even non-Christians show love. Christians don't have a monopoly over love. Everyone knows it; even those who have never been reached by our Christian faith know love. Without it none of us would have survived into adulthood. Our mothers especially would have shown us love when we were weak and we survived because of it...

"Members of every family will protect their relations from outsiders. A father loves his children and children love their parents. We love members of our communities. If two members of the same village meet in a different town and one runs into trouble, the one in trouble can count on the support of the other person from his village. That is natural...

"In our workplaces, in our neighbourhoods, people will return love to those who first showed them love...

"So love is not a quality of only Christians. One may ask that if love is known not only among Christians, then why should Jesus preach it? Well, he acknowledged the fact that throughout history mankind knew and also exercised love. He challenged Christians to make our love different. We should love proactively and put no barriers to our love. Non-Christians love their kith and kind. They return love. Christians are asked to expand the boundaries of their love and to love everyone. Not just their family members. Not just their friends. Not just those who have shown them love. Not just those who share the same faith with them. Christians are commanded to love everybody. If you are a Kenyan and you are walking in the streets of Nairobi and you see someone being attacked, it doesn't matter if the person is not Kenyan, a true Christian will go to the aid that person. That is Christ's commandment to us regarding love..."

She thought of Dan and his mission to make a difference in the lives of people he did not know. She remembered an incident in Kadoma. Judith, from Tanzania, felt sudden cramps in her tummy and had to the rushed to the hospital. It was late evening but Dan accompanied the hotel staff who sent Judith to the hospital. At the hospital he paid for all her drugs and stayed till she was in a stable condition and could see people. It was past midnight but he stayed till he could talk to her. He took her husband's phone number and called him the next day to inform him about Judith and also assured him that there was nothing he would be expected to do and that everything she needed was being done for her.

He facilitated the sessions the next morning standing on his feet till the break when he made a quick exit to check on Judith's condition. When she was discharged he paid for her to extend her stay by two days and paid to change her flight date so that she was sure she was strong before she left.

"I will try to get my organisation to refund the money you spent on me to you," Judith had told him, uncertain she could convince them to do that and very certain she could not refund it herself. But it was too much money to spend on a stranger.

"Don't think about the expenditure on you. I will try to claim it from the organisers. If I don't succeed in getting a refund I won't worry."

He also arranged for Judith to attend a training session in Ghana that covered the same issues treated in the Kadoma training. This had allowed Judith to attend the Salima training.

She exchanged mail frequently with Judith and she knew how Judith thought of what he did for her. "It was certainly not because he was the facilitator. As the facilitator he had his obligations but he went miles beyond that obligation. He is just an extra kind-hearted man."

Show proactive love. Expand the boundaries of love. Dan did all that.

When the communion was being offered she felt only love in her heart and she knew she qualified to take communion.

She sat in one of the pews close to the altar so she was among the last to leave the church. She knew her parents would be in church today because they said they would come to give support to their friend's daughter whose infant child was baptised during the service. She expected to meet them outside and offer to take them to Carnivores that evening. Her dad knew the place very well and she had been there before, just once before she and her parents took Dan there. She thought it would be nice to go with the old couple.

Her head was raised looking for signs of her parents, expecting them to be with Jennifer and her husband and Martha, her mother. Martha and Diane's mother had been friends for many years now. Both sold flowers. When one received an order too large for her to meet alone she would rope in the other woman to help her meet the supply. Diane and Jennifer, however, had not been quite close.

She was still looking up and around for her parents, looking out for her mother's cream coloured silk dress, when she saw Jane and Teddy right in front of her, just about two metres ahead of her. She turned into a statue. But for only a few seconds. She became alive and did the only natural thing to do, continue to walk forward which meant towards them. Teddy saw her first and he did freeze as he stopped immediately. Teddy and Jane, each carrying a child, had been walking forward too, and therefore towards Diane. Jane turned to look at her husband when he stopped. Then she turned and saw Diane who had continued to walk towards them. Jane smiled and held out her hand. Diane smiled too and also held out her hand. They shook, smiling at each other.

Diane shook hands with the younger of the two children whom Jane was carrying, the boy. Then she turned to Teddy who was carrying Samantha, the older child, a girl.

"Good morning, Auntie Diane," Samantha greeted first.

So Diane took Samantha's hand first and responded, "Good morning, Auntie Samantha."

"Me, I am a small girl. Am I your auntie?"

"Yes, Auntie Samantha, you are my auntie. My aunties are small girls."

"No, you are my auntie. I am not your auntie."

"But I also want an auntie," Diane said, "and it is you I want to be my auntie."

"Me, I don't have money to give you to buy toffee and biscuits and ice cream. I am a small girl."

They all laughed. Even Teddy joined in even though he was terribly uncomfortable.

Diane held out her hand and smiled, just a tiny smile, "Hi, Teddy. It has been a long time. How are you?"

He held out his hand but it had no life in it. "Yes, yes, it has been a long time. I am fine. And you?"

She took a deep breath, "Well, I am alive as you can see. I am healthy. I am okay."

Jane hugged Diane. "Hey Diana girl! I heard you are now an international trainer. A woman who attended your training said you trained a team that came from the four corners of Africa and she said you were great. Nobody told me you had gone into training. Congratulations. I hear you are one of the best in Africa."

Diane smiled. Of course Jane had been ostracised from their circle of friends and some friends were even angry with Diane for having anything to do with Jane. The proud Jane had really been shoved out of the circle she had once been a proud member of. Diane was not convinced it made any difference to Jane but friends said it hurt her to have been cast out. With her being out of the circle she heard news items about members of that circle only very late.

"It is true that I am into training and we did train a team that comprised people from different African countries. But I am not sure I am even among the best in Kenya let alone in Africa. And I am sure they would have told you that there was a lead trainer who was super."

Jane was excited. "Yes, they told me about him. They said he was a powerful trainer too and very knowledgeable. I heard you made a perfect pair." She moved closer to Diane. "Diane, please tell me. Are you going to marry him?"

"Marry him? Did they tell you he was not married?"

"No, I did not hear anything like that." She dropped her voice to a conspiratorial tone. "But don't tell me you are not going to marry him."

What she said next just came out of her mouth. She did not think about it but when she did think about it later she was glad it came out that way. "Jane you are married now and won't be looking to marry again. So if I were going to marry him, there would be no risk my telling you because you will not be interested in him. No, I am not going to marry him. We will be training together for some time even when I win my own contracts because he is such a great facilitator but we have never discussed marriage."

"I hope he proposes to you anyway."

Diane smiled and just said thanks.

"Auntie, you did not buy me my dress." That was Samantha and Diane smiled.

Trust little children to remember what you tell them jokingly. She did promise to buy Samantha a dress she was crying for her mother to take off a girl for her when she ran into them about five weeks back. She fished in her purse and gave money to Samantha telling her, "I did not go to the shop where they sell the dress. That is why I did not buy it for you. Use this money to buy it. Let Mama take you there and buy it for you."

"Thank you, Auntie. I don't know the shop."

"Mama knows there."

Then she noticed commotion on the shoulder of Jane. The little boy also held out his hand for money. Diane laughed and took out some more shillings from her purse for him. "Please stop at two children otherwise the next time they tax me I will have to sell my clothing to raise enough money for them.'

That brought Jane even closer to her. "That reminds me, Diane. I have been meaning to tell you this since I set eyes on you. You look very beautiful. The dress is very beautiful and it fits you perfectly." She felt the texture. "This is not Kenyan made, is it?"

She told her where it came from and who gave it to her.

"Wow! And you can claim there is no marriage in the making?"

"From how many people did you receive gifts who did not ask you to marry them?"

Jane was unruffled by the question. "They may not have done so but the intention was not far away."

"Sorry, in this case the intention does not even exist."

She patted the two children and waved at the adults. "Have a nice day."

It was when she was leaving them that she saw that the crowd had frozen and all were engaged in staring at them.

It was very embarrassing for Teddy. When Diane left he looked round and all eyes seemed fixed on him and his wife. He took in not just the looks but the silence that accompanied the looks. The looks and the silence told him how the crowd felt about him. Jane, however, did not seem to notice anything wrong. The truth was, Teddy and Jane had different characters. Even though Teddy seemed happy to have married Jane, he had the impression that people shunned his company and that some previously close friends had been cold towards him and Jane. He was aware of the fact that his decision to marry Diane's friend had moral implications for him and Jane. Jane did not see this at all. In public she did not have the sense that Teddy had that people were looking at them with accusations in their looks or that they were not as warm in the way they received them. She did not see this. Because she did not look hard in people's faces.

So while Jane wanted to go on and say hi and socialise Teddy was firm that they should leave. Jane resisted and it looked like they would create a scene. Seeing that Teddy was obstinate about their leaving she gave in.

Jane sulked as she followed her husband who felt the crowd opened up for them to pass because they wanted to be rid of them. He felt eyes bore their back and when he got inside the car he actually looked round and was convinced that people were looking at them.

Diane walked over to her parents who were standing with Jennifer, her husband and her parents. Her mother hugged her and pressed her head against her bosom. She had never done this to Diane in public and she promised to ask her why she did that. But not in the presence of the others.

When they said 'bye to Jennifer and others and walked towards their cars Diane proposed the evening out at Carnivores. Her father looked at her a while before asking why Carnivores.

"Well, because we have been eating indoors, either at my place or yours. I just asked myself why not go out occasionally. It was nice going out with Dan but why not just the three of us?"

Her mother smiled. "It may also give men the chance to see and be attracted by Diane."

They laughed and Diane said, "Mama, I was not thinking about advertising myself."

She remembered the question she had for her mother only when she was driving home.

They enjoyed themselves eating at Carnivores. They found that it was less work for them and they had a wide variety to choose from. They were together as a family and had the privacy they expected at home while at the same time being part of crowd. It was more fun, they found, than being at home. They were therefore surprised when a man walked up to their table and asked if they would mind his sitting with them for a few minutes. They said no, they did not mind and he sat down. It was when he sat that Diane recognised him as a priest in their parish. "I came over to tell you," he pointed at the parents, "what a wonderful daughter you have. I think most of us in the parish know about her and Teddy and Jane. We recognise her as the symbol of Christian strength and virtue for the relationship she has maintained with Jane and Teddy. What she demonstrated this morning was exemplary. She is very rare and you must be proud to have her as a daughter."

Both parents agreed. It was her mother who said, "We worried about her sanity when it happened. We knew how much she loved Teddy and she suffered emotionally. But her maker gave her strength. First we are thankful to God, to the many people who prayed for her and touched her and we are certainly proud of her. We sure were happy to see how she conducted herself this morning with the two."

Diane understood why her mother hugged her in the morning.

Chapter Fourteen

Dan opened his eyes with the crowing of the cocks. The pattern of the cock crows had not changed since he noticed it in his childhood days. At first a solitary cock would crow. That was what his people called the early cock crow. The same cock might repeat the crow about three to six times. Then a second cock would take it up and join the early cock to inform the new born day that it was welcome. And also to inform all living things that the new day had arrived. Over the next thirty minutes or so the cocks in the whole neighbourhood would be testing the strength of their voices with their crowing. The pattern hadn't changed.

When he was growing up in this house he could sleep through the early morning noises of cocks crowing, guinea fowls crying up on the neem tree, of animals chasing each other in the kraal and cows lowing in neighbouring houses. But since he left home, those early morning noises woke him up each time he came home.

He would have loved to sit up and lean against the low wall that ran round the platform and observe the day break. Listen as the crying of the guinea fowls intensified. Listen as the cows started to low. Listen as the goats and sheep got restless and began to bleat. Watch the sky brighten and become orange and eventually give up the sun. He would have loved to sit up and watch other people rouse from platforms in other houses and fold their mats. He would have loved to watch the bad habits of the men as they invariably put one foot against the low wall and urinate at the back of the house.

He did not sit, though. He picked his mattress and pillow and went down to his room where he lay on the sofa in the sitting room. It was still quite cool and he knew he would fall into a deep sleep if he lay on the bed in the bedroom.

He went round the families in the house and exchanged greetings with them. They all asked if he had enough rest from the tiredness of the previous day's travel. Then he returned to his room where he boiled water on a kerosene stove and prepared coffee for breakfast. He also fried an egg which he ate with his bread. He bathed quickly and put on navy blue corduroy trousers and picked his dungaree overalls and joined his father for the trip to his father's turkey farm.

His father was the example of what he expected of his uncles and cousins and other distant relations. He told them time and again that almost all the requests he received from his relatives had been requests for consumption purposes. That was, besides those he supported in education. He complained that by that attitude the family was putting its weight on just one person. "No matter how broad his shoulders are, he can't carry all of you. No matter how strong his bones are he can't take the weight of all of you," he told them more than ten times. "Nobody has ever come to me to say I have thought of this activity and after turning it over in my mind have come to the conclusion that if I had X cedis and did A, B and C it will support me and my family forever. If you all thought of income earning opportunities and put all the money I gave you into such activities this family would have gone very far. You wouldn't need me. But what do I get? Request by a very small boy who should not have married because he has never even sewn a new pair of trousers for himself has gone ahead and married and can't even buy cloth for her. Request for money to buy sheep to be given to in-laws because someone who should not have married had gone to marry and had not done any of the customarily required acts consuming a marriage. Requests for money for funerals. What will happen to those of you who have chosen to depend entirely on me if say on this trip back to Tamale I am involved in an accident and die?"

While his father chuckled at the suggestion his mother spat. In their tradition if you don't spit out the saliva in your mouth when you say something bad you are inviting it upon yourself or the person you were making reference to. The idea of her only child dying so soon was not something any mother would welcome. The other members of the family sitting under the neem tree who heard him did not like it either. Dan dying?

His father was different and that was why his father understood him and supported him in many of the things he said to relatives who were a nuisance to him.

Five years previously Dan asked his father what his father could do to support himself. He pointed out that farming did little for him. His father was very hardworking, Dan pointed out, like all the farmers in the village and in Navrongo in general. But they did not harvest enough to meet their needs throughout the year. So why not consider anything else? Because farming was the only thing they knew.

One day Dan told his father of a farmer in Nalerigu who did not cultivate crops but spent his time raising turkeys. "He is better off than most crop farmers," Dan explained. "He gets more money from the sale of turkeys and eggs than most farmers get from the crops they produce. So he buys all the foodstuffs his family will need and he still has plenty of money left to cloth the family, pay medical bills and educate his children."

When Dan was leaving for Tamale his father told him to come back some other time and send him to see the turkey farmer he told him of so that he could study him. That was one other thing he liked about his father; he was considerate. Some other relation would have come to him one day and asked to be taken to see the farmer he talked of. His father gave him ample notice. When coming the next time. Prepare to send me to see him.

So Dan found out about the farmer and sent his father to see him. Even though his father talked to his brothers and cousins about what he was going to Nalerigu for nobody showed interest in turkey farming and nobody came with him. Dan bought some gifts for his father's 'teacher' and the two men spent about three hours together talking mostly through sign language. But they seemed to understand each other and his father left quite keen to take up turkey farming. The result was this venture which turned his father in old age into a prosperous man. The irony was that his father was the one person who did not need this enterprise. If any two people had a right to demand remittances monthly from Dan his parents were those people. And, in fact, he did remit handsome sums to the old couple. His father did not need to raise turkeys to live comfortably. But Dan had thought it would be good for the old man to have his own business and take pride in how it could support him. And that was what his father had done.

The old man returned from Nalerigu with some turkey eggs which he put under a hen to hatch. Fourteen of the chicks survived and grew into adult turkeys. He kept close watch over them and collected their eggs which fowls brooded. He did not sell the turkeys or the eggs. He acquired land on the way to Kajelo and put up a structure for a turkey farm. It was a simple structure. It had compartments where the turkeys could lay eggs. The main part of the farm was a large fenced area where the birds spent the day roaming. He fed them there and gave them water. Sometimes he opened the gate of the fence and let out the turkeys, especially during the rainy season when the grass was green. There were larger compartments into which he herded the birds in the evening.

He had hands who helped him especially with bringing food for the birds, cleaning the cages and compartments and fetching water from the borehole.

When Dan was at home he drove his father to his farm. They both left home in ordinary clothing, this morning Dan was in his navy blue corduroy trousers and a deep blue open-necked T-shirt. At the farm he put on the overalls, like his father. Father and son were ready for a day together on their farm.

Dan's name was known very wide for his commitment to work on his father's farm whenever he came home, which was frequently. On market days men and women from the villages beyond Saboro would stream past the farm on their way to Navrongo market, greeting and admiring the father and his son. They admired the relationship, the harmony, that existed between father and son. They admired the son who drove such an expensive vehicle, meaning he was a 'big' man and yet would spend the day working alongside his father as if he was illiterate and had never left the village all his life. Some women did not feel ashamed to stop and openly watch Dan engaged in various activities. They would watch him sit on the donkey cart and guide the donkey to pull them to the borehole. They would stand on the road and admire him as he carried two buckets of water at a time from the drum in the cart into the fence and poured it into a container from which they would later fill the turkeys' drinking troughs. They watched as he brought out the troughs and washed them and refilled them with water. They watched him as he mixed the feed and filled the trays. It was dirty work, not meant for a highly educated, big man who drove a big car. But there he was before their eyes doing just that.

Dan remembered the day an elderly woman approached them and asked Dan how many wives he had. Both Dan and his father were amused by the question, his father amused because of a second reason he and Dan knew.

"Why do you ask, Mother?" Dan asked her.

"Because of the way you work," she replied as she leaned against the fence. "You work so hard I think you need about three wives to be able to take care of you effectively."

Dan and his father roared with laughter. The woman was a very jovial person and before she left she asked if Dan would not drive her to the market since she had never sat in a car before. Even though it was a joking request Dan also decided why not go along with the joke and offered to drive her. Her colleagues roared with laughter and delight when they realised what was happening. Fortunately for Dan there were only four women in that group so he did not have problems with space. When at the market he was going to get down in his dirty overalls the elderly woman protested. "You are a big man. You should not get down in this crowd in your farmer's attire."

But Dan got down and helped them to get down. When he gave them money to buy food for the house they simply found it unbelievable. The elderly woman walked to the driver's window and spoke to Dan in a low earnest voice. "My son, God will give you the three wives I said you deserve. And each of them will give you ten children who will be as hardworking as you and as concerned for and respectful to elderly people as you are. I don't have anything to give you. I give you my blessings."

Today was not a market day so Dan and his father worked without interruption. By the time they had finished the morning chores it was past eleven and Dan was happy to lie in the camp bed next to his father. He always looked forward to this moment of quiet intimacy with his father. Those were the moments he knew he loved his father.

The morning chores had over the years grown longer. Dan admired his father's sense of initiative and his drive at an advanced age. The number of turkeys he kept grew in number till at any time he had about two hundred and fifty birds laying. He sold some of the eggs. A single turkey egg sold at the same price as a live guinea fowl. He put some of the eggs under fowls to hatch. He also sold some of the birds.

Two years after the turkey project was started the old man Apeatu, simply called Atu by the younger generation, decided to add pigs to the farm. He said that he noticed that there was a large demand for pork. And that anyone who bred healthy pigs would sell them easily. He went to Navrongo Secondary School and Notre Dame Minor Seminary and Secondary School where he observed how they bred their pigs. Dan took him to the Veterinary College in Pong Tamale where he also observed how to raise healthy, wholesome pigs. Atu bought five pigs from Pong Tamale, one boar and four sows, as his parent stock. He controlled these too, limiting the number he kept for breeding and selling many of them to institutions and individuals.

He introduced guinea fowls here too.

The pair, father and son, retired to their reclining chairs under the shady bread fruit tree only after they and the farm hands had cleaned the places where turkeys and pigs lived and had changed their water and changed their feed. Dan did not mind cleaning the pig sties, despite their stench. Women returning from fetching fuel wood, or picking shea nuts or *dawadawa,* would pause and watch with open mouths as Dan cleaned the sties and gave the pigs water and food. As he emerged from the sties drenched in sweat they would ask each other how this man would have been working if he had never been to school. They liked to say of him that he worked as if he had no blood. And they always went back to the fact that he was doing all this despite being a big man.

With the morning's chores done, Dan and his father lay side by side in their camp beds and rested. Dan loved the quiet time with his father. In the past whenever Dan found himself alone with his father Matilda and the children were sure to come up as an issue. Dan remembered a difficult session he had with his father about Matilda and the children. It was the second year after the break up and his father asked if Matilda had remarried to which Dan had said no.

"Why don't you ask her to come back?" Atu asked. "I remember that it was her who asked you to move out. You still wanted her at the time of the separation and you tried to see her several times to patch up the differences. If she has not married again why not try to get her to come back? Maybe she has not remarried because she wants to come back."

Dan laughed at the very idea. "Atu, Matilda cannot come back. Matilda and I cannot ever live together as wife and husband again. It is just not possible. It is true that I very badly wanted her back after she threw me out of the house and declared the marriage ended. At the time I wanted her back. But not now."

Dan did not find it difficult to call his father Atu. In Kassena culture people were called by their names, even the elderly. But as a sign of respect elderly people were called by shortened versions of their names. His mother was Jango, but everybody called her Anu Ago, Mother Ago. His father was Apeatu to his peers and Atu to the younger generation.

"Why not now?" Atu asked. "Don't tell me she slept with other men since then because that is not a good excuse for refusing to take her back."

"We have just grown into two different people who have nothing in common," Dan told his father. "We can't live together because our interests, our ideas and our very way of life, are different."

"What has that got to do with marriage, tell me?"

"Atu, a lot. I know of the practice at home where a woman will bring her relative to marry a young man in the family she has married into. The young man and the young woman would not have seen each other before and may be different people, the way I have said Matilda and are I. But they will live and stay married till ripe old age. It is different when we are away from the home. Here you can live with the woman and have very little contact with her. Your time with her is only when the two of go to sleep. You hardly chat with each other. It is not the same with those of us living away from home and the bigger family. We spend a lot of time with our spouses. Your wife is your sister, your best friend and your aunt. If you don't relate well it is hell for the two of you. And for the children if there are children."

His father did not agree but as they kept talking about Matilda returning, his parents came to see that they would not ever be able to influence a reunion of the two.

So they asked about the children.

"I made attempts to see the children soon after we broke. After all they are my children," Dan told his parents in answer to their query about the children. "You both know it was Matilda and her mother who prevented me from seeing the children. They will not entertain any suggestion to take the children away from Matilda."

Turning to his mother he said, "Anu Ago, you even have quite painful experience in the hands of Matilda's mother over these children."

Dan's mother came to Tamale after the break up when Dan said he was not allowed access to the children. Matilda's mother had come to Tamale too and was taking care of the children and had forbidden Dan from setting foot in the house. Jango was convinced she would be able to talk to Matilda's mother and that between them they could reach an understanding based on their culture.

That was not how things had turned out. Matilda's mother prevented Jango from seeing the children. She was inside the room with the children when Dan and his mother knocked at the door. She asked who was out there and they identified themselves. But instead of asking them in she came out and closed the door behind her. She was not in the least friendly, not even to Dan's mother.

"Yes, what do you want?" she asked them.

"That is not how to receive people," Dan's mother complained. "In our culture you will receive us, offer us water and then we exchange greetings. It is only after that we will tell you our mission."

The other woman was unmoved. "What if I don't go through that unnecessary process? I asked you a question; what do you want?"

"Well, we came to see our children," Jango said, the effort to restrain herself very visible in her face.

"Did you come to eat them or to see them?" Matilda's mother asked, very cool when she said it as if she was saying a very ordinary thing. "You mean you came after my grandchildren to eat them?" She struck her chest to emphasise the fact that the children were her grandchildren.

Jango was shocked at the unprovoked attack on her intentions. Marian opened the door and poked her head through the opening and started to say something but her grandmother pushed her back and shut the door.

"You are an elderly person," Jango said. Dan could see that her mother was strained under the effort to maintain her calm and not accept the fight that the other woman wanted. "You can't be serious about us coming to eat the children. They are your grandchildren but they are his," she indicated her son, "children. Why did he not eat them earlier and he will now come seeking to eat them?"

"Who gave him the children?" Matilda's mother asked. "You made reference to culture earlier on. I hope you know the culture you made reference to. How can you have children in Kassena culture when you have not married the woman?"

"He married her," Jango said rather loudly, her anger with this annoying lady showing.

"From whom? Are you Kadua's mother? Oh, so you stole my daughter and gave her in marriage to your son, is it? Go back to the culture and take your lessons in it. You don't marry a woman on the streets. You marry her from her home, her parents. And so far as I am concerned my daughter has never been married to anyone. She kept men and had children. I don't know their father. Now leave."

Jango had heard about the behaviour of the woman when Dan's family sent the delegation to discuss the performance of the second stage of the marital rites. But she had not expected that a woman her age would behave the way she was doing towards them.

She decided to also become foolhardy. "We are not leaving till we see the children. If it comes to eating you will rather eat us."

"Oh, I thought you respected yourselves which was why I gave you so much respect. Now that I know that you don't respect yourselves we shall see."

It was only at this stage Dan said a word. He knew his mother-in-law and what she was capable of doing. So he gently tried to pull his mother away but she refused.

Matilda's mother went into the yard and started clapping loudly to attract attention. Which she did very well. "Witches! Witches have come to eat my daughter's children! Witches! Leave this house and leave my children. Witches!"

Dan was not surprised at all by her behaviour but his mother was shocked and was almost paralysed by the action of the other woman. An amused crowd had gathered and Dan gently steered his mother through it, with insults and accusations and hand clapping following them. He felt like melting under the heat of the eyes. His legs felt like giving way under him but he managed, somehow, to keep walking.

His parents remembered this alright but that did not persuade them to give up action to claim the children.

"How can you leave your children with their mother just because their grandmother is difficult? Are they your children or the grandmother's children?"

"Atu, it will take a long, costly and embarrassing battle to get the children. I can imagine their grandmother organising people to stand outside the court each time the case is being heard to shout and boo at us. It is going to be a big public drama case that will attract the whole of Tamale each time it is coming on. The children will be subject to so much ridicule it will not do them any good and we will be muddying their future. I don't want to do that."

"Are you afraid for yourself or for the children?" his mother asked.

"Both. It is going to be a case in which this whole family, those of us who will be in Tamale to go to court, will be subject to public ridicule. The old lady will stage free drama each day and Tamale is going to be turning out in numbers to laugh at us. You are right that I am not going to like being the one or one of those the town is entertained with.

"But I am also concerned about the children. It will hurt them and hurt them badly. They will be in papers. Their colleagues in the area they stay in and in the schools they attend will be making fun of them for years to come. Their names and their story are going to be etched in memories for a long time. People they are going to meet later in life will have fun at their expense. I am not going to subject the children to this treatment."

"You just slept with Matilda and brought the children to this world," his father told him. "You don't own them. The family does. That was why it was us and not you who went to discuss the marital rites. You were in Tamale and nobody even asked you to come home. This is our case and not your case."

"Unfortunately Atu, this is my case. You have two options in pursuing this case. One is to seek judgement from the traditional system by going to the chief. Before the chief you can get judgement delivered in your favour. You performed the first rites. That means the family of Matilda accepted and acknowledged that we were married. The chief can then ask that we provide animals and take the children. But it will not be an enforceable judgement. Matilda and her mother will not come home with the children. The chief has no power to force Matilda to come to his court with the children. He can only pour his anger on the head of Matilda's family, the old man back at home. But that will not bring the children. No, it won't. The chief can't send his elders or anybody to go to Tamale and arrest Matilda and the children. So using the traditional system can only result in a judgement that can't be enforced."

"You mean the chief can't force Matilda's father to bring the children?" his father asked incredulously.

"The chief can order the old man, the head of the family or Matilda's father and threaten them with a sanction, most likely a fine of an animal. He has that authority over the old people but not over Matilda. If you go to the chief to get the children back, sorry you won't get them back. Matilda and her mother will not return them, you know that. You will only get someone in the family in trouble."

The old couple digested that.

Dan added, looking at his mother, "You know that woman and what respect she has for custom. Both of you were told how she behaved even with the men in the house when the delegation from here went to the house to discuss the offer of the goat and dog. She did everything that defied culture."

As they thought about it he went on, "The second option left to you to claim the children is going to court, using the national, legal system and not the traditional system. However, I will need to initiate the action. That system recognises only two parents, the father and the mother. In that system children belong to their immediate parents and only in the absence of those parents can next of kin come in. But I have told you I am not going to start anything that will create so much ridicule for the children."

His father softened his tone and said, "You should understand us. We – not just I and your mother but the elders of this family – are accountable to our ancestors for every member of this family. We will be stranded on the way in the hereafter and not reach our ancestors if we die leaving those, or any other, children unclaimed and not united with the family."

Dan could see clearly the conflict of beliefs. He understood the belief that when people died they went to join a community of members of the clan already departed. Those in leadership position in the family would be asked questions about their leadership of the family. He was unable to tell them sorry, but I don't share your belief about the hereafter. He knew what he believed was not important. They believed and that belief would affect the way they saw things.

But Matilda and the children had stopped coming up over the years. His parents had to accept, even if painfully, the fact that he would not reconcile with Matilda and would not take her back even if she offered to come back. They also knew they could not make him initiate court action to take the children back. The children would remain in limbo unless something happened to make the children themselves come back. Or, as he told them, if their mother died.

In the village people did things according to the sun and not clocks. So it was past midday when his mother came to join them and to prepare their lunch. When the farm was started and she had to bring her husband lunch, she prepared it at home. But you can't prepare a meal at home and carry all of it away without sharing it. So she chose to rather come to the farm and prepare it. They built a small kitchen and Dan got them a good quality kerosene stove.

They all sat together under the shady bread fruit tree, the couple, Dan and the hired hands, and had their lunch, chatting and laughing. After lunch Dan washed the utensils used for cooking as well as what he and his parents ate in while the others washed their own items. Then he and his parents lay back in their chairs and enjoyed a family communion. Dan enjoyed this even more than the time alone with his father.

But this afternoon as he lay quietly between his parents, looking up at the leaves and through them the sky, he thought of his children. The scene in the Tamale Secondary School assembly hall came back to him. It occurred to him that if at this age he cherished the presence of his parents, both parents, for children the age of Marian and Junior, and for children who had not known parental care, they would value time with their parents even more.

Before the meeting with Marian the previous weekend he was thinking only of providing money for the children's needs. He had not factored spending time with them into what he must do for them. They needed money for their various needs. Here is the money, and he had shouldered his responsibilities to the fullest, he thought. It was as simple as that, easy to do and he was not afraid to do it. After the second meeting with Marian, and now as he lay feeling the pleasure of the presence of his parents, he knew he had a tall responsibility. Except that he could not absolve himself of it; he could not in any way get out of that responsibility. He had to shoulder it.

His mind began to play tricks on him. His life was filled with his work. Every space of it was taken by his work. He had never been a father. Over the four years that he lived with Matilda and the children he had never really played the role of a father to the children. He had spent that time living inside an *akpeteshie* bottle. Now he must act as a father and act it effectively. To teenage children he did not know. He remembered Marian's questions and accusations and that made him even more uncomfortable about his responsibility.

He was almost dozing off when his mother patted his knee and said, "I almost forgot to give you this message. Kada said I should ask you why you did not say good bye to her daughter."

"I didn't say good bye to Kada herself. Why didn't she ask me about that? And say what kind of good bye? I am not leaving today so why say good bye to anyone?"

"No, you are not leaving today, but her daughter left today."

Intriguing was all he said in his head.

Chapter Fifteen

Dan spent an anxious week preparing for the visit of his children. On the Monday he spent more time than was healthy behind the computer looking up sites from which he could get advice on children. He found a lot of general information but nothing very close to what he wanted. He spent the afternoon preparing his notes for the presentation he had to make at Mole on Wednesday and Thursday. He visited more sites on the Tuesday morning, downloaded and read lots of materials which he printed and carried along with him to Mole. He shared the evening between his notes for the presentation and the materials on children. He did not realise till he started reading the materials that he had printed more than two hundred pages.

After reading through twenty pages he gave up and decided he would not read the rest. He learnt nothing specific but learnt something general – he would never find material that would describe how he could relate with the children. He realised that relating with one's children was like leadership. Each was context specific and since no two contexts were the same nobody could ever write a script for a father. Each father would have to discover the nature of each of their children and find out the best way to relate with them. But saying that made his task even more intimidating. Marian had said that her brother was not the same as her. If he was confused how he was going to manage his relationship with Marian given what he perceived to be a complex nature he now had to add to that managing a relationship with her and her brother who was different from her.

He smiled at himself. He had agreed before, not today, that he could not learn how to manage or relate with the children from books, literature or anybody's experience. Yet when the day for meeting the children got close he had been so worried stiff by the uncertainty of how the meeting would be to try to do the impossible – seek what was learnt from experience and not from other people.

He concentrated on his presentation and shut his mind on the impending meeting with the children.

He did nothing serious the Friday evening and spent the evening reading. He went to bed early and still got up late the next morning. The children came just before 11:00 a.m. He opened the door and saw Marian standing there in uniform. He held out his hand and welcomed her. Junior was behind her and it was when she moved to come into the house that Dan saw him fully. The boy stood there looking at his father and his father also looked at him. Something let itself loose inside him and he felt a feeling he could not describe. It made him say involuntarily, "Junior!" At the same time he stooped and picked up the boy even though he was not that small. He lifted him and held him against his chest. The boy looked up and away from his father's face. When he turned to go into the house with him he caught Marian smiling at them.

He put the boy down and asked them to sit down. They sat for more than two minutes in uncomfortable silence. He said welcome again and they again said their thanks. After that he did not know what to say or do.

It was Marian who broke the silence. "Dad, do you stay alone here?"

"Yes, Marian, I stay here alone."

"It's a big house."

"Yes, it is." He offered to take them round the house. He started from the upstairs where there were three bedrooms, each with its bathroom and toilet. They came down the stairs where there were three rooms used for various purposes, in addition to the sitting room, the kitchen and the guest toilet. The first was what he called the guest room. A second was the study which also held an assortment of books, cassettes and pamphlets in addition to a computer.

"I spend most of my time in the house here," he explained to the children.

"Doing what, Dad? Are you doing further studies?" Marian asked.

"Yes and no, Marian." He looked at Junior but he was lost admiring the books and equipment in the room. "If you mean am I doing say a Masters the answer is no, I am not doing studies of that kind. But I read a lot, on a wide variety of subjects. I use here to prepare the materials for my training sessions. I also spend a lot of time here writing reports, analysing information from interviews and so on." He explained his work as a consultant.

He showed them the next room which he called the studio. It was his recreation room and he had various instruments and equipment in here. He showed them how the karaoke worked and he sang the Temptations' *My Girl* for them. The children were impressed and curious. They asked a few questions.

"Dad, so there are no children staying here with you?" Marian asked when they returned to the sitting room.

"Which children do you want to come and stay with me?"

"Your nephews and nieces. Your brothers' children. Your sisters' children. I am sure there are a lot of children in the village who will like to come and stay with you here."

He thought over that. As usual, Junior was looking somewhere around the room and avoiding eye contact with his father.

"I am an only child," Dan told them. "I have cousins and their children would have liked to come and stay here. But they can't come and stay with me."

"You are an only child, Dad! Oh! So we have no cousins? But why can't your other relatives' children come and stay here?" Marian asked. "You don't like children, do you? You are alone in this big house. There are many rooms. Three children could sleep in each of the bedrooms."

He noticed the fact that Junior looked sharply at him and then looked away. He offered them soft drinks.

He did not immediately answer, aware of the effect his answers could have on the children's perception of him but he decided to be frank with them. In their relationship with each other they needed to understand each other, he told himself. They could only understand each other if they each frankly told the other what they thought and how they felt.

"It has nothing to do with whether I like or don't like children," he answered, looking at both of them. "I live alone here and travel a lot. Even when I don't travel I bring home a lot of things to do. There is no woman in the house to control children staying here. I can't afford to bring my relatives' children here because I won't be able to manage them. I won't have the time.

"Marian, I support many children in school. In order to earn the money that will enable me to support them I need a quiet home in which I can plan my work. Between the financial support they get from me and their coming to stay here I will imagine that the financial support is more important to them."

"What about them coming to spend holidays with you?"

He chuckled. The persistent questioner, he noted. "Marian, things are not as simple as you think. We are all different people with our respective likes and dislikes. There are things we can each do and things we can't do. I have lived a long time alone and developed a routine in my life. My life is centred on work. If I allow one child to come and stay here with me, I will find it difficult to care for him or her adequately. I leave home early for work. I come home late from the office and I spend a great deal of my time at home in the study. That is how I am able to cope with my work. I won't have time to care for a child staying with me.

"My work is very important to me. But it is equally important to those children who you want to come and stay here. I pay the school fees of a lot of my cousins' children. I support a lot of members of the extended family financially. And that support is possible from the amount of work I do. I am good at doing my work and earning money and supporting my relations. I am not good at playing host to them. So they must accept from me what I can most afford to give.

"If one of my cousins' children comes to stay with me once, the next holidays there will be half a dozen cousins who will want their children to come and stay with me. If I can't care for one child staying here things will be worse if I have to care for say four or five children staying with me."

He looked at each child and found Junior paying him very close attention for the first time. But he looked away again when Dan looked at him.

Again it was Marian who spoke. "Dad, can Junior and I come and stay here?"

"Why do you want to come and stay here?" he asked her.

She shrugged. "Because you are our father. Because this is our home too, isn't it?"

Poor me, Dan told himself. He had this critical daughter leading the interrogation and this blank faced son observing the process. Junior was listening to him with obvious interest in what his answer would be, he was sure.

"No, you can't come and stay here," he told them, knowing that Marian would have additional questions.

He waited for the questions but Marian initially just sat there looking at him. Junior did the same, with no hint what his feelings were.

This time, in the game of waiting out the other, he won as Marian asked, "Dad, why can't we come and stay here?"

Dan smiled but the children did not smile back. "Several reasons, Marian. I can't walk up to your mother and say I want the children to come and stay with me and she will say sure, have them. If I want you to come and stay with me, I will have to fight your mother and fight her in court. It won't be good for any one of us. It won't be good especially for the two of you. It will be an interesting case in Tamale and the press, both radio and the newspapers, will take up the story and follow each court session. Each hearing day will attract hundreds of people. They will watch you as you come to court. Of course they will watch your mother and me as well. Your story will be all over the school. You will be a story to your school mates and wherever you go people will follow you with their eyes and giggle and have fun at your expense. The eyes of the crowds will bore through you each day you are coming to court.

"The family will provide drama for the town and for the country. Do you want that?"

The children said nothing.

He went on. "Marian, Junior, taking you away from your mother will mean we want your mother to die in a very short time. If we go through that painful and ridiculing process successfully and the two of you are taken from your mother to come and stay with me, and your mother has to live with losing you, that fact will shorten her life. Your mother, whatever her faults, took care of you when you were helpless and even gave you education up to this point. Do I want to cause her avoidable pain? The answer is no. Do you want to cause her pain? Do you want to be the cause of her early death?"

"Why do you say Mama will die early if we come to stay with you?" Junior asked. "She doesn't like us."

Dan smiled, hearing Junior talk.

In response he only put his index finger to his lips. "Junior, your mother likes you," Dan assured him. "If she didn't want you she would have dumped the two of you on me many years ago. I know you feel she does not treat you well…"

"She does not treat us like her children," Junior told him. "She does not like us."

"Junior, if anything should happen to either of you and you go on admission to the hospital, your mother will not leave your bedside. It is then that you will know that no matter how much she shouts at you, how much she acts as if she does not like you, she really likes you. If anything should happen to either of you and say you die, your mother will be deeply affected. She loves you in her own way."

There was silence as the children did not answer. Junior was looking at the ceiling, whatever he was thinking not showing through his face.

Without any warning Marian asked, "Will you take Mama back?"

"No!"

The answer did not come from Dan. So both Marian and her father turned to the source of the answer, Junior. He looked back, blank. Dan smiled.

Marian asked, "Why did you say no, Junior?"

"If you want him to take Mama back she has to stop drinking and she has to stop shouting at people."

Dan only shook his head. He smiled and said, "In a way Junior is right. Your mother and I are now two completely different people. Our differences will not make us have a healthy relationship if we came back together. We simply cannot come back together. It is not I not taking her back but she will not want to come back because our lives will be one long conflict."

"Dad, do you have a girlfriend?"

Junior looked sharply first at their father and then at his sister. "You ask a lot of questions, Marian. Why are you disturbing uncle?"

She turned to him. "Who is uncle? Maybe he is your uncle, but he is my father. And I don't know anything about him. How will I know anything about him if I don't ask him questions? Is he your uncle?"

Junior shifted restlessly. He could not look at his father straight in the face.

Dan looked from one to the other, each so different. He smiled. "Junior, I am your father. I am not your uncle. Or do you want me to be your uncle?"

"No, Sir."

"He is not Sir. He is Dad."

Junior looked uncertain.

"Marian, I have a girlfriend."

"But why can't she come and stay with you? Why don't you marry her?" Her mind went to Veronica Baah.

"Why can't she come and stay with me? Because she is still a student and she even needs an exeat to go out of school. Why don't I marry her? The same reason; she is still a student. And she is only sixteen years old. I am waiting till she reaches eighteen."

Both children looked at him. Marian said, "She is only sixteen years old? A student? Which school, Dad?"

"Tamasco."

The two children looked at each other and looked at their father.

"Tamasco?" the children asked together. Marian asked, "In our school? Dad, what is her name?"

"Marian Wepia."

Junior laughed and clapped his hands. Marian got up and walked over to him murmuring, sat next to him and laid her head on his shoulder. "I am not your girlfriend. I am your daughter." She looked up into his face. "You said you cannot take care of children who come to stay here because you will be too busy with your work. If you had a girlfriend staying with you she could take care of them. If Junior and I want to be coming here how will you take care of us? Is it because you are alone that you don't want to take us from Mama or do you believe Mama loves us and if you take us away she will suffer?"

He had thought about the demands of re-establishment of the link between him and the children. It would require giving up some things he loved. It would require his changing some of the routine of his life. Like today when he decided he would not lift a finger to do anything official so that he would be entirely available to the children.

"The two of you are my children," he told them, looking dubiously at Junior. "I will make the time to be here for the two of you when you need to come here. I am your father. I owe the two of you what I don't owe to the children of my cousins. Whenever you want to come here I will have to make the time to take care of you."

"So it means we can always come here?"

Junior flashed him one of those looks.

"No, Marian…"

She protested. "Oh Daddy!!"

"Marian, you are in school. You must concentrate on your studies. Which means you must leave the school only when it is very necessary. When you are not in school, and you want to come here, it is your home. Call me and we can arrange for me to find the time to be here for you. I may sometimes not be there because I travel a lot. I may have committed myself to do something and I can't change it. But whenever I can block the time, when you are not in school and you want to come here, I will be here for you."

"Uncle… Dad, what about me? I am not in boarding school. Weekends I am free. Can I come?"

"Junior, let me know whenever you need to come here. I will buy you a GT phone card and show you how to use it. Call me anytime you need me and we will arrange when you will come."

"Is it true I can call you Dad?"

"Junior, I am your father. Call me Dad."

Junior nodded. His father asked him to come over and he did. His father made him sit next to him and he pulled both children to him and held them in a warm embrace for a few very pleasant moments. It felt heavenly, having the two children pressed to him. Father. What a feeling. It felt good. He wasn't sure acting it – acting father – would be that easy. Or that acting it would make him feel that good. He made a resolution in his heart; if he failed it would not be because he did not try hard enough.

Still holding them in that embrace he spoke, "Marian, you asked if it is because I am alone that I don't want to take the two of you from your mother or if I really believe that she will suffer if I take you away."

Both children sat up.

Dan went on. "I have given you many reasons why I will not try to take you from your mother. One is the good of the two of you. Your mother will not just give you up if I ask for you. She won't. I will have to go to court. As I explained earlier, if I go to court you will be ridiculed. I will be ridiculed but the two of you will be worse. Your grandmother will be coming to court everyday entertaining people with her own concert party performances. You will be at the centre of the drama. It will hurt you. And not just now but for a long time in your life. I will not try to take you from your mother because of you; I will hurt the two of you. I will hurt myself.

"But Marian, believe me that if your mother should lose you it will hurt her. I can provide your needs without taking you away from your mother. I will make the time to be able to be available to the two of you. When you are on holidays we can spend a lot of time together without my having to take you away from your mother."

They sat in silence for a long time. He was not sure whether the children believed him or not but he told himself that there were some things he just had to say no to.

"Dad, why did you and Mama divorce?" That was Marian but the attention Junior gave him confirmed his personal interest in the question.

Dan regarded her for a few moments before he replied. "We have been down this road before, haven't we, Marian? And I told you I will explain things to you one day but not now. I will tell you one day, but that day is not today, I am afraid."

When he went to bring them more drinks Marian looked round the room and the corridor leading to the other rooms. "Dad, why do you call the room downstairs a guest room? What about the other bedrooms upstairs? Aren't they guest rooms too? You sleep in only one room."

"It is the purpose for which the rooms were originally intended that gave them their names. The rooms upstairs are meant for the family. If your mother and the two of you were here, your mother and I would have had the main bedroom. You would each have had one of the bedrooms upstairs. If we had a guest the guest would then have the bedroom downstairs."

Marian shook her head. "This house is big for you alone. And it is very quiet. We live in a single room. The compound is crowded and very noisy. It can be very dirty. The women in the house take turns to wash the bathrooms. Some of the women are lazy and don't scrub the floor properly. Sometimes the floor is slimy and slippery." She looked round the room again.

He did not know if she was complaining about the condition in which they lived as contrasted with the condition in which he lived or she was making a matter of fact statement. He felt sad knowing the contrast between how he lived and how his children lived. He felt sad that over the years he had left the children to live in very poor conditions. Things had to change. He had to change their condition. He had thought about it. He would have to find out what to do for them. It occurred to him that he could not change the condition of the children without the cooperation of their mother. He could not change the condition of the children without changing the condition of their mother.

"Let us talk about the two of you – your education, your future, what you need to support you and what I should be doing for you."

He listened a lot and the children did the talking, Marian mostly and Junior hardly. He asked a lot of questions and developed a lot of ideas. When they had done a lot of talking he led them to the kitchen and set them various tasks, slicing onions and vegetables and blending tomatoes. They helped him to prepare fried rice and spaghetti bolognaise.

While they were cooking he asked Junior, "Can you cook?"

But it was Marian who replied. "Dad, he is a boy."

"So?"

"Boys don't cook."

Dan turned and looked at Junior who kept his usual indecipherable looks.

"You will learn how to cook here," their father told his son. Addressing both of them he said, "Don't believe in any theories of

239

what girls should do and what boys should do. Except get pregnant and breastfeed babies men should do everything women do. Junior, you need to learn to cook, wash clothing and clean the house properly. By that I mean be able to sweep it thoroughly, mop the floor, remove cobwebs and dust the furniture. You need to be able to do that for two reasons. When you enter university you are going to be on your own. You will have a room which you need to keep clean yourself. When you start working you will be on your own. You will need to take care of yourself. If you don't learn now you will be handicapped when you don't have your sister and your mother to do things for you.

"The second reason, Junior. When you marry, you will most likely marry a working woman. You will both spend your day working hard and earning income for the family. Each of you will come home tired. There is no reason why your wife should be the one to still come home and do all the housework. You will need to take part in doing the work. You should be able to cook if you are home and your wife is working. If your wife travels as part of her work and you are left alone with the children you should be able take care of them and the house. So start now learning to take care of yourself and the house. You will learn cooking and taking care of the house here."

On the spur of the moment he told his son, "You will be coming here weekends to help me clean the house and we will cook together. Okay?"

He rubbed a hand over the boy's head and the boy grinned. Marian just looked on amazed and unable to say anything.

He set the table placing plates and forks and knives in three places. Marian sat on his right and Junior sat on his left. He told them, "One of the rules of this house is that everyone eats with fork and knife."

"O-o-o-h Daddy!!" the children said in chorus.

"Mmm! It's so delicious," Junior announced after the first mouthful. "Man pass woman."

Marian protested. "I won't argue because it is Dad." She turned to her father. "Dad, is it because you are such a good cook that you decided not to marry again?"

He smiled. "Before you leave here you would have assigned over ten reasons why I won't marry and why I don't want you to come and stay here. No, Marian. It is because I lived alone for a long time that I learnt to cook."

They spent the afternoon playing games and telling stories. At one time they found themselves chasing each other round the room, Marian chasing Junior and their father preventing Marian from catching him.

He showed them round the house. They spent time under one of the two summer huts he constructed behind the house. He told them he liked to lie on a camp bed under one of them, especially the one next to the big mango tree because of the breeze. Weekends if he did not have work that required the use of the computer or a table, if he only had to read, he preferred to lie in the summer hut and let the air bath him.

At 4:00 p.m. he led the children out to the car to drive them back so that Marian would be in school before the five o'clock deadline for return of students. He stooped and asked Junior to climb on his back. He carried him that way out while Marian protested. "Why carry such a big boy?"

Their father disagreed. "He is a baby."

Marian again protested. "Ah! Twelve years old and he is a baby?"

Looking over his shoulder at Junior Dan asked the boy, "Do you have a younger brother?"

The boy grinned. "No."

"Do you have a younger sister?"

The boy again grinned and said, "No."

Turning to Marian their father said, "Then he is a baby. He is his mother's last child so he is a baby."

Their father opened the door and dumped Junior in the front passenger seat. He went back to bring the things he bought for the children from Kenya.

Junior turned round in his seat and smiling broadly told his sister, "He carried me. Mama will skin me if I asked her to carry me."

"Dad is different," Marian told him. "Let's wait and see but he seems a good man."

Their father was surprised to come out and find Marian standing by the door and not in the vehicle where he had left them. "I also want to be carried," she told her father.

"You are too heavy," Dan protested.

"Junior is heavy too but you carried him."

He stooped and she got on his back. He tried standing pretended she was too heavy and he moaned and moaned. Then he fell on his knees.

"Dad, I am not heavy. I will not get down. You will find the strength to carry me."

In the vehicle Junior was smiling at them, very amused. Their father carried Marian to the car, opened the back door and dumped her on the seat. He wiped imaginary sweat and exhaled deeply. He gave the clothing to the children, jeans and T-shirts with various animals typical to Kenya. Each child had one pair of jeans and two T-shirts. In Bolga the previous week he also bought two pairs of jeans and some shirts and dresses. The children were excited about the gifts. Marian hugged her father from behind.

He drove to Moshi Zongo, guided by the children, where Junior got down. Marian got down and was going to take the seat Junior had vacated when she suddenly screamed at her father to take off. Their mother was nearby and had seen the children get down from the vehicle and recognised their father. She picked a stick and was running towards the vehicle apparently to hit one of the glasses. Marian's shouts alerted their father but instead of taking off he put off the engine and reclined in his seat. People standing nearby rushed and stopped Matilda. She struggled with them but they managed to take the stick from her.

Marian could not understand her father. She did not know why he did not take off but instead killed the engine and settled back in his seat. While the people wrestled with Matilda, Dan got down and Marian watched him with unease. He calmly walked up to the crowd and spoke to his former wife. He was very calm and did not seem to take the threat by their mother seriously and it puzzled Marian.

"Matilda, listen to me and listen very well…"

"Stupid! Get out! Who are you to tell me to listen? Listen to what?"

"You drink but you are not mad," her former husband went on as if she had not spoken. "I would not have stopped you from doing whatever it was that you wanted to do with the stick. But there is something called the law which is intended to protect weak and law abiding people like me from bullies like you. If you hit the vehicle

I was going to park it here and go for the police. They will lock you up till your drinking buddies can bail you. Then they will send you to court where you will be made to pay the cost of damage plus a punitive fine. If you can pay that you will be free. If you can't you go to prison.

"You don't want me to relate with the children. But if you go to prison I will get to keep the children because I am their father. I was a coward in the past and the children suffered because of that fact. I now intend to do the right thing for them no matter the cost. If it means the two of us being at each other's throat be assured that we will bleed to death, if that is your wish."

He walked back equally calmly, leaving a near hysterical Matilda screaming all manner of insults and threats after him. Marian called Junior aside and asked him to visit her the next day in school, after church. For the drive back to the school she was very quiet, unsure of this man who had been all friendly and playful with them all morning and afternoon but suddenly becoming a different person, a hard person, to their mother. The transition from child friendly father to steel husband was too much for Marian's sixteen year old mind. Her initial worries about who their father was came back, even more strongly this time.

When they arrived at the school her father said, "I know you and your brother are going to be worried about the romance between your mother and me. Your mother and I are like a match stick and the part of the match box against which they scratch the match stick to light it. Whenever we come together there will be sparks. I can avoid her. Which means not seeing you and your brother as frequently as you need me. The second option is to make her accept the fact that I have to see you. And she has to live with it. I could not have made it easier than I did. I have to be hard when being hard is necessary."

All Marian could say was a meek "Yes, Dad."

When they were leaving his house Marian had decided that on arrival on campus she would invite her two friends to come and meet her father. With the state of her mind after what happened in their house that thought perished. It came back after he had driven off. She turned and stood there looking at the receding vehicle hoping something would make it come back. Nothing made it come back.

243

She bowed her head in thought as she walked to the dorm. The contrasting images of her father kept flashing before her mind's eye. The quiet, intense looking man who drove her from his office to school when she first met him. The firmness in his voice when he told her he would see her either in the school or in his office and not his house. The irritation in his voice when she called him on the phone for the first time and he asked if she did not have a name. The impatience in the same voice when he asked why she was calling him if there was no problem with the cheque. His almost admitting he did not miss them when she put that question to him. His admission that he did not like to have children in the house. Then, worse still, this calm disposition when their mother was certainly going to bash the windscreen of the vehicle. And even worst still the very calm manner in which he had threatened their mother. Threatened, to her, that is.

Then flashes of other, positive, images. That he did not argue when she told him who she was. She accepted the queries he made as necessary. His settling her fees for the two years without arguing. The extra amount he gave her. The help he got for her to enable her cash her first cheque. The education he gave her when she first called on the phone. His weeping when she told her story. The pleasant nature of that very morning and afternoon spent with him. His pleasantness when they were with him. His open invitation to Junior to come visiting weekends.

Mercifully the other two Musketeers were not in the dorm and she had the luxury of lying in her bed and continuing to go over the events since her first contact with her father. Who was he? What kind of relationship would they have with him? What should they expect from him?

Dan also spent the evening going over the events of the day. The two children were clearly different. Marian continued to show he would have to learn fast to relate well with her. She would be stubborn but so far she had not exhibited the rotten kind of stubbornness. She would challenge him and he would have to learn to meet the challenge. He was not sure if he would not do something terribly wrong with her. He was haunted by the wrong he had done them over the past twelve years by abandoning them and how they had suffered as a consequence. He was determined not to make mistakes again if he could avoid them but he was also resolved that that resolve should not lead him to do what would make the children go down the wrong road. Would he always know what to do? Not necessarily always; but in critical times would he be able to make the right, the most appropriate decisions? How could he be a positive influence on their lives, doing the right things for them but also knowing when to hold them by the collar of their dresses and pull them back?

Junior. Ah, the unknown personality. His head lolled back and rested on the cushion of the chair. He spent a long time going over everything he could remember about the boy but all that told him very little about him. He was a mystery. His sister had said of him that he was different from her. She was right. And that fact made him even more worried about his relationship with the children. Would their differences affect the way they related with them? Would he relate better with Marian because she was open and talkative and leave Junior behind them? Or would he relate better with Junior because he was not always asking questions and openly disagreeing?

This house is big for you alone. And it is very quiet. We live in a single room. The compound is crowded and very noisy. It can be very dirty. The women in the house take turns to wash the bathrooms. Some of the women are lazy and don't scrub the floor properly. Sometimes the floor is slimy and slippery.

The contrast between his standard of living and the children's standard of living. Things were getting even more complicated than he had ever thought about relating with the children. They could not be left to continue to live the way they were living now. But even as he thought about what to do he did not see an easy way out. If he wanted to take the children from their mother he would have to destroy everybody. Matilda and her mother would fight him for the children. They would create the most sensational court scenes Tamale had ever known. They would put him, the children and themselves at the centre of public ridicule. It would be a painful thing.

He also thought that whatever Matilda's attitude to the children she would suffer more than he would without the children. She needed them and losing them would cause her real pain. He was convinced it could lead to her early death.

So he brings the children home. What did he do? Each would have a bedroom to themselves. They would not lack for any of their physical needs. But he would be away from home a lot. He could cut down on his travels but he could not cancel them altogether. How would they be looked after the many times he would be away from home? What did he do? Marry in order to have someone at home to look after them? But he did not love anyone right now and he would never again marry without love. And he was not sure he would ever love.

Assuming he had someone he loved and married her. What would her relationship with the children be like? Healthy? One long conflict?

So what did he do? Leave them with their mother? It seemed to be the only option.

Mother never talks to us. She is either screaming at us or insulting us. We never do anything right in her sight. Her friends are all drunkards so they are like her. Some of them also shout at us and insult us. But it is mother who makes them insult us so because they are protective of their own children. We are the dust bins into which they dump any garbage they dare not give to their children… Mother spends so much of her money on drinks so that sometimes we don't have food in the house. Sometimes she comes home so soaked with drink when I am in school there is nobody to prepare food for Junior.

Not pleasant conditions in which to leave the children. How did he address that?

Will you take Mama back?

No… If you want him to take Mama back she has to give up drinking and she has to stop shouting at people.

It was true they were so incompatible their coming back together was completely out of the question. From her action when she saw him with the children he was sure she did not consider a relationship with him anything to be interested in. He did not want her either. They could not live together.

So how did he address the condition of the children? He did not have an answer by the time his eyelids were laden with sleep and began drooping. But he did have some ideas. He envied those families which lived together with their children. He envied the fathers. He envied the mothers and he envied the children.

Before his eyes closed in sleep however, a smile started from his lips and spread to cover the whole of his face. Being with the children had not been all challenges. It had been fun cooking with them. It had been fun playing with them after the meal. It reminded him of the words of a French song they learnt in the junior forms in secondary school. *Mon grand père est vieux.* That was the French version of the popular English song *My Grandfather's Clock. Nul enfant sans joie.* It had been translated to mean there is no joy where there are no children. He was not sure how true this was because he felt he had felt joy even without the children but the joy of the afternoon had been different. Maybe they would bring a different kind of joy he had never known before.

In the afternoon of the next day he called on Auntie Gina. She was Regina but the children called her Auntie Gina and Dan called her so too. She was not really Matilda's sister but a cousin of some sort. They came from the same clan in the village. They had a common ancestor several generations back and at the time must have lived in the same house. As the children and grandchildren of the ancestor multiplied they separated and built different houses and started their families. Several generations later the descendents of this common ancestor still came together to perform funerals and sacrifices.

Auntie Gina was a nurse too but a sober one. She was a senior officer and was respected in the Ministry and in the regional hospital.

"What brought you to this my humble dwelling?" Regina asked when her children let him in.

"From my house to the front of your house it was the car that brought me. From there into the house my legs brought me," Dan said looking very serious as he spoke.

Auntie Gina was used to him and only smiled. "Sometimes I forget how stupid you are."

"The next time I am coming I will remember to hold a sheet of paper in front of me that says 'Please remember I am stupid.' "

He accepted water but refused drinks.

"Now tell me why you called to give me ill luck on a Sunday afternoon," Regina told him after he drank the water.

He shook his head. "You know the English believe that if you meet a black cat it will bring you good luck? Well, they also believe that if a stupid person calls on you on a Sunday afternoon you will become a millionaire or you will live for over one hundred years or you will become a millionaire and live for over a hundred years."

Regina was older than him by close to ten years but the age difference did not make any difference to their relationship; they joked with each other. Dan told her the reason for the visit. "Our children have found me…"

Regina cut in to ask, "When you say 'our children' who do you mean?"

"I mean Marian and Daniel Junior. They found me and established contact. You know why I have not seen them all these years. Anyway, they found me and they came home yesterday. And they made me feel very guilty for being a coward and leaving them to suffer all these years while I lived a life of luxury. All that has to change. Their lives have to change. They could change in a number of ways. One is for them to come and stay with me. It will be very good for me and the children." He paused and looked at Regina. She said nothing. So he went on, "But that won't be good for Matilda. She can't survive without the children. She needs them more than I do. I am used to living alone and I am willing to let them live with her."

He paused again but Regina refused to ask questions or say anything. After almost a minute of silence he continued, "But the children cannot live in the condition in which they live right now. She can't afford anything better for them but I can. And if they are not going to live with me she will have to make that change happen. With resources I will provide. But I will be providing the resources because of the children and not for her drink. So she will have to ensure that the children do have enough to eat."

He again paused for a long time and again for that length of time Regina said nothing. "The children will have to have enough in the house to eat and to ensure their basic needs are met. I will pay their school fees, provide uniform and even buy them clothing. I know that if they are sick and they need an operation or need costly treatment I will bear the cost." He opened the purse he had put on the seat and took out bundles of money. "This is two million cedis. It is the first monthly payment because I don't know her bank account. Ask her to give me her bank account and I will give a standing order for the transfer of two million cedis every month into the account."

Regina interrupted him at this stage. "Excuse me, Dan. What are you telling me?"

"That what I am asking of Matilda for the children will require money. And I am going to be giving her two million cedis every month."

He stopped and looked and listened to her.

"Do you know that is more than her monthly salary?" Regina asked not hiding her surprise at the amount Dan was offering to give to Matilda monthly.

He smiled and looked down. "I am proposing to give her what I think is reasonable for their upkeep. I expect her to spend less than half of that on the needs of the children. But I am not just offering to give her money for the children's needs. There will be more than enough left for her to spend as she chooses. That is why I am saying she will have to ensure that there is enough food and soap and things like that in the house for the children to use.

"And there is one other condition," he added. "I need to have access to the children. As I said earlier, the children have suffered enough because I did not support them over the past twelve years. They made me feel guilty when we met yesterday. And I promised myself they should not continue to suffer. I will be giving Matilda the money promised monthly. But I will want to have access to the children so that they can discuss their problems with me. And so that I can support them. Matilda will have to accept the right of the children to have access to me whenever they need me. She should not prevent them from coming to me. And she should not prevent me from seeing the children."

"Why do you think she will want to prevent you from seeing the children or the children from seeing you?"

"I know she will. I am not just thinking. When I went to drop Junior in the house after the children came to me she came threatening to break the windscreen of the vehicle. Some people had to restrain her."

Regina picked the bundle of money and turned it over before putting it back on the table. "Why don't you want to talk to her yourself?" she asked.

"Auntie Gina, I don't expect Matilda to listen to even you. I expect her to argue with you and say all kinds of unreasonable things. As for me she won't even give me the chance to talk to her. And I am not keen to join her to provide free drama to the public."

As she walked him to the vehicle she asked, "What if Matilda refuses to let the children see you or to take the money?"

He paused and looked at her. She could see he was thinking. He was. He was asking himself if he should tell Gina the truth or just tell her that he would wait and worry about crossing the bridge when he got there. "Auntie Gina, I will tell you a fact that I am sure will be lost on Matilda. Marian is sixteen years old. And Junior is twelve. Both are very intelligent children. In the records of the Births and Deaths Registry in the Tamale office I am recognised as the father of the children. If she tries to sit on the happiness of the children, they will make good witnesses on the witness stand. They will convince a judge that their mother is not fit to keep them. In that case instead of the children just seeing me, they will be taken away from her and they will come and stay with me permanently.

"She can refuse the money. I will give it to the children themselves. I will ensure they have food and provisions but that arrangement won't be good for anyone."

Chapter Sixteen

Sunday began in Tamasco with students being roused out of bed very early. It was not an idle day. Two of the Three Musketeers would normally go to church. Leila was Moslem but joined her friends sometimes. Her father was born a Moslem but her mother was converted. Gonjas were both Moslems and Christians. Leila's aunt, her father's younger sister, who was born a Moslem, married a Christian and became a Christian. Her father had a good relationship with his sister and her husband, despite the difference in religion.

When she went to Tamale Secondary and became friends with Marian and Carol who were both Christians she thought of going to church with them a number of times but initially refused to go. She knew that the mosque was a sacred place and not everyone could go inside one, at least not at the time of worship. She thought the church would be the same. When she learnt that it wasn't and her friends encouraged her, she went with them once. And after that she went with them several times later. Whenever she felt like some adventure she went with them.

She asked them questions about some of the rituals they went through. The first time she went with them she joined them when they were making the collection. The church accepted her money. But when they were going out the second time, this time they said for communion since both were communicants, they explained that she could not take the communion.

She learnt some of the prayers, like the Credo, Glory Be To God and the confession prayer.

This Sunday however she chose not to go to church so two of the Three Musketeers went alone to the St Peter and Paul's Catholic Church, which was what the church built inside the school was called. From church they went for breakfast and then the three came together to do their homework. When they were done they grilled Marian for information about the visit to her father the previous day. She told them about his house and the fact that he lived alone.

"He likes music and he has a system that allows him to sing along when a song is playing. He works at home as well. And the house is big. It has three bedrooms and a guest room but he lives there alone. There are security guards. He cooks himself and we cooked together. He is a good cook."

"What food did you cook?" Leila asked.

"Fried rice and something he called Spaghetti bolognaise."

"W-o-o-w!" Leila exclaimed. "Your father cooked it? Really? He must be a super cook. Doesn't he have a girlfriend?"

Marian shook her head. "We learnt that he lives alone and he does his own work. He washes his clothing himself. He has a washing machine but he irons himself. He does his own shopping. He likes to be alone in the house."

"Does he like you? Do you like him?" Leila again asked.

Marian looked at the sky and followed a flying bird before turning to face the two friends and said, "I think he likes us. We played after the meal and he even carried Junior on his back. But he is difficult to read. He will be hard. I like him. At least I can talk to him. I asked a lot of questions and he answered them. I like him but I am afraid of him."

It surprised her friends and she told them of the incident with their mother. But her friends rather admired him for that.

"Look, Number Two, if he is not very hard with your mother she will not allow you to see him. Don't you want to continue to see him?"

"I think he will be good for you and your brother," Carol said, speaking softly. "Besides the fact that you need someone who is hard to force your mother to let you visit your father whenever you need him, the two of you also need someone like that in your lives. My aunt is very loving but she is hard too. And I think I admire her for that."

"What was your mother's reaction to what your father said? And what did she say about your visiting your father?"

"I know she won't be happy but Dad brought me to school when they were pulling Mama away. I don't know what she did to Junior but now that Junior has met Dad I am not sure Mama can bully him. He will threaten to pack out and I am sure Mama will not want us to pack out. Dad also said the same thing about her, that she will not want to lose us."

The question and answer went on for more than two hours.

Junior came visiting Marian in the afternoon as agreed the previous day. He came at the time their father was visiting Auntie Gina. When Marian came into view of Junior the latter stooped and clutched his private parts. Marian rushed over thinking he was in pain.

"Junior! Junior! What happened? What is wrong with you?" she asked in anxiety.

He moaned. "My penis!"

"What is wrong with it?"

"Mama cut it."

"Mama did what?"

"She cut it."

Marian was confused. "She cut it? Why?"

"Do you remember that Mama said if you ever saw Dad she would rub pepper in your vagina? And you said if we see him she will cut my penis. So she cut my penis."

Marian snorted and smacked her younger brother's face jokingly. "When will you ever be serious?"

"But I am serious. Now that she has cut my penis we can pack to Dad's place."

Marian smiled. "You're right. But remember that your father said you cannot come and stay with him. So you can pack out of Mama's place but you won't have a home. And since she has not done what she threatened to do to me I don't have any reason to move out of her house. So you go alone."

"That is not fair," Junior protested. "God created us together."

"Wrong. He created me first and then created you four years later."

When Junior straightened up and became serious his sister asked, "What did people in the neighbourhood say after Dad and I left?"

Junior smiled. "They asked who the man was."

Marian waited for the answer. Junior did not even look at her. Instead he just looked at the students passing them by on either side of them.

When she was sure he would not provide the information she wanted she asked, "What did you tell them?"

He shrugged. "The truth. I told them he is our father."

"And what did they say?" She did not wait on him to tell her when he wanted to because she knew he would not want to.

He again smiled. "They said he is cool."

It turned out when people knew that the children's father was Dan they asked why the children were left with their mother. Some of the children came over to talk to Junior and to tell him what they thought about their father.

Junior gave her another of his famous smiles, one that covered only half of his lips and lit up his face in a way that gave it a mystery that could mean anything. It could mean I won't mind you. It could mean he did not think you serious. It could mean he found you amusing. It could mean you should not bother him. Oh, it could mean anything. "Dad is hard!"

Marian turned and looked sharply at him. It had been her thought too but it surprised her that he observed how hard their father could be and should voice it. "Very hard," she agreed.

"That is good for mother, anyway," Junior said.

Marian thought about it and agreed. "I just wonder why he stayed away from us and mother for this long time. Remember he said he was a coward and that made us suffer. What did he mean?"

As expected Junior only shrugged. And said, "He was nice to us. He played with us and Mama does not even notice us sometimes. We can't go near her."

"What did Mama say after we left? What did she do?"

Junior suddenly stooped and clutched at the crutch of his trousers. "Whew! As I told you earlier she cut my penis."

"If Mama cut your penis you would have either been in the mortuary or a hospital bed by now."

He straightened up and felt his private parts. "It looks like she did not cut it after all."

She sighed loudly and feigned exasperation. "What does a poor girl do with a comedian brother? Put him on a stage to perform drama?"

Junior shook his head and pretended to be serious and said, "No, you buy him ice cream."

Marian was impatient. "Just tell me what she did and stop staging your drama. As for you and Dad one has to beg you people to give them information."

Matilda had continued to rant after Dan had left with Marian. Marian had expected that. She turned her anger on Junior when they went home and would have talked for hours if Junior had not threatened that now that he knew where his father lived if their mother continued to harass him verbally he would pack his things and go to his father. This had brought out a long wail from their mother.

"I am dead in this house. Whoever showed these children that useless man? It is that witch Marian. Whoever told her to go looking for him? Now every small thing I do I will hear the threat of the children packing and going to their father."

"Didn't she tell you that if you pack to your father your father will eat you, or starve you or roast you?"

Junior laughed. "No, she didn't say that."

"But she used to say Dad is a monster, useless and will kill us if we were left with him."

For answer Junior only smiled.

They parted each holding a different view of the side of their father they saw when their mother threatened him. Marian was scared of that aspect of him, thinking he could be very hard on them. Junior was not worried about it. He thought it was good for countering their mother. If their mother realised that she had a strong person who could be stubborn at times to deal with she would soften her attitude towards the children and their father, Junior thought.

Chapter Seventeen

After meeting with the children the issue of Dan's relationship with them became even bigger and more worrisome. He spent the Saturday evening playing back the conversation with the children, pausing on significant issues and thinking hard about them. One outcome had been his decision to address, in the short term, the issue of the condition of the home of the children. He kept expanding what could and should be done, each time keeping a reality check on the ideas. Each time considering what would be Matilda's reaction to the idea and each time looking for options to overcome Matilda's rejection if she would reject it.

As he thought more about what could be done for the children he found his thoughts growing to include what should be done for Matilda. First, he realised that he could not do things for the children to the exclusion of Matilda. Second, he found himself compelled to do things for Matilda as a former friend and a former wife, and not just because of the children. He could not tell when the idea was born but at a certain point in time he felt convinced that whatever the relationship with Matilda in the last days of their marriage, and whatever their relationship since then, he could not block and delete the period of friendship with and marriage to Matilda. She still occupied a place in his life. And unlike the characters typed on a typewriter which can be wiped off by correction fluid, or the characters typed on a computer which can simply be deleted, Matilda could not be blacked out of his life. So that even if they did not have children, if the children both suddenly died, or if they were given over to him, he still had a duty to contribute to make Matilda's life a better one.

He did not reject the thought of supporting Matilda. As was the case with the children he chided himself for not thinking about Matilda earlier and not offering her support much earlier. He was realistic enough to recognise the difficulties in trying to help Matilda herself. He knew how even trying to start a dialogue with her would be like from her acrimonious reaction to him each time he tried to establish contact with her. Later she would even try to be violent to him whenever they just found themselves in the same place. In the alcohol drenched world in which she lived the real world did not exist so practical considerations were impossible. Everything was driven by impulse, surrealism, whims and what an alcohol induced mind caught.

He put together the whole picture of a relationship with Matilda – not love, not marriage, but one in which he supported her – and a relationship with the children and the result was intimidating. It would be taxing on him. Emotionally, and even physically. He did not mind the financial implication. He was convinced the children and their mother deserved whatever they needed from him. That decision led to his visit to Auntie Gina on the Sunday.

Over the week, in the office, as he travelled to Wa and back and as he prepared for the trip to Kenya, he kept going back to the discussions with the children. He amplified the guilt he felt each time and multiplied the fear about what he should do. Could he clearly define it and could he do it? From Marian he learnt that his responsibility as a father was not just financial. He had a lot more non-financial commitments. He did not think that at the time he knew all of them. Or even that he would get to know all of them in a very short time. The fear then was that, even after re-establishing the relationship with the children he would continue to be an irresponsible father. And the risk worried him.

Now in the air his thoughts were still about the children and the time they had together the previous Saturday. Did he love children? Marian had inferred that he did not. *Did you miss us? You don't like children, do you?* Did he love children? He had confronted this question several times before but could not answer it. He liked children, he was sure of that. He played with children of the staff whenever they came to the office. He took infants and played with them. He would take toddlers and try walking with them either round the office or the grounds. In the family home in Navrongo he played with children but was not intimate with them. Ntim's children liked him and he enjoyed being with them.

But if he had to answer the question if he loved children, he could not give a yes or no answer. He liked or tolerated children. Did he love them?

Did he love his children? Another very difficult question. As he thought and thought over the answer he found himself asking another question. He initially did not want to even raise it because it seemed counter to general thinking on the issue of parent and children relationship. But he was not afraid to ask and confront questions on issues thought to be closed. He was not afraid to challenge generally accepted thoughts. So he asked himself the question: must a parent love his children? It initially sounded heretic but he explored that heresy nonetheless. The heresy did not appear as such to him when he considered what love was supposed to be and how it came about.

What was love? Another of the many questions he had not been able to answer. He was frank enough to say he did not know what love was. He married at the time he married because it was convenient, an automatic thing to do. He could not say he was conscious enough of his feelings and that it was the nature of the feelings that dictated his decision to move in and live with Matilda and refer to her as a wife. He was not even sure if he initiated the process or if it was Matilda who invited him to move in and he said yes. Whatever the case may be he was not sure love was a factor in their relationship.

He was also sure he was not even aware of the children during the four years he lived with them after Marian was born. In his younger days in the senior forms in secondary school and at the university drink had been his love. He did not recall any strong feeling for any girl he could describe as love. Over the past ten years or so, he did develop what he would call lust for some women. He did develop some kind of feeling of like, strong like and even desire, for some women. Did he ever love any of them? He was unsure about love. In the course of running the leadership training, especially when he took up training on women as leaders, he had met many women he admired. He did admire and did like some of them strongly. Some were an inspiration to be with and he could be with them for a whole day, just engaged in conversation. Did he love any of them? He thought he did not.

What was love? He had been made to understand that love was something you felt, that came automatically out of your heart. It was an emotion and not something you deliberately called up. And he understood that was why a man could find a woman beautiful and good mannered and all that and not want to marry her because he *did not feel love* for her. It was the same with women. Marriage, the counsellors advised, must be founded on love. And love was something you felt, not something you called up.

So he would question a man who did not love his wife. A man was supposed to propose to a woman for whom he *felt strong enough* love. And the reason for his wanting to marry her would be that he was convinced he felt enough love for her he wanted her to live with him. He would question the person up to a point and not beyond that. Because if love was a feeling that was not rationally called up, it could change.

So you marry because you are certain you feel love. And you love her because something in her lets loose a certain train of feelings in your heart. Love is a reaction to a stimulus from the woman. And in a woman it is a stimulus from the man. So you must love your wife. What about your children? In their case are you expected to automatically experience love for them? In the case of relating with children was love not expected to be stimulated?

He did not ask these questions to absolve parents of their responsibility to their children. He had no doubt that people who decided to have children must understand and accept their responsibility to the children. And this responsibility included being there when the children needed them, meeting the different needs of the children including physical and spiritual needs. Obligations of parents to children he did not find controversial, but he was not sure about the obligation to love them. But he also held that even in the absence of an obligation to love children, every parent had an obligation to care for their children.

As the plane's engines droned high up there in the skies, Dan continued to engage in his exploration of love and his relationship with his former wife and his children. He became conscious of the headache only when it had grown so intense that he needed to act on it. He always carried first aid medicines wherever he travelled and he now fished out some analgesic and asked for some water.

Dan knew he would be met. He also expected it to be a driver or a junior staff of the bank. Since they did not know each other he expected to be welcomed in a manner one sees commonly in airports around the world. He expected to see someone holding a paper that announced his name. But he did not know which name to expect. Dan. Or Daniel. But he thought Dan or Daniel was too common and they would know that they could be more than one Daniel on the flight. It might either be Dan Apeatu or just Apeatu.

He was right. It was just Apeatu. But it was a lady who held the card and that surprised him. He rolled his trolley towards the woman now that he saw who was waiting for him. It was the smile that drew his attention – the woman holding the paper with his name was Diane. He almost screamed her name. So the bank did not send someone for him after all. Or maybe Diane offered to come instead.

She met him and hugged him, kissing first one cheek and then the other. It was the first time since he had known her that she had done that to him. She introduced another Daniel, the driver of the National Trust Bank who had been sent to come for him. Dan Apeatu shook hands with him and introduced himself.

"As your hostess I thought I should meet you at the airport."

"Mrs Murungi is my hostess, not you."

"If I come to Ghana, it doesn't matter what I come to do, you will be my host. Here in Kenya I am your hostess. For this training session especially since we are working together I am your hostess while you are here."

Dan refused the front seat and chose to sit at the back with Diane. Daniel the driver was a very good driver and he drove very carefully but able to weave his way through vehicles to change lanes if it was necessary. They were booked into a different hotel, Fairview Hotel, and not Silver Springs which he knew very well. Dan thanked the driver when they got to the hotel and thought Diane would have gone with him since she did not have a car. But she said she had. She had brought it and parked it in the hotel and had then been picked by the NTB driver to the airport.

She stood by when he filled the form at the reception. She talked to the receptionists, explaining the fact that a suite had been reserved for him.

"What do I need a suite for?" he asked. He had never in the past taken a suite.

"Well, NTB thinks you should stay in a suite."

He looked at her for a few long seconds but chose not to say anything.

"NTB decided that all the staff attending the training will stay in the hotel," Diane informed him. "But they are not checking in till tomorrow. I will be checking in tomorrow as well."

"Are you coming into residence this time?"

"Yes, and so is Mary. She is taking a suite too. She wants to take active part in the training, both as the Manager responsible for HR but as a learner as well. So she will participate in all the sessions but thought they might be some evenings she would want to discuss an idea with us. And the time after supper would be ideal for such meetings."

She came into the lift with him when the boy took the key and his luggage. He wanted to ask if she was going into the room with him but it seemed obvious and he kept quiet. She examined the room and its facilities, giving it a good pass mark.

"Are you going to bath now?" she asked him, sitting on the bed.

He looked at the watch and it was only three in the afternoon. "No, I will bath in the night, not now."

"I was going to leave you to change if you were going to bath." Since he was not going to bath now, she leaned back on the bed, resting on the left elbow. "So how was Ghana? How is your family? How was work and how are your staff?"

While they exchanged greetings Dan opened his suitcase and brought out what needed to be taken out. Diane informed him, "I will come back for you at seven o'clock. Mary invited you for supper in her place. I accepted on your behalf. We actually competed for the honour to host you this evening. I let her have you since you have been to my place before. We have lunch at my place next Saturday."

Dan turned to face her. "Can I ask for one small favour from you?"

"Of course. Please ask."

"Since you knew you could act on my behalf, can I ask you to go and have the supper on my behalf?"

She snorted. "I am very happy to do that for you. I only hope you will return the gesture. I have also been invited. Since I am going on your behalf and can't eat two portions, will you be kind enough to go and take my place?"

He had turned and was removing things from the suitcase. He walked to the bed and laid down three sets of clothing. One set had Diane's name pinned to it. The second set had Mr Orengo written on it while the third had Mrs Orengo on it. Diane was so embarrassed she could not say anything. She told herself she should have known that Dan would bring her gifts. She could not have known about her parents' gifts but she would have known he would bring her gifts if she had only thought about it. If she had she would not have followed him to the room. Even though Dan was not even thinking about it, she felt as if she had escorted him to his room to take what he brought for her. She felt so uneasy with herself.

Something for each member of her family. And in each person's set of clothing there were a number of items. She quickly checked hers and there were again three different dresses. Her mother had two and her father had two as well.

Because he had it in his mind to sew clothing for them, Dan critically observed Diane's parents when he was with them the last time he came to Kenya. So he could find people whose build was same as Diane's parents when he went to see the tailor and dressmaker. So he was sure their clothing would fit them.

He escorted an embarrassed and silent Diane downstairs. He was going to walk her to her car but when they got down they found Mary Murungi at the reception. She held out a hand. "I came to welcome you," she said with a smile.

"You are giving me such a royal treat. Diane was at the airport with the driver from the bank. My room is a suite. Diane told me you have invited me to supper this evening. And finally here you are in person just to welcome me. I feel like a Duke. Except that there are no dukes in my village."

They shook hands and took seats at the reception and exchanged greetings.

"Please come up to my room," Dan told the two women. Mrs Murungi looked at Diane but she only smiled back.

In his room he again took down his suitcase and opened it. He brought out two dresses he brought for Mrs Murungi and two shirts he had brought for Mr Koech.

Diane was sitting on the bed and Mr Murungi joined her on it. She fingered the materials and examined the embroidery. "Daniel," she said after a long silence, "if I didn't know Ghana I would think that Ghanaian designed clothing is very cheap. But I worked with Barclays Bank before coming to work for NTB. I spent one month in Ghana and therefore know a little about cost of living in that country. And especially the cost of clothing because I was interested in Ghanaian designed clothing. I therefore know that it cost you a fortune to buy me and Mr Koech the clothes. We are paying you for the service we understand you will provide to our staff. We are not doing you charity. Why will you want to spend so much of your fees on us?"

Dan was seated on the writing table and calmly looking at Mrs Murungi. He crossed and uncrossed his legs. "I know you are the HR Manager of NTB and the coordinator of this training. But your official responsibilities would not include hosting me, would they?"

There was silence in the room as Diane pulled a pillow from the bed and laid back, completely lying down. Mrs Murungi said nothing and Dan went back to his suitcase and locked it.

"I initially wondered why you carried a big suitcase for a week's training. Now I know it contains mostly gifts."

Mrs Murungi said appropriate thanks.

Supper was fantastic. The Murungis had four children, two boys and two girls. Mr Murungi was a lively man and talked as if he had known Dan for more than ten years. Dan was grateful for his nature because he did not have to speak. He was happy to listen and laugh.

Diane insisted on coming for him for church service on the Sunday. She came dressed in one of the new dresses he brought her. It looked very nice on her. They met her parents in church, dressed in the clothes Dan had brought them. They looked very nice in them as well and the look on their faces said all the thanks they needed to say. From the church they drove to the old couple's home for lunch which mother and daughter cooked. After lunch they sat together for a chat and talked for more than two hours. Dan was like a son to the couple and he found them very pleasant company.

From the parents' house they drove to Diane's where she picked the bag she had packed for her stay in Fairview Hotel. The two spent the afternoon and part of the evening going over the sessions they would lead. They met most of the participants during supper that evening. They had met most of them during the trip to the bank's branches for the assessment and knowing them before hand was helpful.

When the participants walked into the training room the next morning they were welcomed by South African music which changed to Malian music before the day's first session began.

Mr Murungi kicked the process start by explaining how the training came about. She explained what had been observed as the need for the training which had been confirmed by the assessment that Dan and Diane did. She stated her confidence in the two facilitators after observing them train other people and having had the chance to listen to those earlier participants state their impression of the sessions. She said she expected interesting and undemanding sessions at the end of which she expected the staff to have learnt a lot. She said management's interest was not just in staff participating in the training. Management interest was not just in what staff would say they had learnt at the end of the training. Management was interested in both plus the exhibition of positive leadership attitudes informed by what they had learnt.

"Thanks a lot, Mary Magdalene," Diane said after Mrs Murungi handed over to the trainers. "Good morning and welcome to the first of the five days we will be spending together here. My name is Diane Orengo. I worked for many years as the Gender Coordinator of an NGO. My background is in NGO work and not financial institutions. But four year back I had the opportunity to participate in a leadership training session which completely changed the direction of my career. That training is one of the most important events to have occurred in my life. And now four years later I am happy to be training other people.

"Daniel Apeatu is Ghanaian and a leadership development consultant. He developed the contents of this training that we are going to take you through. He has intimate knowledge of leadership issues on the continent having trained people in many African countries.

The first training session I attended brought together twenty-five of us, all women, from about twenty African countries. We each found the training so useful that not even one of us missed the follow up training. We have since been in touch with each other and it has been very interesting, and even motivating, knowing the changes each of us has gone through as a result of the training.

"I am therefore happy to be part of this team of two that is going to try to influence your view of things in such a way that you will each discover the potential in you, develop a very positive vision of who you want to be and confidently chart the path you want to take to your desired destination. I am even happier that I am going to try to undertake this rather interesting task working with the man who influenced me to make this most dramatic change in my life.

"Like Mary Magdalene, I am equally confident that we will enjoy our five days together. We will not ask you to do anything you cannot do. But we will ask for your cooperation in contributing experiences for the learning process. At the end of the five days how rich in knowledge we would have become would depend on how much we have collectively contributed. Let us therefore be generous in sharing our experiences as the learning will be derived from the experiences we share."

She turned to Dan. "I will now invite my mentor and co-facilitator, Dan Apeatu, to lead us to introduce ourselves."

Dan shook his head as he got up and the participants followed him with curious eyes. "Thanks, Diane." Turning to the participants he said, "But I will strongly advise that you ignore all that Diane said of me and don't expect very much from me. Diane and I make a good team and I am proud to be facilitating this training with her. I am confident that we will make the sessions as interesting and beneficial as possible as I am sure your contributions will ensure that we all learn a lot at the end of the five days. Between all of you, you have enough experience to make us leave here very rich in our knowledge of leadership. So while I ask that you moderate your expectations of me, and your expectations of Diane, I have very high expectations of you. I assure you, however, that the expectations are not unrealistic."

He paused and looked at the NTB staff as they murmured about this last statement. "In a learning process such as what we are going to go through in the five days, we need to work as a team right from the beginning. We do that through more intimate knowledge of each other. It can however be assumed that staff of the same institution some of whom have known each other for more than five years would have intimate knowledge of each other. The assumption is sometimes, but not always, true. Let us have two volunteers to do an exercise for us. I want two people who think they know each other very well to volunteer for this exercise."

After some hesitation and murmuring two ladies, Rose and Mavis, stood up.

"How long have you known each other?" he asked them.

"Six years," they both replied.

"How well will you say you know each other?"

"Very well," one said.

"Very, very well," the other said.

He made them stand about five metres apart and facing each other. He gave each of them a card and a marker pen. He asked Rose if her parents were still alive and she said yes. "If you walked into a quarrel between your parents, which of them would you believe was the cause of the quarrel, your mother or your father?" He turned to Mavis and asked her to anticipate what her friend's answer would be and write it down. The participants were amused that Rose took a long time writing while Mavis was done in less than a minute. He collected the cards and read them. Mavis wrote that she expected her friend to blame the mother for the quarrel. Rose wrote that neither of her parents liked provoking the other so she would make inquiries about the cause of the quarrel first. The staff laughed.

Now he asked Mavis to write down her most preferred dress colour and why she preferred it. He asked Rose to also write down what she thought was her colleague's most preferred dress colour and why she preferred that colour. He collected the cards and read them. Rose said Mavis most preferred black because it was a simple colour. Mavis said she most preferred green because it represented fertility and blended well in most environments. The staff roared with laughter, Rose and Mavis laughing the loudest.

"Did we learn anything from the two exercises?"

They poured out the lessons they had learnt and both Diane and Dan knew they had a team that would participate actively in the learning process.

"The exercise we are going to use to introduce ourselves is called Three Truths and an Untruth," Dan told them. "Each of you will say four things about yourself. Three of those things will be true while one is false. Please say things that will let the other staff learn something fundamental about you. Everybody knows your position in the bank. You probably all know who is married and who is not married. You probably all know who is Luo, who is Kikuyu and who is Maasai. So don't say things that are obvious to the others."

He offered to start. "Diane already told you my name. It's Dan Apeatu. I am Ghanaian. Four things about me one of which is not true. One, I come from a large family in which there were six educated members before me. Two, I was a drunkard somewhere in my life. Three, I am my parents' only child. Four, the ethnic group I belong to is one of the smallest in Ghana. Which one of those statements is false?"

Mr Murungi was sitting next to Diane and she turned to ask if she could tell which was the false statement. "He certainly has never been a drunkard before. Even though I know he drank before he was not a drunkard. And he doesn't even drink now."

"I thought so too," Mrs Murungi said.

When hands went up and he called the first person it was the one she said was false. She said he had never been a drunkard before.

He smiled. "Does anybody have any other thoughts?"

"You are not an only child," someone suggested. And yet another one suggested that the ethnic group he belonged to was not small.

He smiled and told them, "I am my parents' only child. I don't have siblings. I come from a very small ethnic group, one of the smallest in Ghana. I got introduced to alcohol in secondary school. It was and still is common practice for young people to drink, but moderately, where I come from. However, in Sixth Form I drank more than moderately and in university really developed an addiction to strong drinks. When I started working I became a serious drunkard. I got so drunk many nights I could not make it home and spent the night in the bushes on the way home. When I kicked the drink problem I also found the leadership course and it transformed my life."

You could almost see eyes straining to pop out of their sockets. He went on, "I come from a large family but am the first educated person from that family. I am the first in the large family to have tertiary education. I thought that would have been easy to pick as I am sure a lot of you are pioneers in education in your families as well."

Mrs Murungi looked at Diane but she only shook her head.

The exercise was very successful and very revealing. The staff started clapping spontaneously when the last person had finished with her introduction.

In the evenings Diane and Dan went over the day's sessions and picked issues to address in the subsequent sessions. They agreed to create a session for those that could not fit into any of the remaining sessions. On the Wednesday evening Mrs Murungi joined them for a discussion that lasted till almost midnight. The response from the staff had been more positive than Mrs Murungi had expected. She therefore thought she could take advantage of the interest to develop follow up training sessions, sessions that would build on what the staff would learn from this first training. She wanted to know if the pair of training facilitators could think of issues that would be covered in follow up training. Dan explained that the content of any further training would only be determined by the staff and the bank. They would have to find out what the staff thought were areas of further interest and what their overall future interest was. The content would also be determined by what the bank thought was its objective in developing this group of staff.

"For a one off training like this," he explained, "the exercise we conducted was enough. If you think the staff would want further training and if the bank would support it, I will suggest a more comprehensive leadership development plan. This will be based on the bank's long term vision for the staff. There will need to be a framework within which the training will fit. You started with this group. Is this the only group the bank will target for leadership development? And for how far in leadership? We could do a presentation on possible options to bank management. Management can look at its overall HR policy and resources available and make choices. But if you can afford you will need to train more than this group of staff.

"One limitation of most training on leadership is that nothing is done about the followers. But followership development is becoming as important as leadership development. And for good reasons. One, the future leaders of any organisation would include some of its current followers. Increased appreciation of their role as followers makes them better leaders as they understand followers better. Secondly, it has been recognised that success in any situation requires not only appropriate action by the leaders but appropriate action by the followers as well. A good leader leading a pack of very bad followers will always be one mile ahead of the team. The team can only make very slow success. The importance of followers is increasingly resulting in training programmes to develop the quality of followers…"

Both Mrs Murungi and Diane were open-mouthed when he finished. "I hope I haven't precipitated a landslide that will bury me," Mrs Murungi said.

"No, I am sure you have started something you should be proud of in the very near future," Dan assured her.

Mrs Murungi praised the two trainers and told them they made her proud by the quality of their delivery and the impact they made on the staff. She said this was one training she had not worried about from the planning to the current stage. She had never felt anything could go wrong and she had expected the staff to feel relaxed throughout the sessions and they appeared to be just that.

Chapter Eighteen

They called her Auntie Gina. Others called her Mama Reggie. Very few people knew her by her real name. Regina Kaba was a staff nurse when Matilda came to Tamale to attend the Nurses Training College. As an older relative of Matilda living in Tamale and in the profession Matilda was training to enter, she felt an obligation to guide her cousin. She would call Matilda to her house and spend more than an hour giving advice on the pitfalls of the profession and the dangers of the extent of interest Matilda had in alcohol.

"Sadly nurses don't have a good reputation. Many people hold the view that nurses make bad, unstable wives. They hold the view that nurses are fun loving and therefore don't settle down in stable relationships. That is the view already held of the women in the green uniform. Let the public see you with one man today and a different man the next day and it confirms their preconceived view of you that you must be a cheap flirt. It doesn't matter that one of the men is a relative and the other is your friend's husband. That does not mean that if your brother comes to take you out you must say no because of that erroneous perception of nurses. But it does mean that if you take life seriously you will be wary about the way you live your life. You will be cautious who you are seen with in town. You will be cautious the places you go to.

"A lot of people drink alcohol. There is nothing wrong with drink provided it is taken in moderation. Beyond that it is not good for anybody but it is even worse for a young spinster. It can give you an image that is negative, so negative nobody would want you for a wife. If taken in quantities that are not moderate it can lead you to do things that are inconsiderate…

"Enrolled nursing is regarded as auxiliary to nursing. But it gives you a foothold on mainstreaming nursing and a career in health. There are opportunities for you to sit the GCE privately. Many Enrolled Nurses have obtained GCE passes and gone on to become State Registered Nurses. I will advise that you take the Enrolled Nursing as the starting point of your career and not the final stop…"

Regina was an interesting woman. A single mother of two, she told younger women that she learnt a lot from her experience. If she had the opportunity to wind back time her life would have been different. She did not want others to go through her sad experience and end up the way she had. She therefore shared her regrets with anyone who had ears to listen and to advise them against doing certain things. She was a rare woman, willing to prevent others from treading the path that led to her current destination which she did not like. Some people would be happy to see others walk down the slippery path on which they had slipped so badly, waiting to see their destruction. Not Regina. She drew a lot of women to herself, gave them advice and a shoulder to lean on whenever they needed anchor in bad weather.

She did not reject those who rejected her advice. She did not shut the door on anyone who did not listen to her and later suffered as a consequence. If the person turned to her, she welcomed her and gave her support. That way she had been able to help many women learn from their mistakes or get over their misfortunes and turned their lives around.

Unfortunately it did not work with Matilda. Her advice to Matilda during her student days against drink and the male company she kept was not taken. She cautioned Matilda continuously about the way she gave herself up to men and her love for drink. When Matilda was raped, Regina stood by her, inviting her to her house and helping her nurse her feelings. She took her to see a doctor for a confidential test for STDs. She visited her in her room and made her feel accepted. She used the painful event to remind her of the advice she had been giving her in the past. Matilda seemed at the time to listen to her and to find value in what she heard. But later events did not suggest she heard anything Regina said.

Many younger nurses and young women in Tamale found Regina a loving mother whose house was home to them. Sadly, her closest relative did not find her a mother and did not find a home in her house. Their relationship over the years had not improved. Regina never gave her up and would stand by her if she needed it but she stopped trying to influence her life.

When Matilda met Dan and they started their drinking relationship Regina felt sorry for her, convinced the relationship could only deepen Matilda's drink problem. When they declared themselves married Regina saw prospects for Matilda so she called her and advised her. She told her that her husband had a very good future both in the Ministry and outside the Ministry.

"But that bright future can remain an illusion for the two of you and your children if he continues to drink the way he does. You can help him give up drinking and turn his and your future into a very bright one. But before you can help him give up drinking you have to stop drinking first. Only then can you influence him to stop. If the two of you go on drinking the way you do now I don't see how you will raise a healthy family."

Regina had thought that her cousin's relationship with Dan was God sent after all. She doubted if any man would have married her with rape in her records and an addiction to strong drinks. If she could give up alcohol and then help transform Dan, which Regina was willing to help her do, then she would have had a gift she could not otherwise have dreamt of. She continued to advise Matilda but over time the latter became openly defiant.

When Dan was packed out of the house Regina sat with Matilda on three occasions to find out what the problem was. As with other people who tried to intercede to save the relationship she told her cousin that there was no reason and she did not need any reason to terminate the relationship. Or did she? Regina agreed she did not.

Initially when the marriage ended, Regina sat with Matilda to discuss the relationship between the children and their father but Matilda would not listen to her. She screamed at her when she wanted to point out the difficulty she would face bringing up and educating two children on her salary as a junior nurse. Regina would know because she was bringing up two children as a single parent. And she was a senior nurse, not one at the bottom of the rung like Matilda. She tried to explain to Matilda the difficulty she would be creating for the children if she cut them off from their father. She pointed out to Matilda that she had no right to dim the brightness in the future of the children by preventing their access to their father when she could certainly not provide their needs. The first meeting had ended up in screams from Matilda. The other two times did not end in screams as Regina came prepared not to push too hard if her cousin would not listen to her.

When Matilda's mother visited her daughter Regina thought the older woman would be more reasonable but found in her an even more unreasonable and stubborn person to deal with. In fact the woman had called her names, asking why she thought Matilda could not care for the children if Regina looked after two children without the help of their father. She had swallowed the insult to explain that she was telling them how difficult things would be from her experience. Secondly she was a senior nurse and earned more than Matilda did. She also did not spend so much of her income on drink but she still found it really hard to meet the cost of the family of three alone. She told Matilda's father her fears when she went home but his wife seemed too much in control of Matilda that the old man had been unwilling to interfere.

So Regina sat on the touchline and watched the sad story of her cousin and her children. A number of times she wanted to intercede on behalf of the children and let them meet their father but the wrath of Matilda and her mother prevented her from doing what she knew was right. If Matilda's father feared his wife and daughter she did not see wisdom in her invoking their wrath.

She thought of supporting the children but could not do so as the burden on her was more than her resources could meet. In addition to the two children she had to bring up and educate, she was solely responsible for the upkeep of her aged parents. Her father was asthmatic and her mother had high blood pressure. She had to keep sending them the appropriate drugs, ensuring that they had enough drugs by them all the time. With advanced age their father suffered more frequent attacks and so could not do a lot of the work that he did when he was younger. Regina had a brother who stayed at home with the parents but the term useless did not adequately describe him. He would have put his weight on Regina if she allowed him. He could not even take care of his children and it was his wife who had to work extra hard to support the children. Sometimes the husband would take money from her, resulting in quarrels. He accused the wife of being hard fisted, hoarding her money while he suffered. In addition to the rainy season farming, his peers cultivated vegetables under the Tono Irrigation Project. He was too lazy for that. His peers raised poultry and livestock, mostly small animals, goats and sheep. Regina asked each time she went home but at no time could anyone point at a single fowl or guinea fowl that belonged to her brother.

With so much responsibility on her she could not afford to support Matilda's children. When Marian confronted her one day about their father it put Regina in a tight corner. Someone had told her that their father was well to do and was very helpful to others. She told Marian that if they contacted their father he would take care of their education. But their mother had warned the children never to contact their father. She had told them many horrible things about their father. Marian contacted Regina to tell her the truth about their father and to seek her advice about contacting their father. She explained the difficulties their mother had paying her fees especially. Regina had thought for a long time, unsure if to tell the girl what she knew to be the truth about their father or if to evade the question altogether. She was not sure what would be the reaction of Matilda. And what her mother would do as well. Both still referred to Dan falsely as a useless man even when he was reformed and was now doing very, very well while his former wife was still leading a meaningless life. In the end Regina chose truth over fear. And she told Marian that she thought their father would be willing to help them.

Despite her belief that Dan would help his children she had not expected the decisions he had made about supporting Matilda. Two million cedis was a colossal amount by all standards. She could not tell how many men living with their families gave that amount monthly for the housekeeping. It was more than her own salary. That was very generous.

He was right about one thing, though. He could not have approached Matilda and asked for a discussion on his supporting the children. She would not hear it. Regina could not tell why Matilda and her mother wanted the children to have nothing to do with their father when she could not support them. She was struggling to keep Marian in school. She complained several times about Marian's unpaid fees. Many a woman who was separated from a man with whom she had children would even take the man to court to support the children. Matilda and her mother would not want the man to support the children.

Now she had a big task in her hands, take the first remittance from Dan to Matilda and to convince her to accept this and the subsequent remittances. Most women would have been ecstatic. Matilda would threaten World War Three from this gesture. Regina was very happy for the children. Their father seemed determined to maintain his relationship with them. He had not threatened but she understood from their chat that he would not be stopped from seeing and supporting the children. Whatever it was that had kept him from seeing and supporting his children he was now doing the right thing for them and their destiny was sure to change for the better. She was happy for them. She would have been happy for Matilda as well but Matilda did not even know what was good for her let alone appreciate it.

It took her many days to be able to agree on the best way to talk to Matilda. She consulted her trusted friends and sought their advice. So for more than a week after Dan had given her the assignment she had not been able to meet Matilda. Dan was far away in Kenya holding his training for the staff of the National Trust Bank when Regina decided to meet his former wife.

She decided not to see Matilda in her house and to see her at a time she was sober. So she went to the ward she worked in and told her she would like to see her when her shift was over. She started to ask what it was about but Regina only told her it was something that required that they went to Regina's house to talk. She asked Regina if anyone from her family was dead but Regina told her if that was so she would not leave it till after work.

There was impatience and irritation all over Matilda when she came to Regina's office when the afternoon nurses took over in the ward. As they walked to Regina's house which was a Ministry of Health allocated house not far from the hospital Matilda harassed her cousin with questions and curses and threats. She talked non-stop till they reached the house. Somewhere on the way Regina also became irritated and asked if her cousin never got tired with talking. Matilda retorted that she did not talk till people like Regina provoked her. If they did not want her to talk they should not provoke her, she told Regina.

"I can't understand people like you," she told Regina who just kept on walking. "Do you think I am mad? Will I be talking to myself or start talking to someone who has not given me cause to talk? You cause me to talk and then turn round and accuse me of talking too much. Who wouldn't talk if someone came and called them to her house without telling them what it was that they were going to discuss? What is difficult with telling me what it is that you want to discuss with me? Am I a small girl for you to just ask me to follow you? You are older than me. Far older than me, I admit but not so old that you treat me like a small girl."

Some silence. Then, "When I talk you won't even mind me. It won't make you tell me what you are going to tell me. I am not a small girl. If my mother or my father is dead why can't you hint me? You are a snob. You treat me snobbishly and then wonder why I talk. I talk to complain. And if you don't mind me I will continue to complain. If I ever came to you and asked you to follow me to my house without telling you why we are going there will you go with me? I am even subservient enough to follow you and then you complain why I should be talking, asking you to tell me what we are going to do in your house. Is it too much for you to tell me?"

Another round of silence. Short-lived though. "Sometimes you behave as if you are my grandmother and not an older sister. You treat me as if I were a very small girl in comparison with you but you know I am not a small girl. I am almost forty years old, remember that. How can you expect me to behave like a pet dog, just trot after you? Do you recognise the fact that I am human and an adult too? No, you don't. You are used to treating nurses like children because you are a senior officer and we always have to say yes Madam to you even if you are wrong. But that is at work. Must you carry that into our personal relationship as well?"

Another spell of silence. Then, "You complain that I speak a lot. But just look at you. You won't be moved to respond to me, to treat me like a human being…"

"Matilda," Regina was forced to make a statement, "I know your mother. I know your grandmother. Neither is talkative. Your mother talks but not non-stop. Your father can be mistaken for dumb. From whom did you inherit this talkative trait?"

Eventually they made it to Regina's house where she offered her cousin a bottle of Star beer. "I know beer is like water to you but that is what I am going to offer you," Regina said when she had poured the beer into a glass for her.

"Look at this!" Matilda exploded. "You provoke me but don't want me to talk. Who told you that beer is water to me? Do you want to tell me that I never buy beer for myself? Who told you that? You provoke me by making false allegations against me and don't expect me to react. You push me to talk and then you turn round to accuse me of being talkative."

Regina put the bundles of money given to her by Dan on the table in front of Matilda and asked her to check it.

"What is it for?" she asked instead of counting it.

"Just check how much it is," Regina insisted.

"Two million cedis," she said after counting it.

"Your children's father came to see me two weeks ago. He gave me a message for you…"

"This money? And who is my children's father? My children have no father."

Regina watched her in silence. Matilda turned the bundles over and looked at Regina but said nothing.

"So how did you get pregnant? You got the pregnancies from drinking water?"

"It is none of your business how I got my pregnancies," Matilda retorted.

"Matilda, you need to grow up and try to see the real world and not look at it through the fog in your eyes. You can say your children have no father. Please yourself till your false world crumbles around you.

"Anyway, yes, he brought the money. But he also brought a message with it."

"I don't want his money." But she did not throw the money at Regina. She kept fingering the money.

Regina laughed. "Matilda, why don't you grow up? I asked that we come here immediately after work because you would still be sober by then."

"You see the insults that provoke me to speak. And when I speak you call me talkative. When am I not sober?"

"When you drink which is most of the time you are not at work."

They argued over this for about five minutes till Regina kept quiet and watched her cousin talk and talk.

"Dan came to see me and gave me a message for you. He gave me two million cedis to be given to you. He said he proposes to give you that amount every month for the upkeep of you and the children…"

"For the upkeep of who? Who told him the children are not being taken care of? How did they survive over this number of years and why can't they survive now? The children don't need his money…"

"You don't need his money or the children don't need his money?" Regina cut in, losing her patience. "You know very well that the children contacted him. And they contacted him because they need him and they need his money."

She threw the money at Regina. "Then let him give it to the children."

Regina picked the money. "He told me that if you said no to the money that was what he would do, give it directly to the children. But as you can see, the children don't need two million cedis a month. So the money is intended for you and the children. But if you say no he will contact the children directly and arrange to give them what they need. The children will not lose. How much of the money he is offering will you spend on the children's food and soap a month? The rest is for you. The children need the money and they will take it. They won't need two million cedis a month so he will have a fat balance from it. He gains. The children don't lose. You lose."

"The children won't touch his money," Matilda said weakly.

"Says who? Matilda, be real. The children will abandon you for their father. They will be happy to be able to feed better at home. They will vote for their father against you. Why fight battles you can't win?"

Matilda was silent. Regina put the money back on the table in front of Matilda.

"Listen, Matilda, and listen well," Regina said, pulling the lobe of her ear for emphasis. "Your former husband is offering a package beyond your dreams. You know that Dan could not see the children because you said he could not see them. You know that he did not contribute to their upkeep because you would not hear it even as you are rejecting his offer right now. You know you prevented him from supporting the children, it was not his fault. You know it."

She continued without giving Matilda the chance to make objections. "Now he is offering to remit two million cedis every month to support you and the children. Every month. For your food and other household needs. He will pay the children's fees. He will clothe them. Those costs are not included in this money."

"He thinks he can buy the children from me? I don't need his money."

Regina got up and walked round her cousin. "You need the money he is offering. You can pretend you don't need it. The children are not so unrealistic. They need the money and they will not reject it. They are not babies and they are not toddlers. They will vote between you and their father with their feet. You cannot prevent them from seeing him. You cannot prevent them from taking money from their father. You cannot prevent their father from supporting them. If he cannot support their welfare in the house through you he will support the children directly. The children will think you a wicked mother if you refuse to take money for their welfare when you are broke most times of the month and the house is empty of food and provisions. When the children were young they were toys and you had control over them you could keep them away from Dan. They are no more the helpless kids you can control. Have you ever considered the fact that they can pack and move out to their father? If they do that what will you do? Their father doesn't need to buy them from you. He can have them for free."

Matilda looked away, saying nothing.

Regina returned to her seat and faced Matilda. "Matilda, since you came to Tamale I have tried to be a good sister to you. I have better relationship with people who are not related to me. But not with you who are my nearest relative. I am still going to try to give you advice even if you won't take it.

"You keep saying that Dan abandoned the children for twelve years. You know yourself that he did not abandon them. He tried many times to have discussions with you about the children but you refused. You can tell outsiders that he abandoned the children for twelve years but you know I know the truth so don't keep trying to sell me that crap. I don't buy it. For twelve years you suffered with the children while their father could afford to support you. You caused yourself needless pain in the process. And caused the children equally needless pain in the same process. Whatever your reason for deciding not to have anything to do with Dan, that is your decision. The children don't know it. Even if they know it they may not agree with you. Especially not since they are suffering and you cannot meet their needs."

Matilda made to interject and Regina paused, but her cousin thought about it and changed her mind and closed her mouth instead.

"I know what you wanted to say," Regina went on. "You were going to ask me who told me the children are suffering. You can pretend all is well with you but you can't pretend for the children. You know very well that they came to me a number of times in the past and they would have complained to you about their needs in the house. As I told you earlier, when you meet outsiders you can sell them any story you want but don't try selling me any story that is not true. I know how the children feel. You can deny it here but that won't stop the children from feeling the way they feel. And if they feel unhappy, if they feel you are unable to meet their needs, no matter how strongly you deny it, they will do what they can possibly do to get over their suffering. And if their father can offer them relief they will take it. Be realistic, you are not dealing with infants. You have complained to me about how the children were becoming defiant to you. That was before they met their father. Do you expect to be able to stop them from contacting him whenever they need anything you cannot provide? What do you think will happen between you and the children if you try to stop them from seeing their father? They will fight you. And eventually pack out if they can't stand the situation in the house. Do you want to lose the children? You have been preventing their father from having access to them. Do you want to lose them completely to him?

"Very fortunately for you their father is offering you the means to satisfy them and still keep them with you. He is offering you a package to change your own life, not just the life of the children. To change your own life as well. He is offering you two million cedis a month, more than your salary. Even more than my salary. How much of that will you need for food, soap, pay your light and water bill? You will still have a good balance. I am sure never in your wildest dreams did you ever consider that the situation he is offering you is possible. And now you get it as a gift and you sit before me to bluff. I will advise you to stop being unnecessarily difficult and accept the offer."

Matilda said nothing. She sat there playing with the money and not looking at her cousin.

After more than a full minute of silence Regina continued, "He makes some requests from you, requests I consider valid and reasonable. One, he is worried that you will spend all the money he gives you drinking and the children will still suffer."

"Nonsense. He can't dictate how I live my life."

Regina laughed. "He is not dictating how you live your life. Understand that he lives in Tamale and knows the cost of living. He knows how much reasonable expenditure on food and necessities for you and the children is. He is giving you more than that. Which you are free to spend anyhow. He is not dictating how you spend even the excess of the money he is giving you. But he is right to be concerned about the children not getting their needs despite his remittance. He is acting within his rights to ask that you don't let the children lack what the money can provide. He said he will stop remitting you and start giving money directly to the children if the children don't get basic things like food, soap to bath and wash with, toothpaste and so on…"

"Nonsense! Did the children tell him they lack those? Before he met the children again were they starving? If they were starving they would have been dead over the twelve years that he … that he has not been seeing them."

Regina chose not to contest that. "The second request is that he wants to be able to see the children. He will be paying their fees and he will provide their clothing as well. He wants to support their education and that means he must be able to meet the children and discuss their performance and any help he can offer. If they need anything that is reasonable and you cannot afford it he will want the children to be able to see him about it."

"Did the children have my permission to see him? Or does he not know that I know that they have been seeing him?"

Regina looked at her cousin, thinking that there were certain things about her she had to accept and not expect that they would change. "He knows you know that alright but he also knows that you are against it."

"Why won't I be against it? Why not…?"

Regina told her calmly, "That is what he wants changed. You may not like their seeing him. He can't stop you from feeling the way you feel. I won't either. But there are certain things you have to accept. You will only be punishing yourself if you want to stop the children from seeing their father. You can't stop them. You can't stop even Junior who is the younger of the two children. Marian is now a young woman and it is time you begin to recognise her as such."

For the first time Matilda was forced to face reality. She was defeated and she knew it. It had been there in her subconscious knowledge but that day it was forced into her consciousness. The defiant attitude of the children started before they met their father. Auntie Gina was right; she could not expect to control the children. They were showing signs of rebellion and threatening her with packing to their father. Threats. Would they stop at the threats or would they one day carry out their threats if they were pushed?

She lowered her head in thought and Regina left her to her thoughts. When Regina asked for her bank account number to be given to Dan for the transfer of the monthly remittances she gave it without drama.

Chapter Nineteen

That Wednesday evening it was close to midnight when they went to their rooms. Since Mrs Murungi, Diane and Dan were all on the same floor they went up together and said goodnight. A minute after entering his room Dan's phone rang. He did not pick the handset immediately, unsure who could be calling at that hour and who would have known he had just returned to his room. It continued ringing so he picked it and forgot all his phone manners and said the hello in a manner that could not be described as courteous.

"Are you already undressed?" the voice at the other end of the phone asked.

He hesitated, thinking. Then he recognised the voice. "Yes, I am undressed, completely."

"That is very fast, the fastest undressing I have ever known. Well, I am coming over so you may want to wrap the bed sheet or something around you."

He wanted to ask if she must see him that night but decided not to ask.

She smiled when he opened the door and she came in a minute after she called. "There is a lot about you I don't know. I would have betted my last shilling that you had never been an alcoholic. Nothing about you ever suggested that. This very minute I have discovered something else about you. You have extraordinary speed in undressing and in dressing as well. Less than a minute after you entered your room you said you were undressed already. Now less than a minute after the call you are completely dressed. Great record."

He had nothing to say to such beautifully packaged sarcasm.

She did not come into the room but leaned against the door. "Dan, it may not be my business but I cannot pretend I have not noticed something is wrong with you. I don't know what it is but I believe something is worrying you. It may not be something big, and I sincerely hope that is so. But whatever the size of the issue there is something on your mind. I thought I should let you know that if there is anything I can do to help, I am available. If it is just the need for a listening ear, please let me know. If you need more than a listening ear, I am still available. Have a good night."

"Diane," he called as she turned to open the door. She stopped. "Thanks. I didn't know I was so transparent."

She shook her head. "You are not transparent. I don't know that many people close to you would notice that you are carrying something on your mind. You bear yourself very well. I am not sure any of the people we interact with every day would know that something seems to be eating you. But I have met and interacted with you three times previously. I am beginning to think I know you. I am also very sensitive, especially about you. That is why I can tell all is not well with you."

He stood there sheepishly looking at her. He looked at her without seeing her. His mind was somewhere and she could tell his mind was somewhere. When he woke up from his thoughts he said, "Thanks. I will remember your availability if I need you. Have a good night too."

She smiled and opened the door and went out. As she closed the door she looked at him through the closing space. He was still rooted to the spot where he stood, his mind clearly somewhere. She wondered what it was that could engage his thoughts in such a captivating way. She had guessed there was something worrying him but initially she thought it had to be her imagination. He was still jovial and as lively as she knew him to be when he did his presentations. He was effective and listened effectively to participants. He had not made any slip so far and she did not think he would make any. But she kept looking at him and sometimes he seemed to temporarily fly away into space, absent from his immediate environment. It did not occur frequently and when it occurred it was not for long. But she had never noticed this in him in the past.

When she thought of talking to him she did not ask if it was her business. It never occurred to her that someone may ask if it was her business if anything worried him. She only hoped that he would say she was mistaken. And that he was fine. His answer confirmed she was right and now being right disturbed her. It worried her that something worried him. She still had him on her mind when she fell asleep but she did not dream of demons chasing him. She had a sound sleep.

He had a sound sleep too when he finally slept. When Diane left him he stood facing the door for a few more minutes, looking at and through the door. He asked himself if he was so transparent. She had said no but he had to be transparent to a certain degree for even the most sensitive to observe he had worries. Earlier at the beginning of his career as a leadership trainer he resolved not to let personal problems seep through his mood whenever he had to train people. He told himself that if he could not get rid of his worries from his face and his communication he had better not go into a training session. He had succeeded very well, he thought. Till now.

Before he slept however, he turned his thoughts unto another revelation from the two minute encounter with Diane. She had a spotlight on him. And she was good at reading him. More than good. *If he needed a listening ear…* With that offer in mind he fell asleep.

It was normal for people in Dan's training sessions to reflect on the process from the third day. It happened during this training as well. On the Wednesday evening, after supper the participants sat in groups over drinks and the topic of their conversation was the training. It was so unlike any they had attended. It didn't seem to ask very much of you unlike other learning and experience building processes. They did not seem to exert themselves.

"You don't really notice how much is demanded of you, how much you are made to work. But now, looking back at the three days so far, I can see we have done a lot of work. We have been made to do a lot, but a lot of very interesting and sometimes obvious work," a participant called Nathaniel told his group.

Agnes, a sharp woman close to thirty years agreed. "They have been seemingly small tasks. They have been seemingly unimportant things. But they generate so much thought when you have gone through them you learn a lot. And the lessons just flow into you. You don't have to strain yourself to see the issues in an exercise."

"I wish all training programmes were like this," moaned George who worked in the Mombassa office. He was not a participatory person and had felt very uncomfortable when they had been told at the beginning of the training that the learning would be derived from their collective experience. "It is so unfair of trainers to impose methodologies we have not been used to on us, and expect that we would be comfortable and good in them. Your primary school teachers make you repeat things till you get them committed to memory. Later in life your teachers lecture you and then pose questions, expecting you to recall your learning and use that memory to answer the questions. In your professional life they take you through the rudiments of your work. They may teach you the theory and practice of your work and later watch you do it under supervision till you are comfortable enough to do it alone. Or till someone is comfortable about your ability to do it alone.

"That is the history of how you have been learning. Then without any practice, you are taken to a session and told in order for the learning to be successful you must magically be able to understand the impediments to your understanding things, remove the impediments yourself and then see what lessons you had previously not been able to see. Using what skills or what experience from the past?"

The group roared in laughter. Very soon the small groups understood they were each discussing the same issue and so tables were joined to form larger groups and the discussions, aided by a few more bottles of beer, became more animated as the evening grew.

"This training is very good but we will need a follow up training."

"We will need follow up trainings, not just one."

It was an interesting agreement because just about the same time, Mr s Murungi was proposing the same to Diane and Dan.

Dan was in the conference room when Diane came down the next morning. After the greetings he told her, "Thanks for many things. One is the offer of yesterday. But one stronger reason is your concern for me to the extent that you notice slight signs of disturbance in me. I appreciate it."

She shrugged. "You appreciate very small things."

He smiled. "Size is relative and it is determined by where you stand to look at it. It may take you very little effort to do a thing for someone. But that act could have such a tremendous impact on the person. Secondly, the value of an act does not depend on its size. If someone voluntarily picks a pebble and told me he wanted to show his affection or care for me but had nothing and was giving me the pebble, I would value the pebble as much as I would value a gift of ten thousand dollars. Why? Because they both represent the same intangible feeling in the hearts of the givers. What I am valuing is therefore what the gesture manifests and not the gesture itself."

"I won't argue with you. You have a very philosophical attitude to life."

"I will interpret that to mean I have a very life-like attitude to life."

She changed the topic. "I have been meaning to ask this you." He stopped working and listened. "Why do you treat my sister so painfully?"

He raised an eyebrow. The question was obvious.

She hit his arm jovially. "Don't pretend you have not noticed anything."

"Oh no, I can't do that. I have noticed a lot of things. You are standing in front of me. You look very fresh, refreshingly pleasant fact considering that you have been working hard for three days now and you went to bed very late last night. You are wearing a pink coloured dress even though Valentine's Day is long past."

"What is your middle name?" Diane asked, looking serious.

He looked equally serious. "I have so many I don't find it easy to choose one when asked."

"Is naughty one of them?"

"It is the most preferred one. That one and Stupid."

Jean was about thirty too. A beautiful woman who seemed to enjoy flirting. But it seemed the relationship she expected to establish with Dan was more than a flirting one. She seemed to have been smitten by a bug for him and she expressed it in many different ways, unfortunately none of them verbal. She stood close to him as often as possible. During the breaks you could find her next to Dan. She would position herself in such a way that he bumped into or brushed against her breasts when he moved. She stood next to him when he went to prepare a cup of beverage. Many times their shoulders touched. Many times their hands touched over the sugar container or when they made to take spoons. She sat at the same table with him more often than any other participant did. She engaged him in idle chat more often than the other participants did. When she was not at the same table with Dan she positioned herself so as to be able to see him. Or even face him. When their eyes met she would smile.

Diane believed Dan was sincerely oblivious of her interest. She was sure he did not notice many of the small details she, and maybe other participants, especially the female ones, had observed. And he did not read anything in the few he had observed.

So she told him. "Jean has her eyes on you."

"Meaning?"

"She admires you. She is either infatuated with you or genuinely in love with you."

He looked at her dubiously.

She turned his face away. "Don't look at me that way. I know it for a fact. And trust my judgement because I am a woman."

He shrugged. "We will be out of here in two days, won't we?"

"Yep! We will. But we may be back together if the discussions with Mary yesterday lead us to further training." She was going to ask what was wrong with love but checked herself. She did not know about his marital status. A question came up in her mind; if she would have him as a boyfriend if he was married. She dismissed it.

Mr Koech joined them on the last day, the Friday. Diane and Dan had planned for the last day to end at 1:30 p.m. From their experience in the past they knew that participants who had homes in Nairobi would want to leave on the Friday after the last session. They may prefer to take supper with their families than eat the hotel's food. They envisaged that if the last session ended early enough even those from places not so far away from Nairobi would want to leave that same day too. With news of the duration of the last day shared in advance, some participants checked out of their rooms during the morning's coffee break and left their luggage in a room provided by the hotel.

The actual training activities for the day ended at midday. The evaluation questionnaire was then administered after which they followed a closing session programme done by Mrs Murungi. Three participants were asked to speak on behalf of the staff. Mrs Murungi would make her observations after which Mr Koech would speak. Then Dan would respond on behalf of the facilitators.

The three participants were agreed on many things. It had not been as tiring as they had expected. They learnt a lot more about themselves and about each other than any of them would have expected. It was interesting to discover that they really did not know themselves and discovery of aspects of them they had been unaware of was very helpful to them. They had learnt a lot to make them develop greater ambitions than they came to the training with and they could see their future development tied to their commitment to the bank. They described both facilitators as humble, very knowledgeable on issues of leadership.

"It is the unanimous decision of all of us that this training is only the beginning of our journey to become true leaders, to be like the two trainers," said Agnes who was one of the three chosen to speak. "I previously asked why they chose to call themselves facilitators and not trainers. But after observing them for five days I think I understand why – it is part of the humility that being a leader makes of you. Let me not go off track. We are all agreed that we have a long road ahead of us. We are determined to travel on that road. None of us will turn back. But we need help from both the bank and the facilitators on our journey. We will need follow up training and we ask both bank and facilitators to commit themselves to this. We will need support from the bank in the form of opportunities to practise what we will need to develop certain skills in us...

"Whatever we become in future, we will remember this training as the turning point in our lives. We cannot thank the facilitators enough for what we have learnt, both lessons and attitudes. Their humility and their practical demonstration of leadership qualities further reinforce the teaching from the two..."

After the other two speakers Agnes came forward again. "To demonstrate in practical terms our appreciation of the gift of knowledge we have received from the two facilitators we offer them, from deep down our hearts, token gifts. We invite them to step forward and receive them."

Diane was given a beautiful dress. Dan was given an equally beautiful shirt, a tie and cuffs.

Mrs Murungi spoke briefly. She was happy to hear the comments made by the three previous speakers. As she sat through the training she had felt the same herself but since the training was meant for all of them she had been anxious to find out how her colleague staff felt. She had had very high expectations of the facilitators having seen them train before. She had been sure she would not be disappointed…

She turned to the issue of follow up training brought up by all three staff who spoke and told them the discussions she had had with Diane and Dan about further training. She had shared this with Mr Koech and she would let him comment on it. The staff clapped both in anticipation of and to force a yes answer from their boss.

Mr Koech was also brief. He told them of his initial scepticism about the wonderful nature of the training when Mary Magdalene first described it to him. He said his doubts disappeared when he had the chance to sit in some of the sessions of a training that the facilitators were conducting at the time. Like Mary Magdalene he had had high expectations from the facilitators. And he knew those expectations had been met when he spoke to some of the staff during the break and when he listened to the three staff speak on behalf of their colleagues. Mary Magdalene had discussed the need for further training with him and between them they agreed the bank would support further training. The staff stood up and clapped. He smiled and went on. They had decided to invite the training team to a discussion with management and some of the participants on the following Monday. Their intention was to institute a long term staff development programme based on this initial training but also covering lower levels of staff. The staff again stood up and clapped. He was happy to hear that staff saw their personal development linked to commitment to the bank. It was what an MD would most want to hear from his staff.

The bank also presented gifts to Diane and Dan. Mrs Murungi knew Diane was not married so they gave her a gold necklace and a gold plated automatic *Seiko* watch. To Dan they gave two such watches, one for men and the other for women. "One for you and the other for your wife. So that you can tell her how much the organisations you work for appreciate your services to them…"

Mrs Murungi sat next to Diane and she saw her writing points on a pad so she asked what she was going to do with the points.

"They are for my speech," Diane replied.

"But you won't be making a speech. I spared you the task. Dan is the one we have asked to respond for the two of you."

Diane went on writing, shaking her head. "If Dan has not suddenly changed, I will be making the speech instead. You wait and see."

After receiving his gift Dan stood in front of the conference room to make a speech. "I am too overwhelmed with emotion to make a coherent thank you speech. There is a story in my country…"

Everybody started laughing. He smiled too. "Since you know the story I will skip it."

But they pleaded with him to tell it. Over the five days they had come to expect his stories and they would ready themselves to laugh when he started, knowing he told such humorous jokes.

"The story has it that a departing foreigner was, maybe like me, overwhelmed by the gifts given to him and to his wife during the send off party. When he had the chance to say thanks on his and his wife's behalf he said, 'I want to thank all of you from the bottom of my heart and from my wife's bottom.' "

The participants roared with laughter.

"So I want to say very sincere thanks from the bottom of my heart," he saw Diane begin to shake her head and he smiled, "and from my co-facilitator's bottom."

While the room burst into another round of laughter, Diane said, "No, I object. From the bottom my heart too, like you, and not my bottom."

Another round of laughter.

"Seriously, I have not conferred with Diane but I know that like me she is overwhelmed too. You didn't have to do any more than pay our fees. The work we did was the service we had been contracted to provide. We take the gifts from participants and from the bank as indications of personal friendship and we feel highly honoured by your offer of friendship."

He looked down at the watches in is hand. "Sadly the culture of gifts requires that we don't consult people to whom we intend to offer gifts. If I were consulted I am sure only one watch would have been offered to me." At least three people held their breaths and Diane looked sharply at Jean. "I don't have a wife. Maybe it should have come out during the exercise to introduce us but divorcee is not a status you want to hold high as if it were the flag of your country, a symbol of pride. But I have someone who would equally appreciate the gift and to whom I can teach the lesson of how rewarding it is to make a vocation of one's job."

He did not miss the exchange of looks between Mrs Murungi and Diane. He also saw Diane again look at Jean. When he looked at Jean he saw that she had literally poured out both eyes on him.

He put the watches in his pocket and brought his hands together and Diane tapped Mrs Murungi and alerted her to expect something.

"A team achieves the best results when it recognises individual strengths and shares responsibilities according to these strengths..."

"Here comes the assignment for me," Diane whispered to Mary.

Mrs Murungi did not have the time ask how Diane knew.

"Between my co-facilitator and I, Diane is better in making appropriate speeches." He noted how Mrs Murungi turned sharply to look at Diane. He knew there was some secret they shared. "I will not want to dilute the quality of our response so I will ask Diane to make the response on our behalf."

Diane did not object but walked up and took over from Dan. "Even though Dan has already expressed the gratitude of both of us for the unexpected but highly valued gifts from you, now that I have been offered time to say something I will like to add my voice to his. So from the bottom of my heart and from my co-facilitator's bottom..."

She did not complete it because the room exploded in laughter. Even though they had not discussed the follow up training she was sure she could make a commitment which she did. She said other things as well, including praising the participants for their active role in the learning process. "How many of you have ever seen the T-shirts with the inscription 'If You Can Read This Thank a Teacher?' "

Three hands went up. "Each time I look at the dress, the watch and the necklace you have given me, I will remember this scene here today and I will say thanks to you. And each time I see those items I will also say thanks to Dan who made me the facilitator that I am today." They clapped. "You will notice the extent of his humility by the fact that throughout the five days, anytime he made reference to me he said his co-facilitator, thus putting someone he tutored and mentored at the same level as him."

Mrs Murungi informed Dan and Diane that Mr Koech was arranging lunch for the five of them in his house the next day. She was checking out that day but Diane said she would stay because she was sure they would start their report writing process that evening by collating issues to include in the report.

"Workaholics," Mary teased.

Diane shook her head. "It is not me. You heard him. His work is his vocation so you can understand his attitude to work. Anybody who wants to work successfully with him should expect to work eighteen hours a day."

Mrs Murungi looked at Dan who was busy bringing down some of the flip chart papers they had put on the walls. She shook her head. "Some people are committed to humanity and not just their countries. He," she indicated Dan with her head, "will slave himself to deliver the highest quality service even if you gave him a task in Greenland."

Diane agreed. "You're right. He loves humanity, not just his country."

"Did you know he was divorced?" Mrs Murungi asked, turning once more to look at Dan.

Diane shook her head. "The last time he was here and I took him out shopping on the Saturday, he bought gifts for his staff and his children, two of them. He bought nothing for a wife but I did not ask him anything."

"Do you know if he has a fiancée?"

"I don't know anything about his private life. Maybe he has. I don't know."

"I asked because of the statement he made about giving the ladies' watch to someone who would appreciate it."

"His first child is a girl. She is sixteen years old. He could be referring to her. But he could also be referring to a female friend or even a fiancée."

"I thought you just said you knew nothing about his private life," Mrs Murungi said, smiling as she looked at her friend. "It seems you know a bit about his private life."

"Well, I know he has two children, a girl aged sixteen and a boy aged twelve. I don't know anything about his love life."

Mrs Murungi decided to become mischievous. "So you wouldn't know if he loves you?"

Diane shook her head. "I will definitely know if he loved me. He *does not*."

Mrs Murungi turned and looked at Dan busily packing things. He seemed so passionate about his work she was not sure he had any romance in his heart. She turned and looked at Diane and wanted to ask her if she loved him. She decided against putting the question.

Jean was one of those who did not check out. But she was disappointed because Diane was with Dan throughout the rest of the afternoon and the evening. They started discussing the contents of the report over lunch and continued after lunch, in the conference room.

During lunch Dan caught Jean looking at him. When their eyes met she smiled. Dan forced a smile too. Diane saw it and smiled too.

"I am sad for her," he said softly to Diane.

"Why? Why should you feel sad for her?"

He turned and looked lazily at her. "Nobody should make another person suffer because of him. Unfortunately I am not capable of giving her what she wants."

Diane decided to play devil's advocate. "What does she want and why can't you give it?"

"You know what she wants. I can't give it because I am married and romance is not part of my life."

Diane cocked her head. "Are you married or divorced?"

"Both. You know about the divorce. But I am married. To my work."

She laughed. "It is rare to meet someone who admits they are married to their work."

"I am married to my work and that is a fact."

She searched his face when she asked, "So you don't expect to marry, do you? Well, a second wife if your work is your first wife."

He shook his head. "Diane, marriage is not in my mind. It has never featured in my plans since the divorce. I have to fall in love first, see."

"But Dan, you have a lot of opportunity to fall in love. You interact intensely with a lot of women. You can be closeted with young women for a week or more. And you are in touch with them for a long time even after the week together. And I have noticed some, not as openly flirtatious as Jean, but virtually show unconcealed admiration for you. You have the opportunity to fall in love."

He shook his head. "Unconcealed admiration is not love. You can admire someone without falling in love with the person. Besides, I have a very demanding wife. Diane, I am convinced my work will always be between me and a wife. I don't want to marry if I can't give my other half as much of myself as is reasonable."

She looked away and nodded. "Always the considerate person."

After supper he told Diane what had been troubling him. Before meeting her he spent time thinking of how much to tell her. In the end he decided to tell her as much as necessary. He recognised her as a friend he could trust.

He told her the condition under which he entered into the relationship with Matilda and the children they had. He told her the story of their separation and the fate of the children and why he remained separated from the children for twelve years. He did not exonerate himself.

"... When my daughter first contacted me and made the demand on me I was quite willing to shoulder my responsibilities. But I did not understand the extent of those responsibilities. I only thought of paying the children's fees, clothing them, meeting their health needs and so on. The girl is rather assertive and made it clear that they demanded more from me than money. The range of demands on me, the weight of the burden on me is what has been worrying me...

"I have never really been a father before. During the four years that I lived with the children I was not ever sober and so did not play father to them. I have no skills in managing children. I don't know if I will know the right thing and if I will be able to do what is right for them."

He paused and looked away. Diane did not say anything.

"For twelve years these kids have suffered and they continue to suffer. I am their father and I have an obligation to ensure that they have the best possible in life. I have an obligation to ensure that. I understand that providing money alone won't ensure that. I learnt that from my daughter. And I am unsure of my ability to do more than provide money. If I am not able to do that what happens to the children?"

A pause again which again was not interrupted by Diane.

After a very long pause he said, "Christ asked what it would profit a man to gain the whole world and lose his soul. I have achieved a lot. And continue to make other people different, for the better. What does that amount to if I can't do the right thing for my children?"

He told Diane why reconciliation with Matilda was out of the question and why he did not think taking the children would be good for anybody. He acknowledged the contribution the children's mother made over the period that he was not in touch with them. It was clear he had told her as much as he wanted to tell her.

A very long silence. While Dan sat back in his seat and looked at the sky Diane looked at the table. She picked her drink and took a sip. She was lost in thought. He had an interesting history, she thought. She smiled at the thought. She had asked him to tell him his worries. She had offered to be an ear. Now he shared what a man would tell only someone he called an intimate friend. She defined the problem in her head. He would have liked to give his children the best a father could give. But he was not sure what he could do for the children which would come close to that. First because he did not know what to do. And secondly because he was not sure he could do it even if he knew what to do.

She wanted to get up and walk round his chair and wrap her arms around him from behind, like a loving mother, and assure him that everything would be alright. And tell him what she thought about him – that he would find and do the right thing for the children. She looked up at him, seeing a person different from the Dan she had known. This was a very human Dan. A vulnerable Dan. Diane admired the man she had thought knew everything. She now admired him even more as he sat there showing his human weakness. At the same time she felt pained that, like him, she was not sure she knew how to help him.

She looked at him and put down the glass. "I wish I hadn't asked you to share what was worrying you with me," she said at last but the smile told him she did not mean it.

She had drunk only a bottle of *Tusker* beer so far and she asked for another bottle. He took fruit juice. "Why don't you touch alcohol at all now? Are you afraid you may not be able to control how much you drink or is it that you now just don't like alcohol anymore?"

He sipped his juice and replied, "I thought I told you before why I don't touch alcohol at all. It is both reasons you just mentioned. The best way to give up a habit is to give it up and not say you will moderate it. I could drink and resolve to moderate the quantities I drink. It may work. It may not work. I don't want to find out whether it will work or not. But it is also that having given up drink for a while I don't fancy the taste of alcohol. I don't."

She sat back in her chair and looked at him before looking round. Jean was gone. At one point earlier in the evening she had caught Jean looking at her and Jean had given her a look that seemed to suggest Diane was trespassing on her property. Jean had since left but Diane did not notice when she left. She had been absorbed listening to Dan.

"I can see both sides of the problem," she said as she turned her chair to give her more room to cross her leg. "My parents are not only my friends but my best friends. I am thirty-two but still enjoy my times with them. As you talked about the children and the way they feel about your role in their lives I tried to imagine my childhood but without one or the other of my parents. In their case, the way you said the children feel about their mother it looks like they grew up virtually without a parent they could relate with on intimate basis. It also looks like, from the children's perspective, they don't expect that kind of intimate relationship with their mother. They don't think it possible. They have only you. They can talk to you. You listen. They will expect an intimate relationship with you, a relationship in which you not just listen to them tell you their needs but in which they can just be around you as a friend. In such a relationship you can't keep them at arm's length. You have to embrace them.

"On the other hand I can see your worry as well. In addition to your fear that you may not know what to do and how to do it, for me there may be an unstated fear. This afternoon you told me that you think your work will be between you and a wife. I can see it between you and the children as well." She was looking at Dan and she detected an imperceptible nod. "You have lived this life organised around your work and that is now so well organised that the children will seem like an intrusion to disturb that organised life. You said if you cannot give as much of your life as is reasonable to a wife you will not marry. You have a choice over marriage. But you don't have a choice over your relationship with your children because you already have them. So now your worry stems partly from your having children to whom you can't give as much of your time as it will be reasonable to give."

For a spinster with no experience managing children, he thought, her analysis was very good. He had never thought of the children as an intrusion into an orderly life but now that she said it, he admitted that it was an unconscious but deep seated fear.

"Sorry I can't help you very much," she said. "I don't have any experience with children so I don't have anything useful to share. Besides, I guess relating with the children is like leading. Just as a leader would lead effectively if he chose what was appropriate to the context, your relationship will be based on your context. And like all contexts, it will be unique. A father of twenty children will not be able to advise you because your children may not be like any of his twenty children. Relating with two children who grew up missing their parents will not be like relating with two of twenty children. I know a bit about you, but I don't know even ten percent of what anyone advising you needs to know about you in order to advise you appropriately. I am afraid you will have to decide yourself what you should do in each situation as it comes up.

"I am even afraid you may not be able to develop a very practical plan how to deal with relating with the children because you cannot foresee what will come up. At this early stage in your relationship with the children you don't know them enough to predict some of the demands they will make and to make a rule about responding to their demands. You can't foretell the possible events that will come so you cannot prepare yourself for them. Situations you cannot predict will come up and you will have to deal with them as they come up."

She stopped and looked at him. He knew she was not done so he did not say anything and they sat in silence for a while.

When their eyes met she smiled. "Does that scare you?"

"I will feel scared or not when you have finished."

She shook her head slowly. "I will not say that I would not worry if I were you but I will certainly suggest you don't worry. Why? Because worrying does not help, for one. It does not solve any problem and it does not leave you with a clear mind to find solutions. You are looking ahead and imagining monsters arising out of your relationship with the children. It is your imagination that creates the worry. The children won't know this but I should be happy if I were the children because your worry is a sign of your concern for them. Personally I have no doubt that as situations develop you will manage them well. You are a perfectionist. That is what I think, having seen the way you plan and carry out your training. You want to be able to assure that everything is right and that the result is the best in the circumstance. I am not sure any parent can say they *have always* done the right thing for their children. You are afraid that you may do the wrong things or do things wrong sometimes. Of course you will do the wrong things sometimes and you will do the right things wrong sometimes. Which parent doesn't?"

She paused again and took a sip, just a small one. "Scared?" she asked him.

He only smiled, the kind that involves the lips being drawn without showing the teeth.

"I am not worried about you not knowing what to do for the children and how to do it. My worry is more about your willingness to give up some of the things you do for the sake of the children. You are concerned about the children but you are totally committed to your first love, your work. Even before you said you were married to your work I could tell that you don't just work; you are married to work. You live for it. But sorry, you will have to slow down in order to make room for the children. It may be difficult, knowing you. You can decide which jobs to take and which not to take because they will upset your order of work. But in addition to the obligation for you to fit the children into your time table you can't even do so allocating specific times for them and tell them you are available to them only during those times. Their needs cannot be programmed. You have to learn to accept them into your plans and you have to learn the use of flexi-time with them. You have to expect upsets to your carefully planned use of time. You can't be dad through remote control. Being dad is not only about paying fees and impatiently giving the children an ear. It is about being on call twenty-four hours a day, three sixty-five days a year."

She leaned forward. "Dan, it means you have to change yourself but change yourself for a very good and very necessary purpose. Your work cannot be more important than your children. You can make choices about your work but you cannot make choices about the children's demand on you. Even if the children had a supportive mother they still need a supportive and not passive father. If what you have said about their relationship with their mother is true then their need for you is even stronger."

When she stopped talking he closed his eyes and took a deep breath.

They were at their table till past midnight. She asked if Dan considered supporting his former wife to enable her support the children better. "You can't think of their welfare only in the needs you can meet directly. The condition of the home affects their welfare."

Dan explained what he had done not only in support of the children's needs in the home with their mother but also in support of the welfare of their mother. "One of the facts that dawned on me when I was forced to think of my relationship with the children is my obligation to their mother. Not just because she is their mother but also because she was once my wife. I feel I owe her and should support her as Matilda and not as the mother of my children…"

She told herself he had gone farther than she could recommend and asked herself why she thought he would not have thought of the condition of their current home.

When they went up to their rooms it was almost one in the morning. Dan turned to say 'night at the door to Diane's room but she insisted on following him. He raised eyebrows but said nothing. She came into his room, took his hands in hers and tilted her head upwards and gave him a kiss. On his lips and not his cheek as he would have expected. He was about six inches taller than her but with the high heeled sandals she wore she did not have to raise herself on her toes.

"It is to say thanks for taking me into confidence on such a personal and important issue. I am honoured that you should consider me close enough to you to let you share so much of your personal life with me. I understand your worries but I know you will make the relationship a pleasant one for the children and for you as well."

She was looking up into his face all this while. He looked back, looking directly and intensely into her eyes. She raised her lips again towards his. He saw them coming. He did not avoid them but when they touched his lips he did not respond either.

She spent many minutes in bed seeing him as he sat there narrating his problems. She could still see the human Dan she had never seen before. She could still see him as he listened to her, so intense in the attention given that, looking back at it from her bed, she was not sure if she was saying things so worthy that he had to listen that way.

He did not sleep for a long time. He recalled almost every word she said. He played back some parts of their discussion. He found peace in her counsel. Her face so close to his when she kissed him remained that close even when he closed his eyes in bed. Her eyes sparkled through his closed eyes. Her lips were forever parted in his mind's eyes. With that picture only millimetres from his face he slept.

He woke up early on the Saturday despite going to bed late. He tried sleeping again but tried as he did he could not sleep. He got up, had his bath and started working on the report based on the issues agreed with Diane. They agreed he would develop the first version and send it to her for her input. She wanted to return the document to him for him to then finalise it and send it to NTB but he convinced her to consider the edition she would come out with as final and to submit it. They had also agreed with Mrs Murungi and Mr Koech on a week in May when Dan would return for the discussions on longer term training. Before then the bank management would consider the bank's staff development plan and resources they would be willing to commit to staff training in leadership. Diane and Dan would, after reviewing the outcome of the exercise with staff on areas of further training and discussions with the bank's management on staff development, then develop a proposal for the consideration of management. The proposal would not be based on the resources the bank would be willing to commit but management knowing in advance how much resources the bank can commit would enable them make informed decisions on the proposal the two would submit.

He wanted to call on Diane but was not sure if she was up. So he went to her door and left a post-it note on her door for her to call him when she came out. Then he returned to his room and went back to work.

She did not call till over an hour later. They went down to breakfast together. He put his hand over hers when they sat down at the table. Jean was not in the restaurant. It seemed the rest of the bank staff left early that morning. "Thanks very much for the healing effect you had on me yesterday."

"Dan, I am not sure I said anything of value to you yesterday."

"Let me be the judge of that. But don't underestimate the therapeutic effect of wise counsel. And don't estimate the wisdom in what you told me yesterday. You listened to me critically and you told me things I valued."

"I am not sure I told you anything you don't already know."

"Reaffirmation can be more than you need in some circumstances. Diane you told me things that enabled me to confront myself in a way I have not done since I met the children and started worrying."

Chapter Twenty

It was one of those rare Saturdays when he did not go to the office. The office staff knew that he did not wake up early on Saturday. When staff needed him on Saturdays they would normally catch him in the office. Those who only wanted to pay a social visit came on Sunday when he returned from church.

The previous day, on the Friday, Mercy asked if he would come to the office the next day, as usual. He told her no, he was learning to either do no work over the whole weekend or do it at home. He asked if she needed anything and she said she needed nothing and that she only wanted to know if he was going to take a rest.

He was at breakfast on the Saturday when he was informed by the security guard that he had visitors. Mercy had come visiting with Khadija. Their visit saw Dan in the kitchen again. Mercy would take bread toasted with egg while Khadija asked for omelette. They trooped into the kitchen and offered to take over the preparation but Dan said they were guests and would not prepare their own meal. They watched him as he chopped onions, green pepper and tomatoes expertly and beat them into the egg. He did a very good toast for Mercy and a nice omelette for Khadija. Khadija confessed that she had never eaten bread toasted that way and Mercy praised him for his cooking skills.

It was when they came out of the kitchen after washing up that Dan noticed how Khadija was dressed – in a tight-fitting dress that hugged and accentuated her bust and made her breasts stand out. It was cut low at the chest so the beginning of the mounds of her breasts was pushed above the dress line. The dress hugged her trim stomach and flanks and announced very loudly her well formed hips and buttocks. It was drawn tightly around her thighs, giving up the secret of the shape of the thighs but it reached down to her ankles so her thighs were, mercifully, not exposed.

"My friend said you were so nice to them on the way to Accra when you picked them to Accra. She said you were very patient stopping for them to buy foodstuffs and taking them all the way to their home. She has been asking me to bring her to your house for her to say thank you in an appropriate manner."

He raised eyebrows. "So Mercy, you came all the way here with her just to say thanks. You know that you could have received the thanks on my behalf." Turning to Khadija he said, "Mercy qualified to have received the thanks on my behalf. She is part of me."

Mercy shook her head and shook it vigorously. "I am not part of you. I don't know who is part of you. I am part of my husband. I can receive his thanks, not yours."

"I have given you authority…"

"I decline the authority, please."

Khadija was amused. Was this boss and subordinate?

Mercy asked to be shown the washroom and Dan led her there.

"Don't you feel lonely living all by yourself in this big house?" Khadija asked when they were alone.

"I'm used to it," he told her.

"Can we go out for lunch some time next week?" she asked him, tilting her head as she said it.

He didn't know what that gesture meant. But he could not say no outright. He didn't have a reason to say no. So he said, "I can't predict how the week will be like, crowded or just moderate. Let us see how it turns out to be."

They stayed for over two hours. Mercy remarked that the house was too big and asked if he would show them round. He did and they purred at almost everything they saw. Mercy said she was not surprised at the well equipped study. She said they all knew he worked as much at home as he did in the office. The music room surprised them. He played them Kenny Rogers' *Till I Can Make It On My Own* on the Karaoke and sang along for them. Mercy had never heard him sing and she marvelled at this secret he kept so well. They had heard him humming in the office, but not singing. Why, he sang so well.

When they left, on Mercy's motorbike, he wondered why they came. Just for Khadija to say thanks? That must be someone who appreciated things, he thought.

He decided to walk along the neighbourhood road, now that he had come out. He walked along the road to the end of that stretch, where it turned right to join the main road. This road was rectangular in shape. It branched off the main road, turning right from town. That stretch was about one hundred and fifty metres. It then turned left and ran between rows of houses on either side. This stretch was more close to three hundred metres. At the end of the stretch it turned left again to rejoin the main road.

He walked the three hundred metres stretch up to the end and turned towards the main road. He walked up there and stood watching the vehicles, motors and bicycles go up and down the road. He stood there for over twenty minutes and walked slowly back. He smiled at the lifeless neighbourhood; silent houses, no sign of movement from within. It was past midday and those members of the neighbourhood who wanted to go shopping, drinking, visiting or to the office would have gone. Those at home were either cooking, cleaning, doing their laundry or just lazing inside the house.

He smiled again, a typical residential area. Everyone kept to themselves. Most people in the neighbourhood knew who lived where now and what the person did. They said hello when they met on the road but nobody visited other neighbours.

The gate to number 30 opened just when he was passing it. Out came Wilhelmina followed by a younger woman. The younger woman held a shopping bag. Wilhelmina smiled broadly and it forced an equally broad smile from Dan. How the face contrasted sharply with the contorted face of the woman he carried to the hospital two years ago.

"Denise is my cousin," Wilhelmina introduced the younger companion to Dan. "She is the member of the wider family I am very close to. She is staying with us for a month. She works at the Noguchi Medical Centre." She turned to her cousin and said, "You heard Adams and I speak about God sending an angel in the form of a neighbour when I lay dying by this very gate."

"Oh, yes, Daniel you said he was called." She offered a hand. "So nice to meet you. I've been here for only two days but I have heard a lot about you."

She had a very beautiful voice. And her hand was soft.

"A lot?" Dan asked. "Wilhelmina and her husband know very little about me."

"Dan, we know a lot about you. You will be surprised how much we know."

He pretended to shiver. "You make me afraid. Does what you know include all the women I raped before and the teenagers who died from trying to abort my pregnancies?"

"We will find that out yet. But right now we don't know about them," Wilhelmina said, wearing her smile.

Dan sighed. "Then I can breathe till you find out." Turning to the woman introduced as Denise he asked, "How have the two days been so far?"

"Rather quiet. This is my first weekend and I am watching how it goes. What are you doing the rest of the day?"

"Daniel is a workaholic. He goes to work on Saturdays as well so I am sure he will be on the road to the office in the next few minutes."

"Workaholic? Please don't give me a bad name. Me workaholic?"

"I'm not sure saying someone is workaholic is giving him a bad name," Denise said.

"I don't think I am a workaholic. I work weekends only because that is the only way to keep pace with the work."

"You work weekends? That sounds like workaholic to me. So are you going to spend the rest of the day in the office?" Denise asked.

He shook his head. "I am staying home today. I hope."

"Why 'I hope?' What can make you go to the office if you choose to stay at home?"

"If any of the staff need help to do work that cannot wait till Monday, sorry I have to go work with him."

"I hope you don't have to go to the office today. I will call in the afternoon if you are at home."

She didn't know it but that statement made him wish he were going to the office.

Wilhelmina turned round to look at Dan before they set off on her bike. She remembered the events of that day and subsequent days two years ago. They were events that changed their relationship. It had shown them a side of their neighbour they did not know about, hidden by his seeming disinterest in anything but his work.

Dan was driving to work that morning two years ago. The road was empty and it reminded him yet again about the contrast in living uptown and downtown. During his first visit to Zimbabwe the agency that had contracted him to conduct the training for it made one member of its staff take him on a tour of Harare. He had been struck by the red brick buildings and large commercial farms that made Harare seem more European than African to him. He had also been struck by the fact that the residential areas seemed empty. It did not feel African at all. Africa is known not for quiet, empty neighbourhoods but neighbourhoods full of life, with people idling, walking away or returning, with fun and laughter, with people playing games, selling things. That was what he thought about Africa contrasted with Europe.

He had made this observation to his guide who only smiled, initially. That afternoon he took him to a different part of the same Harare, the neighbourhoods which had been reserved for blacks allowed in Harare during the period of apartheid. There he saw a different Harare. Besides the obvious unauthorised additions to the original structures he saw crowds of people engaged in all manner of productive and idle activity – and being busy about it.

He was reminded yet again about this contrast in life in Harare as he drove through the quiet neighbourhood on his way to the office that morning. He imagined the streets of Old Cemetery Road, Hausa Zongo, Builpela and Ward F at this time of the morning. Certainly they would be crowded with people. Children loitering on their way to school, some eating their breakfast. Women and girls returning from fetching water. Children, some in torn shorts, with bowls in hand going to buy food. Cyclists and motorists weaving their way between pedestrians and vehicles.

Where he stayed was Tamale's version of the red brick residential areas of Harare.

As he drove past number 30 he noticed that the gate was open and a lady was coming out of the house on her motorbike. He knew the lady by face and, if he met her in town, could tell that she lived on the same road with him. She lived there with a man who also rode a motorbike, a bigger bike. Besides that he knew very little about them.

He waved as he drove past. The lady did not wave back, which was unusual as she usually waved back. Most residents did not visit each other but they did respond to any form of greeting. He continued to look at the woman from the driving mirror. Unusual that she did not wave back. Maybe she did not see him.

The bike seemed to lurch. Maybe it was having problems and her mind was on the problems hence her not having waved back. It seemed to stop. The woman seemed to lean on the handle bars while a girl ran out of the house to her. Strange, he thought. He almost hit a cyclist who hurled insults at him. He heard the insults because he rolled down the glasses of the vehicle. When the morning was cool he kept the glasses rolled down to let in fresh air. When he looked in the mirror again the figure he saw was very small. It seemed woman and bike had fallen and the girl who ran out seemed agitated. It was too far and he could not be sure.

Just drive on, a voice inside him told him. He was curious though and kept looking. He decided to reverse to be assured things were alright. They weren't. The girl seemed to be crying and the woman was still lying on the fallen motorbike. He sped back, still in reverse and braked sharply. He jumped down and pulled the motorbike to free the woman. The girl who was becoming hysterical was relieved to have someone take over. He quickly lifted the woman and put her in the front passenger seat of the vehicle. He adjusted the seat to recline and allow her to feel more relaxed. He rolled the bike inside and asked the girl who was at home with them. She said nobody. He asked her to lock up the house and come with him. They drove back to his house where he asked the security to keep an eye on the other house.

In the car he asked the girl what happened. She explained that her aunt was riding out of the house when she screamed and clutched at her lower abdomen. She braked the bike but fell with it. Pain in the lower abdomen that caused her to pass out.

At the hospital he relied on the girl to provide the limited information she could afford. Dan did not even know the woman's name. The girl gave the name of her aunt but did not know her age. She was still carrying her aunt's bag and Dan looked through it. It had a driving licence and he got the age from there. Her husband was in The Gambia for a workshop, the girl said. So there was nobody to give the consent needed for operations. Dan explained that he was not related to the woman.

The doctor diagnosed ruptured appendix. Since this was an emergency they rolled her into the theatre for the operation. They told Dan the cost and he agreed to pay. He drove the girl back home and asked her to pack a few things to be taken to the hospital for her aunt. He helped her list what would be useful. It was not something he knew a lot about, what a woman on admission at the hospital would need.

He rang his office and told Brenda to pass the word that he would not be in the office the whole morning. He was not sure of the afternoon but would let them know later. He then went to the bank, took money for the deposit required for the operation and went back to the hospital and paid. He asked the nurses what would be useful to bring and they told him. She would be on drips when she recovered from the effect of the anaesthesia so she would not need food and she would not need water. With that information he went back and helped the girl to pack. He left her at home to take care of the house while he drove back to the hospital. She was wheeled to the ward but she had not gained consciousness yet so he could not talk to her. He arranged for her to be put in a side ward which they said would be more costly but he insisted on it.

He went to the office, seeing that he could not be of any more help even if he stayed. He drove back at 4:00 p.m. and sat by her bed. She stared at him, not knowing what to say. She was still on infusions and was not allowed anything else for twenty-four hours. He asked how she felt and she in turn asked what happened. He described what happened.

"You brought me here?" she asked.

"Yes. I and the girl in your house. She called you auntie."

She still kept looking at him. "Yes, Nelly. She is my distant cousin's daughter. How do I say thank you? You didn't even know me. You have been seeing me, I know, but we never talked. It was very generous of you to do that much to save my life."

"Are you Christian?" he asked her.

She thought a few seconds before answering. "Yes, I am."

"We live in a neighbourhood where for some reasons we hardly say more than hi to each other. But we are neighbours, aren't we? And Christians are told that what distinguishes them from others should be the fact that they love their neighbours, and even their enemies, as themselves. You should have expected me to do exactly what I did."

They talked for more than thirty minutes. He asked if she knew how her husband could be contacted. She said no. She knew he was in The Gambia but she did not have his contact number there. He told her he had only wanted to call and inform him about her sickness and to assure him he did not need to worry about it.

He continued to pay for her medicines and tipped the nurses generously. So generously they treated Wilhelmina like royalty. She was discharged before her husband returned. On his return husband and wife came over to thank Dan. He received them warmly but flatly refused to tell them how much he spent at the hospital. The couple was shocked. Spending so much of his time to send her to the hospital, to be her anchor at that moment when she needed help the most. But to refuse to take back all the money he spent on her, which must have been a fortune, was more than they had a right to expect of him. They looked at each other, each showing the confusion in the face.

Dan learnt lessons from that event and went round the houses in the neighbourhood to invite residents to a neighbours' meeting. He met a retired colonel in the neighbourhood living three houses away who said he had been thinking of such a meeting himself. He was happy to host the meeting and Dan was happy to let him host it, more people may come for the meeting if he hosted it.

The meeting was a success. Before the meeting Dan thought of what would be the purpose of a regular meeting of residents. He thought of the irregular flow of water. He thought of the inability of the residents to get prepaid metres from the Volta River Authority. He thought of the problems they had with garbage collection.

From it they formed a neighbourhood association. Over the next two years they found strength in the association and used it to improve services to the neighbourhood. Meetings of the association improved with more residents attending when they saw the services they could get through the work of the association. Residents knew each other better. When a resident organised an event in their house they invited other residents. Residents were more supportive of each other.

Two other residential areas also formed neighbourhood associations when they saw the achievement of this association.

Wilhelmina and her husband told all this and more to Denise. Those were the things Denise said she had heard about Dan that morning when they met. Dan said bye to them as Wilhelmina picked her on her motorbike. Denise turned round and looked at him and waved at him. He waved back and walked on.

The phone rang only five minutes after he returned home. "Hello, Dan Apeatu here," he said into the phone.

"Dan, you never called me. You never got in touch." It was a female voice but he did not recognise it.

"Who is on the line, please?"

"It's Rosemary."

He thought hard trying to recollect who she was. He knew three people called Rosemary but could not tell which of them would be on the line. "Rosemary," he repeated. "Which Rosemary?"

"Now tell me, how many girlfriends do you have called Rosemary?"

"They aren't many. I have only six girlfriends by that name."

He heard laughter at the end other end. "Well, I don't know if you consider me to be one of the six. I am Rosemary Agyegekwaga"

She wasn't. He had not even thought of her at all. She accused him of not calling her even though she left her phone number with his aunt Kada. She said she was sure he had driven through Kumasi many times and asked why he had not bothered to look her up. He smiled because he could not tell her the truth which was that she did not even cross his mind the number of times he drove through Kumasi.

They exchanged greetings and she asked when he was coming through Kumasi. He was going down very soon but could not tell her the truth because he did not intend to look for her. Certainly not when he was going to be with his children.

"I miss you, Dan. I have been thinking about you. But I am not sure you even remembered me at all."

His sigh could not have been heard at the other end of the line, but he sighed, a sad sigh. Romance did not feature at all in his thoughts. It had no place at all in his life. But how could he tell her the truth? No, Rosemary, I did not remember you at all because my life is all taken up by my work. It fills every space and leaves no room, not even a tiny space, for me to think of socialisation.

I miss you. What did she know about him to make her want to see him and to miss him when that did not happen? Undoubtedly what Kada would have told her. Kada had said she expected Dan home. And it had been because of Rosemary. She may have conceived of matching them. So she may have talked a lot about Dan to her 'daughter.'

He was totally out of his element in a conversation of this nature and so did not know what was appropriate response when a lady said she missed you and you did not miss her but did not want to hurt her.

He wiped the perspiration from his brow when he put down the receiver. Gosh! A romance! He thought he was too old to be indulging in romances. He hoped that was not what Khadija had in mind too. He thought his life would be hell if she too, like Rosemary, had plans for a relationship with him. If he was sure he could not manage a single romantic relationship, he was sure he would die in two.

Denise came in when lunch was almost ready.

"Hey!" she exclaimed. "You prepare your own meals. No, Dan, you need someone to prepare your meals for you."

"Why do I need someone to do that for me?" He tilted his head and looked at her as he put the question. "I can cook so what is wrong with me cooking?"

"Dan, leave the cooking to women. Concentrate on your work and come home to eat. Cooking is not for workaholics."

"Good," he told her. "I am learning. Your cousin would have told you I don't have a wife. I either cook or eat out. I prefer to cook."

She shook her head while deeply inhaling the aroma from the simmering lunch. "You left out a third option. A girlfriend can cook for you."

He smiled but chose not to encourage the topic and so said nothing. He turned their attention to getting the meal ready.

"Wow!" Denise exclaimed with the first mouthful of food. "You are a really good cook. Nice aroma, great taste. I am here the whole of this week. Let me help you cook."

She stayed till 6:00 p.m. By the time she was leaving it was clear she wanted an intimate relationship with him. He knew he did not want a relationship with marriage as a possible result. But he could not have a relationship with Denise that did not expect that as a result because he did not think it fair to fool around with a relation of his neighbours. On more sober reflection he admitted he was sure he could not even manage a love affair. He would not know how to handle it even if he had the time, which he would not have anyway.

That night in bed he gave thought to love in his life. There was Jean. He hoped she had given up any hope of an affair with him. Then there was Khadija, at present only mysterious since he did not know if she had more than friendship in mind. There was Rosemary who was the one who had put her feelings in words. And now Denise. With his worry about the relationship with the children he was convinced he would not be mad enough to accept a love affair.

Chapter Twenty-One

"Dan, you are going on leave for how long? Four weeks? What will you do with four weeks' leave?"

"What is wrong with going on leave for four weeks?"

"You've never taken more than a week. Why four now? Tell me, are you going to marry?"

"Hey! You must be a clairvoyant! How did you guess so easily? I have kept it a secret."

"Marry my foot!" But she kept looking at him and he looked back. She shrugged in the end. "Anyway, I am happy that you are taking leave. I also hope that you will be taking real leave every year. I mean real leave, not the one week rests you take and work through them."

"So from worrying that I am taking too many days you now worry that I will not be taking that length of leave in future, is that right?"

"Dan, you know I will not answer any question you pose to tease information out of me. Take what I said anyway you want it."

He went back to working on the computer. Brenda pulled a chair and sat in front of him, her back to the office door.

"Seriously, Dan, you have never taken more than a week's leave at a time and I was wondering what has happened to make you need four weeks' leave."

"Did you know I have children?"

She stared at him. It was not something she expected to hear from him. For some reason she did not ever associate him with children. She did not know his background and did not ever investigate, either by asking him or … She realised she did not know anyone who said they knew Dan intimately from whom she could have engaged in positive gossip about him. Did she know he had children? No, she never thought of him having children.

She shook her head. "No, I didn't. Do you have children?"

"Yes, two."

"Two! A wife then?"

She was surprised he shook his head. How can you have children without a wife? He was not the type who would have children with a woman and refuse to marry her. Or was he? Involuntarily she shook her head. Maybe he was a widower. Most likely. Widowed.

"No, Brenda, I don't have a wife. We divorced. The children have been with their mother since. But I am back in the lives of the children and I want to take time off work to give them some of the things they needed from me but which I could not give them."

She gave him the thumbs up sign. "Great! I will say that four weeks is too short. They need more than four weeks of you. It is fantastic to hear you talking about other things than work, especially family. If you exhaust your leave days and you need more time with the children please use some of mine."

He smiled and said nothing.

She walked to the door and walked back. "One more question. It is your private life and I know you have been a very exceptional boss by the amount of liberty you allow me to take of you. But by allowing that you have made me a friend and not your subordinate. Will you be back in the life of the children's mother as well? If she did not remarry."

"Yes and no, Brenda. We had nothing to do with each other and that was why I was kept out of the lives of the children. Now I have to support her to keep the children. And I also have to support her for her own sake, a former wife and a former friend. But it won't be possible for us to come back. We are incompatible." He held up a hand. "It is not my work. It is who we are. Maybe one day I will tell Brenda my friend more of it but I don't have the time now to tell you that."

She walked behind his desk and rubbed his shoulder. "Sorry to hear that you had a divorce in your life. And thanks for telling me."

She walked back to stand in front of him. "When you asked me if I knew you had children I told you the truth, which was that I did not. But now I remember that once when you were in Kenya and extended your stay there, a girl called to ask about you. She initially said she was your daughter but when I asked her further she said she was your sister's daughter but she called you her father."

"Do you remember her name?"

"Unfortunately, no I don't."

"Do you remember where she called from?"

"I am not sure I asked. You were not in and I don't remember if I asked her anything other than who she was."

"Did she say Marian Wepia?"

"I think so. But I can't swear that was the name. She said you had told her you were travelling but would be back by a certain time and she should call."

"That was my daughter. I don't have a sister."

She tut-tutted. "Oh dear! I owe this girl an apology."

Dan got up and went to prepare a cup of tea, Kenyan tea. "No, you don't. I do. I didn't let the office know I had a daughter. It was not your fault. It was mine."

He had to send out a memo to all staff, both Leadership Development and Training Centre staff, to inform them he would be away on leave for four weeks. He designated heads for the two places while he was away. Both places were soon buzzing with questions about his taking *four weeks' leave.* One reason he told Brenda about the children was the fact that he did not care if word about them spread. The second reason, but one he did not think about, was Brenda's mature attitude. She would not be in a hurry to share this information about the personal life of Dan. So the whispered questions about his leave went unanswered.

On the Friday he went through his desk and pulled out drawers, throwing out things he now realised should not have been kept in the first place. He collected the items in a heap and was surprised how big it turned out to be. He shredded them and returned to admire the neatness and order on his desk.

He slept till late the next morning. He had told Marian he would come for her at ten o'clock. The school vacated the previous day, the Friday, and the students were going home that Saturday. Many students took taxis home and Marian could have gone home in a taxi too. After all she had been going home on her own the past four terms. But Dan decided to go for her and to send her to school each time school re-opened. It was an impulsive decision but he did not regret it.

Most of the students had left by the time Dan drove into the campus. Marian was waiting for him, and with her were her two friends. They met her father for the first time even though they had heard a lot about him from Marian. He drove them to their respective homes where they left their luggage but came with him. He waited in the vehicle while they took Marian's things home. Junior was at home and he ran to his father who lifted him up before putting him down. Dan took all of them to his house where they all went into the kitchen and prepared lunch. He put all of them, including Junior, to work performing various chores. It was an interesting experience and eating it was even more interesting. When he drove them back they chose to go to Leila's house. They spent the rest of the day talking about how pleasant it had been to be with Dan.

Before they left Dan wrote a letter for his children to send to their mother.

Dear Matilda,

I am writing to ask for permission on behalf of Marian and Junior. I want to take them on a tour of Ghana. It will improve their knowledge of their country and they will see how people in other parts of the country live. It will also be a very pleasant way for them to spend their holidays.

I plan to leave with them on Monday and we will be away for a week. We should be here on Holy Saturday or Easter Sunday.

Thanks and greetings.

Daniel Apeatu

He spent the Saturday evening worrying about the trip on Monday. He was not sure how it would turn out to be. He was not sure how he would fare being thrown against the children with all their questions about their relationship. Would they come back with their backs to each other or would they find a strong bond with each other? This trip was going to be the test of his fatherhood and he did not expect to do well.

On the Sunday afternoon Marian and Junior went to Dan's house and he took them to his study. There they went over a large scale map of Ghana and he showed them the route they would take and the places they would visit.

The children came to his house at 7:00 a.m. on the Monday. He took one look at their bag and he felt sad. It was old. Its type had gone out of fashion many years back. He did not know what clothing they carried in that bag even though he had bought them a few recently.

He was happy he had decided to set off so early. They would arrive in Kumasi early enough for him to be able to change their bag and buy them clothing.

He had thought the children were leaving Tamale for the first time in their lives. It was true. But when they went past Lamashegu and both children started staring at what they saw he realized they had never even come this far in Tamale. So his commentary started from there. He explained what Nulux Plantations did when they drove past the company's office and cotton ginnery. He pointed out the road to the public cemetery to them. He chuckled when they approached Datoyili.

"What is funny, Dad?" Marian asked.

"This village is called Datoyili," he told them. "In our secondary school days Navrongo Secondary had a student population of a little over one thousand. Only about one hundred were from the district. There were more students from Northern Region than from the district."

He paused and concentrated on the driving as he swerved away from a sheep crossing the road. "There are many villages in Navrongo that end in *nia*," he went on. "We have Korania, Vunania and so on. The term nia simply means the people of. So that we have Bavugunia which is a village founded by Bavugu. When the community was started people would have been referring to the people there as the people of Bavugu, the founder.

"Students from other parts of the country used the names to tease us, saying every village was a nia. They made fun of us saying we were not creative in naming settlements. Then I came to Tamale and Dagbon and found that the way they name their settlements is not different. We just went past Datoyili. We have Chogomanayili, Sognayili and Jisonayili in Tamale alone. In other parts of Dagbon we have Nakpayili, Afayili, Kuntumbiyili, Gunayili and many others. Yili means house. The place is named after the first settler. So if I am the first settler in a particular place the place may be called Apeatuyili."

The children laughed.

"So that will be our village?" Marian asked.

"No, it won't be your village because you are not Apeatu. You are Wepia, remember?"

They protested.

"It is not just Dagbon. In Sissala belle is the common name. So you have Wellembelle, Bugubelle, Naabugubelle, Sorbelle, Tukurubelle and so on. Among the Gonjas it is pei. They have Yapei which we will be going to soon. They have Buipei, Gentilpei, Gurumpei, Sisilipei, Kawampei and again many others ending in pei."

They drove over the Volta River at Yapei and again at Buipei. After Yapei they came to Damongo Junction and he showed them the road leading to Damongo and explained where else it led to besides Damongo. Beyond Damongo was Mole Game Reserve and he assured the children he would bring them there on their return from this trip.

When they entered Brong Ahafo Region they came across settlements that had Akura attached them – Sarikyi Akura, Alhassan Akura, Kurawura Akura. Some stretches of the road were so straight they saw far ahead of them. At Kintampo they stopped to visit the waterfalls. They were excited seeing the water fall down the rocks. The caves amazed them. They stopped at Buabeng and visited the Monkey Sanctuary. They were taken round the sanctuary and the guide explained why the sanctuary was created. He also explained the way man was destructive, destroying other species and the environment.

They had lunch at Techiman and arrived in Kumasi at about 3:00 p.m. He drove to the commercial part of the town where he found a place and parked the vehicle. He went out with the children and bought them suitcases and clothing. He bought them pyjamas and night wear for Marian. He bought them footwear, shoes and sandals. There was just time to drive round the town and feel the difference between the smaller, more serene Tamale and the metropolitan Kumasi. They went through traffic they had never experienced in Tamale and which they could not have imagined no matter how hard they had tried to stretch their imaginations. They drove past the University of Science and Technology and he turned into Silicon Hotel. He was not sure there would be accommodation there but he had not made any previous arrangements because he was sure they would always find accommodation in one of the many good hotels in the city.

Silicon had rooms. He asked for two suites and Marian asked why two. He told them she and Junior would have a room to themselves.

"But, Dad, we don't' want a room to ourselves. We want to share the same room with you."

"You are adults and must now have your privacy. That's why I wanted you to have a room to yourselves."

Marian took his right arm and Junior took the left. "Dad, we don't want privacy. We want to be close to you."

The front desk officer was entertained by the man and his two children. She did not doubt the fact that the man was the father of the children. The resemblance with the boy was very striking. Even though she wanted more of their rooms to be taken she supported the children. And they won.

As the porter led them to their room Dan told the children, "In Europe and America I can't put the two of you in one room. No child older than eight years old should sleep in a room with another person."

"This is Ghana, Dad, not Europe or America. We haven't been close to you for twelve years. This is our first opportunity to sleep in the same room with you, to feel you so close and you worry more about our privacy. We choose intimacy over privacy."

"Marian and Junior, laws are made from experience and for good purposes. You will be surprised that the incidence of children being abused is very high, worldwide and not only in one place or a few places. By children being abused I don't mean that they are insulted. I mean older people may fondle the breasts of girls, play with the private parts of the children and even have sex with them. It is also a sad and surprising fact that most of the children who are abused this way are abused by close relations. It is, again sadly, sometimes their own parents, an uncle or a friend of the family. So the laws on children eight years or older having their own room is to protect children from being abused."

"But you won't treat us that way, Dad," Marian told him. Junior agreed. "We both know that you will not treat us that way."

Their innocence and faith amused him but also made him sad. They were vulnerable and he had a charge to protect them and educate them to reduce their vulnerability. His responsibilities would seem to grow with intimacy with the children. "Children, listen. Many adults now roam the world traumatised by stressful incidents from their childhood.

Many children have been abused by people they trusted and who they expected to protect them. When they are taken advantage of instead by people they trusted it shatters their trust in humanity and the effect sometimes lives with them forever. Many children are molested by people they believed could not do that to them. It includes parents."

"Parents?" both children asked together.

The room was big and there were two double sized beds in it. Junior stood and stared while Marian exclaimed, "My, oh my! Aren't these beds monsters!" She looked at Junior. "If we had a room to ourselves you would have had to sleep in one of those monsters alone. It would have swallowed you up in the middle of the night."

Junior pressed on the mattress and then said, "No, this monster eats only girls."

Their father chuckled. They inspected the room and he explained things he knew they did not know. He showed them how the cold and hot water taps worked. He showed them how the remote controls, both for TV and air conditioner, worked. He explained the use of the shower gel. As he explained things to them he realised how far behind he had left the children, his children.

Silicon Hotel provided cables in each room where lodgers could log on to the hotel's Internet service. So he sat at the table and set up his laptop computer as the children stood around him and watched. He showed them the wonderful power of the Internet. He showed them how to read the news in Yahoo. He showed them how to use the Internet search facility. He typed in Universities in South Africa and clicked on go. They were thrilled by the results.

He then took them to his mailbox and showed them how to use the Internet for correspondence. He explained how the box was set. "The headings on the left allow me to go to that particular part of the box I am interested in. The *Sent* box contains all mails that I ever sent but which I have not deleted. The *Trash* box contains mail I deleted. The system will send all mails it suspects are not genuine to the box called *Spam*. The Inbox is like the post box in the post office. It contains mail coming to me. Those items in bold print are the mail in the inbox that I have not opened yet. The information on this page includes the name of the sender, the subject of the mail and date on which it was received."

"Dad, there are so many women on your list," Marian observed. "Are they all your girlfriends?"

Junior looked at him and chuckled.

"Yes, Marian, they are. I am sure you now understand why I am not married. I have difficulty deciding which of them to marry."

He scrolled down the page. "What I am doing is called scrolling." The children watched with keen interest.

"Diane Orengo's name appears a lot. Who is she?" Marian asked. Junior looked at her sharply and turned to look at his father.

"Diane? She is the one I finally decided to marry. Don't you want me to marry her?"

"If she will make a good wife to you and a good mother to us, why not?"

He froze. If he ever had to marry he would need someone who would make a good wife to him and also be a good mother to the children. Mm. It would be difficult, he told himself. As if marriage ever crossed his mind.

"Diane is my partner," he told them. "She is Kenyan and we have been training people together. We have some work to do together very soon. A bank in Kenya wants us to do an assessment and discuss long term training of their staff. Diane and I communicate a lot because we work together."

When he closed the programme and shut down the computer Junior asked, "Will we be able to use the computer the way you use it?"

He rubbed his head and said, "Yes, you will. You will acquire computer skills. We all need computer skills in all we do. If you are a doctor for instance, you can use the Yahoo search to find out the current information on a particular disease, latest drugs for any disease and so on. Marian, I hope you will want to attend holiday classes in the Science subjects when you come home during the third term holidays which are quite long. I will pay for the two of you to attend computer classes as well."

They shouted and jumped and raised their hands.

They went down for supper and he had to help the children choose foods. He introduced them to hot and sour soup which they liked a lot. They agreed to ask for a plate of rice each and ordered three different sauces, shredded beef, shredded chicken and shrimps. The children enjoyed all three sauces. They had ice cream for dessert.

After supper he took them out for a drive through the city. Kumasi by night he called it. He took them through the commercial part of the town, now completely emptied of its human contents. He took them to the residential areas and the slum parts of the city. He took them to New Tafo which had a hectic night life. Then he drove them back to the hotel and to their first night together.

The children, as would be expected of any child wearing a pyjama for the first time in their lives, were excited about the pyjamas. They had their bath and went to bed. The children chose to sleep on each side of him.

"Dad, we don't know any Kassena stories," Marian said. "Please tell us stories."

"Once upon a time," he said in Kassem. *Asunsoala kampo.*

The children did not know the appropriate reply. He taught them. *Kan ding.*

"Three toads went and sang praises of the chief…"

"Dad, was this the chief of the toads or a human chief?"

"Marian, in Kassena story telling you don't ask such scientific questions. Just listen."

The children promised not to ask questions again.

"The chief was happy with the toads and gave them a cow. They tied a rope around the neck of the cow and started on their journey back home, pulling the cow behind them."

The children laughed, imagining three tiny toads pulling an unwilling cow behind them. Their father smiled too but did not interrupt the storytelling. "Halfway home the toads met the hyena who asked them where they got the cow from. The three toads told him how they got it. The hyena was a nephew of the toads. He told the toads that as a nephew he was entitled to the foreleg of the cow.

"Now let me explain some things to you. In Kassena culture, if you visit your maternal uncle's house at a time they have killed an animal, they will give you one of the forelegs. Different members of the family have a particular part of a slaughtered animal they are entitled to. Please understand that in traditional society animals are killed mostly only to perform sacrifices. So the distribution is very strict. At the time of sacrifice of an animal, if a daughter of the family who is married comes home, she is entitled to the waist of the animal. If any daughter of the family is divorced and is staying at home permanently, any time they kill an animal they must give her the waist.

"If any of you should go to my maternal uncle's house at the time they have killed an animal they will give you the part that they would have given to me if I went there. You replace me.

"Another thing you need to know, in Kassena folklore, the hyena is a symbol of greed and stupidity."

He adjusted himself on the bed. "The toads explained patiently that the hyena could not take his share of the cow since it had not been killed but he said then they should kill it. And he killed it for them, skinned it and cut it into its parts. Then he started taking all the meat. He took one of the forelegs. Then he said if his first son visited the toads when they killed an animal they would give him a foreleg. And he trusted they were generous enough not to deny the son his share of the meat just because he was not present. So he took the second foreleg for his son. He told them if his mother were around she would have been entitled to the waist. If they were generous to him and his son he was sure they would be even more generous to their own sister. So he took the waist."

The children laughed.

"He found an excuse for taking all the pieces."

"Greedy animal!" Junior said.

"Yes, Junior," his father admitted, "the hyena was greedy. He rolled all the meat in the skin and was going to go off with it when the oldest toad said they could not pour so much blood on the earth without pacifying the earth. Now, again understand that in Kassena traditional belief, the earth has a spirit. The sky has a spirit. Rivers have spirits. So the toad said after pouring so much blood on the earth they needed to pacify its spirit. He explained that they would have to use the liver to make the sacrifice. So the hyena fished out the liver from the pieces of meat and gave it to the toad to perform his sacrifice. You can be sure that he was impatient to go home with his meat and have a feast. When the toad told them that the liver had to be roasted the youngest of the toads offered to go and fetch fire for them to roast the meat. He pointed at smoke coming from a house about half a mile away. You can imagine a toad hopping to go fetch fire half a mile away. You can equally imagine the impatience of the hyena in the circumstance."

The children again laughed. But as promised they asked no questions.

"So the hyena offered to go fetch the fire instead and bounded off. On his return he saw two of the toads dead, lying on their backs with their feet pointing skywards. So he stopped fifty metres away and asked the live toad what had happened but the toad would not tell till the hyena came closer. The hyena moved slowly forward asking to be told the story behind the death of the toads each time he came closer. When the hyena was ten metres from the toads the remaining toad explained what had happened. 'When you went away a wind blew through here that required that people died in pairs. My brothers had no patience and decided to die together. But I decided to wait for you to return so that we die together.' "

The children roared with laughter. And broke their promise. "What did the hyena do? Did he agree to die with the toad and leave his meat behind?"

"He threw the coal at the toad and told him that if he would not die alone he was welcome to live forever. Then he ran off as fast as he could to get away from that spot where people died in pairs. The two supposed dead toads got up and together with the other one took their meat home."

The children could not stop laughing.

They asked him to tell them another story and he told them another interesting story. All three laughed over it. He realised that in story telling the narrator enjoyed it as much as his audience even though the story already existed in his head and he knew it already. Story telling was sharing fun and not just giving it to others.

The children asked a lot of questions on story telling among the Kassena. It made him tell them a little about his childhood and how life in the village was.

"Dad, we know very little about Kassena culture," Marian told him. It was one of those statements that sounded like accusations to him. It was a fact but he took it that he was responsible for that lack of knowledge about their own culture.

He put out the lights, patted their heads and wished them good night.

"Dad." It was Marian.

"Yes, Marian."

"I want to say thanks. Thanks for bringing us on this trip. Thanks for telling us the stories. Thanks for the clothing and the suitcase. We have never had a day like this before. Thanks."

Before he could reply he heard, "Dad." It was Junior.

"Yes, Junior."

"I want to say thank you too."

He embraced both children. "It has been an interesting day for me too. Thanks to you too."

They did not know how much he meant it. Maybe he did not know it himself. Almost two hours after the children were breathing regularly in their sleep their father was still very much awake. He felt the joy of the trip so far. When he told the children the stories it dawned on him that storytellers enjoyed their stories as much as the people to whom they told the stories. Now the same realisation dawned on him. The children said thanks for the clothes, the suitcases and what he did for them. As he lay awake with the children's hands on him, he admitted that he probably felt happier than the children. He had given the children material things that could be costed. He could not cost the value of the happiness he felt that evening, being with the children.

Another realisation. He had always felt happy with his work. He loved it and it rewarded him with fulfilment and satisfaction. That day he found something different, real happiness, real joy. And it had to take his children for him to discover the fact that there was happiness out there to be discovered, to be enjoyed. There was life to be lived. Today he was not only taking the children around; he was living a life he did not know existed.

He remembered Marian telling him they did not know the culture of their own people. It still sounded an accusation to him. He did not think that that was the last time his guilt would be brought up. But he was less afraid of what would come up between him and the children during this trip. Their thanks just before they slept still rang in his ears, and the words were so sweet. It was an indication of the ground they had covered between them. It was indication how much the children had come to accept him.

He slept with a peaceful smile on his lips. He looked to the rest of the journey with the children with a lot less apprehension and a lot more expectation than he felt when he first set out with them.

He put one hand over each of the children and closed his eyes.

Chapter Twenty-Two

It was one in the afternoon. She had just come back to the nurses' table from administering the midday medication. Patients were admitted to the hospital for many reasons. One reason was to give them the rest they needed to help their recovery. That was one reason why nurses fought with relations of patients who followed up to the hospital in hordes to visit outside visiting hours. Patients whose condition was serious were also admitted so that they could be under close observation. They could be given fast attention if their condition was deteriorating. The third reason was to ensure that they took their medicines in the right dosage at the right time.

So it grieved Matilda seriously when her colleagues acted lazy and did not administer the drugs to people on admission at the right time. She was paid to provide services for patients. If there were no sick people there would be no hospitals and there would be no nurses. And they would not have been entitled to the salaries they received at the end of each month. It pained her when patients were treated as if the nurses were doing them charity and they were a nuisance to nurses.

Patients on drugs to be taken three times a day had their drugs at six in the morning, at two in the afternoon and again at ten in the evening. That was eight hourly. Those who had to take their drugs four times a day took the drugs at six in the morning, midday, six in the evening and again at midnight. She had just returned from administering the midday drugs.

She went through the files on the nurses' table. From the information on the files of the patients on admission in the West Wing, which she was responsible for, she checked the medicines in the trolley to be sure that she had each patient's drugs and that the drugs were all there. She wheeled the trolley between the beds and started administering the drugs to those on eight hourly medication.

She finished shortly after two o'clock and returned to the nurses table where her colleague was writing the report for the morning. The report consisted of information on each patient, their condition and what the morning nurses had done for them.

The first afternoon nurse came in fifteen minutes after two and the morning nurses started handing over to him. He was a male nurse.

Matilda was down in thirty minutes and on her way home when she met Kachana. They hadn't met for a long time. Kachana avoided Matilda after they quarrelled many months back. Kachana liked to ask questions and make observations Matilda did not like. But after a long time Kachana thought they should put the past behind them so she invited Matilda for a drink. The Tamale office of the Ghana News Agency was across the road from the hospital. There was a bar there where they also sold meat and soup. Nurses and other hospital staff went there in the afternoon to eat soup and have a drink or two.

The two ordered a plate of soup each and two bottles of Star beer. Matilda yawned. It started a conversation for the next thirty minutes. Kachana admired Matilda for her attitude to work. So it was good that they started with her work. Work was safe ground to tread on. Sometimes Kachana would contemplate where Matilda would have been in her career if she had been more serious. She loved her work. She knew it. She learnt that she was intelligent. If she had been more serious with life than she knew her to be, she could have done further studies and risen to the top of the profession. Now she was mired at the very bottom of the profession, an auxiliary nurse. It surprised her that anyone would be happy to be somewhere very low when they had the potential to be high.

The conversation about the work was very lively. Kachana listened as Matilda complained about the attitude of her colleagues. She asked questions about what they were expected to be doing and was impressed with Matilda's in-depth knowledge of her work. But they could not remain on safe ground forever. Kachana asked about the children. And it took them to quicksand.

"Now that secondary schools are on holidays, what is Marian doing at home?" Kachana, who was also a mother of two, asked. Her first child, a girl, was one year older than Marian and was in her third and final year in senior secondary school. She loved the children and she

329

and her husband did a lot to ensure the children had a comfortable home and good education.

Matilda clapped her hands and wailed. "Please, Kachana, don't give me a heart attack. The children don't care about me. They want to make me die before my time. Ask about something else and not the ungrateful children."

Kachana digested the answer. It was not unexpected. However she was unsure whether to let Matilda know how her attitude to the children could also make the children die before their time or let sleeping dogs lie. She decided to tell her the truth.

"Matilda, I know your children. They are very respectful. They are more respectful than the children of some of your drinking friends. But your friends help you to treat your children in a way they will never treat their children. Your children respect you. But you don't see the respect. What have they done to want to cause your death before your time?"

"They've gone off on holidays with their father!" It was a scream. "Can you believe that? They have found that man they call their father and they have allowed him to take them, he says, to show them the country. After abandoning them all this time he just walks back into their lives and walks off with them."

The agitation showed strongly in her face. And Kachana smiled that such a natural occurrence should cause her so much pain.

She put a hand on Matilda's hand. "Do you know how many children will love to be taken round the country on holidays? I would have thought that it is good for the children that someone is taking them to show them the country. If someone would do it for my children I will be thankful to him. I can't afford it and I know my husband can't afford it either. He doesn't have the time too. I don't know how long they will be gone. But many women would feel relieved to have their children taken away for a while to give them some rest."

"You can talk that way because your husband did not abandon you and your children. Dan abandoned the children. Why should the children accept him so easily when he walks back into their lives? The painful thing is that they looked for him. It wasn't even that he walked back into their lives. They went and looked for him as if they were starving or burning without him."

"I don't know the conditions that made them go to look for their father but I can understand generally why they should go looking for their father. Can you go back to your childhood days? At the age of the children how would you have felt if your parents only communicated with you through shouts and insults. You grew up in a home in which they talked to you. People chatted with you. All your children know from you is screaming and insults. Matilda, that alone could have pushed any children to look for a father, if only to find out if they could establish a relationship in which someone talked to them.

"Another good reason, I guess, why your children would want to meet their father is money. You have complained to me in the past about Marian pestering you for her fees. You have said that the amount she mentioned gave you headache and you could not afford it. If you could not afford it I would imagine she would want to contact her father to see if he would pay her fees. It is natural. It is to be expected. Unless you say they searched for him for some other reason which you can describe as frivolous I would say they had to look for him. It was to be expected. If this is what would make you die it is not the children who are causing it. It will be caused by you not accepting what is natural."

"I know your position about me and my children," Matilda said, her mouth full of meat. "I did not expect you to back me against the children. You will support them even though they do the wrong things. You have supported their father right from the beginning. So I am not surprised you are in support of the children going off with their father."

"Matilda, fortunately some of us were in Tamale when you sacked Dan from the house. You keep saying he abandoned the children. But you know that when your marriage ended some of us were against your decision not to let Dan have anything to do with the children. You prevented him from seeing the children. You prevented him from having anything to do with the children. You know yourself that he did not abandon them. He made the effort to see them, to support them. You said you did not want him in your life and you did not want him to have anything to do with the children."

She paused and looked at Matilda. She was busy eating her soup. She finished one plate and ordered a second one. "The soup is really nice tasting," she recommended to Kachana.

Kachana was not sure if there was a change in Matilda or it was the tiredness from work that prevented her from being aggressive with her. Whatever it was, the fact that Matilda was not as aggressive as she had been in the past emboldened Kachana so she went on. "Matilda, you have to decide what relationship you want with your children. For many years you prevented the children from contacting their father with stories about what a terrible person their father is. Now they have met him. You say they have gone on holiday with him. You have not had anything to do with Dan for many years. He is a very nice man, besides being well to do. The children will come back with an impression of him that is different from the stories you tell of him. If you continue to scream at them; if you continue to insult them and if your friends continue to join in insulting them, you risk losing the children to their father. And I know you won't like that.

"Marian is not a child any more. She is a young woman and very bright young woman. She is not five or six years old. You cannot continue to treat her the way you treated her ten years ago. Daniel Junior is quieter than his sister but I am sure he is equally intelligent…"

"Who is quiet? Junior?" The expression in her face told Kachana Junior was pain in the ass of his mother. "That boy, more than his sister, has been very naughty since they met their father. All I have to do is open my mouth and they threaten me with packing to their father. It is as if I have been a monster to them all these years."

"And they are right to say you have been a monster to them."

It wasn't Kachana. They both looked up into the face of Auntie Gina. Without waiting to be invited she pulled a chair and joined them.

"My afternoon is spoiled," Matilda complained.

"I have only spoiled your afternoon, Matilda," Auntie Gina told her. "You have spoiled your whole life. You don't want what is good for your life so why worry about only your afternoon getting spoiled?"

Kachana watched them, bowed her head and smiled. Gina ordered some soup and a malt drink. They both knew she drank beer but she was still working and would return to the office. Hence the malt drink.

She asked what had started the complaint and Kachana told her.

"She thinks I am too old and my ideas are dead," Auntie Gina told Kachana. "She thinks I belong to a different generation so my advice is not good for her. You are her peer so she may listen to you. I have never learnt what caused the separation with Daniel. He drank but so did she. And she did not stop drinking so I am not sure she would say his drink was a problem. I am not sure if he was taking her money to drink. Maybe only God knows the reason for the separation.

"But when they separated she had children with Dan. They were her and his children. Right from the time of the separation she prevented the father from seeing his children. I remember the embarrassing scenes even in the church on more than three occasions when he came to the same church service in order to see the children. At no time did the man reject the children. In some cases women run after the fathers of their children to contribute to the upkeep of the children. This man was running after her to support her and the children…"

"Who was running after whom?" Matilda asked.

"Matilda, I know that this man came with his mother to see you and your mother about the children and both of you drove them away," Auntie Gina calmly told Matilda. "I know it for a fact. In fact, the two of you embarrassed them. That was after he made many futile attempts to have a discussion with you. He was running after you."

She paused for Matilda to challenge her if she could. She pretended to be busy with her drink, too busy to challenge her cousin.

"You accuse me of spoiling your afternoon. You worry about the short afternoon but didn't worry about the fact that for many years you put yourself through unnecessary pain. And you forced the children to go through the same avoidable pain with you."

"Did I ever come to beg you for anything?"

"No, you didn't. But did you ever worry about the children? I heard you say the children behave as if you were a monster to them. You never came to beg me for anything but the children suffered…"

"Did they come to beg you for anything? Did they come to tell you they were suffering?"

Auntie Gina's calm disposition did not desert her. In fact, in many very trying circumstances she kept her calm. "No, they did not. But why did they contact their father despite your threats? Why did Marian have to go in search of her father if they got all they wanted from you?"

"People are never satisfied. You can't judge what I do for the children by what else they want. If they want to live like a prince and a princess and I can't afford it is that a crime?"

"Marian only asked you to pay her fees for her. Is asking that you pay her fees wanting to live like a princess?"

Kachana repeated the advice she had given to Matilda already.

"Your friend doesn't know what is good for her," Auntie Gina said. Turning to Matilda she said, "I thought Dan's gesture towards you would have made you wake up and think. If you did you would have realised how much you missed over the twelve years that you refused to acknowledge Dan as the father of the children."

She turned to Kachana and told her about Dan's offer to Matilda for her upkeep and the upkeep of the children.

Kachana screamed. "That is more than my salary. If my husband ever gave that much for housekeeping I will sing for him each evening when he is eating his supper."

Between the two women they gave Matilda various pieces of advice. She listened but seemed defiant.

"Look here," Kachana advised, "I already told you Marian and her brother are not children any more. You must recognise that. You have said so many things about Dan, many negative things about him. You may believe in your stories. But you must remember two facts. One, you cannot meet the needs of the children. Even if you were not drinking you cannot provide a comfortable home and pay the fees of the children. Not on your salary, you can't. Furthermore, you drink. Whether you drink for free or spend your salary on drink, if I were the children, whenever you are unable to provide any need I will take it that it is because you drink that you don't have enough money to meet my needs. I won't be happy with you. Two, Dan is not the monster you paint him to be. You could not have expected to keep the children forever away from their father when you could not meet their needs. You did not want them to contact their father but you created the conditions in the home that would force them to look for him. And once they found him they would know he is not a bad man. You say he is taking them round on a tour of the country. They will come back convinced that he is more concerned about them than you are. They will come back thinking he loves them more than you do. It won't be because of his money. Taking the time to be with them and go round with them is an indication of love. If he doesn't shout at them or insult them they will want to be with him and not with you."

She dropped her voice. "Matilda, listen to us. We are telling you all this for your own good. If the children come back and begin telling stories about their father and the trip, understand that they built a good relationship with him. Understand that they are getting closer to him than to you. You will need to change your attitude towards them or one day they will carry out their threat to move out and join their father."

Auntie Gina took over. "She doesn't even know her luck. Dan is willing to leave the children with you and support you financially. And generously too. If you don't change your attitude to the children he can take you to court to ask for custody of the children. If the children pack to him and he decides to keep them you can only get him to return them if you go to court or to the Department of Social Welfare. Whether you go to court or Social Welfare, they will invite the children as witnesses. If both of them complain that you drink a lot, and that you hardly talk to them but shout and insult them most of the time, if they say that your drinking companions insult them as well, the court will judge in favour of your former husband."

Like the others Gina also ordered a second plate of soup. While they went to bring the soup she looked at her cousin and for the first time since she knew her, she saw a subtly subdued Matilda. "Sorry, you have little choice. You pushed the children to their father. If you don't want to lose them completely you have to change your attitude towards them. If you lose them you also lose the monthly remittance their father has agreed to be giving you. Think about it and make your choice."

"I looked after those two children alone for twelve years," Matilda protested. "I am not rich but they did not die of starvation. They did not wear the best clothes but they did not wear rags. I could not pay Marian's school fees but I did not make her drop out. If they had not gone to school at all their father could not have taken them at this age to school. You accuse me as if I did not do anything for the children at all."

Kachana had something to say but deferred to her older colleague who was a closer relation. "Matilda, there are a number of things you should be aware of," Auntie Gina said. "One is the fact that right from the beginning Daniel did not refuse responsibility for the children. The conditions the children had to go through which you said you managed very well were your making. You created them when you rejected a role for Dan in the lives of the children. Two, you did well for the children by sending them to school. If you had not kept the children in school till the time they found their father when they found him it would have been too late for him to give them a good education. You did well, in many respects, for the children. But you risk losing the love the children should have given you for that by your stubborn attitude to their relationship with their father.

"When Dan came to me he acknowledged your strong and positive role in the lives of the children. He said it was one reason he would never want the children separated from you. But grow up, you risk incurring his and the children's displeasure to the point where they will gang up to have the children moved from you, that is what we have been trying to tell you. Stop and think sometimes, Matilda. Assuming on this trip with the children their father tells them how many times he tried seeing you in the past to discuss his relationship with and support for the children. Assuming he tells them how his mother came all the way from Navrongo and together they met you and your mother who did not even receive them. And the children know that over the twelve years you did feed them, you put them in school but they lacked many things they could have got if only you had allowed their father to play a role in their lives. Stop and think sometimes, woman. You are no more Marian's age. Even Marian thinks ahead, at her age."

Chapter Twenty-Three

Father and children woke up late the next morning. As on the previous evening, they went into the bathroom one at a time to brush their teeth and bath. He had advised the children about decency in their dressing when the three of them were together in the room. They each created space for the privacy of the others when they needed to change. He was sure that in the single room they lived with their mother privacy would not be a value but he had to make them learn to respect it in orders and to demand it for themselves. He found that having a suite helped because two of them could be in one room while the one who needed to dress could use the main room.

When they walked to the restaurant for their breakfast the children were dressed in jeans trousers and jackets worn over T-shirt. They looked great in their outfits and he was proud of them. For breakfast the children ordered fruit juice, omelette, toasted bread, oats and cocoa drink. Their father had the juice too but while the children took pineapple he took orange juice. He also had beef sausage, toasted bread and coffee. The children asked why the breakfast was called Continental breakfast and he told them he did not know. He was frank with them when he did not know something.

When they checked out he joined the main Kumasi-Accra road and drove towards the centre of Kumasi. He had to ask for instructions how to enter the University of Science and Technology. It was quite complicated but he eventually made it. He did not know the university having never come inside it. They discovered it together and he found the halls with the children. Queen Elizabeth Hall, simply called Queen's Hall. Katanga Hall. Unity Hall. Africa Hall. Republic Hall. They found the lecture halls together and he asked for directions to the bookshop where he bought books for the children. Marian selected her own books while he bought abridged versions of books such as

Treasure Island, The Prisoner of Zenda, Silas Marner, Robinson Crusoe, The Gorilla Hunters and *Kidnapped* for Junior. For Marian he also bought textbooks.

They drove together to the Military Museum which Dan was visiting for the first time himself. Their guide was a captain of the army and he told them the interesting story of the Museum which was originally a fort. He showed them the peephole through which the British soldiers could see the Ashanti warriors without showing themselves. They saw pictures of scenes from the two world wars. They saw various weapons that had been used by the British army in Ashanti. The captain showed them two guardrooms. He opened the door to what he termed the guardroom for minor offences. He asked Marian to go in and look inside. Once she stepped in he banged the door shut and locked it. At the same time as the door banged they heard Marian scream inside. But the guide was apparently used to such attitude because he remained very calm when Dan and Junior were agitated by her screams. He opened the door after a few seconds but when she came out after those few seconds she had beads of perspiration on her forehead.

Junior offered to go in and the captain opened the door for him. He closed it when Junior went in. He came out a few seconds later laughing at his sister as if to say look, I did not scream.

From the museum they went to the regional hospital which was not far from the museum. They were taken to see the sword which legend said had been driven into the ground on that spot by the fetish priest who had been instrumental in the founding of the Ashanti state, Komfo Anokye. Many people had tried to pull it out of the ground without success. History had it that when the legendry Mohamed Ali visited Ghana in the 1960s he tried unsuccessfully to pull the sword out.

From the hospital the trio went to the zoo. Dan told the children what he knew about the animals at the zoo. Dan asked for directions to the Asantehene's palace and parked in the car park in front of the house and they walked round inspecting it. Even though they were told they could go in and see the former palace which had been built by the British they did not go in because they did not have time.

He drove to Ahinsan, known as the industrial heart of Kumasi. They went into a sawmill and were shown how logs were sawn into the boards that came out and were used for making furniture and for construction. He took them to the Naja David Veneer and Plywood mill and they saw how they turned wood into plywood and why plywood was stronger than ordinary boards. He showed them the breweries which brewed lager and stout beers. He did not know the difference between stout and lager beer and he admitted his ignorance when the children asked him.

They had lunch at Joeffel's and then set off on the next stage of their journey. They found that this road turned and twisted as against the straight road on which they drove from Tamale to Kumasi. They drove towards Cape Coast and stayed the night at Elmina Beach Resort. Here again they took a suite. In each hotel the children registered as Marian Apeatu and Daniel Apeatu Junior. Questions would have been asked about him staying in the same room with a sixteen year old girl who was not his daughter. That evening they had shrimps and lobster and boneless fish. The children were hearing the names of fish such as grouper, snapper and barracuda for the first time.

That night the children again asked their father to tell them a story. This time they knew the right response when he said the once upon a time in Kassem. "The hare is considered the most intelligent and most cunning animal in Kassena folklore. The hare and his family were starving. He needed food immediately otherwise the family would starve. So he went to the lion to borrow a bag of millet, promising to pay at harvest time. But the hare did not have a farm so several harvest times later he hadn't paid. The lion began to harass him and he decided to avoid the lion. He could not go out to feed and would starve if he did not get the lion off his back.

"He thought and thought and thought and eventually developed a plan to outwit the lion. He went to the buffalo and asked for his skin. The buffalo was naturally reluctant knowing that the hare was a trickster and when he gave up his skin might be the last time he saw it. Hare covered himself in buffalo's skin and went pretending to be eating grass where he knew for sure the lion would pass. When the lion was passing by he saw a highly emaciated buffalo, one so emaciated his skin dragged behind him. He became curious and went near to have a closer look. He noticed that the buffalo even struggled to chew the grass. He got nearer but kept a reasonable distance between them. From that distance he asked buffalo what had happened to him."

"But this is hare in buffalo skin and not the real buffalo, right?" Marian asked.

"Right," her father answered. "But we will continue to call him buffalo. Buffalo slowly raised his head to look at the lion as if even the effort to raise his head required more energy than he had. In a very soft very sick voice, he responded to the lion's greetings. To the question what had happened he told the lion that he had been sick for two months and that that day was the first day he had come out. He told the lion that it was a miracle that he was out eating since his family had given up hope that he would live.

"Lion was curious and kept asking what caused the sickness but the buffalo only kept sighing. When lion moved a few steps towards buffalo he stopped lion, explaining to lion that his sickness was highly contagious. Apparently reluctantly he told lion that it was the hare that spat on him in anger."

The children burst out in laughter.

"He told lion that the saliva of the hare, especially when the hare was angry, was very poisonous. And that he was the only one known to have survived from such venom. He sighed and slumped on the ground, apparently exhausted by even the effort it took to speak to the lion."

The children went on laughing. They wanted to ask questions but kept quiet, remembering the lessons from the previous night.

"For many days the lion avoided the path that went close to the hare's house. For many days the hare looked out for the lion to see if his trick worked. One morning the hare was upstairs in his house when he saw the lion going past his house, using that path that was far behind the hare's house. Hare got up and hailed the lion, greeting it. But lion quickened his steps and called back saying he was in too much of a hurry to even tarry and exchange greetings with the hare."

The children laughed and clapped their hands. The trick was working.

"But the hare was insistent, inquiring about the health of lion's wife who had been sick. Lion broke into a trot. 'Some day we will exchange information about her health but today I am in a hurry. Her health is improving.' Hare smiled but did not let the lion off so lightly. 'Friend lion, I have been looking for you to return your bag of millet. When a friend has been generous to you it is good that you don't stretch the person's patience. The bag is ready but you know I can't carry it myself so I have been looking for you to inform you to stop by for it…' But lion did not slow down and he did not let hare finish. 'I am sorry I forgot to tell that the bag of millet was a gift and not a loan…'"

The children again roared with laughter.

Their father went on. "This was interesting because the lion had before then been harassing the hare for repayment. So when it suddenly became a gift and not a loan only he could tell. But the lion went on, 'What are friends for? If one cannot help a friend in need what is his use?' At that time he was getting out of the range where he could be heard. Hare simply smiled and clasped his hands and wringed them. He knew that from that day onward he was free to roam and not live in fear of meeting the king of the jungle."

He and the children laughed. Marian said, "Folk tales are interesting. But they leave a lot of questions. It is assumed that the lion did not meet the buffalo for a long time before he saw the hare in the buffalo's skin. Was there no fear that he would meet a healthy buffalo say only two days after the hare had borrowed his skin and put the fear of God in the lion?"

Dan sighed. "Marian, you are studying Science and you have a scientific mind. Traditional societies don't have your scientific mind. Story telling is an art intended to entertain and sometimes teach a morale. So even in scientific communities storytellers go against what are scientific principles in order to create what is entertaining. You have animals and human beings doing business with each other and talking to each other. So you have Little Red Riding Hood being able to talk to the wolf. In your scientific world the wolf would have just pounced on the little girl as early as he could and not go lie in her grandma's bed and go through the rigmarole that the story said they went through. Even in novels written under supposed scientific contexts, readers are expected to exercise what is called the wilful suspension of disbelief…"

The children found Kassena stories interesting and asked a lot of questions about the art of storytelling in what was their culture but which they hardly knew. Their father explained as much as he could. "Storytelling serves many purposes in our culture," he told the children each of whom was resting on one elbow in order to look at him. "Stories were told in order to share certain values and teach lessons around those values. Kassena culture values being helpful to even people one does not know. There are stories told in which people have been unkind to strangers and suffered disasters as a result. In some of the stories a spirit turns into a human being to beg for help from a known miser. The miser refuses and calamity falls upon him. In orders a good hearted person gives away the only piece of food he has to live on to someone he does not know but who seems worse than him and the good he does changes his condition for the better. So they help to capture and share and keep for posterity cherished values.

"Storytelling also helps to keep families together. I remember how much I looked forward to the evening when I was in primary school. The reason? I longed to hear a new story. Sometimes we found as much fun in the stories we had heard several times as we did in the new ones. Some members of the family told already known stories in a way that you could not help but be entertained by them. Storytelling time brought families together and bonded them. I can't imagine the number of conflicts and grumblings that must have been avoided in families by using that space of time to create fun, to amuse and to educate…"

The children showed a lot of interest in the stories and were happy to be learning about their people. It seemed in every stage of his relationship with the children he would find something to be guilty of. He and Matilda had left the children suspended, without roots. They had made them children without an identity. Now the children were seeking their identity. They now wanted to know who they were, what the group they belonged to was like.

Before he closed his eyes in sleep he knew that telling stories would be a nightly ritual on this trip. He would activate and polish that part of his memory that held the stories so that he would have at least two interesting stories to tell the children each night.

When the children dozed off in sleep he lay there thinking of evenings in his childhood sitting around the fire and listening to stories. He enjoyed listening to stories and his aunt Kanuga told such beautiful stories. She knew so many of them and she had a way of telling stories that made everyone listen when she started one. She could make the hair on your body, even the hair that you did not have, stand erect when she told stories of horror. She could make your ribs ache with pain from laughter when she told funny stories.

Dan had never had the opportunity to tell any of the stories he had heard from his parents' generation. Now, through Marian and Junior, he was practising an art he had acquired many years ago. Through them he was sharing a pot of gold he had been given many years ago and which had lain idle in his mind. He again sighed. Oh fatherhood!

The next day he took them first to the Canopy Walk. The children and their father had heard so much about the Canopy Walk but even Dan had never been on it. The Walkway was constructed of boards held by rope high above the top of trees in a dense forest. To many people it seemed an interesting experience to walk on it till they found themselves on the swaying walkway. Imagining walking several metres above a dense forest and looking up into the open blue skies and down on top of an endless umbrella of trees would seem fascinating to a lot of people. One's imagination could be scaring when there is nothing to be scared about; or it could be romantic when reality had no element of romance.

Father and children had a good laugh as they watched many fainthearted people come all the way to go up on the walkway only to chicken out at the very last minute. But it really required courage to go on the walkway when they watched people wobble their way forward, the tension in them radiating from their body as steam from a boiling kettle.

Father and children went up on it, with Junior the most courageous among the three. Only one person was allowed at a time. Junior went first, followed by Marian so that their father would be able to support either of them who might need help.

Dan felt afraid when he had gone only twenty metres and felt the walkway swaying under him. When they arrived at the other end and got down Dan and his daughter sighed loudly with relief. Once on solid ground he found his fear unfounded. The walkway was held by many solid ropes. Even if one of them broke there were still many others to hold the weight of a man.

Dan bought them coconuts and they drank the cool sweet water and ate the soft and equally sweet flesh.

343

Next they drove to the Elmina castle and were taken round on tour. He had never been to any of the castles and he found the history of the castle as fascinating as the children found it. Elmina was called Edina by its citizens. The Portuguese who were the first to come to the then Gold Coast landed first in Edina. They called it the mine, *La Mina* in Portuguese. The natives had been struggling for many years to get it officially called Edina but it still remained officially called the mine, Elmina.

The castle had an interesting but sad story. It changed hands as the different European countries fought for supremacy over the country. It was taken over at a point by a scheming local chief, but for only a brief period of time. On the parapets of the castle facing the sea there were still cannons pointing towards the sea. Rusted cannonballs lay nearby. Their guide explained how the cannonballs were fired at attacking ships.

But the harrowing part of the history of the castle was its use as warehouse, so to speak, for slaves. Slaves were stored here till ships arrived to take them across the Atlantic to lands they did not know. People who did not know each other, who had been captured in different parts of the country, torn from their families, men from their wives and children, women from their husbands and children, were all thrown together here in dungeons, chained to prevent their escaping in such a fortified place. People who did not speak the same language were lumped together in the holds of the castle.

They were shown where the governor stood and looked down at the human cargo. Some people's loved relations. Merchandise to their captors. If he saw a woman he admired he would ask for her. She would be taken out and given a scrub before being sent in to satisfy the big man's lust. To the children it probably meant nothing. But Dan's imagination took him many years back to a room in which a bewildered black woman, uprooted from her roots, made to walk on foot for days over many miles, living each day in fear of what would happen next, was having sex with a white man she loathed and feared. While the white man enjoyed his act, heightened by his power over her, the woman would hate everything that happened. Going through this was more pain added to the pain of her forceful uprooting from her family.

They learnt that women who got pregnant were released and just left in the town. Abandoned in a town in which they knew nobody and were saddled with sickness that could lead to their death and responsibility if they delivered successfully.

The lowest point of the tour lay outside the castle. They were taken through a tunnel that led outside the castle unto the shore, only a few metres from the sea. Canoes would be berthed there to cart the slaves to the waiting ships. They called that stage the Point of No Return. All those who got to that point lost any hope of ever escaping. They were transported in the canoes to the waiting ships to be packed like Moroccan sardines on a journey in which thousands died.

When they left the castle Dan told the children what happened to the slaves when they arrived at the other side of the Atlantic. "They were treated like animals. They were taken to markets and sold the way you would sell animals. The men were advertised as bulls or boars who could work hard and breed children for their owners."

The castle had a sobering effect on the children. It had an even more profound effect on Dan who could stretch his imagination to live the lives of those who went through the pain.

They drove through Cape Coast, amazed how hilly the town was. They visited famous schools they had heard about. Mfantsipim, the first secondary school in the country and producer of most of the greatest citizens of the country. All the schools were on hills, they noticed. They drove up Ghana National, went on to St Augustine's College and Adisadel.

They spent the Wednesday night in Takoradi the swingers' city. On the Thursday they went to the village they had all heard so much about and wondered how it would be living in it, Nzulezu, the village on stilts. This was a village built over water. The houses were therefore built over stilts to raise them off the water. They had to park their vehicle somewhere and be taken by boat there. Initially the boat ride was scary to the children, especially Marian. She did not hide her fear but Junior laughed at her. They were taken round the village by a volunteer guide and the two children were fascinated by the houses on stilts and how children played. They asked a lot of questions about the community. When they had to leave the children felt reluctant. Marian exchanged addresses with a girl from the village who was in secondary school in Takoradi.

It was an exciting day for them, because travelling through the thick forest was itself exciting. But as they drove back Dan worried about mosquitoes in that village.

They went back to Elmina and spent another night in Elmina Beach Resort. Again that night he told the children two stories but they slept early since they were going to wake up very early the next morning. He looked for signs of tiredness in the children but he found them excited rather. If they were tired their excitement masked it.

They hit the road at five the next morning and drove through Accra to Akosombo. They joined in the activities planned by the Volta Hotel for the Good Friday. It included a boat ride to an island in the River Volta. It was fun as there were music and various games throughout the journey. At the island there were various games and father and children had a swell time. Dan could not remember ever having so much fun on the Good Friday. He felt guilty that they did not go to church and he did not think that not taking the children to church on especially such an occasion was what a good Christian father should do. But he hoped their maker would understand and forgive him. He made a mental note to suspend going for communion and go for confession at the next earliest opportunity.

They had a wonderful day and the laughter of the children kept ringing in his ears. The sight of the children mixing with other children and playing games with other people they did not know filled his heart with joy. It was good for them to broaden their horizon. Here again Marian made friends and exchanged addresses with two girls.

They returned to the hotel in the evening and checked in. They stood at the rails of the restaurant and watched the green beautiful hills surround the hotel. They looked at the dam and its giant equipment just next door. They would not have the time this time round to visit the hydro-electric generating plant and he knew they would have to come again. He would certainly have to come again with the children. The next time they would plan to visit only a few places and stay longer to discover each place.

The children were now getting used to the exotic foods they had been introduced to on this trip, especially the seafood. After supper he made them stay around the restaurant for more than an hour. On the way to their room he made them stop at the car park where the air was filled with the fragrant scent of lavender. They leaned against rails that ran round the car park and breathed in the beautifully scented air. He told them about the tree that exuded the scent. "It is called the Lavender tree or Lady of the Night. In the day it does not produce any scent. In the evenings it exudes this scent you smell. If you ever stayed in my house till this time you would smell the same scent." It was a lovely evening, a beautiful ending to a very pleasant day.

They stood there for a long time sometimes talking but most of the time just enjoying the company of each other, strengthening the communion of the children and father. Several times on this trip Dan's mind played games with him. If Matilda had not been who she was it could have been a happy family. He would have been thinking seriously about a reunion with her now that he had found pleasure in the company of the children. He had thought of him and Matilda coming back but ruled it out definitively. They had developed into different personalities and they were undoubtedly incompatible. But the second reason, and even more important to him, was the fact that Matilda had lived a very loose life after the divorce. He could not imagine him having her back after so many very low men had had their fun with her. She had acquired a reputation he would not want associated with his wife. And finally, she drank and was addicted to it. After this long time in the bottle as they say it, she could not get out of it. For her it would take more than the shock that woke him to wake her up. If she was sacked from her job she would rather drink herself to death.

If they had not been drunks and lived in the clouds when they married they could have been a happy family, he thought several times. That evening at the Volta Hotel in Akosombo he wished there was a wife and a mother to make the happy family complete. He also thought that it would not happen. He would not have Matilda back. And Marian had underlined the impossibility of him marrying again when she described the qualities of the woman he needed to marry – one who would make a good wife to him and a good mother to the children. Now that he had come so close to the children he took Marian's statement very seriously; he would not marry any woman he was not very sure would be close to the children. After all that they had suffered because of him and Matilda, and now that they had discovered happiness he did not intend to let anything, or anyone, disturb their happiness. He could not undo the harm of the past but he could prevent any future harm. He knew he could never forgive himself if he allowed the happiness of the children to be compromised.

He told the children stories while they all stood bathed in the scent of the lavender trees.

They left very early in the morning for Accra. They found some shoppers who could not resist the temptation of making money even on a festive day. Dan bought more clothing for the children. But he also bought some textiles for their mother as well. He asked Marian if she knew the size of her mother's footwear. She did so she guided her father to buy footwear as well for her. They bought a suitcase and loaded their mother's gifts in it.

They arrived in Kumasi late in the evening and found a room again in Silicon Hotel. The next morning they attended the Easter church service in Kumasi. They had a choice of many places and he chose the St Peter's Cathedral. The children loved it – it was so huge, far bigger than the Cathedral in Tamale.

After the church service they drove to Tamale, arriving at about four in the evening. Auntie Regina had come to visit Matilda when the children lugged in the suitcases. The joy of the trip showed in the non-stop smiles the children flashed at the three women. Dan did not come in, not desiring any confrontation with his former wife. Children in the neighbourhood helped Marian and her brother to carry the suitcases.

They gave their mother her suitcase. Auntie Regina who had started saying good bye when the children came in postponed her departure to see what was in the suitcase for Matilda. Even Matilda was moved by the contents of the suitcase – dress materials, textiles, night wear and footwear. For once Matilda did not say disparaging things about the children and their father. Regina could not tell whether there was a change of attitude in Matilda or it was fear of the children that made her silent. Whatever it was, she was happy for the children. She had never seen the children so happy.

Dan went back to the market when he left the children in their mother's. He bought guinea fowls and goat meat. He got a Moslem to slaughter the guinea fowls because of Leila, his daughter's friend. He spent the evening in the kitchen preparing food for the children and him to send to the Catholic organised picnic the next day. He woke up very early the next morning and completed the cooking. He wanted to prepare spaghetti, knowing how much the children liked it. But he knew that the children could not sit in the open under the cynosure of the public and struggle eating it. Instead he prepared yam balls, fried rice and used the goat meat to prepare what was called light soup. It was well spiced. He also packed a box of assorted soft drinks and cold water.

By 8:00 a.m. he had finished and packed the food in food flasks and was ready for the church. The children, all four of them including Leila, were in his house by 8:30. When Dan asked about her going to church he learnt that she had sometimes gone to church in school. She wanted to go with them.

They all drove to the Kamina barracks where the church service and the picnic were going to be held. It was his first picnic even though he had been in Tamale for many years. After the church service they went their separate ways, enjoying the different activities taking place. He agreed with the children to return to the car at 1:00 p.m. for lunch. He gave them money to buy whatever they needed and asked them to go their own way and have fun. But Junior chose to rather go with him.

Dan walked round to find out what sort of fun people had in the picnic. It was interesting how people enjoyed themselves. There was all kind of music and people had many different games. Various plates of food were on sale. With Junior trailing behind him he visited the Dagaaba dancers, then went to see the Frafra dance. It was one day of great fun, played out in various forms. They met people Dan had not seen for a long time. Again through the children he was learning. This one day off in a year, to join the crowd and meet people he had not seen for a long time, to just stop everything and unwind, would bring so much healing when he returned to work he would be more productive. He knew all this, at least the theory. A good leader takes time off to renew themselves physically. There was no better way to renew oneself than to give up all work and do something entirely fun.

Junior clung to his father. Occasionally he would pull his father's hand and sometimes he would get on his father's back. Dan was happy to carry him. And Junior was happy to be carried so he climbed on his father's back as frequently as he could.

The children were completely lost in the crowd. It was the first time Marian had come to the picnic. In the past she did not have nice clothing to come into a crowd like this. Besides their mother could not give them any food to bring to this place where most people were expected to bring food. They found their friends and went from place to place, amusing themselves.

Occasionally the three girls would run into Junior and his father. They would introduce whoever they were with. Marian would say Dan was her father and she would say it proudly.

When Dan and Junior returned to the vehicle almost thirty minutes after the agreed time they found the three girls and two of their friends leaning against the vehicle. They brought out mats and sat under a tree where Dan served the food. They ate the light soup and kept going back for more of it. Dan encouraged them to eat the other foods before they filled themselves with the soup. When they tasted the yam balls they wanted to continue eating. When they tried the fried rice they ate so much of that as well. In the end they could not take more than a can of soft drink each. The two friends of the girls giggled when they learnt that it was Dan who cooked it. But the four children who already knew how good a cook Dan was did not find it funny that he had cooked so well.

After the meal the three girls also offered to go with the Dan. So all five formed a band that went round. Dan felt like the father of a large family. That afternoon he realised that he was going to be the father of not only two children but four. He realised he could not relate with his daughter without taking in her two friends and treating them as the sisters they have been to her. He could not separate them. But it brought back his worries; how he would fare managing four young people. He planned the next set of activities with all four children included in them.

They left the picnic grounds after 5:30 p.m. That evening in his bed, Dan recalled the little people in *Who Moved My Cheese*. He felt like writing on the wall: HAPPINESS HAS MANY DIFFERENT FACES.

Chapter Twenty-Four

Dan woke up very early and prepared breakfast. He was expecting the children and he was not sure if they would have eaten. He had bread toasted with eggs, bacon and fruit juice and beverage ready by the time the children came in. The children screamed with delight when they saw him. He was dressed in blue/black corduroy trousers and a navy blue polo shirt he bought in Kenya. He placed a baseball cap on the table but did not have it on when the children came in.

The dressing was one of the signs of his freedom. When he woke up that morning he told himself that he was truly free and so should dress to announce it. When he looked at himself in the mirror he liked what he saw. He first put on a cowboy hat. The hat had been given to him more than five years previously and he never wore it. He tried it and the image he saw in the mirror looked very nice to him. He smiled – the children were really changing his life. But he put it back and took an equally deep blue baseball cap instead.

Over breakfast he saw Leila and Marian lean close to each other and talk for a minute or so. Marian then leaned towards Carol and talked to her for a while. He noticed Carol shake her head. He ignored them and went on eating.

Till Marian said, "Dad, where did you learn cooking?"

"In Ghana," he replied and went on eating.

Marian's friends laughed at her. Junior did too but Dan pretended nothing was unusual. Leila leaned and whispered to Marian, "Your father is a very good joker." Marian nodded.

"Ah Dad!" Marian protested. "I know you learnt to cook in Ghana but I am sure you understand the question."

"Maybe I don't. I have thick skull, you know. You will be surprised how little I understand. So ask your question again."

She rolled her eyes and breathed in deeply. "Okay, I will. The first time I ate bread toasted with eggs was here. Carol and Leila are eating it for the first time. Here. We have been asking each other where you learnt to make this toast. And to cook such delicious light soup and spaghetti and yam balls and fried rice and I am sure many other dishes."

"But you don't want me to say I learnt my cooking in Ghana, which is where I learnt it."

"No. Who taught you?"

"Difficult question," he told her. "I picked one thing here and learnt to prepare another recipe from somewhere else."

When they cleared the table and washed up, the children insisting on keeping Dan out of it, he shooed them out of the hall. When he put on the deep blue baseball cap to complete his all blue dressing, the children exclaimed and instantaneously clapped. Even the security guard on duty smiled. He knew the master of the house to dress well on weekdays and to dress neatly but very informally on weekends but he had never seen him dress in what in Ghana was called Yankee style. He looked well in it though and looked like one less serious with life but ready to enjoy it.

When he stopped at Dungu to buy yam, the group of people who sat under the tree and in nearby sheds virtually 'poured out' all their eyes on Dan and his troop of children. "Your children are nice," an elderly woman could not help telling him. "Are the girls triplets?" He told her no. He smiled, with pride. Only a few months back, he told himself, he did not even know the two children. Now he had four. And when he looked at them he admitted they were nice. He would be the envy of many people. For the umpteenth time he sighed and in that breath was the word fatherhood.

He played music and told them he had a lot of music that reminded him of the days when he was young and free and happy. The children loved some of the songs but did not like others. He played a collection of Jimmy Cliff songs and relived the happy feeling of his childhood. Songs like *Suffering in the Land, Struggling Man, I Want to Know, House of Exile, Number One Rip Off Man* and *Vietnam* were among his favourite songs and he still enjoyed them. When he put on Johnny Nash's collection again songs like *Comma Comma, Let's Be Friends,*

Cream Puff, What a Feeling, Birds of a Feather and *Reggae on Broadway* brought back nostalgic feelings of his school days.

Long stretches of the road to Bolga were, like some stretches of the road between Tamale and Kintampo, very straight and on very level ground. When they drove past Nasia he asked the children to remind him on the return journey to stop there and buy smoked fish.

When they drove through Walewale he pointed out the road leading to Nalerigu where history had it that a chief built a wall around the town. Remnants of the wall could still be seen, he told the children, even though he had not been to see the wall himself. He promised to take them to see it one day. Leila turned and whispered to Carol who was in the back seat with her and Junior that her father did not take his children anywhere. And he did not promise taking them anyway. "Even if he ever did we know he would not keep his promise."

Their first stop was at a ranch in a town called Wulugu. As they approached the ranch they came across a road sign with a cow on it. It meant animals crossing but Dan remembered something funny about that sign and he shared it with the children. Ghana Broadcasting Corporation had an educational programme through which it sought to educate drivers and the general public on road signs. The education team members would stop drivers and show road signs to them and ask them what the signs meant. In one of the series a driver was shown the sign with the cow between two lines and he said the sign meant that there was a restaurant nearby. Another was shown a twisted arrow which meant the road bent one way and then the other way. The driver said it was a warning to drive carefully because there were snakes ahead.

"He is the funniest man I have ever met," Leila leaned above Junior to whisper to Carol. "He doesn't act like a father. He is like a friend."

Carol nodded. She had been thinking that way too.

The ranch had cattle but it was not the cattle he stopped to show the children. The ranch also stocked ostriches, birds that were not native to Ghana. They parked the vehicle and walked over to the fence and the children were delighted to see the big, long legged and long necked birds. Dan took pictures of the children with both his digital and ordinary cameras.

"Welcome to Bolga," he told them. It was not yet 11:00 a.m. so he drove to the Commercial Bank and asked Ntim's secretary to see him. She waved him aside and went on being what was commonly called 'busy-fee,' being busy doing nothing. They crowded the space around her but that fact did not seem to bother her. Ntim came out of his office to talk to some staff when he saw Dan. He was angry when he heard they had been waiting for more than five minutes because he had been free and the secretary had not called him to tell him he had visitors.

"Understand that it is not all visitors to the office who come to ask for favours or to borrow money," he told her. "You should ask visitors the purpose of the visit and call the person they have come to see and let him decide whether he is free to see them or not. Someone we need urgently can walk away because of your attitude."

They went outside to transfer the yam from Dan's vehicle into Ntim's.

"You know I ever married?" he asked Ntim.

Instead of replying Ntim only smiled. "You forget that Gloria once asked you if the experience from the first marriage was so bad that it made you not want to go through a second experience. Yes, I know you married." He darted a look at the children, unsure he had so many children from the marriage before it broke down.

Dan chuckled.

"What is funny?" Ntim asked. The children looked at him with the same question on their minds.

"No, we did not have four children."

"How do you know that was what I was thinking?"

"If I were the sleuth Sir Arthur Conan Doyle created I would have told you, elementary, Ntim, elementary. Have you ever heard of Edgar Alan Poe?"

He shook his head. "No. Who is he? Or who was he?"

"He was a writer."

"No, I've never read him. The writers I have read the most are Nevil Shute, Alistair Maclean, Arthur Hailey and Frederick Forsyth. Never heard of Poe."

"Poe was many things. He was a poet. He wrote short stories. But I am referring to him now because he was the father of deduction. He pioneered, even before the creator of Sherlock Holmes, the ability to follow a person's train of thoughts by observing his body language. You admitted knowledge of the fact that I had been married before. And went on to prove the fact that you knew it by referring me to what Gloria once said. And then you came back to the fact of my marriage. And at that point you hurriedly looked at the children. The question was in your face. Did he have all these children from that marriage?"

"I know you to be a wizard accountant and not an investigator." He again took in all the children.

Dan offered to answer the unanswered questions. "We had two children. When my wife and I separated I was separated from the children as well. They found me this year. And brought two more children along with them. So now I have four children." He asked the children to introduce themselves.

Ntim smiled when Junior introduced himself. Even if he had not said he was called Junior Ntim would have picked him out as one of Dan's children. The resemblance was striking. He introduced Ntim to the children.

"Your dad was a break," Ntim told them. "We were course mates in the School of Administration but he was far ahead of us. He was consistently the best student in the class and had the best class in our batch. He was the only student to have made a first class that year." He paused and turned to look at Dan. "Should I?" he asked Dan.

"Should you what?"

"Tell them about the other life."

"My life is now an open book. You have already told them what I would not tell them."

"Even in those days at the university your dad drank heavily. He drank everything – palm wine, beer, wine, gin, *akpeteshie* – he drank all of them. He would stagger to the hall and struggle to climb up the stairs. But when he woke up at dawn and read, and in the afternoons and those few evenings when he was not drunk, what he read stayed forever in his mind. Remember that at the university you get a good grade not because you can recall all that you read. You get a good grade because you can recall that you learnt and apply it. So your dad had a brain for seeing connections and making applications, even in his alcohol flooded brain. Now that he has given up drinking he is again doing wonders."

Like Dan he also stretched his arms and took all the children under the arms. "Study hard and make your dad proud. Your dad is a very kind man. And I know he will support you if only you work hard. So work hard and make yourselves proud and make him proud, okay?"

They all said okay.

"When are you coming back?" Ntim asked Dan.

"Around 4:00 p.m. You know I don't like driving on the highway in the night."

Ntim looked at the children. "You know Gloria would have loved to meet the children. Are you reconciled with their mother?"

He shook his head. "It's just with the children."

"Is reconciliation in the making?"

Dan looked at the children and shook his head. "We are incompatible."

Among the four children only Carol knew Navrongo. The rest were visiting the town for the first time. "I chose today for this trip because today is a market day and there is a lot of drama on market days. People get drunk and take over the road and perform very interesting drama for free."

"Daddy!" Marian protested.

"Marian, what is wrong?"

"Dad, Leila is here. She will observe all those happenings and use them to mess Kassenas when we go back to Tamale."

Dan nodded understanding. Leila was Gonja and Gonjas and Kassenas made jokes about each other.

"I didn't have to come here to see what is obvious about Kassenas," Leila told Marian. "Every Ghanaian knows that when Kassenas eat groundnuts they can do all kinds of infantile things. Like think that because yams are white when you peel them yams are fatty."

"Dad, do you see that she has started?"

When they were leaving Ntim had told the children his wife would be happy to meet them. "The children especially will love to meet you. Dan is their favourite uncle and they will like to meet his children."

Marian pondered over the bits they had learnt from Ntim. This was the second time she had heard of the intelligence of their father.

The lady at Barclays in Tamale had told her her 'uncle' was a break. Ntim went farther than that. She took a quick look at the man who was their father who was still an enigma to his children.

She hoped they would be introduced, through their father, to networks of social relationships that would make them stop pitying themselves.

Their father had been a drunkard too. Dan, a drunkard? She had heard it before, from friends of her mother. Now Ntim confirmed it and their father had not denied it.

Navrongo. Home. She turned round to see if Junior was affected by the trip as much as she was. But as usual he kept a face that said nothing of his emotions. She looked at their father. Birds of a feather; they hardly showed their feelings on their faces.

They bought ice blocks before leaving Bolga and they drove straight to the Tono Irrigation Project. He took them to the landing bay which was where fishermen brought their catch and sold it to women who then sent it to Navrongo town or Bolga for sale. The women initially agreed to let Dan buy the fish directly from the fishermen but when he brought out two large cold boxes and they realised how much fish he wanted they realised he was not a small scale buyer. He bought only tilapia. He filled the two cold boxes and put the ice blocks on top of the fish.

He drove them up the embankment of the dam and explained how it worked. "This is the largest irrigation project in the country," he explained to the children. "It irrigates about 2,500 hectares or so. I am not very sure of the figure but it is over two thousand hectares. There was a river here that flowed throughout the year. They dammed it here, building this embankment, and creating the dam."

He took them some distance from where they had been standing and showed them how the water was controlled. "This wheel you see here controls the valve that controls the outlet from the dam. When they turn the valve to open it, water goes out through this main canal. There are other smaller canals which branch off this canal. They are controlled by sluice gates. The smaller canals feed even smaller canals which form a network that allows water to feed the fields."

He took them to one end of the embankment and showed them the spillway. "The dam can take in only a certain volume of water. In years when the rains are very heavy, the dam may take this maximum volume and yet still have water coming in. The excess water flows out of the dam through the spillway. Water from the dam can be intentionally pumped out to reduce the pressure on the embankments. If the walls holding in the water collapse, all this water will gush out and cause untold destruction."

They drove down and went to see how the water was fed from the main canal to other, smaller canals. They met farmers and some workers who helped to explain how the irrigation process worked. The children asked a lot of questions. They drove back to the main road and turned towards Sandema. He went off the main road and took the children to see farms on which they were harvesting tomatoes.

"The impact of this project on the economy of the town is fantastic. Over one thousand farmers are able to earn extra income from the dry season tomatoes cultivated here. The town has fresh vegetables throughout the year. There is fish throughout the year as well. Some years back fish farms were introduced and fish farmers bred fish for sale. I don't know why that collapsed. Tomatoes and rice are the main crops cultivated here. During the rainy season it is rice that is mostly cultivated. In the dry season most of the land is put to the cultivation of tomatoes."

The children saw tomato fields stretching as far as their eyes could see. They bought two crates of tomatoes, very cheap. The girls, who knew how much tomatoes cost in the market in Tamale, talked excitedly about the cheapness of the vegetable on the farms.

Dan drove back to the centre of the town, through the market which was now filled with people. The vehicle had to literally beg for permission to drive through as both men and women had taken over the road. They drove past the district hospital, past the teachers' training college and turned right at a point about a kilometre from the college. The children wondered where they were going so far out of town. Marian thought it must be his house and felt excited about meeting her grandparents on her father's side.

She was wrong. After about ten minutes after turning right, he stopped and they came out and he showed the children more fields under tomatoes.

"You mean the project extends as far as this?" Leila asked, snuggling close to him.

"You can drive for more than a mile up this road and you will still be in fields under the project."

He drove them to Navrongo Secondary School and showed them the classes he sat in. He showed them Luther King house which was where he lived for the seven years that he was in that school. It was empty as schools were on holidays.

He drove them towards town and stopped to show them the Navrongo campus of the University for Development Studies. "It was agreed during the establishment of the university to locate the Administration, Medical School and Agric faculty in Tamale. The Applied Sciences Faculty was to be located here while the Wa campus was to host the Integrated Development Studies Faculty."

He drove them back towards town and drove into the campus of the training college. He told them that it was among the earliest educational institutions in Northern Ghana.

Even this far from the market the road was busy. The children saw people already returning from the market while some were then on their way to the market. They saw old men in white smocks, their white beards matching the whiteness of the smocks, riding bicycles, a chicken or a guinea fowl tied at the back. They saw many women, many of them elderly, riding bicycles, their wares tied on the carriers behind the bikes. They saw children, some barely more than ten, riding bikes to or from the markets. They saw men returning home and pulling behind them animals they had bought in the market, the animals protesting against their relocation to new homes by stubbornly refusing to follow their new owners.

There was a lot to see and be entertained by on the way and in the market. He took them to the Catholic cathedral about half a kilometre from the hospital and told them the main church building was a historic monument being one of the earliest cathedrals in Northern Ghana.

It was about two in the afternoon and even though the children had not complained he knew they would be hungry. So he took them back into town. He bought hot bean cakes which they took to a bar he said sold the best tilapia in Ghana.

359

"How can the best tilapia be sold in Navrongo?" Leila challenged him.

"You will judge for yourself," Dan told her. "I have eaten tilapia in different places in Accra. In Blue Gate in Accra which is famous for its tilapia. In Achimota and in North Kaneshie. I know how their tilapia tastes. So I am well placed to judge."

He ordered the largest size for each child and ordered drinks for them while they waited for the fish to be coal grilled. They ate their bean cakes and they found them very nice tasting. Even Leila commented on the taste of the cakes.

"In the Upper East Region, cooking is an art people have taken to very high levels. The best roasted beef or goat meat in the country can be got in Bawku. It is very soft, even though coal roasted. All the broth is still trapped in the meat and with the first bite you can feel it oozing out of the meat into your mouth. From the look of the meat on the grill you would think it is not well cooked. But when you eat it you will find that it is just right. In Bolga there is a place called Kings and Queens where they do chicken and cabbage so well even when your tummy is full you will still find enough space to store at least a quarter of a chicken. And the best tilapia, as I told you earlier, is done in this bar."

They served them giant tilapia fish done with spices and cabbage. Their father had a smile spread on his lips as the children attacked the fish in silence. When their eyes met Leila smiled too and said, "It is very nice tasting but I don't know if it is the best in the country."

"I'll give you time to find out," Dan replied.

"The only places I know are Tamale, Salaga and Bole. And now Navrongo. So I can't find out."

They enjoyed the fish and cabbage. Leila asked how the cabbage was done to make it taste so nice and Dan explained

"If you marry your wife will suffer," Leila said.

"Why?" Dan and Marian asked at the same time.

"You will know more about cooking than she does."

"We can change roles then. I cook and look after the house and she works."

"She works?" This time it was Leila and Marian who asked at the same time.

Dan looked across at Junior and the girl Dan now thought in his mind as Junior's sister, Carol, the two quiet members of the team.

He next took the children to a must visit site in the region, the crocodile pond of Paga. After the market in Paga they turned right and took a narrow lane that led to the pond. Young men came around as soon as the vehicle showed up driving towards the pond. Dan bought a young chicken more than three times the price he knew they could get it in the market. They could see the young men had a close relationship with the reptiles and even gave some of them names. The young men called out a crocodile and it came gliding through the water and came out unto the land. Dan took its tail to show the children that it was safe to do so. Thus encouraged by their father they all crowded round the giant reptile and put hands on its tail and body while their father took pictures. He squatted on its back to encourage the children to do same but only Junior posed that way and he took pictures of him. They watched in fascination when the chicken was thrown to crocodile. It opened its long mouth and caught the poor bird between teeth and crushed it with such a crunching sound it made Leila and Marian turn their faces.

He drove the children to a site that was said to be where slaves were camped before the long march to the coast. They saw dents in the rocks that the slaves were said to have used in pounding grain. "Now I am sure Marian and Junior have a better picture of the lives of the slaves. Many of them were captured here or even farther north. The stories of the pain in those who were captured and the relations they left behind were terrible. When I was a kid and growing up in the village, the family would tell stories of how babies were taken off the backs of their mothers and smashed against rocks before their mothers were marched off into slavery. Some even more cruel captors would ask mothers to pound their babies in mortars.

"From here they walked over five hundred miles to the castles in the coast. These days, even in the comfortable buses ran by the State Transport Corporation, people find the journey long and tiring. In those days the slaves walked barefoot, and chained, from here to the coast."

When they were leaving Navrongo it was past 4:00 p.m. It was when they were leaving the town that Marian asked if they were not going to the house.

"Which house?" Dan asked

"Your house. Our house."

"No."

She kept looking at his face for a whole minute but he did not turn to look at her nor did his face give away what he was thinking. She thought it wise not to raise the issue with the others in the vehicle.

There was silence in the vehicle for a long time. They stopped in Bolga to buy onions and watermelons.

When they got back into the vehicle Leila leaned forward and said, "Dad, did you notice how people have been looking at us wherever we go? I noticed it when we stopped to buy the yams. All the women at the bay were looking at us when we were buying the fish. When we went to buy the tomatoes and when we went to the bar to buy the fish, it was the same. Those young men at Paga could not seem to have enough of us."

"Maybe they were asking if all of you were my children and if the three of you were triplets. Maybe they were saying what beautiful girls."

"Mmm!" Leila said. "Or they were admiring this father who loves his children so much that he collects of all them and goes on an excursion with them."

"I don't know about that," he told them.

"I know about that," Leila said, putting a hand on his shoulder. "You are a loving dad."

Before he could say thanks he heard, "We know about that. You are a loving dad. You have been very nice to us. And you know so much and you have taught us so much. We learn a lot from you each time we are with you."

He did not say anything for a whole minute. The last speaker was Carol, the silent one. Yet, she was the one who paid the last compliments. Even Marian turned and looked at her and smiled.

"Thanks, Leila and Carol," he managed to say after a long silence. "I thought I was happy when I lived alone. I still think I was happy. But I have found a new type of happiness with you around. It has been fun having you people around me. So I am not just giving to you; I am receiving a lot from you to give me joy."

He noticed the different titles Leila called him since he met her and Carol. On the first day he met them, when he went to the school on vacation day and took them home he was Mr Dan. By the time they finished cooking and ate and he drove them home he had become Uncle Dan. On the day he took them to the picnic he started as Uncle Dan and ended as plain dad. And dad had stayed.

The last stop on their way home was Nasia where Dan bought smoked fish.

By the time it was dark enough for them to have to use the headlights they were entering Tamale. He drove them to his house where they prepared supper together. He had prepared meatballs with sauce. He heated it and now prepared plain rice and spaghetti. The children ate till they were too full to even get up from their seats. While they washed the crockery he found plastic bags and shared out the fish, both fresh and smoked fish, the onions and tomatoes for the children to send home. He then drove them home and left them in front of their houses. It was almost 10:00 p.m. when he returned to the house.

The next day Marian came to visit. Without Junior.

"Where is Junior?" her father asked.

"He will come later."

"What was he doing?"

"But it is not all the time that we go to places together, Dad."

He accepted it and said nothing.

"Dad, why didn't we go home yesterday when we went to Navrongo?"

He looked at her, remembering the question the previous day and the look she gave him when he answered. Was that why she came? And was that why she came alone?

"We didn't have the time to go home."

"We could have cancelled the trip to Paga to go home if we wanted to go home."

"Well, I didn't have any thing to do at home. That was why we did not go."

"But Junior and I have never been home before. We would have loved to go."

He said nothing for a long minute and they looked at each other.

"Marian, I will take you home when the time is ripe for me to take you home," he said sternly. "Yesterday was not the time to take you home."

She thought over it. "And when will the right time be, Dad?"

"I don't know but it was not yesterday."

An awkward silence followed after which Marian asked, "Dad what is it that will be wrong for us, Junior and I, to go home now? Why won't you want us to go? We could go on our own, you know?"

He hadn't thought about that. But now he did. They did not have to depend on him. If they didn't have to depend on him he needed to convince them not to go. He needed to tell her why he did not want them to go home now.

"Marian, people at home have very strong cultural beliefs. To them you belong to me. In the current world thinking on rights, children belong to both parents and not to one alone. Your mum and I therefore have equal claims to you and must have equal access to you. Traditionally that is not so. You belong exclusively to me. If husband and wife are separated therefore, the children must be in the custody of their father. My family has been suggesting going to the chief to grant custody of you to our family. I have said no because if your mother loses you it will kill her. My family has come to accept the fact that I will not be part of any action to seek custody of you from your mother. But if you go home, it is going to renew the pressure to demand custody of you. It may embolden them to even initiate action without my consent."

She digested that while she looked at him. "Dad, we can't come and stay with you because mum will die. We can't go to what is our home because they will initiate action that will kill mum. We have two sets of grandparents. We know mum's mother. We don't have a healthy relationship with her. All she does is insult us, big head, long ears. We will not ever dream of going to spend any number of days in our maternal uncle's home. We can't go to our own home because you don't want us to. So it means we can't come to the town we come from. We can only come as strangers, to see the town and go back that same day. Let us say we come here one day on an excursion with our mates and they ask us where our home is, what do we say? We are lost because we don't even know our home. We don't know where we come from."

There was silence as Dan chose to say nothing.

"Dad, it is you and mum, we don't matter. It is what you want or don't want. It is what will make mum happy. What that means to us does not matter, does it?"

"Marian, I have never taken more than a few days' leave from my work. I took four whole weeks to be with you. I have never gone round the places I went with you. I found them in order to bring us closer. Within the short period that we found each other, Marian, I have done enough to show that the two of you matter to me."

He did not shout. He said it with an even voice but in the tone of the voice she sensed his unhappiness. She knew he felt offended by her accusation. She thought about it and knew that he was right. They did matter. He had given them more than many parents had and her two friends had told her that much.

She got up and walked up to her father and sat next to him. She rested her head on his chest and looked up at his face. He did not smile. "Dad, I am sorry. It was unkind of me. I am rather thinking of myself and am not thinking of you." A tear rolled down her face and her father put his arm round her.

"Marian, you are impatient. You want everything at once. But things don't work that way in life. Your mother will come to accept the fact that you belong to both of us. My parents will come to accept same. Then you can go home without your mother worrying about her losing you. Then you can go home without my parents feeling they must seize you. But we have to take one step at a time."

She looked up into his face and nodded, as more streams of tears flowed beside the first one. He put his arm around her shoulders and pulled her to rest her head on his chest.

He waited till the tears dried. Then he spoke. "Marian, I want you to understand me. I love my parents and will not want to create opportunities in which I have to say no to them. Both parents of mine will want to see the two of you taken away from your mother. They have given up on putting the pressure on me because they came to realise I would not budge. Let me go home with you, let them see you with me, and let them know that we have re-established contact and they will be all over me asking me to claim you. They will revive the efforts they made some years back.

"I am in a triangle formed by you and Junior, your mother and my parents. My parents will want me to take you from your mother. You may say why not. Your mother will say nonsense."

She chuckled and lifted her head and looked into his face. He smiled at the combination of smile and tears in the same face.

"If your mother died today I would claim the two of you, I assure you," he said, still looking down at her face. She buried her head again in his chest. "But besides the reason I gave the last time for not wanting to claim you from your mother, I want you to understand that we will be unfair to her if I took you away from her. Whatever you feel about your mother please understand that she kept you alive for twelve years when I was not present in your lives. She put you in school till I met you and can now take over the payment of your fees. I respect her for that and in all I do I will acknowledge her role in your life and education and will want to protect her interest.

"I can explain that to you but I can't tell my parents that. It will not make any sense to them. That is why I did not think it wise to take you home. Marian, listen carefully. People will ask me why I am not insisting you change your surname back to Apeatu. Is that as important as taking leave in order to take the two of you round for us to develop a closer relationship?"

She sat up and looked at him.

He nodded and went on. "Do you need to change your surname in order for me to know how much you recognise me as a father and how happy you are to have me back in your lives?" He widened his eyes to emphasise the question and shook his head to signify no. "I am not concerned about myself and your mother alone. I am concerned about you the children. From where I stand in the triangle I have to think about you and your brother, my parents and your mother."

She hugged him and let her head lie on his bosom. He stroked the back of her head.

Chapter Twenty-Five

It was past 8:00 p.m. when Dan parked outside Aunt Polly's house and walked to the door and knocked. He expected Carol to come to the door and open it. He was ready to say hello Carol when the door opened and all he had to say remained frozen in his mouth. For many seconds he could not say a word. When you have prepared so well for a certain situation and you meet an entirely different situation you can be dumbfounded. He did look like a fool before the lady who also stood looking at him and wondering why he was there and could not say a word.

"Good evening, Madam," he managed to say eventually. "I came to see you."

The disbelief was apparent in the lady's face. "You came to see me? Do you know who I am?"

He had recovered. "Yes, you are Auntie Paulina."

She was still doubtful. She looked at him for many more seconds before clearly reluctantly opening the door for him.

The surprise was partly because he did not expect Auntie Polly to be the one to open the door. He reasoned that the two occupants of the house would be in the sitting room at that time. And that when they heard the knock it was the younger of the two who would open the door. Things had not worked out that way. He saw no sign of Carol in the house. But it was the image of the woman who stood before him that caused the confusion in his mind. From what he had heard about Aunt Polly, that she stayed indoors and spent a lot of time reading and studying, he had expected to see a plain old maid. Instead, the woman who stood before him was young and beautiful. Her shapely body stared at him through the transparent nightgown she had on.

He had to look round the room to take his eyes from the white pants and the rest of her inviting body that the loose gown only kept drawing attention to.

"Sorry for my intrusion into your quiet evening," he said when he sat down and his hostess remained standing. "My name is Dan Apeatu. My daughter is a friend of your niece Caroline."

The transformation in the face of his hostess was sudden and great. "Oh, you are Daniel Apeatu! I have never met you. I have heard about you but I don't know you. Sorry I was not expecting anybody at this hour. People hardly visit us and almost never in the evening."

Dan felt sorry for her discomfort and tried to reassure her.

She sat herself in one of the chairs, one that was forty-five degrees with Dan's. Even though Dan did not have to look across at her it did not make him feel comfortable that he had to sit talking to her with her in clothing that announced rather than concealed her body.

She cast one downward look at herself and got up and excused herself. "I was dressed for the night."

Dan was relieved. She came back with a cloth wrapped around her under the nightgown. It covered her breasts and reached down to her ankles. She was a very shapely woman and Dan guessed in any dress the great shape would show but the way she came back dressed made him more comfortable than the way she was previously dressed.

She welcomed him and asked if he would drink water. He said no, having just come from the house. They exchanged greetings.

"I am sure we have not met," Paulina said.

"Yes, I am sure we have not met. I am not great at remembering faces but I am sure if we had met before I would have had some impression that I saw you somewhere when you opened the door."

"I am relieved," she said to Dan's surprise. "I have heard many people talk about you. I have been told many times that I must have met you but only don't know that you were the one."

Dan assured her he was sure they were meeting for the first time.

"Thanks for the gifts from Navrongo," she told him.

He tilted his head. "Gifts from Navrongo?"

"Yes, Carol brought many parcels when you came back with them last week – fresh fish which was wonderful, smoked fish, tomatoes, onions and watermelon. I asked her if you shopped for her alone."

"Well, you don't have to say thanks to *me* for those items. I gave them to Carol who said thanks. So if she in turn gave them to you, your thanks should go to her and not to me."

"Daniel... I hope I can call you Daniel."

"Please. Call me Dan."

"Thanks. Call me Paulina. Dan, I have a lot to thank you for. A lot. For bringing my niece home when they vacated. For the wonderful day they had at the picnic. I don't go to places like that. I live a very quiet life but that is not what I want to impose on Carol. So I asked her to go last year but she refused. She went this year because you were taking them there and she came back very excited. I'd never heard Carol talk excitedly about anything. Till you took them to the picnic. Then when they started coming to your house she had a lot to talk about – what you had told them or done to them. She talked excitedly about the trip to Navrongo, about the things they learnt, about how much you told them.

"Dan," she leaned towards him, "you can't tell how much influence you are having on her, and very positive influence too. She showed me the textbooks you bought for her and Leila. They have been coming to your house regularly since their return from Navrongo and she has been telling me how they spend their time. I am proud of her. She is hard working and likes studies. But she is becoming even more serious since meeting you. Two days ago all three girls were here in this very room talking about their studies. I heard them ask how you would feel if they did not make it to medical school.

"The last thing I want to share with you and to say thanks. Carol is my late elder brother's daughter. I love her and have been doing the best I can for her. You have become a father figure in her life. You can't imagine how important it is to her. And therefore to me as well. So both Carol and I have a lot to thank you for."

Talk of the devil. Carol made her entry on the mention of her name. They both turned towards her at the same time. She stopped in her tracks, surprised to find Dan there. Like her aunt she was in a light nightgown. Her aunt asked her to go back and dress more decently. Dan was relieved. Carol was relieved too because she had been unsure whether to run back or come into the room and greet Dan.

Dan sighed. "I am used to Auntie Polly because that is the name I have been hearing from the children since meeting my children."

She laughed. "Polly makes me feel like a puffy cheeked child. Don't ask me where I got that image from; I have it and that is that."

Dan laughed too. "Well Auntie Polly who feels like a puffy cheeked child, thanks for what you said about Carol and I. I am glad to hear I have some influence, positive influence, on her. Carol is a wonderful girl – quiet but very observant and more mature than her age. She is the least emotional of the three girls. And she can look at things from a perspective you expect from only someone far older than sixteen.

"I have four wonderful children who are teaching me things no textbook can teach. They are teaching me a lot about real happiness which I have never come across in a book. Being with them is a wonderful experience that is best felt. I am discovering the joys of fatherhood, joys which are different from the satisfaction you derive from achievement in your profession. I took time off work to make them happy and ended up finding more happiness than they probably did – from the simple things I knew but took for granted, like the irrigation project in Navrongo. But also from the glorious company of these teenagers. I did not know how exciting it is to be plotting graphs about the future with children, seeing potential that can be developed and feeling how wonderful it will be to see it developed…"

Carol came in at that moment, this time dressed in a long dress that was not transparent. She came over and greeted Dan, calling him Dad.

After responding to Carol's greetings he turned to Paulina, "I don't know if you have heard the joke about the boy who was sent to deliver a message. When he arrived at the home where he was to deliver the message a party was going on and he was invited to join. He enjoyed himself, forgot to deliver the message and returned home only to describe the good time he had at the party. The Kassenas say that adults don't dance among flowering bean plants. So I won't behave like the boy. Let me get the main purpose of my visit out of the way first.

"When we set off for Navrongo last week it occurred to me on the way that if we had an accident you and Leila's family may not know that the children were travelling with me. I would be hard put to come and explain things to you. I don't want to make the same mistake twice. I want to take the children to the game reserve at Mole and I came to ask for your permission to go with Carol…"

"You don't need my permission for you to take Carol along," Paulina cut in to say. "I am happy for her to be with her friends and am happy for her to be going on trips that are both entertaining and educative."

"Thanks," Dan said. When he turned and looked at Carol she smiled. "We are leaving on Friday. We will come back on Sunday. That should give us enough time to go round the park as well as watch from the main hotel."

"I am however worried about the cost to you," Paulina told him.

Dan assured her not to worry. "For twelve years I denied my children what a father owed them. I can never make up for that. No amount of my time or expenditure on them now will ever make up for what I withheld from them. It doesn't mean if Marian comes up to me to ask for one million cedis to give to her boyfriend or to buy the latest fashionable shoes I will be parting with the amount because I owe them. But they deserve all that I have been doing for them so far. And the cost will not go up very much with Carol and Leila joining. And now that I consider all four my children Carol and Leila are not additional costs."

He leaned back in his seat. "Auntie Polly, you know…" He saw Carol smile at the name. He smiled too. "She is my auntie too." They laughed. "I am not only taking the children round for them to have fun. I have been to Mole before. To train people. I saw a few animals but have never gone round the park. This is going to be my first time going round the park. Going round Tono with the children was fun. Going to the crocodile pond was fun not only for the children but for me as well. So I am having fun. Don't worry about me."

He asked to leave ten minutes later. He said he was calling on Leila's family. When they went outside – Carol and her aunt came out to see him off – he turned and asked Paulina, "Did Carol resemble her mother or your brother?"

"Carol? Even though she is a girl she is the one among the children who resembled her father the most."

"I bet you resembled your brother too."

"Yes, but how did you know?"

"Carol resembles you a lot."

Leila's younger sister was the one who opened the door for Dan when he knocked at their door.

"Are your parents in?" he asked when he was let in.

"My mother is in but my father is not yet back."

"Can I see her?"

She did not know him so she asked, "Who should I say wants to see her?"

He shrugged. "Tell her your boyfriend."

"I beg your pardon, Sir."

He had walked past her and sat on one of the chairs. "Tell her the man you have been waiting to marry you has come and you want to introduce me."

She looked uncertainly at him. Initially he looked back, his face serious but he could see she was confused so he smiled.

"Tell her a Kassena man with no name has come to see her."

She looked at him curiously before going to call her mother. When she came back to the sitting room Leila was right behind her. "Daddy!" she screamed and ran into Dan's arms. "You are welcome. Our mother is in but Dad is not yet back."

"My wife has already informed me about that," Dan said, looking serious.

Leila disengaged herself. "Who is your wife?"

"Oh, your younger sister. She is going to tell your mother that she wants to marry me."

The girl smiled but said nothing now that she guessed who he was. She had heard her sister and her friends talk a lot about him. Marian's father.

Leila's mother was younger than he had thought she would be. They shared jokes after the introductions, each teasing the other. Leila and Mouna watched the two adults and laughed. Dan told his hostess the purpose of his visit and asked for permission for Leila to come with his children.

"Can I say no?" Leila's mother asked. "If I say no Leila will pack her things and sneak out through the window in the night and join you and your children. Since she met you all we hear in this house is you. You said this. You are that. You did that."

Dan looked at Leila with a falsely strong frown. In a deep voice he said, "Leila, now I know that you have been telling lies about me. Don't tell your parents things I did not say. Did you hear that?

They laughed.

"She is enjoying the holidays and she is learning a lot in the process, according to her," Leila's mother continued. "We will like to take the children to the Game Reserve. It will be educative for the children. Their father is hardly at home and is busy chasing contracts which he can't get. So if you are offering to give her what we should have given her but which we can't give her, can I say no? Thanks in advance.

"I have only one caution," she added with a smile.

The children smiled too because they knew she had something jovial to say.

"I know your caution," Dan said. Turning to Leila he said, "Your mother is wisely cautioning me not to promote you to be Kassena." He turned to her mother. "Your caution accepted."

Leila's mother shook her head. "My caution is, don't go and look for a Kassena husband for her."

"Mama, can I go with them?" Mouna asked. "I have never seen an elephant."

"Look at her," her mother said. "Am I the one sending Leila to the Game?"

"Sure, you can come along," Dan told Mouna before Leila could retort. "As in the case of Leila there is only one caution from your mother. And that is that I should not try to falsely raise your status in life by asking Kassena men to marry you."

Mother and daughters came out and saw Dan to his vehicle. They shook hands and said 'night.

Dan carried packed lunch and they stopped on the way and sat under trees and had their lunch. During one of the training sessions in Mole he learnt that the staff of the Motel hardly had the chance to go to towns where they could shop. So he bought rice, plantain, sugar and cooking oil which, on their arrival, he gave to the matron to share to her staff. They took three rooms, Carol and Marian took one room, he and Junior took another while Leila and Mouna shared one too. They took rooms in the chalets next to what was called the observatory.

The observatory was a concrete platform with metal rails around it on which visitors sat to watch the animals that came to drink water at the dugout below. From that point they could also see long stretches of the park beyond the dugout. From there one could see animals as they sauntered towards the water.

The excitement began that afternoon. They stood at the observatory and looked down at the dugout where animals came to drink water. During the trip down south with Marian and Junior, Dan had bought two powerful binoculars. They were able to rent two more from the motel. So they looked down at the dugout and Dan pointed out crocodiles that sometimes swam out of the water. Most often it was the head that stuck out of the water. They saw duikers and water bucks. They saw monkeys which played all the way to the drinking point. They saw other animals their father could not name.

They saw more than half a dozen elephants approaching the water. The children watched in fascination as the big mammals came seemingly sluggishly towards the water, their large ears flapping. They watched with equal fascination when the grey coloured animals started to troop inside the water. Could they swim or would they sink? They seemed too huge to float. Dan chided the older girls, telling them that objects sank in water not because of their size but because of their weight. Oh Daddy was all he got in reply. But Leila gave him a look that said this man knows a lot and is observing us like a teacher; we must be careful and not act stupid.

It was a fascinating half hour as the animals played with each other in the water. The elephants were good swimmers, the children learnt. After the first dip when they surfaced, their grey coats were black and the children observed it.

"It is their natural colour," their father told them. "When they leave the water they coat their skin with clay to keep off insects and ticks. It is that clay that gives them the grey colour."

Towards the evening they went with a guide round the park to see other animals. "The dry season is the best time to visit the reserve," the guide told them. He carried a gun and was dressed in the khaki uniform of the game wardens. "In the dry season there is very little water anywhere in the game. The little pools would have dried up and the dugout is the main source of water. One can therefore see a lot of animals by sitting at the observatory or going down to the dugout. Again, during the dry season the long grass is withered and it is possible to see far. In the rainy season the tall grass hides the animals."

They saw what the children called bush pigs. Warthogs, the warden told them. They came across a herd of buffaloes crossing the road they were driving on. They stopped to let them pass. The children stood up and craned their necks to see them better. "They are like cows," Junior said.

"In Kassem the buffalo is called bush cow," their father told them.

One hour later they came across a solitary buffalo only some five metres or so off the road. It was feeding but it stopped and raised its head to look at them in a manner none of them would describe as friendly. One of its horns was loose and hanging down. The guide was tense and he asked Dan to drive a few metres ahead. He adjusted himself to be able to bring the gun unto his lap.

"It is an old buffalo," the guide said. "When buffaloes grow old and can't keep pace with the rest of the herd they are driven out of the herd. That single animal seems to make the rest of the herd vulnerable. It slows down their pace. They tolerate it for a while but not forever. At a point their patience is exhausted and they kick the old bugger out. Such animals are dangerous. First, they grew up in the comfort and security of the herd. Now they have neither the comfort nor the security being with the herd brings. They are more vulnerable and therefore more liable to attack you than they would if they were in a herd."

They returned quite excited by the scenes from the trip and the children romped round the car park for a while as Junior climbed on his father's back.

"The world's only twelve year old baby," Marian called and Leila went to pull him off his father's back.

"Sometimes you are the world's only sixteen year old baby," Junior said from the back, showing no sign that he intended to climb down. Even Mouna made to pull his leg but he hitched up his feet.

Visitors and staff laughed at this playful family. Once again the children observed that they would be an attraction to others. They were getting used to their celebrity status, though.

When it was getting dark they heard a shout from the rooms beyond the swimming pool. They were sitting at the observatory and had been looking at the few animals that still came to drink. They got up hurriedly and ran towards the sound, Dan leading and holding out his hands to keep the children behind him. A big, old elephant had come very close to the rooms and was feeding on the leaves of a tree close to the bar. It seemed a popular friend of the staff as they came out and talked about it.

Like the buffalo they saw earlier in the bush, this elephant was also a loner detached from the rest of the herd. It was not dangerous, but could be approached easily. According to the staff it came frequently to their living quarters and was not destructive. They called it *Onipa Nua*, man's sibling, because it preferred the settlements to the bush. They had the chance to watch how it fed. It would harvest the leaves with its trunk and twist the trunk round to bring the leaves to its mouth. For many minutes the family and other visitors watched, talking in low tones, as if afraid loud talk would make the elephant angry or drive it away.

After supper they again rubbed the insect repellent lotion on their bodies and went to sit at the observatory. Not that they expected to see anything but it provided a good place for a family of six to sit comfortably and talk.

"Dad, we hear you tell very interesting Kassena stories," Leila told Dan. "Please tell us some stories."

"Okay, I will. But before then each of you is going to answer a question."

"Please Dad," Leila pleaded, "don't ask us difficult questions."

"Leila you know me. I am stupid and can't even think of difficult questions. Besides the fact that I won't know the answers myself."

The exclamation from the children showed how much they believed or disbelieved him.

"What do you want to be when you complete school?"

The three older girls all said they wanted to be doctors. Mouna said she wanted to be a businesswoman, owning big shops but Junior said he did not know.

Then the next round of questioning began. "Leila, why do you want to be a doctor?"

"I want to be a doctor because doctors are respected and they are rich. Their work is very important."

"Teachers' work is also important," Dan reminded her. "Will you want to be a teacher as well?"

"A teacher? No. My mother is a teacher and even though she does not complain her colleagues complain. Teachers are not well paid."

Dan thought about that and decided to go on to the next person, Marian.

"Me? Why do I want to be a doctor? I like their work. But I decided I wanted to be a doctor because I want my children to be able to go to private primary schools. And I will need money to pay their fees. I want to be able to pay my children's fees when they go to secondary school, even if it is southern schools. I don't want to be poor."

"So do I take it that you want to be a doctor because you think you will get more money from being a doctor?"

She fidgeted. "Well… I like their work. They save lives."

"Carol. You want to be a doctor too. Why is that profession your choice?"

"When my mother was sick and dying I wished I could save her. They would not send her to the hospital and I could not do anything about it. At that time I wished I were a doctor and could help her. I like the power doctors have. You see a very sick person sent to the hospital. The person cannot sit, does not smile, cannot eat and is very weak. In three days a doctor can make him smile, sit up, maybe even get down from the bed and walk and make his relatives feel happy. I want to make people get better and to make their relatives happy."

They listened to Mouna who said she wanted to be a successful businesswoman and make a lot of money. She wanted the opportunity to build houses and send her children outside the country to study.

"Many years ago, secondary schools had teachers who were responsible for providing guidance and counselling services to students. The role of the guidance and counselling officers was to guide students prepare for the profession that would match their knowledge and nature. For some professions you need several years of training to qualify you to enter them. For law you need five years and to be a doctor it is six years of training. The study is very narrow and very specific. When you join the profession and practise for say ten years and find that you are not happy in it, what do you do? Accountants can't switch jobs easily. Lawyers can't switch easily. Doctors can't either.

"I am sure you are asking why would someone feel unhappy in their profession. Because they chose the wrong profession. Because they entered into the profession for the wrong reason. Do you fear blood? Are you squeamish? If you are medicine is not the profession for you. It is good to want to be doctors. Medicine is a noble profession. As Carol said it is a life saving profession. It is not a profession for making money. It is true that doctors are better paid than other professionals. They are better paid than teachers. It takes less than six years to train teachers. But doctors are not as rich as some of them want to be. They are not as rich as people think they are. If you want to be a doctor to be rich it is the wrong reason for choosing that profession.

"If you want to be rich, be like Mouna and choose business. Business is for making money. If you want to be a doctor because you want to be rich let me know and I will begin to put money away in your name so that when you complete school you can start your business and make your money. Medicine is for reducing pain and suffering and saving lives. Do you love people more than you love money? If the answer is yes then you are ready to be a doctor. If the answer is no then medicine is not the field for you. If you become a doctor because of money you will be one of those doctors who will watch patients die because they cannot afford to pay them. You will be one of those who will feel angry to be called away from playing tennis or drinking beer because a patient has been brought in very critical condition and if a doctor does not attend to them immediately they will die. You will be one of those doctors who will leave a patient on admission for weeks because his or her relations cannot raise the fee you are charging and won't care if you hear that the patient has died.

"If you want to be a doctor because of wealth in your very first year you will be thinking of a deep freezer, video decks and big TV sets, executive furniture and by the second year, if not in the very first year, an expensive car...

"You have this year and next year to think about what I have told you. Ask yourself questions about what you want to be and why. Medicine is a good field but for saving lives and taking away pain. If you go into Medicine to become rich you will kill people and cause untold pain. And that is what doctors are supposed to prevent..."

The children asked a lot of questions and he answered them patiently. He told himself that he had a lot to learn about the children. And he had a lot to do to influence who they became in future.

He told them two stories and they all laughed. It was a very pleasant evening, another of those that made him not regret taking his leave. Another of those that reduced his worry about relating with the children. Another of those that made him think he should have encountered the children much earlier than he did.

He had to shoo them to bed. His room was in the middle, between the rooms of the children so that they all had easy access to him in case any of them needed him in the middle of the night.

No one needed him. He woke them up early for the early morning drive round the park. The guide explained that different animals had different habits. "Few animals come out in the open in the heat of the day," he said. "But while some animals prefer being out in the early mornings others prefer the evenings."

As with the drive the previous evening they saw a few animals. They saw what the guide called elephant dung. They were huge.

They came back to the motel for their bath and breakfast. They learnt from one of the servers that they had been nicknamed the Happy Family.

"But we are not happy," Dan protested.

"Aren't you?" the matron who was supervising the serving of their breakfast asked.

"No, we are not."

So she asked the children one by one and all of them said they were happy.

"Thanks for saving me," she told the children. Turning to Dan she said, "If they had said no we would have had to give a new definition to happiness. They made that unnecessary with their answers."

"Don't take Dad seriously," Leila told the matron. "He is always saying opposite things. We are very happy. We are a happy family because we have a loving and playful dad."

"So if I told the matron that you are a boy but only dressed in girl's clothing, would that be being opposite?" Dan asked Leila.

"Of course, Dad, you will say that," Marian came to the rescue of Leila. "But you know she is a girl and you know the matron knows she is a girl."

Over the next few minutes they were busy pouring hot water, mixing beverage, plastering butter on bread and hardly talking.

"Am I welcome to join this closely knit family?"

They all looked up and saw a white lady they had seen around the motel and the dugout the previous day.

The children all looked at their father who said, "I am sure there is space for one more addition to the family. Welcome."

She pulled a chair and joined them, sitting between Leila and Carol.

"I have a confession to make," the white lady said.

"Mmm! You will have to wait till they can call a Catholic priest for you. I am sure none of us is qualified to hear confessions much less grant absolutions."

The lady laughed. "Well, it is not that kind of confession. I have been wondering since I saw this group yesterday if the children are all yours."

"Well, yes they are."

A server brought the white lady some breakfast items.

She looked at the three older girls especially. "The three girls must be triplets then."

"No, they are not," Dan said, feigning seriousness. "I was married to the mother of one of them but had two girlfriends. Coincidentally all three, my wife and my two girlfriends, got pregnant at the same time. The result was the three girls who are the same age today."

The laughter of the children gave him away.

"Sorry I have another confession to make," the woman said. "I sat behind you yesterday in the night when you asked the children about their professions. I came out to just sit and listen to the cries of the birds of the night. But instead I found you more interesting to listen to. I didn't intend to eavesdrop. Eavesdrop is the word? Yes, it is. But I could not help listening. I heard what you told the children about why to choose a profession. Let me say that you are too responsible to keep two girlfriends who would be getting pregnant at the same time as your wife."

"That was what you learnt about me yesterday. I am talking of sixteen, seventeen years ago."

At that point they introduced. She was Canadian, French Canadian and was called Monique. Dan explained his relationship with the children.

She said she was a lecturer at the Institute of Renewable Natural Resources and was an ornithologist.

"So that explains why you were interested in the cries of night birds. While we are here for the big animals your interest is birds."

Dan saw the look on the faces of the children so he asked Monique to tell them what an ornithologist did. She told them. Dan was interested in what she found in the park. "In a habitat such as this there must be a lot of birds but will there be enough variety to make it worth the while for someone interested in birds to visit?"

"Bird watching is not popular here," Monique observed. "So I can understand why the bird variety in the park is not included in the brochures advertising this place. There is a good enough variety of birds for anybody interested in birds to be attracted here. People come all the way here to see how many animal species? I don't know. But there are more than one hundred and fifty bird species here."

Dan whistled. The children stopped eating to listen to Monique tell about the birds. Without her knowing it, she had stimulated their interest in birds. They sat talking after breakfast till almost midday. They all drove down to the dugout with a guide and Monique continued to educate them about birds.

He drove the children a few miles out of the park to Larabanga. Larabanga had what was believed to be one of the oldest mosques in the country. It was apparently built by the slave raiders. Dan drew the attention of the children to the strange relationship between religion and some of the most heinous crimes humanity committed.

"You know," he told them, "in the Second World War, there were priests praying for the German soldiers as they went out to fight. They were not praying for the souls of the soldiers in case they did not come back alive. They were blessing them and asking for God's guidance for them to go and kill. On the other side, among the French, British and other Allied soldiers, there were priests offering prayers for their soldiers for the same purpose. All of the priests were supposedly praying to the same God. I am sure he would have been confused.

"But here is evidence that the raiders called themselves religious, but they raided villages, killed many people and separated many people from their loved ones and took them away and sold them to be taken to places they did not know."

The children shook their heads. He drove them beyond the village to an interesting stone. It was perched a few metres off the road. But the road made a sharp twist round the stone. "Legend has it that the road was to have been straight, passing over where the stone is. The workmen removed the stone and constructed the road through where they removed it from. But they came back the next day to find the stone returned to where it had been when they removed it. They again removed it but came again the third day to find it had returned to its original spot. They removed it yet again but it returned yet again. They left it and diverted the road."

He drove them back and they drove round the park for the last time that evening, with Monique in the vehicle, and this time they watched more than animals as she made them stop occasionally to watch birds. They had supper together but she left Dan with his children for their second night together at the observatory. He told them stories but most of the night was spent discussing Dan's work. The children were fascinated by it; that he travelled to other countries and trained people, including senior bank staff.

He shooed them off to bed again, this time before midnight. They woke up early, had an early breakfast and left. Monique was up and she came over to bid them farewell. Leila whispered to Marian in the vehicle that she noticed that Monique did not have a ring on her ring finger so she should arrange to marry her for her father.

"I thought he is your father too? Why don't you initiate it and we will support you?"

Dan asked what they were talking about but when Marian was about to say it Leila clamped a hand on her mouth.

They attended church service at Damongo, Mouna joining the other girls for the first time in a church. She looked round the room throughout the service and found their kneeling and standing and sitting amusing.

The children had lots of stories to tell when they got back to Tamale. And Mouna, who missed the Navrongo trip, joined them in the talking this time. She also took the lead in Dad did this and Dad said this which had become a mannerism with especially Leila and Marian.

When Dan woke up on the morning he had to go back to work he had mixed feelings. He felt rested mentally. He felt rested even physically. He asked himself why he had not been taking holidays before. He thought it would be nice to take holidays more often. But like Nina in the song of the same title by ABBA he knew that if he took frequent holidays the fun would go away.

He felt anxious about going back to work after such a long absence. A part of him dragged itself to work while a part of him was anxious to check what was waiting to be done and to get it done.

"And so how was it like to have a holiday?"

He was startled by the sound of the voice. He had not heard the door open. As was the case before he went on leave, Dan was the first to arrive at the office. He came in fifteen minutes before work was due to start. He came to his office and started his computer and was engrossed in checking his mail when he heard the voice, the voice of Brenda.

He sat back in his swivel chair, clasped his hands behind his head and leaned back in the chair. And gave off a deep sigh. "So good I felt angry with the killjoy who made it end for me by saying all good things must come to an end. I wish I could go on and on."

Brenda had walked in while he talked and made herself comfortable in the chair in front of him. "You are welcome to take another four weeks' leave."

"Sometimes I forget how generous you are. Thanks for the offer."

Chapter Twenty-Six

He carried an A4 size coloured picture of Diane with her name written under it and held it up in front of him.

Diane came pushing the trolley in front of her, her eyes searching for Dan. She wore a dark coloured suit and white shirt. She looked more like a diplomat than the often relaxed woman he had known in Kenya.

She saw the picture and the name and told herself that Dan had sent someone and to make sure the person got her right he had given him her picture. She rolled the trolley towards the man holding the picture. But when she looked into his face she could not help but burst into laughter. It was Dan himself.

He did not smile back. The man beside him looked at him, perplexed but Diane did not know what perplexed him. Dan came round the metal barrier and came up to her, still holding the picture with her name under it.

"Excuse me, Madam," he said to Diane, looking the word seriousness itself. "We have been assigned to meet and pick Her Excellency the Kenyan High Commissioner to Ghana, Diane Orengo. I can see you very strongly resemble her. Are you Her Excellency?"

The man he had been standing with and who had a perplexed look on his face had come forward with him and still looked somehow confused as he stood by him, looking alternately at Dan and at Diane. Dan looked so serious nobody would guess he was joking.

"No, I am not Her Excellency," Diane said, also pretending to be serious.

"You resemble her a lot," Dan said.

She ignored him and dealt with the man who was with Dan.

"Welcome to Ghana," Dan said giving up his jokes.

"Thanks." She hugged him and they exchanged kisses on the cheeks as they did when she met him at the Jomo Kenyatta Airport in Nairobi the last time he visited Kenya.

Dan had hired a vehicle for the pick-up of Diane and the man who had stood by him was the driver.

"I am sure you are doing great teaching leadership. But don't you think you would do better as an entertainer than a teacher?" Diane asked in the vehicle.

"I don't have to think. I know the answer."

"And it is?"

"It is no."

"I expected that from you, Dan. But I have sometimes seriously considered you in drama and thought you would be great in that field. You will make people laugh. Jokes come to you naturally. And making people happy is a rare gift. The world needs more of people who make others laugh, who make others happy."

"Thanks. I can make people laugh without taking up drama. I use it in my training sessions and participants, in addition to laughing and feeling happy, go away learning useful things as well. One of the very first persons to participate in the training sessions when I started some years ago was a young man from Northern Nigeria working with a Ghanaian NGO. He came to me several times later with ideas he was turning over in his mind. He left Ghana three years ago to go and start an NGO in the State of Gombe in support of Pastoralists education. Early this year they got two million dollars over five years for their activities. Their aim is to introduce a flexible educational system that would allow the children of the pastoral Fulani to have access to quality education. Do you know how many children will have a different future as a result of the initiative of this one participant of my training sessions?"

They stayed in Bayview Hotel near the Tetteh Quarshie roundabout. When he took her to supper after 7:00 p.m. he warned her about the amount of spices found in West African food. "Those of us who come from West Africa find East African food rather bland. People from East Africa find our food too spicy. We have a lot of pepper in our sauces, mind."

It was good she had been warned but she found his statement that they had a lot of pepper in their sauces the understatement of the year.

They went by air to Tamale the next morning. She came out dressed in a shirt and corduroy trousers and black shoes. The diplomat was gone and in her place was a younger, very sprightly girl from whose steps and the face lit by the smile exuded life itself. The transformation into different personalities was not lost on Dan. He could see in his mind's eye the girl who sat and absorbed the sessions on leadership with rapt attention. He could move on to the next slide and see the calm, composed and mature person in skirt and jacket leading training sessions in conference halls in hotels in Kenya. He could move further to the slide in which was the homely woman in beautiful social dress hunched over the dinner table in Carnivores. A later slide had the legal and diplomatic looking Diane wheeling her trolley down the aisle in Kotoka International Airport. And now, ahead of him in the queue, the exuberant young woman living free.

When they began the descent at Tamale Dan looked over Diane who sat by the window and asked her if the landscape resembled that of any place in Kenya.

She looked at it critically and told him frankly, "Maybe it does. But I don't know Kenya myself, I must admit. I know Nairobi but Nairobi is not Kenya."

He poked her arm. "So you are a sleek city dweller. Do you like music?"

She hesitated. "I like music, but I am not like you. Why do you ask?"

"Do you know a country music singer called Dan Seal?"

She shook her head. "Never heard of him. Maybe I have heard his music but don't know it is Dan Seal. I know Don Williams and Kenny Rogers. They are the only country musicians I know."

"Yea, they are the flagbearers of country music, aren't they? Dan Seal also sings very good country music and he comes very close to Kenny Rogers and Don Williams in my list of favourite country musicians."

"But why bring him in here?"

"In one of his songs he talks of a girl he admires and who admires him too. But he said everybody said she was not his kind of girl; that she was a city kind of girl. You."

She hit him jovially. "I should have known you by now. But I am not sure I can say I know you."

"I know you anyway."

"Really?"

"Really. You are Diane Orengo."

Dauda was waiting for them when they arrived. On the way Dan told Diane about the accommodation arrangements for her stay. "There is the training centre which will be accommodating all the participants and you can stay there if you choose. That is if you don't want to stay in my place. There are a lot of free rooms in my house and even though it is not a hotel I did not feel comfortable putting you at the training centre. You can look at the rooms in my house first."

She turned away from the window through which she had been looking at the flat grassland outside and looked into his eyes. "Oh, so I am going to stay in your house?"

Outside the window, on both the right and left hand sides of the road, there were scattered trees, short trees compared to the tall timber of the forested south. April had given way to May which was itself ceding the right of way to June. The early rains of April, called stray rains because they came outside the rainy season, and the rains of the early rainy season in May had caused a change in colour in the ground between the trees. A beautiful green carpet of young grass had been rolled over the dark brown earth. Sheep and goats could be seen eating grass and sometimes ignoring the cars that roared past but at other times raising their heads to say hi.

"Yes. I live there alone," Dan told Diane, "and there are many vacant rooms. The two of us will not even half fill the house."

She made faces. "I am going to live in your house alone with you!"

She regretted making that statement when she again looked into his face. She had meant to pull his leg but the seriousness in his face told her he was taking what she said very seriously. When he spoke she felt even sorrier.

"Diane, I had not thought about it." He looked down into her face. "I just made assumptions without thinking about how you would feel. I apologise for taking you for granted."

She sighed and clasped her hands before her. "Dan, you pull legs the most but you don't realise when someone is pulling your leg. I feel honoured that you should receive me in your home and not in a hotel or the training centre or somewhere else. It makes me feel ashamed that I did not think of you staying with me when you came to Kenya. I will be very happy to stay in your house."

"You don't have to stay there to please me. If you feel uncomfortable in any way, please…"

She turned her back to him and lay on him. "I don't feel uncomfortable staying in your place. I feel honoured to be welcome into your house. Dan, recognise when others are teasing you and take what they say at its value."

He felt ashamed of himself and wanted to hold her to express it but restrained himself at the last minute. After a minute when Diane remained slumped against him and he felt her soft body pressed into his, he became intensely aware of the woman in her and hoped she would sit up. His mind went back to his younger days. He would have put a hand round her. He did not know what it would mean to do so now. He kept hoping she would sit up. She did not.

Dauda stopped in the centre of the town and got down, handing over to Dan. Dan offered to drive Dauda to his house but he said he preferred getting down where he got down because he was going to spend the rest of the day with friends in town. Dan took over and drove them home.

Diane got down from the vehicle and looked at the house, thinking it was bigger than she imagined it when he said he lived there alone. She admired the colour, barely noticeable, almost like cement. The sitting room was very beautiful, very rich, she thought.

"You have a choice between two rooms upstairs," he informed her as he hauled her bags up the stairs. "I am torn between the joke in what you said about living here alone with a man and the serious part of it. I may put you in a dilemma sometimes and also find myself in a dilemma sometimes because I am a child of conflicting cultures. One is the African culture in which space means different from the Euro-

American now globalised culture. In the culture of my upbringing reducing the space between you and someone means friendship, it means acceptance at the same level. In the latter culture it means not respecting the other person's privacy. There is a bedroom downstairs and you can have that one if you choose."

He stopped and turned to face her. "Listen, Diane. Feel very free to tell me how you feel. If you feel uncomfortable about anything, believe me, I will respect your feelings. You are not a prisoner here and don't take anything you are uncomfortable with. I am not imposing anything on you. I have made assumptions but I can be wrong."

She walked past him. "Can I look at the rooms I have to choose from?"

"There is a bedroom downstairs too, if you prefer being downstairs."

Dan himself occupied the bigger bedroom at the end of the passage. So she had a choice between the bedroom in the middle and the one just by the stairs. Both were big. She took the one next to Dan's. "So that if I scream in the night," she explained, "you can hear me and you can be there in less than a minute to fight the monster that will be eating me."

"Fight it? You don't mean it. Encourage it to eat you faster, you mean?"

He put the bags on the bed and she went into the bathroom. She left the door open and he went to close it, thinking she wanted to use the loo but she poked her head through the door and spoke to him. "Spotless," she announced.

She came back into the bedroom and sat on the bed. "I am not sure I will ever wake up from this bed. I could sleep in it for a whole week."

"I will leave you," he said as he made for the door.

"No." She got up from the bed. "Please, show me round the house."

He pointed to the door next to her's. "I live next door," he told her.

She walked to the door. She had wanted to ask if she could go in but she later changed her mind and they made a tour of the rest of the house. They came downstairs and she looked at the guestroom.

"This is the other room you can have if you prefer to live downstairs," he said.

"I've made my choice and I told you why I prefer that room."

She admired both study and studio. The study did not surprise her as much as the studio did. She knew of his love for music but did not know he sang as well. She was surprised at the resources in the study though. It was well stocked and she gazed at the volumes of books that crowded the shelves.

They went out and looked round the house. She asked what he did in a wooden structure he had put up near the wall at the back of the house. She was curious because it had an air-conditioner, a split A/C.

"That is the gym," he told her. She wanted to see it and he went back into the main house for the key. Inside it she found all kinds of equipment for exercises. Machines with belts he could walk and run on and go nowhere. So he could jog as much at home as people in Europe go jogging on roads and in parks. There were dumbbells and other muscle building equipment. There was a punch bag as well. On a table in a corner were a large tape and a collection of music.

"Do you have a tape recorder by your bed playing very cool music throughout the night while you sleep?" she asked him, looking up from his collection of cassettes.

"This is your first day here. And you did not go into my bedroom. How did you know that?"

She only shook her head in reply. Impossible character, she told herself.

"My, oh my! The house is too big for one person. Doesn't it haunt you?"

"Why should it haunt me? I built it with genuine money, money I earned from genuine, sweaty work. And the land on which it was built was not a grove or a shrine. Why should the house be haunted?"

"Most often the feeling of haunting is a state of the mind. It may not be real but it exists in people's mind. The fact that one is alone living in a big house can provoke such fears in the mind."

"Fortunately for me I don't have a mind."

It came naturally after what she said and he looked very serious. "Sometimes I have the impression that you can predict what one is going to say so you rehearse your responses in advance. The humour comes so naturally. Is there anything anyone can say to you that won't generate an immediate humorous response?"

"A lot, I would say."

"Give an example."

He smiled and she knew he had something up his sleeve. "If I got a phone call from your parents or if I were in Kenya and went to see them and they told me you were dead, I would not be able to tell them anything humorous in the circumstance."

She snorted. "Why do you have to use my death as the example?"

"I could use my death as the example. But assuming I use my death then I won't be able to tell you how I can't be humorous because dead people are generally not humorous."

"Why do you use the example of death at all?"

"Oh, and why not death? Death is a complement of life and walks in our shadow. We ignore it and think we keep it far away by banning it from our conversations. But that is not true. Please let me assure that you won't die just because I mentioned death in connection with you. If you were intended to live to be one hundred you will still live to be a hundred."

"Where were you brought up? In Europe? In a very urban community?"

"Why do you think I would have been brought up in Europe or a very urban community?"

"Why are you so Ghanaian?"

"Why am I so…? Oh, I see. Because I am Ghanaian. Why are you so Ghanaian? You also just posed a question to my question."

"Because I am in Ghana." Becoming serious she said, "I was brought up in Nairobi which is an urban community. But the culture in which superstition is rife still influenced me. Like my beliefs about death. You don't seem so influenced."

"I was brought up in a traditional community and superstition was quite strong. Still is. You don't whistle in the night lest spirits stone you. When I was in my teens and in secondary school I and my peers in the village would go into town for entertainments and return late in the night. Sometimes after midnight. When we approached places said to haunt people we would feel our scalps tingling and feel some cold creep up our bodies. And there were a few of such places on our way from town said to be the dwelling places of spirits. There was a place where they said at certain times of the night a tall figure reaching up to the skies and wearing a white flowing gown would suddenly appear before you. There was a famous fruit tree where they said late at night you could be chased by a braying donkey. There was a borehole on the way home where they said you could hear people fetching water and talking but you would not see anybody. We did fear."

"I thought you told me you did not have a mind. How could you fear?"

"I told you I do not have a mind but I did not say I never had one. I had a mind, one of the best, when I was growing up. Then I had an accident and it died. I was sleeping once and my head slipped from the pillow and it hit the foam mattress on which the pillow was lying. And my mind died." He sighed, a false sigh of sadness. "It was such a terrible thing."

She feigned sympathy. "I bet it was."

Dan arranged with Mercy before he left for her to prepare *fufu* and light soup for their lunch. Dan had informed her about the East African's dislike for pepper and strong spices so she prepared the soup with as little pepper as possible. She joined them for lunch and Diane ate a lot of the soup, complaining though about the pepper even though to her Ghanaian host and hostess there was very little pepper in it. They had a lively chat and the two women got along very fine.

Mercy had been brought by one of the vehicles that the training centre owned but since Dan was going to go to the office after the meal they asked the driver to go back. So while Dan and Mercy washed the dishes Dan asked Diane if she wanted to change for the trip to the centre. She did not and so stood by and watched Dan wash the dishes while Mercy rinsed them. A window to another aspect of the life of her mentor. He was at home doing the washing. And he did not feel that because Mercy was a subordinate and a woman she should do the washing. He had led in clearing the table and now led in washing, insisting he was the host.

The women sat together at the back of the vehicle while Dan, who described himself as their chauffeur, drove. Mercy explained landmarks on the way to the office. Dan showed her round New Horizon Leadership. They went to the room they were going to use for the training and inspected the facilities and agreed on sitting arrangements, position of equipment and other arrangements. While Mercy showed Diane round the training centre Dan checked which of the participants had arrived and welcomed them. They looked inside the rooms and Diane went into the bathrooms and felt the mattresses. Hotel standard, Diane felt.

They walked round the grounds and Diane noticed that the area was forested. There were fruit trees, shade trees and ornamental trees. Beautifully trimmed hedges enclosed grassy lawns that were also well kept.

"So who owns this training centre?" Diane asked Mercy.

Mercy explained the relationship between the training centre and consultancy office. "Dan owns both but they are kept separate."

Mercy explained that both were very busy. "We have about 80% occupancy throughout the year. Sometimes there is a clash in requests to use the place. We provide excellent services and facilities, I am proud to say. We replace bed sheets very frequently. We don't wait for customers to start complaining about the facilities in the rooms before we change them. We replace the ACs very frequently. When we repair an AC twice we replace it. The place is in very high demand for use by organisations looking for meeting places, venues for conferences or to train their staff."

"You must be making a lot of money from the centre and for Dan," Diane observed.

"And for ourselves," Mercy replied. "Users of the facilities, when they are leaving, will normally give us envelops to express their appreciation of the services we provided. Since we have conferences and meetings going on here all the time you can understand that the constant donations are substantial additions to staff remuneration. We are paid fantastic salaries. No staff of this facility will leave this place to go and work anywhere else in Tamale because no other facility pays anything close to the salary this centre pays. And at the end of each year Dan gives the most fantastic bonuses around here. Every year we look forward to the Christmas for many reasons. One, people rent the facilities for their end of year get-togethers and we share in the fun and the food and drinks. Two, Dan throws the most lavish end of year get-together for all staff and their families. Then he gives the heaviest envelops. We can all normally plan very lavish Christmas celebrations with our families because we know the bonus is very generous."

As they walked back to Dan's office Mercy asked Diane, "Are you going to marry Dan?"

Diane stopped so suddenly it surprised Mercy. She looked hard at Mercy and saw the surprise in Mercy's face. "Did Dan say I was his girlfriend?"

Mercy put her hands on Diane to emphasise what she was going to say. "No. But he has never had a female visitor. He is free with us in the workplace but his life moves from workplace to his home and back to workplace. We don't know of any woman in his life. And you can be sure that everybody here will be happy if we ever hear that he is going to marry. My question is based on a strong wish to see him married."

The muscles in Diane's face relaxed and Mercy heaved a sigh.

"Dan trained me in leadership and encouraged me to take up leadership training. He is my mentor and, I must admit, one of my best friends. But I am sure he has no interest in me beyond supporting me to grow in what I am doing. So sorry to disappoint you but no I am not going to marry Dan."

"Ho! So sad. I don't know you but I thought when I saw you and Dan together this afternoon that you will make him happy if you married him…"

"Marriage is not in Dan's plans. And I am sure he is happy as he is."

When Dan walked out with her towards the vehicle she commented on how the grounds were well designed and well kept. "I did not know you had such very good sense designing the area around your buildings."

Dan laughed. "I don't have that sense. I engaged a landscape designer. He designed the layout and helped us acquire the plant species. Instead of struggling to reinvent the wheel you can always use the knowledge of the experts. That is what we did."

As they drove home from the centre Diane could not help stealing a look at Dan occasionally. The man who owned and ran such exotic facilities was as simple and meek as a week old lamb. That his staff loved him came out strongly in almost every word that Mercy uttered.

She examined the interior of the vehicle for the first time. The glasses of the windows were not controlled by rollers but by switches. The seats were covered in very good quality synthetic leather. The dashboard was very clean, very neat. The man's love for order and neatness shouted loudly from everything she had seen so far that day.

The torture began that evening.

They cooked the meal together in the kitchen. They bumped into each other and sometimes at the sink their shoulders would be rubbing against each other. He had not thought of and was not prepared for that amount of physical contact with a woman he had come to be very intensely aware of that afternoon. At dinner he was troubled by the radiance of her face lit up by smiles across the table from him. Again as they washed up he experienced the repeated physical contacts. She did not seem to notice. She did not seem to mind. They were accidental but this was the first time he was forced to be so close to a woman and to interact so intimately with her. It bothered him. It disoriented him.

After supper she went up to her room and had a bath before coming down. And the torture continued. She wore a light nightgown through which her white pants glared at him and again through which her nipples made faces at him. Well, that was how he saw it. She stretched on the sofa and he was convinced he would not be able to maintain reasonable conversation. But the evening passed agreeably well and they had very lively conversation. They laughed often and when her laughter rang out it carried with it the unalloyed freedom she felt.

That evening they returned to Diane's sore issue. It started with a review of the participants' list. There were more men than women. The number of women in development work was increasing, they discussed. They went on to talk about the growing number of career women. That brought back Diane's problem. Diane's path to her situation was different from that of many women, they said. Many young women were now busy developing their careers, acquiring higher degrees and doing more professional courses. Many young women now would argue with their boyfriends to put off the marriage because the time proposed would affect an activity the woman needed to undertake in furtherance of her career. Some lost their men because of that. Others were so busy they did not develop the deep friendships out of which marriage was born. And as their careers developed the older they became. And the men around them got married. Those men who did not marry preferred the younger women with little substance and not the older better established, more independent and more assertive women.

Like Diane at a certain age they also had to make hard choices. Diane's dilemma came up again. Dan could see it was a big issue for her and felt she would have appreciated some help. But he felt morality was one area he felt unable to draw firm lines. He knew the criticisms against moral relativism – the theory that morals were determined by the context of a people and moral values would differ from culture to culture – but had not yet come across any universal standards for making moral value judgements. And from the many instances he had been present when people argued over issues of morality he had observed that the context of their upbringing had been very important in shaping their values.

"Diane, to me morality and ethics of that nature are personal choices. I understand your situation. It is not your fault that you are not married. You want children. Need them. Someone may argue the need but I won't. How do you get them? Most men your age or close to your age will be married. Do you go and borrow someone's husband to make you pregnant? Will I recommend that? Or will you look for and sleep with a young man just out of school who is not yet settled and has no attachment to any woman? And what will you tell him? I need a child and want to sleep with you to make them but am not asking you to commit yourself to me? Or do you look for a widower because he won't have a woman from whom you are 'borrowing' him?"

He stopped because he saw a smile on her lips that was not there before.

"Or am I going to look for a divorcee because like the widower he will not have a woman from whom to 'borrow' him?"

"Or a divorcee provided it is not me."

She laughed. "Why not you?"

He shook his head. "You know the story about me and the children. I cannot survive another life with unclaimed children out there somewhere, who will not know me even if their mother will be someone like you, able to provide them luxury. What I have learnt from these children is the fact that children need not only material things to make their life complete. Knowing and relating with their parents is also very important. So in addition to the moral issue, if you have children in purely convenient relationship, one which ends with the pregnancy, you should expect the children to pester you with questions about their father. And you must have satisfactory answers to their questions."

They remained silent for a long time.

"So what do you do?" He did not answer for a long time and she knew he did not expect her to answer him so she kept quiet. "Diane, you have hard choices. But you are better placed to make those choices because each option has implications you have to live with."

When they got up to go to bed she bent down to adjust the cushions she lay on and pointed her back to Dan, the glare of her pant even stronger with the gown drawn tightly against her. He had to move away as the pressure against the flap of his trousers was obviously growing. She put a hand on his shoulder as she walked by him up the stairs to their rooms.

At her door she turned to him and told him, "Dan, I don't know how you feel after our discussion this afternoon. It was nice cooking with you and watching you cook in the kitchen this evening. I have had a very nice evening. In a hotel or at the centre I would have had a cooked meal. After the meal I would have had to retire to my room or spend the evening watching TV. The evening would not have been the same as what I had here. I hope you will see the joke I made in the car as it was intended to be, a joke. I am very happy here and I am glad you brought me to your home. Thanks."

She gave him a peck on his cheek. This time it was his cheek. Then they said 'night.

He had his bath and opened the door quietly and went downstairs to the study and spent the next two hours going over the training sessions. Even though he had gone over them on the Thursday before he left for Accra he still went over them, going over his checklist. He had trained with Ibrahim before and he had trained with Diane before. He had trained this group before and this was a follow up training. But all those facts did not make him feel relaxed.

When he went to bed thought of Diane in her nightgown lying only next door kept him awake for more than an hour. He asked himself if he was going to endure this every evening she was there in the house.

He did not know that his ordeal was not during the evenings alone.

On the next day, the Monday, he got up early despite the fact that he slept late. He went down and started making pancakes when Diane came down, dressed as she was the previous night. Again they bumped into each other as they found themselves next to each other in many places. When she bent down and started to sweep the kitchen he had to keep changing his position to have her behind him all the time.

They were the first in the office and Diane asked if this was the time he usually came to office and he said yes. Brenda was the next to come and she came into Dan's office. Dan introduced Diane and the two women had a chat.

Before she left the office Brenda told Diane, "You are very welcome to Ghana. Enjoy your stay. If you have any questions or need anything come over to Brenda. I and the rest of the team will do whatever we can possibly do to make you feel comfortable here. And please, be as at home here as you feel in your own home with your own family in Kenya."

"Good morning to you all and welcome to Tamale and the Horizon Leadership Development training session," Dan said when the participants were all seated. "This group is odd, but not in a negative way, among the groups that have gone through the leadership development programme. Most groups have 25 participants which is the magic number I am comfortable with. In a few cases organisers have insisted on more than the 25 and we have agreed on the maximum I can take in a session, 30. So all the groups I have trained have either had 25 or 30 participants. This group is 27."

The participants laughed.

"You are midway between the ideal number and the maximum number. I am very glad to see all 27 of you back for the second session. I am sure we have all heard and some of us would even have sang the song *Count Your Blessings*. But I am sure we really hardly stop to count our blessings and name them as the song exhorts us to do. I want all of you to observe moments of silence in which each of us will travel back in time. Let each of us go back to our infancy, as much of it as we can remember. And recollect all the children we can remember from how far back our memory can send us. Let us recall who died." He paused for them to think before going on, "Let us go on to our primary school days and on to our middle school days. How many of our mates and children in the communities we grew up in who would have been our peers but may not have been in the same school with us died?" Another pause. "Let us come from there all the way to our present time. How many of our colleagues, friends, relatives close to us in age and neighbours we knew died?" Another pause. "If we will go back to our primary school days again, can we remember children in our communities, in our neighbourhoods, who did not go to school at all? How many of our mates had dropped out of school by the time we reached primary class six? How many of the children in our community were in school by the time we got to middle school? Unless you came from a rich or educated family and so had the rare opportunity at the time to go to one of those preparatory or international schools that prepared students primarily for admission to secondary schools, how many of your mates went from middle school to secondary school?..."

He went on and on with them. Till he told them, "If you can bring together all the children in your community who were your peers, you will find that you are very far ahead of a lot of them. Have you ever counted the blessings that make you different from them? From the last time you came here for the training till now, do you know how many Ghanaians have died? Do you know how many people as young as you have died since then? You are all alive. Let us imagine that one of you, each of you should imagine that it is not you but someone else in this group, had died last month. The rest of you would still have been here having the training. But can you imagine the effect of that death on the rest of you?"

He had been walking round and almost talking to each participant as he went round. Now he returned to the front of the room and told them, "When I say I am glad to see all of you back, I mean it. We could have been missing one or more of you. You could have missed me."

They growled disagreement.

399

He smiled. "I am not immortal. I could have been dead. When I wake up to see the sun each day, I give sincere thanks that I woke up. So, it is very nice to see all of you, including Ibrahim and I, back for the follow up training session.

"You know Ibrahim already. The two of us facilitated the last training session. I am sure you know Ibrahim more than you know me and he doesn't need introduction."

"We don't know him," someone said from the back. "He needs to be introduced."

Dan and Ibrahim smiled. His sense of humour was being played back for him. His smiled broadened. Diane did not smile. She did not know what was going on.

"How many of you here don't know Ibrahim?"

Many hands went up. But when the participants laughed and looked at Ibrahim Dan was forced to look at him too. Ibrahim's hand was up too.

"We have an interesting phenomenon taking place before my eyes," Dan said, still wearing the broad smile. "Many participants are saying they don't know Ibrahim and raise their hands to indicate this. While their hands are up, indicating they don't know Ibrahim, they are laughing at Ibrahim who has also raised his hand to indicate that even he does not know Ibrahim."

They all laughed. Diane saw the fun and now joined them.

"Well," Dan went on, "over the next five days, I will share the honour of facilitating the learning with Ibrahim, who is this gentle creature here." He had walked up to Ibrahim and now put his hand on his shoulder. Walking back towards Diane he continued, "We have a third facilitator for this second training session. Diane Orengo is Kenyan who has trained people in leadership on her own and had co-facilitated training sessions with me. So for this session I have the honour to assist two very able facilitators."

The laughter again.

Diane fitted into the training team and shared a lot of experiences with Ibrahim. She found him pleasant and easy to talk to. Ibrahim, on his part, found her very knowledgeable, and very humble despite her knowledge. He observed her facilitating and answering questions and admired the ease with which she did everything. She offered help with the distribution of handouts, post-it and collected the written notes when others were facilitating.

They did not go home at the end of the day's session. Dan kept them in the office, telling her they would be joining the participants for supper. The three of them went over the day's sessions, brought together their observations and agreed the next day's processes. Dan commended the two for their great work that day.

"He is always praising the efforts of others but plays down everything he himself does," Ibrahim observed when he left the room with Diane. Diane agreed.

The lights in the restaurant were switched off and candles were put on the dining tables. Tables for the participants of this training session were set aside from the tables of the other lodgers of the training centre. There were fresh flowers on the tables of the participants, Diane observed. Almost all the participants were in and the food had been served but no one was eating and Diane wondered why.

Dan had sought and engaged Ferdinand Quao, one of the participants some minutes before they were called for supper. They discussed a lot of issues and had been so engrossed in the conversation that they forgot of supper. Dan suddenly looked at his watch and said, "Gosh, we are late for supper. Let us go."

He led Ferdinand back to the restaurant and opened the door for him. Immediately they entered the other participants stood up and broke into song: "Happy birthday to you. Happy birthday to you. Happy birthday dear Ferdinand, happy birthday to you."

Ferdinand stopped in his tracks, paralysed and dumb. God! Who knew his birthday?

They brought him a bottle of champagne and he shook it and popped it. He had never popped champagne on his birthday. A giant birthday cake was wheeled in and he was helped to cut it. He was given a bouquet of flowers, with three cards, one from his wife, one with compliments from the other 26 participants and one card from Horizon Leadership.

On the drive home Diane asked about the birthday. "Ferdinand must have a very loving and caring wife to have organised this day from afar."

"Horizon Leadership Development Services organised it," he told her.

"You did? I mean Horizon did? But there was a card from his wife and a bouquet from her as well."

"Whenever a participant's birthday falls during a training session, whether here or abroad, we acknowledge it. And if we can reach the spouse we would ask for their permission to offer a gift and a card on their behalf." He turned and looked at her. "If you were married, how would you like it to be reached by your husband on your birthday when you are far away?"

Another of the many small but significant things she would always learn about this man that raise her admiration for him a notch or two. She had known him for years now but each time she learnt something new it occurred to her that she would never fully know him.

They did not have to cook that evening so they did not have to spend time in the kitchen where he would have her bumping into him. But she spent the evening dressed as she did the previous evening. And he felt the same way – sometimes he did not even notice her because they were having so much fun he forgot everything else around them, including her. At other times he became strongly aware of her person. Sometimes he felt aroused.

On the Tuesday evening she asked if she could see the children. Marian, yes. She could go to the school. Dauda would send her if she wanted. Junior, he said, would be more difficult. And he told her about their mother's protective attitude about the children. Diane said it was all right to see Marian.

"I brought them some items. Marian can collect them and pass Junior's items on to him. But I will love to see at least one of them."

On the Wednesday afternoon when Diane was not facilitating Dauda drove her to the school.

"My name is Diane Orengo," she said as she offered her hand to the slim girl in front of her. "I came to work with your father in one of his training sessions. But I actually came more because I want to know Ghana."

Marian thanked Diane on behalf of the two children. "It's nice to know you in person," Diane.

Diane smiled. "You mean you know me in some other way?" She did not know what she expected of the girl. Abandoned by her father for several years. Now only re-united with him.

"Yes. We saw your name several times in Dad's mailbox and he told us about you."

"Oh I see."

Diane was staying in Tamale over the weekend and travelling back to Accra the next week. Marian asked if they were going to travel to Navrongo, Dan's hometown. They had not discussed that. She offered to take Diane there on the Saturday if Diane was interested. "If you are free on the Saturday. I have my own money and will pay my own fare."

As if Diane would be reluctant to go if she had to pay for the girl as well. She agreed to go. The girl was offering to make friends with her and she did not see why she should say no. If it was true what Dan said of the children's relationship with their mother being her friend would not be bad. Spending some time together with the girl would not be bad. She could get to know her better and may be able to give Dan some more concrete suggestions to help his relationship with the children. She may learn some things that could help Dan understand the children better. She hoped so. And resolved to insist on going with the girl if Dan said no.

"What about school?" Diane asked the girl.

"I will take an exeat. We will come back the same day. We will be back in time for me to come back to school that same day."

Chapter Twenty-Seven

There were many things she remembered about this visit. Her memory started from the airport with Dan pretending to be meeting her for the first time. She carried with her a positive feeling about being made to stay in Dan's house instead of a hotel. She knew of his attitude to women and had expected he would arrange to keep her at a respectable distance. That he received her in his house, as a friend, but still kept his distance from such close range, added to her respect for her. He did not ever, not even once, do anything she would consider indecent. Instead he had sought to guarantee her space and respect her right to privacy even though she had not thought she needed any privacy in his presence.

She did know about Horizon Leadership Development Services. After all that was what was used to get the consultancies she helped Dan to work on. She had his card and it gave his address as Horizon Leadership. What she learnt when she came to Tamale were the size and structure of the institutions. She did not know it was so big and did such a roaring business. What she was also made aware of, which she could have guessed if only she had thought about it, were the relationship Dan had with his staff and the love and respect they had for him. The number of members of staff who asked if she would marry Dan surprised her. It was like a family, this feeling of concern for Dan.

The reception by the staff had been overwhelming. When for three days she had not consulted Brenda for any service Brenda had sought her out and taken her home for supper. She had taken her into town and had dresses sewn for her. Brenda and Mercy had acted as if she was an old friend. And she left Tamale feeling greatly indebted to them and to other staff who brought various items of gifts for her. She left Tamale feeling she had friends and she must reciprocate their gesture. Just how would be her challenge.

She was happy to have taken part in the training. He paid her fees for her role but she was indifferent to that. It was typical of Dan to want to reward people for any service at all that they rendered. But Horizon paid for her trip to and stay in Ghana. Her role in the training was really not that significant. She knew she impressed from the feedback Ibrahim gave her and from what some of the participants said in conversation with her. But her role was not significant. They could have done without her as they had done in all the previous training Horizon had conducted.

The most memorable thing she was taking away was her time with Marian. When she told Dan she was going to Navrongo on the Saturday with Marian he had been anxious and asked many questions. He offered to go with them and it was good she had thought about it and prepared her defences. He was happy about her offering to be friends with his daughter; he thought she needed a friend like Diane. But he had been strongly suspicious of the intention behind the girl's offer to take Diane to Navrongo.

"Navrongo is your birthplace, isn't it?" she asked him. "She asked if you had proposed to take me there and I said no. She thought it would be good for me to know the town. What is wrong with that?"

"Nothing. Except that I am not sure it is as simple as that. I feel there must be something else she has in mind." He did have queries in the knit brows.

"Something like what?" Diane asked hoping he would help her understand what it was that worried him, what he suspected.

He shrugged. "Diane, I wished I had a faint idea what it could be. The truth is I don't. The little I know about my daughter makes me feel she is intelligent and has her own way of getting things done. She is good at setting traps. I would not fall in them if I knew what sort of traps she were setting. I don't know."

He offered them the use of his vehicle. And Dauda. She did not want an outsider with them. If the girl had any traps she wanted to be the only one to know them and not have someone else outside the family listening. She wanted the opportunity to be alone with the girl and not have anyone else intruding on their privacy. So she said no.

He asked that she drove but she refused initially. She did not have an international driving licence and her Kenyan driving licence would not be valid in Ghana, she was sure.

"No policeman is going to stop you and ask you for your driving licence if they see you driving a vehicle like the one you will be driving. They assume people in a certain class are above certain offences. But if they stop you and ask for your licence, put up a bluff. They will ask for the papers of the vehicle first. Insurance, roadworthy and both are valid. If they ask for the driving licence, open your bag and bring out your purse and look through it. Then bang on the steering wheel and curse. I know you are Christian so I am not asking you to use God's name. Say gosh or something. Then explain you took the licence from your work bag and put it on the dining table to transfer it to your handbag and forgot to pick it. They will believe you."

She smiled and looked at him. She did not know he could be a crook when he chose to.

Marian was with her two friends when Diane arrived. She introduced them and they scrutinised her in the way they looked at her.

"Your father told me about the two of you as well," Diane told them as she shook hands with them. "He said he had two other equally BAB daughters here."

"What is BAB?"

"Oh, it means beautiful and brainy."

"You mean Dad thinks we are beautiful and brainy?" Leila asked.

"The beautiful is obvious, isn't it? Anyone can see that. Dan thinks each of you is very intelligent."

The girls did a dance and shook hands. Obviously they revered him and his positive opinion of them was invaluable to them. She smiled. She was older and quite established. But his positive opinion of her was a treasure to her.

Leila explained what they thought. "Dad is very intelligent. When you are with him you learn a lot. He knows almost everything. And he is a very good teacher. He explains things one step at a time. He goes from one to two to three then to four and so on. He is very intelligent. We look like stupid girls when we are with him. We seem to ask him stupid questions."

Diane shook her head. "Dan says you ask a lot of questions but they are very intelligent questions."

"And he calls us his daughters?" That was Leila again.

"Is he not your father?"

It was Carol who spoke this time. The quiet philosopher Dan had called her. "I am sure you know the two of us," she indicated Leila and her, "are not his biological daughters. We think of him as our father because that is what he means to us. But that does not mean that he thinks of us as his daughters."

Diane understood. "Dan feels he found not only the two children he lost many years ago, but four children he is very proud of. So he clearly thinks of the two of you as his daughters."

"In the school they call us the three musketeers. We have been together since last year when we came to form one," Marian told her

"They call you the three musketeers?" Diane asked with excitement. "I had a very intimate friend too, when we were in secondary school. And because we were inseparable they called us the two musketeers. We are still inseparable today. I hope the three of you remain inseparable too for the rest of your lives."

The three girls again danced on hearing that Diane and a friend had once been called two musketeers. Her wishing that they be inseparable forever pleased them even more. Thank you, Auntie they all said after Carol started it.

"Auntie, please buy us grilled tilapia when you are coming back," Leila said, coming near the woman. "Navrongo has the best grilled tilapia in this country. I am sure it is the tilapia more than anything that is tempting Marian to want to go to Navrongo."

Carol and Marian rebuked Leila for asking Diane to buy her tilapia but she defended herself saying Diane was her Auntie.

In a way it pleased Diane that Leila regarded her as someone close enough to her to make her feel free to ask her for things. But it also pleased her that her friends rebuked her for asking someone she was new to for things.

"They are wonderful friends," Marian said when they left Tamale and were on the highway. "I am really very happy with the way Dad is treating them as his own children. It makes me happy but it makes me even very proud of Dad. And that makes me even happier."

"Why are you happy that Dan is treating them as his children?" Diane asked when Marian did not go on to explain her feeling.

Marian turned and looked at her father's friend for a moment. She turned and looked ahead of her, at the empty road ahead of them. "I am sure Dad has told you about his relationship with our mother and with us the children. When I first came to secondary school my life would have been very miserable if I did not have the company of these two girls. They were my friends and, besides my brother, the only family I had. It was very important to me because without them I would have spent all my time thinking and worrying and feeling sad and very miserable. They are fun, those two girls, even Carol the quiet one. They made me forget my misery. And they gave me family. They were more than friends. I am not sure they know what their friendship at the time meant to me."

She did not turn to look at Diane when she paused. But Diane turned and looked at her. She was looking out of the window. When she turned and looked briefly at Diane she had turned back to concentrate on her driving. "I am very glad Dad has accepted those two girls as his children because they treated me like a sister. I am also very proud of Dad because the two girls respect him. Leila certainly thinks more highly of him than her own father."

Another silence again. Then, "One evening when we were at the Mole Game Park, HIV and AIDS came up. Dad let us discuss it and he gave us very good advice about it. My friends were shocked that he should discuss sex with us. It is a taboo topic in their homes. And when they told Dad he explained to them why adults should discuss sex with young people. He is there for them as he is for Junior and me."

Diane did not regret coming on the journey and she was happy that she insisted on coming alone with this young woman. She learnt a lot from her and understood her father's discomfort. She was welcome to the turmoil of emotions that father and children were still experiencing so early in their relationship. A window was opened through which she could see how father and daughter saw some things differently because of the different positions from which they looked at them. Yet, despite the differences she felt the strong affection each had for the other.

They went first to the crocodile pond where Diane initially refused to go near the giant reptiles. She did eventually when Marian held one by its big rough tail.

They went to visit the irrigation project and were fortunate to come across a staff who offered to show them round and explain how things worked. Diane had never been to an irrigation project before and she found it interesting. She enjoyed the fish when they went for lunch. She had asked for medium sized one but Marian encouraged her to take a bigger one. She was sure she could not eat all of it if she took a big one. Sometimes people did not know themselves. She ate all of it and was glad she took a bigger one. Diane made them grill four more for Marian to take back to school.

When Marian suggested to Diane that they visit Dan's family she did not stop to think about it but immediately thought it would be a good thing. "But I don't have anything to give to his parents. He is very thoughtful and would know what to bring to my parents whenever he is coming to Kenya."

"It will be okay for you to give them money, I am sure."

On the way Marian asked, "Auntie Diane, are you going to marry our father?"

She smiled inwardly. It looked like she would meet that question more than ten times before she left Ghana. Funny how many people wanted Dan to marry. It surprised her at first that they should all be asking her if she would marry him. But on reflection she stopped being surprised. She was the nearest to a female friend Dan had.

Since she had met this question a number of times before she was ready with her answer. She shook her head, turned and looked at the keen eyed girl. "No. I am not going to marry him."

Marian laughed and Diane did not see what was funny. "The way you said it so fast, Auntie, you don't seem to think anyone should be considering you marrying my father. But he is a very nice man, Auntie."

Her answer forced Diane to smile. "Nobody knows more than me how nice a man your father is. It is not that I don't think that it is worth considering marrying him. Your father does not want a wife. He is happy as he is. I know all those who think of marriage for him do so out of love. But he is happy without a wife. So please stop worrying about him."

Marian breathed and looked out of the window again for a while and then said, "Sorry Auntie, but I can't stop worrying about Dad being alone." Turning to look at Diane she asked, "Have you thought of what will happen to him if he falls seriously sick in the night? And if the sickness makes him unable to talk and unable to get out of bed, what will happen to him? Will he be saved if he falls seriously sick and would have been saved if someone were with him and went to get him help? What will happen to him if he dies in the night?"

Gosh, Diane thought, for a young woman her age she entertained adult thoughts.

Before turning to look at the green valleys outside she said, "I worry about Dad living alone in that house each night."

Marian asked Diane to stop somewhere on the road and she got down and talked to a young man. She said nothing when she came back. They turned right about a mile out of town on the road to Paga. Marian made Diane stop the vehicle for her to ask for directions and that puzzled Diane. The younger woman explained that she had never been to the village before. She was going there for the first time, just like Diane.

"I have been to Navrongo only once before," Marian explained, "and that was very recently. Our mother never bothered to bring us. She would have sent us to her home anyway, and not to Saboro which is Dad's village. I am sure we would not have liked to go to her home anyway." When Diane looked sharply at her young companion Marian explained. "Her mother doesn't like us. I don't know if she likes anybody. She hates Dad and the only reason I can tell for her hatred for us is that we are Dad's children. She doesn't like any reference to Dad as our father but whenever she insults us she brings in Dad. *Look at her big head, as if she just plucked it from that stupid man. Very bad children – following in the footsteps of that useless man.* We would not have liked to go to our mother's home, anyway."

Marian asked for directions when they drove further and from the directions given she guided Diane to the house.

Diane took notice of the architecture for the first time. Most houses were built of gravel and plastered with a material she could not tell. Marian could not tell what material was used in the plastering either when she asked her. The roofing baffled her. The houses seemed to have flat roofs but she could not tell how that was done. In almost every house there were one or two or more rooms roofed with metal roofing sheets, aluminium as far as she could tell. Those would be the members of the family who were better off. Maybe salaried workers. Could be people living and working in urban areas who remitted for the buildings to be put up for them.

The house they drove to was entirely different from all the houses they had passed by so far. It made Diane curious and she looked at the houses all round this house and none was like it.

Marian greeted in Kassem and said they had come to see Dan Apeatu's parents. Some hushed discussions while the two stood. Someone got up and offered them a stool but Marian was not sure if they should take it. If they had come to the wrong house they would not be sitting down.

"Who wants them?" a grey bearded man asked. The grey beard was very pronounced as he wore it long. "Who are you?"

Marian had not expected this question. So she hesitated. She started to introduce herself but checked herself in time and introduced Diane instead. "This lady is from a country called Kenya. She works with ..." She was on the verge of saying her father but she stopped just in time. "She works with Mr Apeatu. He goes there to work with her sometimes and she came here to work with him. They worked together this past week. Today she came to visit Navrongo and wanted to greet Mr Apeatu's parents."

Some further discussions in low tones while the one who offered the stool insisted they sat down. Diane waited for Marian to tell her what was going on since she did not understand Kassem but decided not to ask. She knew Marian would tell her what she needed to know.

"This is his parents' house," the same elderly man said. He pointed to a young man of about nineteen and said, "This boy will take you to him. Apeatu has a birds' farm and he spends the day there. His wife has gone there too. But this is their house. Tell her," he pointed to Diane, "that this is Digadam's family's house." He noticed the confusion in Marian's face and added, "You people call him Apeatu. But it is his father who is Apeatu. You school people like to leave your own names and assume your father's names."

They all laughed and Marian knew he did not mean anything bad.

On the way Diane asked if the Apeatu family was rich. Marian did not know. "I only know Dad. I don't know any other member of the family." She was silent a while and then asked, "Why did you ask that question? Because the whole of the house was built of cement blocks?"

"Yes, the house is different from all the other houses, isn't it?"

Marian turned to the boy and asked. The boy spoke good English and Diane and Marian were relieved that they would both be able to chat with him. He told them Dan helped them build it. "He brought someone who helped to draw the house. I remember the discussions he had with members of the family. He would come home and he and the men would talk and talk about how the house should be built. He kept saying they should think about the future when those who were children would grow and would need their own rooms. So they discussed how it should be built. Then he brought someone who also had a long discussion with them. The man went away and drew the plan. Dan then sent money and they bought sand and cement. They engaged people to mould the bricks, people who knew how to mix the sand and cement and mould strong blocks. But we provided labour. And they started building, building for two or three families a year."

Diane remembered a story her father had read and used to make jokes when they were young. She did not know the story, had never read it but remembered the distorted version her father told. He joked, teasing their mother, that a man from their mother's village travelled to Nairobi where he was awed by all he saw. He came across the main hospital in Nairobi and thought it was someone's home. He asked a passer-by who owned the house. But the man could not speak his language and so he replied that he did not understand. I don't understand. The man from their mother's village stood looking at the house and admiring the non-existent I don't understand. At that moment nurses from the morning shift who had just been replaced by their counterparts on afternoon shift came pouring out, beautiful young women in the same uniform and the villager asked whose daughters they were. The man he asked gave the same answer, I don't understand. The villager saw many wonderful things, wonderful to him, that was, and each, he was told, belonged to I don't understand.

She was not interested in the end of the story but Dan seemed to be the I don't understand in the story. He had a hand in many successful things. He made things happen and he made things different wherever he was. Look at the leadership training. Look at the training centre. And now the house.

Dan's mother came to the fence when she saw the vehicle approaching and she recognised it. She was a bit apprehensive as Dan hardly came home at this time. He would come home in the evening and not come from Tamale straight to the farm. While her husband busied himself working and ignored the approaching vehicle she stood by the fence and watched it drive closer. Her fears increased when she saw that Dan was not driving. But she stayed calm and waited for the occupants to come down.

The young man who accompanied them explained how the two had come home looking for Apeatu and Jango and he had been asked to bring them. They were offered seats and the young man insisted on walking back. When Marian introduced Diane they welcomed her. Marian did the translation for them. They asked her about Kenya, her family in Kenya and her stay in the country so far.

"Does she have a husband?" Dan's mother asked.

Marian translated both question and Diane's answer. She smiled as she translated both question and answer.

"Ask her if she will marry my son," Jango told Marian.

Marian asked the question. She knew the answer and could have told her grandmother no, Diane was not going to marry their son. But she just translated the question and translated Diane's answer.

"You said she has been working with my son," Dan's mother again. "Ask her what is wrong with my son because of which she won't marry him."

Marian again smiled. They had gone down this road and she knew all the landmarks on the road. She knew what Diane's answer would be.

"Please tell our mother that her son is a happy man without a wife. Tell her he does not need a wife. He is very busy and very happy without a wife. So she should not worry about him."

"Ask her how a man can be happy when he has no wife. Tell her every man needs a wife. My son's life is not complete without a wife."

"Tell her, Marian, that Dan's life is complete without a wife. Tell her Dan is very happy without a wife. Tell her he is happier than men who are married. Tell her her son is doing very good work and changing lives of people not only in Ghana. And he is very happy with himself without a wife. So she should stop worrying about him. Some people don't need wives and her son is one of them."

"Auntie, can I ask you a question?" Marian asked without translating what Diane had just said. "Will you marry yourself?"

Diane tilted her head and looked at Marian. "Why do you ask that question, Marian?"

"It is the way you are supporting Dad, Auntie. You are not just quoting what he said. You seem to believe that it is okay not to marry."

Diane contemplated her young companion. "Marian, unlike your father I would marry if I met a man I loved who loved me. Your father will probably never fall in love and is too busy to stop and think about love and marriage. But he is happy. And we should all learn not to worry unnecessarily for him."

Marian translated what Diane said and the old man told his wife to drop the topic. "She is not Digadam. When your son comes you can convince him to marry but please let this woman alone. She can't answer questions for your son."

Marian was initially forgotten in the discussion with Diane. It was Diane who was said to work with their son. It was Diane who could marry their son.

But when they took Diane and Marian round the farm the old man asked Marian who she was and spoke good Kassem. They were back to the tree under which the couple had camp beds and chairs and they asked Diane and Marian to be seated. Marian hesitated and Diane could sense that Marian had been asked a question she would have liked to dodge.

"I am Mr Apeatu's daughter," she said after some hesitation.

The old lady sat up in her chair. "I didn't hear you well." She held the lobe of her ear as if by pulling it she would hear better. "What did you just say?"

Marian smiled and told Diane what had just been said. Diane smiled too.

"I said I am Mr Apeatu's daughter."

The old man sat up and looked at the young woman. Attention had shifted from Diane to Marian. The old lady got up and stood looking down at Marian. "You say you are Apeatu's daughter," she said slowly. "His daughter by which woman?"

"His daughter by our mother, Matilda Kadua. He only married one woman, and that was our mother."

The old lady beat the old man to speak. "You mean you are the daughter of the woman my son married and who later drove him out of the house? You are the daughter of the nurse? There were two of you, you and a boy. Is that you?"

"Yes, Grandma."

The old lady stooped and collected the young woman in her arms. She lifted Marian up to the amazement of Marian and Diane.

"The last time I saw you you were only this high." She indicated with her hand. She released the young woman and stood back and appraised her. She sat down and pulled Marian unto her lap. She embraced her. "These laps have been fallow for a long time. They have not had a grandchild sitting on them for a long time. Digadam is my only child. And you and your brother are his only children. When you were small I put you on my lap many times. But since your mother and her mother refused to let us see you and your brother I have not experienced the joy of a grandmother, having her grandchildren on her laps. My child, lie on me." She pulled Marian and she lay on the old lady. "Welcome! Welcome, my child."

"How is your brother?" the old man asked.

"He is very well."

"And how is your mother?" the old man asked further.

"She is also fine. She is very well."

"Is she still drinking the way they said she was drinking in the past?"

"Yes, Grandpa." She made to stand up but her grandmother pulled her back.

"Where are you going to?" the grandmother asked. "The thorns in my thighs have started to prick you, haven't they?"

"No, Grandma, there are no thorns on your thighs. I am heavy and your legs must be paining."

The grandmother pushed her away from her and examined her. "Where is the flesh on you to make you heavy? Who told you that you are heavy? And who told you my thighs are paining? How many years have these thighs been yearning for a child to sit on them and you want to get up after just a few minutes? Children who are not related to me have been sitting on those thighs and I have not complained. Now that my own blood is sitting on them why do you think they will pain? Sit down my child. You can sit on them for the whole day. The only thing I will know will be joy and not pain."

She asked Marian some questions. If they had come back to their father. Marian explained the relationship with their father. She wanted to know if their mother would come back to their father now that the children had reunited with their father. Marian did not know but did not think it would happen. She explained the fact that her mother did not like their father and she did not think their father wanted her back too. They went on talking. Grandmother asking questions, grandchild answering.

"Don't let your happiness at seeing your grandchild blind you to what you should be doing," her husband told her. "Are they staying? If they are not staying you must prepare something for them to eat before they leave."

Still sitting on her grandmother's lap Marian translated what had been going on. Diane said it was really time to hit the road again if Marian was to be returned to her school before roll call. The old couple protested. How could they come and not eat food in Digadam's house and leave. They insisted they stayed for the old lady to prepare food for them. What would they tell Digadam when they got back to Tamale?

"For you this is your house," the old lady told Marian. "But even for you how will you know that this is your house if you don't eat food here? It is even worse if the visitor has to go without eating food. No, you can't go."

Marian explained to an amused Diane who explained why they had to go. She left Marian to try and do the convincing since she could not speak the language. But she watched with amusement as Marian and her grandmother tried to convince each other. She stole glances at the old man who hardly spoke but was nonetheless attentive. This is Dan Senior, Diane told herself. It was when she looked at him this time that she noticed the striking resemblance between father and son. He was older. He had grey hair and lines in his face. But it was the same face, a younger face, that his son wore.

When the old man got up and spoke even though Diane did not understand what he said she knew it was to conclude things.

"Let them go, Ago." Turning to Marian he said, "Explain to the visitor that when she next comes to Ghana she should come and spend a night with us. She knows Tamale but we will like to have her here for an evening, to eat the food we have not been able to provide her today. Tell her my son's guests are our guests too. And we should have shown her that we appreciated her visit and that she is welcome to our home. But we can't insist on keeping you till late and get you into trouble. But we expect her the next time she comes to Tamale.

"As for you, come as early as you can. Death can come for the two of us, me and your grandmother, at any time now. Come again and bring your brother to see us. Come and know your house. Come and know your other relatives and let them know you."

Marian translated for Diane who nodded. She gave Marian the envelope in which she had put the money to be given to her grandparents.

"Tell them that I did not know what to buy for them since I did not know what they would prefer. So they can use this money to buy something for themselves. Tell them whenever I am in Tamale I will surely come and see them and prepare to spend the night with them."

The old man was busy somewhere. He was able to trap four guinea fowls which he put in a small coop. He caught two turkeys as well.

"Tell my daughter," the old man told Marian, pointing to Diane, "that I am her father, just as I am father to my son. Because she is my son's friend she is my daughter too. When people come from outside it is guinea fowls they want to eat. They say they don't have guinea fowls in some countries outside. So her friend will use these guinea fowls to prepare some soup for her. I know he can cook. The turkeys are also for her. That is what I farm

"As for you, everything here is for you. I won't give you anything for Tamale because you are not travelling. Come again and if you want to eat all the turkeys here for lunch we will kill all of them for you."

Marian again translated for Diane who shook her head at the generosity of Dan's parents. When the envelope Diane gave was given to the old man he protested. It made Diane smile. He was giving so generously but protesting about being given things. Just like his son, she thought. The old man fished in his pockets, emptied all of them and found some money for Marian. When he asked his wife for more money to add to what he had for Marian she asked why he could not take money from the envelope.

"My daughter just gave that to me," he explained to his wife. "She asked me to use it on myself. I cannot give it away."

The old man asked if they could take a turkey to Marian's mother. Diane and Marian consulted. Marian was going back to school. Even if she wasn't she would not have wanted her mother to know she came to this house. So she could not send a turkey from this house to her mother. Diane did not know Matilda so she could not go knocking at her door to say she was bringing a turkey from Dan's family for her. She could be asked questions she could not answer. And they both knew Dan would feel reluctant to send a turkey to his former wife.

Even though Apeatu could not understand English he could tell from the voices and faces of the women that carrying a turkey back to Tamale for Matilda would be a problem for them. He told Marian, "When you go back tell your mother that she has turkeys here to collect. So when she next comes to Navrongo she should come over and collect them. Or if she knows of anyone coming from here to Tamale she can ask the person to collect them for her."

When the old man stopped his wife took over. "Tell her to come and visit us when she comes to Navrongo. She is still our wife. She can't have two children with us and leave us. She did not marry again and she does not have any children besides you, we learnt. So tell her that we are not angry with her. She is welcome here whenever she comes to Navrongo.

"As for you and your brother, when schools are on holidays come home. This is your home. Come for me to prepare a good meal for you. I can't die without you eating my food. And you don't know when I will die so when next you are on holidays come home." She embraced her again and kept hugging her.

Before the two women got into the vehicle Marian's grandmother said, "My child, I am happy to have seen you. Today I will sleep. But I will sleep even better when you and your brother come home and eat my meals."

There was silence as the two women drove back through the town and drove out of it on their way to Bolga. Diane was silent, observing that her passenger was looking out of the window and was very pensive.

At last unable to keep her comment and anxious to break the silence she said, "Such a nice couple, don't you think?"

Marian stirred and looked at Diane. Tears began to stream down her face. It was unexpected. Diane pulled off the road and stopped. She waited till the crying stopped before she asked what was wrong.

"Nothing," she said.

"And you're weeping?"

"Yes."

She was again looking out of the window and Diane said nothing immediately.

She turned to Diane and said, "I am just a small girl."

Diane chose to say nothing but to wait till her companion was more composed to be able to tell her what had caused the tears.

"I am not sure you will understand," Marian told Diane. "I am not sure anybody will understand me. My brother is even different and at times I am sure he does not feel as strongly as I do."

Another silence in which Diane continued to observe her friend.

"I am just confused," the younger woman said again.

Again Diane said nothing and waited.

After a few minutes Marian turned to Diane and spoke. "I am sure you saw everything that happened. For sixteen years, or the most part of sixteen years, we knew only one relation, our mother. Our father claims she loves us. But we did not feel it. All we knew were insults. We did not know our father and even today we don't know why he did not contact us for twelve years. Our grandmother on our mother's side was not different from our mother. If she came into contact with us all we got from her were insults because of what she feels about our father."

She was silent and looked away. Diane sat quietly and waited for her.

"Today we found people who love us and it seems have been looking for us. But even they were prevented from meeting us and showing us love. You don't know how it felt sitting like a baby on my grandmother's lap. You don't know how it felt to have someone show me open love. You don't know how it felt to listen to our grandmother tell me how much we mean to her. Before we left she told me she would sleep well tonight. Because she met me. I mean something to someone. She invited me to come with my brother."

Another pause and another silence.

"Dad says we cannot come and stay with him. He spends time with us and when we are together it is clear he cares for us. Our friends tell us they think he is a loving father. But he says we can't stay with him. He would not let us contact his parents. You just said our grandparents are such nice people. But left to Dad and Mama we would never meet them and we would never experience the love they just showed me. I now know that I have a father who would spend time with me and that if I am in trouble he will support me. I am assured of the payment of the school fees. He is interested in my education, I know that. But until today he was my only relative, as it were. I come from a family but did not know the family." She threw her head back when she asked, "Where do I belong?"

Diane made no effort to answer.

"You grew up with your parents. Maybe you met your uncles and aunts and cousins. So you took them for granted. For many years I have had to ask myself who I am. Look at me; I am even Marian Wepia. But I am not a Wepia. Nobody will want me in that house. But I am not Apeatu. That," she pointed behind her, "is my house. But Dad is more concerned about himself and our mother. *Your mother will die if I took you away from her. If your grandparents see you they will renew their pressure on me to take you from your mother.* For the comfort of him and mother we had to be denied our real home."

The tears again.

Diane looked away in order not to weep herself. She contemplated the unfortunate upbringing of this poor girl and her brother. The girl was right; those of them who had not been through what the two siblings went through in their upbringing would not ever clearly understand them. On the other hand Diane knew their father loved them and in making decisions he would not be thinking about his former wife or himself alone. She knew that the children featured strongly in his considerations and that if he had to make sacrifices it would be his former wife for the children. But he would be considerate to his former wife despite their strained relationship. He probably did not understand the girl and her brother enough but he was not only concerned about his and their mother's comfort.

When Marian seemed well composed Diane put a hand on her shoulder and squeezed it and told her, "Marian, I feel sorry for you and your brother. I feel sorry for all the pain you had to go through. I feel sorry for all the pain you still feel and for the mixture of feelings you must be experiencing sometimes." She dried the young woman's tears. "But I don't agree with you about your father. I know Dan and I know how much you mean to him. I know how much he feels guilty and very bad about his absence in your life for the twelve years. He has not and will probably never forgive himself for what he did not do for you for those years. I know how much he wants to ensure that you are happy for the rest of your life. He cares about you more than I know most fathers care for their children. But your father will not want to hurt anybody if he can avoid it. His preventing you from seeing his parents, from knowing what you rightly describe as your home, is based on his consideration for all of you, you and your brother, your mother and he himself. He may be wrong sometimes. He may not understand how much a situation affects you. Because, as you rightly said, for those of us who have not gone through your experience it is difficult for us to appreciate those things that prick you so hard. So he may take decisions in which he thinks he has rightly considered you and your interest and may be wrong. It does not mean he is concerned only about the two of them, him and your mother."

Marian said nothing and Diane paused and composed her thoughts and what to say next. "Marian, in saying things about your father, please consider the fact that because of your experience and the way you feel about your mother especially but also about your father, you can be harder on them than it is right to be. You may be more concerned about yourself than especially your mother. I am sure one day you will develop a strong appreciation for your father and praise him for being considerate to your mother at this time. Dan loves you and your brother. I am not sure how he feels about your mother. But while he will want to make you a princess and a prince he will also want to minimise how much he hurts your mother in the process."

When they stopped in Bolga for Diane to buy provisions for the three girls the two women were talking as jovially as if the scene in the vehicle a while back did not happen. Diane ignored Marian's protests and bought tins of Milo, sachets of granulated sugar, tins of powdered milk, soap, digestive biscuits and packets of fruit juice for Marian and her colleague musketeers.

"Remember that I was a musketeer," she told Marian. "So you are my sisters."

Marian shook her head. "No, you are our Auntie."

"Sister."

"Auntie."

"Sister."

"You can say it one thousand times, you won't change the way we feel about you and the way we think about you. We will think about you as our Auntie, Auntie Diane."

The smiles and laughter were back and Diane was happy too.

"Auntie, I wish you were not like Dad." They were turning into Tamasco.

"In what way do you wish I were different from your father?"

"In the way you think about his marriage. You say it is okay for him to be alone. If you did not think that way, you may have influenced him to agree to marry. You will make an excellent wife for him."

Diane kept on driving and said nothing. Till she parked where Marian directed her. "Marian, I appreciate your concern for your father and your feeling that he needs a wife. It is not a big issue. He is happy. And he is even happier now that you and your brother have come back into his life. Don't think too much about his being alone."

"I am sure I will think about it from time to time, Auntie. He said if our mother suddenly died he would fight for us. I will be in boarding school. Who takes care of Dad and Junior? Who will make the place a home for us?"

As Diane sat looking straight into the face of Marian the latter went on, "See?"

Diane heaved a sigh but said nothing.

Marian opened the door but closed it again. "Auntie, I know Dad loves us. I know he is concerned about us. I am sorry I said he thinks about himself and mother only. I am wrong. But I hope you will understand me and why I think that way sometimes. As for you I can't say thank you enough. You are like Dad. You are so kind. Thanks for all the provisions. Thanks for your kind words. And thanks for being Dad's friend."

Diane rubbed a hand on Marian's head. "Marian, thanks to you too. This trip was great. I feel very happy that I met and got to know Dan's parents. I am happy that I got to know his home. And it was nice being with you. I see why your father is proud of you. I am proud of you too. I understand you. And I am sure your father understands you somehow. You love your father, I can see that. He loves you too. And he loves your brother too. The three of you should be happy together. But you need to be patient with your father.

"Say hello to your other musketeers for me. Study hard. You are very intelligent. And your father believes all of you are intelligent. Concentrate on your studies and make him proud. You will get to know your father by and by. When you know him better you will be proud of him as well."

As she drove away Diane felt trapped in the turbulence of feelings generated by the relationship between her mentor and his children. She sympathised with each side, understood how each person caught in the turbulent current felt, and understood why it would take a while for them to reach a level of understanding of each other that would reduce the friction. She knew Dan liked his children and was committed to their welfare. He had changed a lot since they discussed the children for the first time in Nairobi. He seemed to have strongly accepted the competition the children would pose to his work and he was ready to give up some work for them.

She knew nothing of Junior but Marian certainly felt strong concern for her father. And that could only come from love for him. But they differed in how they saw things, how things should be done and how they interpreted what they saw. She was glad Marian had voiced out her opinion of her father so Diane could influence that opinion. She knew she would try to explain the girl's point of view to Dan and she hoped she achieved success there as well. Between father and daughter they should be able to communicate for each to see where they stood and why and to agree an acceptable compromise.

She was learning about having children and not liking what she had learnt so far.

For the rest of her stay Diane kept reliving the events of the day she spent with Marian. Dan was initially not happy when he learnt they went to his home and met his parents. He had not been amused about the meeting between Marian and his parents. Diane could see he was thinking of what his parents would demand of him now that they met Marian. She told him he had to manage their demand but he could not stand between the grandparents and the children. They should be able to relate without the children having to leave their mother.

Dan drove her back to Accra, to catch her flight. But they had a tour first. She did not enjoy her visit to Elmina Castle. She had read a bit about the slave trade but it happened centuries back. It was, like all history, history. She had heard of the calls for reparation but had not followed them closely. It seemed to her to be one of those rather intellectual activities hard-line leftists thought up from time to time. Going to the castle brought the trade close to her. She saw the human element in the process. It was not just history. But then, she told herself, on serious consideration, all history was about human beings.

"Why do people make this place a tourist place? It holds such a sad history. Why should anybody want to come and visit it? I want to visit the wildlife park and see animals I have only read about or seen in pictures or on telly. It is fun and it is interesting. What is interesting about the sorrowful tale of the slave castles that anybody would want to visit them?"

They were driving back to Accra. She would not eat. She was not hungry, she told him. The effect of the castle on her surprised and worried him.

"I am sorry I took you there," he said, sounding very sincere. "But I don't think tourism is about only fun and positive places. It is all about learning. The castles may hold stories that are sad but they are factual. They preserve in their holds a part of our realistic past. Their stories may make us sick, sad or angry. They may do that. But they make the black and white figures in the history books we read come alive, acquire emotions and play back the tragic drama that we easily gloss over in print. They tell you the story of the pain our ancestors went through without the sensationalism of Hollywood."

She liked Akosombo. She had never been to the Victoria Falls but she had heard it was a beautiful place to visit. She had in her mind to take Dan there when next he came to Kenya. Provided he would not be impatient to be on the next flight to another destination. She enjoyed the panoramic view of hills and green that surrounded the hotel. In the evening they talked for more than an hour after supper. They did not return immediately to their rooms. Dan made them linger around the car park where the night air was filled with the scent of lavender.

"I don't like hotels after staying in a home with you this past week," she complained to Dan. "Hotels separate you. We had more time together in the evenings in your sitting room. In a hotel if we want to go on chatting we either use the reception, which does not give you the same seclusion and privacy a house room gives, or stay in one of our rooms. In some hotels I knew in the UK there were suites that had say two bedrooms. But there was a common sitting room where people could spend the evening together and go their respective rooms to sleep."

He shook his head. "Diane, let me make a confession. I am relieved that we came out of my house. I don't know how I managed the conversation on some evenings with you sitting or lying across from me wearing scanty clothing. You filled me up with the profile of your body. The woman in you came out strongly. Your shapeliness and beauty sometimes threatened to drown the speech ability in me. It was very nice, very enjoyable, living close to you. You are fun to be with and I am sure Teddy does not know the gold he missed for whatever mineral he swapped you for."

Another one of those intense long looks, as usual, with her head tilted. In the end she smiled. Dan observing that she was shapely and that she was beautiful was a huge compliment, she thought. All she said was thanks.

Chapter Twenty-Eight

When Marian told her two friends how the trip to Navrongo had been they all agreed they did not have to wait for the holidays to go there. Their father had discussed paying for some Masters to teach them in some subjects during the third term long holidays. They agreed he would arrange for English, Maths, Physics and Chemistry teachers to teach them when they were on holidays. There were many centres where teachers organised classes during the holidays but their father wanted to have the three of them alone having classes together. It would mean he would pay the teachers extra fees for them to come and take the three but he was prepared to pay for them to have special attention. That way the teachers could concentrate on their needs and teach according to that.

They were also going to start computer classes during the same holidays, he informed them. He made them understand that computers were the technology of the present and they needed to master them not only as a tool for writing but as a medium for unlimited access to information and knowledge.

So their third term holidays would be learning and yet more learning.

They were not worried that their holidays would be spent learning instead of having fun. On the contrary. They were happy that they would have the chance to treat topics they had found difficult and that would prepare them for the Senior Secondary School Certificate Examination only the next year. They wanted to begin their third year confident that they would do well in the final exam and their father, thankfully, was giving them the opportunity to acquire that confidence.

They also knew the holidays would not be all work. Their father had also assured them that there were places not far from Tamale they could all go to and have fun and learn at the same time. They had never been to the water treatment plant at Dalun, for instance, or the source from which the water was pumped for treatment in Nawuni. He said they could visit some of the districts not far from Tamale and he was sure they would find interesting things to see. "We may even go to Salaga, Damongo or Bole even though these are Gonja districts. Who knows, they could be fun as well." The response was the protest it was intended to generate, from Leila. Of course, nobody supported her.

So the three children agreed they would go to Navrongo during their next mid-term holidays which were four days. They ran into an obstacle. Marian was sure their grandparents would want to see Junior. They had seen her before. And they had been excited about seeing her. They would be even more excited to see both of them. And would be disappointed if they went without Junior. Junior himself would not forgive her if they went without him. Especially given her knowledge of what reception awaited them at home. The first obstacle, a very small one so far as the three girls were concerned, was the fact that going with Junior would mean he missed two days of classes. They knew he could afford to miss them. Their key worry was their mother.

They needed not tell her if the girls had chosen to go alone. After all she would never even know they left school and went out of town. But if Junior was to come along did he just up anchor and sail away or did they inform their mother? Carol was all for their informing her.

"We will pray against anything happening to us on the way," Carol explained. "But it will be terribly bad for us if anything should happen to us and your mother did not know that we were going to Navrongo. Besides, we will be rude to her."

Even a deaf person could have heard the rude-to-her-my-foot statement clearly from the snort and look in Marian's face. Carol said they should not assume that their mother would oppose their going. "Things could have changed since Dad came back into your lives," she argued. Another snort of disagreement which she ignored.

Leila supported their telling Matilda. She would tell her parents and she knew they would not object to her going. Carol would tell her aunt. She had not been home for more than a year and her aunt would agree to her going.

Then began another round of debate, who to tell Matilda. The other two girls were convinced it had to be Marian but she disagreed. The mice arguing over who belled the cat. In the end Marian agreed to tell her but she immediately invented the story she was going to tell her mother. She knew her friends would disagree with her so she did not tell them what she was going to tell her mother. When she went home what she told her mother was that Carol was going home for the mid-terms and she and Leila were going with her too. She had conspired with Junior what to say so Junior exclaimed excitedly that he would come with them too. Their mother rebuked him asking if he was a girl to be visiting with Marian and her friends. She asked no further questions and did not expressly forbid Junior from going.

One dull Friday morning in early June four bright eyed children, three girls and a boy, were among the passengers of a Mercedes Benz bus that left Tamale for Bolga. They occupied the back seat so that they all sat together. Nobody doubted the fact that they were students from their carefree and excited talk, from their arguments and from their laughter. From Bolga they caught another mini bus to Navrongo. They went past Nayagenia. Carol came with them to town. They agreed to go first to Saboro for Carol to know where the rest of them were going. They would later come back with her to her village.

Marian did not know it was that far from the station in Navrongo town to Saboro and then to the farm. Leila teased them all the way but Junior was the most expectant among them, running now, hopping later but all the time quiet, hardly speaking. He observed things around them. He threw stones at egrets that followed cattle and preyed on insects that the cattle disturbed. He stopped and talked to four young boys herding animals. June was the rainy season in that part of the country. The grass was green and crops were at different stages of growth. The early maturing millet was pregnant with seed while the late maturing variety and the sorghum were still very young. Groundnut plants were already spreading to cover the ridges on which they had been planted. In fact the early maturing variety had yellow flowers among the green leaves.

When the crops began to germinate animals were not allowed to roam freely anymore. So young boys, most often, but sometimes young girls, were made to herd them. Junior observed what the four lean looking young boys carried for lunch, a handful of groundnuts and a few heads of sorghum.

They walked past the dugout on the way to Kajelo and here the other children began asking Marian if she was sure they were on the right road. She said yes, she remembered the road very well. But they still asked the next person they met and he told them to keep on walking. And that it was no more far away.

Their grandfather was busy putting water in the pigs' sties when they arrived. He came out into the main yard to meet them when he was told he had visitors. He remembered Marian and welcomed them. He did not shake hands because his hands were dirty. When he saw Junior he stopped talking and looked at him so long that all the others turned to look at him.

"When your father was born," he told Marian, "they removed an arrow from my quiver and forged it into a bangle which they put on his hand. They said he resembled me very much. In our custom if a son so strongly resembles the father and they don't forge a bangle from the father's arrow for the boy to wear, the son or the father will die."

Leila started to tease them but she was not used to the old man yet so she stopped.

The old man went on, "Nobody will question if this boy is Digadam's son. It is as if he spat him. How are you, my child?"

"I am fine," Junior replied.

From the sties pigs squealed and grunted. Junior was soon lost playing with the turkeys. He would scream and all the turkeys would respond with cries of their own. He joined the hands fetching water to go and fetch water. He loved the donkey cart and found it fun pumping water out of the borehole.

The girls went round and inspected the enclosures and all joined the old man to fill troughs and carry food. They would not listen to the old man's order for them to just sit and watch him.

He made the hands catch a guinea fowl which he made Leila slaughter since she was a Moslem. They roasted it for the children while they waited for their grandmother to come and prepare lunch.

Leila was impressed. She said, "Marian, you have a very generous family. I thought it was your father alone but now that I have met his father it seems it is the whole family that is generous. You are a princess and you were suffering."

"Look at Auntie Diane who is not a member of the family," Carol observed. "Look at the provisions she bought for us. For all of us and not Marian alone."

When the children's grandmother came in the afternoon the work had been finished a long time back. All the girls and their grandfather were seated under the shady umbrella tree. Only Junior was out with the hands, climbing trees, throwing stones at birds and going off to chat with boys passing with their animals to pasture. They had to go out and call Junior for his grandmother. She would not do anything until she saw him. When her husband said he resembled his father it made her even more anxious to see him. She held him at arm's length and examined his face, turning him first one way and then the other way. As with Marian she sat down and pulled him on to her lap where he nestled like a baby. The girls laughed but after several minutes she took each of them in turn and made them sit on her lap.

"Tell her I am a Gonja heavyweight and not a Kassena lightweight so I will break her thighs if I sit on them," Leila told her friends.

They translated and their grandmother replied, "Tell her if she is truly a Gonja heavyweight she should break them for me. Tell her I have been looking for someone to break them for me for many years. So she should go ahead and break them for me."

She and the girls set about cooking. Her husband had to go back home with the motorbike to bring more food since she did not know about the four extra mouths. "I am worried for the Gonja girl, not the rest of you. I am sure the rest of you will be satisfied with small quantities of food but I have heard that Gonjas eat in buckets."

They laughed and translated for Leila. "I had better catch the next bus back to Tamale. I am alone among you. You will eat me today."

They laughed and translated for their grandmother. She laughed too. "Tell her we don't eat Gonjas here. She can see that we have guinea fowls and turkeys. Their meat is tasty. I hear Gonja meat is sour."

They again translated for Leila and they all laughed. When the girls had the chance to put their heads together and gossip it was to speak about the old lady's sense of humour. "I was wondering how I would be received here," Leila confessed, "even though I strongly wanted to come. Now I know how I am going to be received."

"You mean you know that we will eat you tonight?"

The children enjoyed their lunch, sitting with the old couple and the hands. The old lady kept shovelling chunks of meat unto the bowl in which the children were eating.

When the children explained that they would be taking Carol back to her village their grandfather insisted she came and stayed with them.

"Your father's place has plenty of room for all four of you," their grandmother told them. "Unless there is a special reason for her to go back she can come with the rest of you. How can you come together from Tamale and then on reaching here you separate her from the rest of you?" She turned to Carol and said, "My daughter, come with the rest of them."

So the old lady returned home with four strong young people marching behind her. People were returning from their farms when they arrived at the house. Jango introduced them to two men who had just come back and were sitting outside the house, the dust from the farm still caked on their legs.

She told the children that the two men were their father's uncles. "They are the brothers of my husband, Digadam's father." Marian knew from the first visit that Digadam was the given name of their father and she told the others about the name when she went back with Diane.

One of the two who spotted a grey beard kept looking at Junior, a smile on his lips. Marian remembered him as the one who made the young man take them to their grandfather's farm when she came with Diane.

"You came with the woman in the big car the other time," he addressed Marian who agreed.

Turning to Junior he observed, "Anybody who knew Apeatu when he was a boy will see him in this boy. The face is strikingly similar. The way they walk and even look about them, they are all the same. I don't know if Atu remembered his childhood days when he saw his grandchild but that boy is Atu when he was his age."

Junior only grinned.

It was the time of the day for fetching water and cooking. The old lady showed the children to their father's rooms. There was a sitting room and three bedrooms, each of them with double beds in them. After putting down their small bags the children went out and took containers and went out with other children from the house to the borehole to fetch water. Carol stayed behind to help the grandmother cook.

After filling their grandmother's containers they asked their grandmother who Kanuga was. "We hear she tells very interesting stories. We want to fill her containers so that she will tell us stories this evening. We want to hear Kassena stories. Dad told us some and they were interesting."

When Kanuga heard what the children said she laughed with pleasure. "So you knew about me even before you came here?" she asked, proud of the fact.

The children were made to feel welcome. They could sense that Dan was loved in the family and that members of the family were glad his children were back. They treated the children very well. Each household brought a bowl of food for the children. Their mouths opened each time a new bowl was brought. They could not even eat up what their grandmother had served them. They did not touch the food in any of the bowls brought from other rooms. Their grandmother chided them for that but there was just no space at all in their tummies for an additional morsel of food.

That evening they joined the rest of the family outside and after meals they agreed to tell stories to entertain the children from Tamale. It was an evening of happiness filled with laughter. It was a moonless night and the darkness practically enveloped them as they sat under sheds and listened to stories.

It was like celebration for the family. The Kassenas loved visitors and a whole community would contribute to welcome a guest of a family. It was the first time in a very long time that the family had received four visitors, even if they were young visitors. In addition to that was the fact that to the family two lost members of the family returned to the flock. Dan had been a provider of the big family, providing money for food during years of bad harvest, paying school fees, contributing substantially for the performance of funerals and other family commitments. And now his lost children had come to the family for the first time. It was more than ample reason for celebration.

Family members took turns to tell stories that made not only the visitors but even the members of the family who had heard the stories several times before laugh. As Dan had found out, storytelling provided fun not only to the persons hearing the story for the first time. They provided fun to even the teller who knew and controlled all the twists in the story. So it was fun time for the whole family gathered under various sheds. The joy of the evening was heightened by the pure joy in the laughter of the four visitors.

When it was time to go to bed the children were taken up their grandmother's room. She showed them the flat roof where, she told them, Dan liked to sleep. "But you can't sleep here. In the rainy season if you sleep here mosquitoes will suck all your blood."

The children gazed up the skies and admired the star-filled envelope above them. Carol was the only one who had seen all this before. She grew up in a house which had many of such rooms. Leila was the one who was impressed most. The old lady had to caution Junior who had wanted to skip on the roof. She warned him he could go down with it.

Dan had built three bedrooms in his side of the house. The children took two. Carol and Leila slept in one while Marian and her brother slept in the other. Carol woke them all up early the next morning and explained about the chores in a family in the morning. Junior was made to go out and sweep the yard. Two of the girls went to fetch water while Carol swept the old lady's rooms and washed the pots used for cooking the previous evening. She also helped the old lady prepare breakfast while the other girls went on fetching water for other women.

By that act alone, their taking part in the family's morning chores, instead of lying down and showing off as city girls, they endeared themselves to the whole community. People in nearby houses could not help openly commending the girls for their attitude to work.

They learnt that there were many children in their teens and early twenties from the house. But the children saw only few of them. Majority were in secondary schools or universities and were away in boarding school. There were four old men in the house, Apeatu and three of his brothers. Two of the brothers were older than Apeatu and one was younger. There were six elderly women. The children learnt two of them were widows. There were six of their children, all adults with their own families, also living in the same house.

The children spent the day on their grandfather's farm. He went first with Junior while the girls walked towards the farm. He came back and picked them one at a time, Leila insisting on being the one to go after Junior. It was another joyful day spent with the elderly couple. The bond between the children and their grandparents seemed to grow over the day. Before the afternoon Jango was joking with all of them, teasing them and being teased back as well. It was a very pleasant day filled with laughter and smiles.

The Sunday was what was called, according to Carol, Sunday High.

"Why do they call it Sunday High?" Leila asked.

"Because it is Sunday High," Carol responded.

Leila did not ask any questions. She knew Carol would give her the answer she needed if she had the patience to wait.

"High mass is the last church service on Sunday. It is the mass most young people attend. It is the popular mass. When a Sunday falls on Navrongo market day, even those who normally don't go to church will go to church. The Sunday that falls on a market day attracts more people than the other Sundays do. Because the third mass is popular and is called High Mass the Sunday that attracts the most worshippers is jokingly called Sunday High."

The church was full, with people standing outside. From church the children went to Nayagenia for Carol to say hello to her uncles.

When the children were leaving on the Monday morning they were in love with the people in the house and the people loved them too.

Chapter Twenty-Nine

Christmas that year was very eventful for Dan, Matilda and the children. It began with a surprise for Matilda. The surprise started with a visit from Dan on a Saturday morning. He came with Auntie Gina. Even though Matilda started with her usual hostile query of what he wanted she did not keep it for long. She naturally protested about being taken to a place she did not know. Dan and Gina had only told her they had come to take her to some place where Dan wanted to show them something. Even Gina did not know where they were going and what they would see when they got there.

"Show me what thing? Hasn't the thing got a name? What is so mysterious about it that he can't tell me what it is? And if he won't tell me why should I come?"

She came in the end. Dan drove them through the centre of the town and took them through Kalpohin Estates towards the SSNIT flats. They turned left before the flats and took a road that ran parallel to the flats. He stopped in front of a new and yet unoccupied house and blew on the horn. A Skones Security Company guard came and opened the gate a little and looked out. When he recognised the vehicle he opened the gates fully and Dan drove in.

The house had a big compound and the yard was gravelled. He took a set of keys from the glove compartment and came out.

"This is the mystery," he told the two women. Turning to Matilda he said, "This is your new house."

It was Auntie Gina who spoke. "You mean whose new house?"

"I built it for the children. But since the children live with their mother this is the new house for Matilda and the children."

The women walked silently behind him as he took them round the house. There were two big summer huts, both roofed with tiles. By one of them was a big swing. The chain that held the platform on

435

which people sat to swing was made of thick metal. Obviously the swing was not intended for Junior alone. So it was made to hold the heavier older girl. And maybe her friends.

One of the summer huts was at the front side of main house while the other one was behind it. "When Matilda and her friends are in the house and the children cannot use the sitting room they can have their freedom under one of the summer huts," Dan said. "On the other hand if it is warm inside and Matilda and her friends are using one of the summer huts and the children don't want to sit inside they can also sit in the other hut and still enjoy their freedom."

There was a large poly tank mounted on a cement platform that was more than six feet high. The tank was huge, and seemed to be able to take two thousand gallons of water. "I have learnt that water flows here all the time. But I have had this tank mounted so that even if the taps are closed for two weeks, if you use water judiciously you will still have water in the house."

Various young trees had been planted round the house.

He led them inside. All this while neither Auntie Gina nor Matilda spoke. "When the children came to visit me for the first time Marian asked if I lived in my house alone. Of course I live alone in that house. Then she said something that hit me and hit me hard. She looked at the house and said that they live in a compound house. I don't know what she meant. But they are my children. And I live in a quiet, peaceful house with many rooms in it giving me a lot of privacy. They lived in a house shared with many other families. I felt that my children should live a standard of life close to mine. I had no right to live in that house and leave them to live in a compound house. They deserved better. So I set about building this house."

The sitting room was large, and divided into two compartments. The division was made by a giant mahogany bookshelf built into the wall. Behind it was the dining space. The dining space had a round dining table with four chairs round it. By it was a large double cabin fridge.

In front of the shelf was the sitting place. The ceiling was made of a synthetic material, very beautiful to look at. There was executive furniture, a 4-seater sofa, a 3-seater one, a 2-seater chair and 3 single chairs. At one end was a 27-inch Panasonic TV on a stand on which was also found a DVD player. The floor was ceramic tiles.

A door led to a room on the right of the sitting room. Dan opened it and the three of them went in. "This was originally designed as a study," he told the women. "You will notice that it is smaller than the other rooms. I had originally planned it for a study for the children. But there was no guest room. We had not thought about that in designing the house. But you will have visitors. Without a guest room the visitors may be forced unto the children or the children may be forced into one room. But this house was built to give them comfort, comfort which will be taken away whenever you have visitors if provision is not made for visitors. Your mother may visit. You could have other visitors. This is intended for the guest room."

It had a bed.

He led them back through the sitting room through a door that opened on the left side of the room. It opened into a corridor. The corridor had the same tiles as the floor tiles in the sitting room. In the corridor was a large size deep freezer.

On the right was a door that led to the kitchen. There were shelves on the wall of the kitchen and a cupboard just by the door. In one corner was a gas cooker.

When they left the kitchen Dan opened the first door to the left. It led into a big bedroom. A door inside the room opened into the toilet and bathroom. He tried the shower and it was running. The tap was also running. A big wardrobe was built into the wall. A king-sized bed took one corner of the room. A dressing mirror with a stool stood in one corner. The silk curtains in the bedroom were made of the same material as the curtains in the sitting room and in the study now converted into a bedroom. He tried the lights and the fan and both were working.

Turning to Matilda Dan said, "This is your room."

The next two rooms were similar to this one but smaller. Each had its own bathroom and toilet. Each had a king-sized bed, a wardrobe built into the wall, a bookshelf and a table on which sat a computer. "These are the children's rooms. As you can see, there is provision for them to study here as well."

There was one Mountain brand bicycle in one of the rooms and three of the same bikes in the other room. For the children, no doubt, Auntie Gina thought. He loved the children, Gina again thought. Why four bikes? Maybe for their friends as well. So this man was providing not only for the children but for their friends as well. Well, so that when their friends visited they would not quarrel over the use of the bikes. Such a kind and considerate person. Auntie Gina could not help counting Matilda's loss. If she were still his wife...

He led them back to the sitting room where he sat down and invited them to sit too. He gave Auntie Gina papers, "Receipts for all the items you find in this house – the fridge, the deep freezer, the TV, the deck, the chairs, everything.

"Neither of you have said anything but I am sure you have comments and questions. I also have one thing to say. But I will listen to you first."

"Over to you, Matilda," Regina said.

"Why not you? Why over to me?"

"I am just accompanying the two of you as witness. I have no say in this. Besides, I am too surprised to say anything."

Matilda said nothing. Her head was bowed while Regina openly admired the house. The ceiling was made with material that looked like polished wood but was synthetic. That ceiling type was called T&G. Both style and material of which the shelf was made were beautiful. The house was beautiful. She looked at Dan, admitting that she did not know him. She asked herself who he was. Was he very rich and pushed by his money to show it off? Or was he truly very concerned about his children that he wanted the best for them? She turned to look at Matilda who was looking ahead of her. Again she wondered about her cousin. Was she emotionally sober enough to appreciate her good fortune?

When the two women did not speak for a long time Dan said, "As I said, I have something to say. I don't hate Matilda. But God knows how much I will avoid her because I want to avoid scenes. Because I know we will not meet each other and talk like two rational beings. That is why I will avoid her." She gave him a nasty look and snorted but he ignored both.

"I am glad the children found me. I am glad because Matilda knows that when we separated I wanted contact with the children. I was prevented from contacting them. I have a duty to the children, a duty which I neglected because of the separation. Their finding me has given the children the opportunity to exact from me the duty I owe them. I am happy to shoulder my duty. As I told Auntie Gina when I went to discuss the remittance for the upkeep of Matilda and the children, I don't intend to ask that the children come and stay with me. I am perfectly satisfied for them to stay with their mother. It means a lot of things I have to do for the children have to be done through their mother. It also means I don't just plan for the two children but for the three, the children and their mother. As I said earlier I don't hate Matilda and am happy to provide for her and the children. There are only two conditions attached."

He paused for effect and reaction. If there was reaction it was not verbal. If there was effect he did not notice it. So he went on. "One of the conditions I told Auntie Gina already. I want access to the children. I want to be able to reach them, to see them, to discuss things with them. I have had it so far. I am grateful." Matilda gave him a nasty look and snorted. He ignored both. "The second is what happens to the children with the resources I am making available to Matilda for their collective use. I have not seen any sign that the children are not eating well in the house or that they are suffering for lack of what money can do for them. I appreciate it and will continue to remit monthly to Matilda for their collective upkeep. In fact, I am increasing the monthly remittance because the light bill in this house will be different from the light bill in a compound house where you have only one room. The power used by the security lights alone will cost more than the power used in the one room in a compound house. In the evening there will be lights in the sitting room, in the corridor, in the kitchen, in different rooms when the children are at home. And so on. You will use more water here. Maintaining the compound will be more costly. So I am increasing the monthly remittance.

"You will appreciate the fact that the room that I had thought should be a study for the children has been converted into a bedroom so that if you have visitors they can have a room to themselves. So I have not just been concerned about the children. But I am concerned about them.

That leads me to the second condition; that the interests of the children are not compromised in the use of facilities in this house. Matilda has friends who will be visiting her here. There is room for everybody to feel comfortable here. Marian will be writing her final exams next year. She needs peace to study. Junior needs to begin at this stage to get used to concentrating on studies. I will really be concerned if friends visit and the interest of the children has to be compromised."

Gina looked at Matilda and could tell that she would have liked to make some uncomplimentary statements. But what was there to say, Regina asked herself. The conditions Dan had set, that he had access to the children and that the interest of the children be not compromised in the house were legitimate conditions. Despite the position of Matilda and her mother about the children Regina knew that Dan could not in any way be denied his right to the children. And the children could not be denied their right to their father either. And he was right about there being enough room in the house to make Matilda and her friends and the children all feel comfortable. And if he was spending all this much, the cost of the house and the remittance, and asking only that the children be given good treatment he was right. Besides, she told herself, should anybody have been telling Matilda to treat her own children right?

"I have arranged for Skones to provide security guards," Dan went on. "They will provide two a day. One will come in the morning and another will come in the evening. At the end of each quarter they will send me the bill and I will settle it. In order for the guards to feel happy, I will be offering them personally some allowances, in addition to what Skones will pay them. So that they can be helpful around the house. If you treat them like slaves or servants you may have problems with them. I will do all I can to make them nice and take the security of the house very seriously. If Matilda goes and drinks and comes back and insults them night after night they will not stay. Even if they stay they may not be nice."

"Why do you want to spoil my name?" Matilda found the excuse she wanted to show her displeasure. "How many times have you ever heard that I have drunk and insulted people? If you want you can remove your guards."

"Just tell him to keep his house," Auntie Gina told her. "Why only the guards? Tell him to keep his whole house. Tell him you don't need it."

Matilda ignored her.

There was little to talk about. He offered to get a vehicle to transport their things when they were ready to pack in.

The following Saturday when he went and picked the three girls from school they greeted him like a beloved uncle rather than a father. Leila and Marian ran and met the vehicle even when it was approaching and ran alongside it till it stopped. They hugged their father welcome. Carol, as usual, was the cool one but whose welcome was no less affectionate even if not demonstrated so effusively. He sent the other two girls home before sending Marian home. The two girls, as was the case during the last holidays, kept their boxes at home and jumped back into the vehicle and went with Marian. When they did not go towards Moshie Zongo Marian kept asking where they were going to. When he got to the gate and blew on the horn Marian looked at the gate with a lot of questions in her eyes. Junior was riding his new bike in the yard when the gate opened and the girls were initially surprised to see him there. Marian looked at her dad and asked if he had moved house. He said no but killed the engine. So the children got down, intrigued.

Junior came to meet them and answered their question. "Dad built his house for us. Mother has moved from Moshie Zongo."

Marian turned to their father and asked, "Dad is it true? Is this where we will now be staying with Mama?"

Leila was admiring Junior's bike. It felt solid.

"There is one for each of you in Marian's room," he told them proudly.

"How do you know they are for us?"

"Your names are written on them," he said with a wide smile.

Marian was listening to her brother and Leila. Only Carol stayed to remove Marian's boxes from the vehicle. Marian and Leila ran inside to inspect the house and to see the new bicycles. He waited in the vehicle for them to carry Marian's boxes into the house, celebrate the house and the items in the children's rooms and come out for him to take them to town. Their mother was in the house. She came out and they said cold good morning to each other. She did not stay out but went back into the house after the greetings.

They spent the rest of the morning, father and four children, buying clothing for the children. He bought three sets of dresses for each child. They ate lunch at SWAD Fast Foods before he sent them to their home.

On the morning of Christmas eve Auntie Gina was still brushing her teeth when she heard the sound of a vehicle outside her house. She sent the children to find out who had come so early and what the person wanted. When they came back and told her it was Dan she quickly changed from her morning wear to something more decent to receive a male visitor in and came out to meet him. He was with the four children.

"Are you a tortoise?" she asked Dan.

He thought a while not understanding why the comparison.

"A tortoise moves with its whole house. Look at you and all your children. The car is your house."

The children came over, hugged her and greeted her affectionately.

There were two goats, two turkeys, a coop with twenty guinea fowls, a 50 kilogram bag of rice and five gallon container of cooking oil. There were two half pieces (six yards each) of Holland made real wax prints.

As the children loaded them inside Auntie Gina's house she tried to block their entrance and enquired, "Where are all these items going to?"

"They all said they have been hearing how Christmas is such a lively event in your house. So the goats, turkeys, guinea fowls and all those items that have just gone inside decided they will spend Christmas this year with you. You see how popular you are? Even in the animal kingdom they know about you."

They went inside the house. While the children joined Auntie Gina's children Dan sat in the hall with Gina.

"Regina, I appreciate all that you have done for me and the children. I have used you extensively and you have not complained. I have passed messages and things through you to Matilda. I know you have been talking to her on your own on behalf of the children. I greatly appreciate it. I can't ever say thank you enough so I won't even try to say it. But I want you to know I appreciate everything you have done for me, Matilda and the children."

Auntie Gina in turn said how she appreciated what Dan had chosen to do for the children since they came to look for him. She was particularly grateful that Dan had not chosen to give his attention to the children alone but was concerned with the welfare of their mother as well.

"I am happy for the children," she told him. "Now if they take their studies seriously they will go far in their education. And," she lowered her voice, "Matilda and her friends have changed their attitude to the children since they met you. The children used to complain a lot to me about being insulted by their mother's drinking buddies. It has reduced considerably. The effect of your return into their lives can be seen on Matilda herself. I am not sure she will ever give up drinking but she takes better care of herself now than she used to. I am sure it is because her salary alone could not go far with the amount she spent on drinking. The remittances from you have made a lot of difference. She appreciates it even though I don't expect her to ever admit it. The house will make an even bigger difference, especially in her relationship with the children…"

They talked for over an hour. She insisted he and the children took breakfast with them.

Dan left with the children after the breakfast because he said they had to prepare for the Christmas party that evening. Gina had been invited already and he now asked her to come with her children. To ensure that Gina would come he called her children and told them about the party in his house that evening and the fact that he had asked their mother to come with them. "You come even if your mother decides not to come."

He gave the children an envelope with money for their Christmas.

Auntie Gina did not know how many guinea fowls had been brought till Dan left and she went in with her children to see what would be best to do with the items. It was then they counted the guinea fowls. "Twenty! This man does not expect us to buy meat for the rest of the year, does he?"

Dan went back to the house with the children and they spent the rest of the morning and the afternoon baking, grilling, frying and steaming foods. Even Junior was pressed into service. Nobody complained that he was a boy but was made to cook.

They also chopped vegetables and prepared salads. Dan checked the drinks, plates, cutlery, glasses and serving trays and ladles. He had everything. He had never organised anything like that and he was careful not to miss anything that would ruin the evening for the invited guests. The children had brought the dresses they would wear that evening.

Mercy arrived with even more food and soups at 6:00 p.m. She began setting up tables and service points. The party was going to be held in the yard because the number of people invited would be too many for the sitting-room.

The guests started to arrive at 7:00 p.m. The children had changed into their party dresses and were ready to act as ushers and servers.

Mahama came with his wife and Mouna. Mouna immediately left the adults and went to join her sister and her friends. She helped in receiving guests and serving them. Carol's aunt came with two ladies, one older than her and the second about the same age as Polly. One was a relative and the other was a friend. Both had come to spend the Christmas with Paulina whom they had not seen for a long time.

Six families came from the neighbourhood. There were staff from the office and their families, those who had families. The previous week when Dan sat down to prepare the list of people to invite to the party he realised one painful truth – he did not have friends. Besides his staff, the parents of Leila, Carol's aunt and Auntie Gina the other people present were six families from the neighbourhood, the manager of the Tamale branch of Barclays Bank and a major food supplier to the training centre. Hajia Rukaya came with two of her children. Brenda led the staff. Khadija came with Mercy but she helped Mercy with supervising the service of the food. There was nobody he could call a personal friend, someone he visited or who visited him sometimes, someone he went out with or would call on the phone just to say hi and that it had been a long time. He did not have anybody like that.

There were more than forty people but the service was very orderly and everyone had drinks and food. Mercy supervised the food table and she and the children guided the visitors to fetch what food they liked. The girls held out cutlery and tissue paper for them. They went round and asked people if they could bring them more drink. A collection of music from different parts of the world played non-stop.

When everyone had served the food they would eat, before they drank enough to make them tipsy Dan asked for their attention. "I want to start by thanking you all for coming," he said. "I am sincere about it. In order for you to understand why I feel grateful I want you to imagine how you would feel if you were me, and you worked the whole day with this army of young and beautiful ladies and one gentleman to prepare foods. You are set and ready for your guests by let us say six o'clock. Seven o'clock, no guest. Not even one. Eight o'clock comes and goes and there is not even one guest. Nine, ten and eleven, no guest. How will you feel? So I am grateful you agreed to share your evening with me. Thanks a lot for it.

"This is the first time I am organising a get-together in my house. I am learning a lot about the amount of life that exists outside work and that it is nice to pause from time to time and enjoy it. Thanks to the children for teaching me that. But this get-together is also a celebration and I will explain to you what I have invited you to join me to celebrate.

"How many of you remember the play *A Straw In The Wind*? It was first performed in Navrongo Secondary School but I know that it later became popular in other schools as well."

"I don't know why you Navascans like making claims that are false," Mahama said. "*A Straw In The Wind* was first performed in Tamasco. Navasco only copied it from Tamasco."

Dan did not, up to that time, know that Leila's father, like his daughter, attended Tamale Secondary school.

Dan bowed his head, smiled, picked his glass of fruit juice and sipped from it before continuing with his speech. "If you let me finish what I am going to say you will not doubt which school performed the play first."

"Well, you speak on, but don't try to falsify history. We are listening to you keenly," Mahama warned him.

"If you tell lies," Hajia Rukaya warned, "as you Kassenas do without shame, we will throw your daughter out of the school."

Dan smiled and went on with what he had to say. "Let me repeat the question. How many of you have ever seen the play?"

A few hands went up. "Quite encouraging number. For those of you who have never seen the play, it is about a student boy whose girlfriend met a student who was senior to the boy, a Sixth Form student, and dropped the junior student. The affair with the senior student did not last because the girl found that the junior student was more valuable to her and she loved him more. But when she returned to the junior student he felt so pained by what she had done to him that he would not take her back, despite the fact that she tried very hard.

"When more than a year later the boy, Adda, was called home by his parents, he did not suspect anything till he met the girl, called Anita, in the house. She had gone to complain to the boy's parents that Adda had made her pregnant but was denying responsibility for the pregnancy. She had come with a friend who supported Anita in everything she said. The family chose to believe Anita and Adda was ostracised from the family. An aunt was the only person in the family who believed Adda and who came out to see him off, praying that his innocence would one day be established.

"He went through torture in the class when word got to the school that he had made a girl pregnant but refused responsibility for the pregnancy. He spent the holidays in the school doing odd jobs till he completed and went out into the world, suffering first one misfortune and then another. For four years he was blown about from one place to another, like a straw in the wind, till he met a family that adopted him and gave him a home.

"Just about the same time Anita had an accident and was sent to the hospital. On her deathbed she called Adda's father and confessed that she had told a lie for Adda."

His audience reacted with exclamations of anger at Anita.

"Pained by what he had done to his son, pained by the loss of his son, and guilty that he had not trusted his son, Adda's father went out in search of him. But when he found him Adda would not come home because to him where his father said was home was not home for him. It did not hold love for him. He rejected what his father called family because he felt a family trusted and protected its members. Prevailed upon by the family that adopted him, drawing his attention to the importance of forgiveness, Adda agreed to return to his home. The climax of the drama was when Adda was confronted by his mother, the one whose rejection of him pained most throughout his stay away from home. His soliloquy whether to reject or accept his mother, his admission of the pain she must have gone through and his decision to forgive her, and when he finally took her in his arms and they wept over each other brought the curtain down on the play."

The audience showed it was a moving play by its reaction.

"I played the part of Adda when we first performed it in Navasco. The Entertainments Master of Bolga Girls Secondary had come to visit a friend in the school and saw the play and insisted we came to perform it in their school the next week. We could not go the next week but did go to perform it two weeks later. I did not act in Bolga Girls. Instead I sat with the audience to see how the play affected people. Students wept. And when eventually Adda and his mother hugged each other and wept over each other some students cried real tears while others laughed and clapped."

He paused and sipped his juice. And then went on, "I did not want to be introduced at the end of the play since my role was an invisible one but the cast insisted I joined them for the curtain call and the introductions. A member of the cast would introduce themself by saying, 'My name is X. I am in Form Four Science,' and the audience would roar Doctor! Or Engineer! If they said they were in an Arts class the audience would roar Lawyer. Or Accountant if the student said they were in a Business class. I was at the end of the queue since I only went up for the introductions. I told them my name and my class, which was Lower Sixth Arts, and they clapped and shouted Lawyer at me. Then I went on to tell them that besides directing the play I was the one who wrote it."

He paused. And looked round the crowd which gasped. So he wrote a play as a student and it was taken round other schools?

"The students started to clap. It was thunderous. Then someone started insulting me and threw an object at me. 'Bad man. You are very wicked.' And the girl influenced the rest of the students. Before long the stage was flooded with all kinds of objects aimed at me."

"It is true. It is very true. He is not telling lies and he is not exaggerating. I was there. I was a student in BOGGISS at the time," the older of Paulina's companions told the people around her. She had stood up and all eyes were turned on her. "That play was moving.

Nobody in the crowd kept dry eyes. We all wept when we were watching it. And when he said he wrote the play they asked why he should write such a wicked play. They said he was a wicked writer. They called him a bad man. They threw anything they had at him."

"Why do you leave yourself out? Why do you tell what happened as if you did not take part in throwing things at him?"

The woman protested her innocence vehemently, gesticulating with her hands to emphasise her denial. "I did not throw anything at him. I knew that it was not real and that it was a play he had written. No, I did not throw anything at him. But the other girls did throw things at him, anything they had – handkerchiefs, papers, pens, anything they had."

Dan smiled while the exchange was going on. He sipped his juice, in very small quantities, but said nothing till the exchange ended.

"The reason I took you back to the play is that somewhere in that play, when Adda's mates heard what had happened to him, as would be expected from some students, some of his classmates teased him. Someone would walk up the front of the class during night studies and say, 'There will be a meeting for all those who are hiding babies in your chop boxes in the toilet at midnight. Note that only genuine fathers with babies hiding in their boxes are welcome. Remember to bring along your napkins and feeding bottles.' Another student would go to the front of the class and say, 'I have been asked to inform you all that it has come to the notice of the authorities that some students have refused to claim the babies they helped some innocent girls to bring into the world. The authorities wish to let you all know it is an offence under the school's rule for any student to impregnate a girl. But it is even more offensive to refuse to claim the product of your lust.' Yet another would go forward and say, 'A newly delivered baby boy has been dumped in front of the Headmaster's office with the name, address and photo of the father stuck to the cloth in which the baby is wrapped. Will all students whose wives are expecting please go to the Headmaster's office to inspect the baby after night studies.'"

Paulina's friend stood up again. "While all these announcements were being made, on stage Adda would pretend to be busy studying. The whole class would laugh but he would not even raise his head from his books. When the class was quiet he would raise his head and gaze at the ceiling. You could see he was worried. You could tell he was not responsible for the pregnancy. At the end of the scene in the class he went to the front of the class and spoke to his mates. We all wept over his speech."

"Look at her. She is including herself in this but she refused to admit that she threw things at Dan. If you wept then you threw things at him too."

"I did no such thing. Dan is not going to beat me or insult me if I say I threw things at him many years ago. So if I did it why should I deny it? I didn't throw anything at him."

Again Dan only smiled.

He went on. "That scene was drama. It was not real. It was created. I thought about it and put it down on paper and students went on stage and pretended it happened. But even the make-believe drama was so painful to some people they wept."

He paused, looking round. There was silence. Then he went on. "Those of you who only got to know me recently only know the gentleman in me. Or something resembling a gentleman."

"Is that not a contradiction?" Mahama asked. "How can a Kassena man be a gentleman?"

Again Dan only smiled and went on. "Only few people who are close to me today, like my aunt Regina, know the other life I led some years back."

"Don't call me your aunt," Auntie Gina protested with a smile. "You will make people think I am old."

People laughed and some turned to look at her.

"Sorry about that, Mama Regina," Dan said to a roar of laughter.

"You are a naughty in-law!"

Dan responded with, "That is the understatement of the year."

Increased laughter.

When it died down Dan went on, "In an earlier phase of my life I was a drunkard and lived in *akpeteshie* bottles. I married and together we had two children, a very beautiful girl…"

"Who is beautiful? Who do you call beautiful?" Hajia Rukaya asked.

While Mahama protested the rest of the guests laughed. Dan waited for the laughter and protests to die down. "I know Mahama will protest again but the truth is we gave birth to a very beautiful girl and the most handsome boy God has ever moulded."

More laughter and protests and some talking. During which period he kept quiet again but wore his smile. And sipped juice, always in small quantities. "I can vouch for the handsomeness of the boy because he took my father's face and even more importantly, he took my face since I found my father's face so handsome that I took it."

Even Brenda joined Mahama to protest and the laughing and animated talking went on for a while.

The smile disappeared from his lips and he looked at the clear December sky above them, not seeing whatever was up there. When silence returned he continued with his speech. "Then my marriage broke down and for twelve years, in spite of the rules of Navrongo Secondary that forbade a father, a product of the school, from not claiming their children, like a lit candle caught in the wind, I went out of the lives of those nice children who I and my wife chose to bring forth. For twelve long years I did not know what they ate, if they ate at all, what they wore to cover their bodies and if they were in school. I would not even know them if I met them. Like the candle in the storm, I just went out of their lives and left them in total darkness about who their father was." He paused for effect. "For twelve long years." He again paused for effect.

"My children and I have since been reunited with each other. One thing I want to use this event to do is what I have just done, make a public declaration of my guilt regarding my relationship with the children over the twelve years and acknowledge what pain they must have gone through, to be abandoned by a father as if they were faeces. I want to be able to live with myself and to do this I want to share with you a part of my life that is not so noble, that is not in any way honourable. That is one way I intend to purge my conscience and find peace with myself. I will one day explain myself to the children and we will talk of forgiveness. But they are still too young and dependent on me to have the freewill to forgive or not forgive. But until that time of reconciliation this public act will be the indication of my genuine remorsefulness about what happened to the children."

A different atmosphere had certainly descended on the party. When he paused there was no laughter and no bright faces.

"But this party is not all about remorsefulness and regrets. It is a celebration, a celebration of the reunion of father and children. Some of you would think how lucky these children are, to have found their father again. What you would not know is how lucky the father is, to have found the children. Lucky because they opened a wider window in my life and through it I can see the world as I had never seen it. And through them I have found joy and happiness as I had never known them. So I am inviting you to celebrate with me and the children the joy of finding each other."

He beckoned to Marian and Junior to join him and they walked towards him. "At this stage, let me introduce the children." The two children stood one on each side of him. "Ladies and gentlemen, please meet my children, Marian and Daniel Junior. For those of you who don't know I had children, let me introduce them. If you meet them anywhere please, know that they are my children."

Auntie Gina looked at the children standing by their father and felt happy for them. Marian had certainly put on some flesh since she met her father. The skinny girl was being swallowed by a fatter girl. And with the additional flesh the beauty that could not be seen in the skeleton of a girl was manifesting itself. As for the boy he was the spitting image of his father, there was no doubt about that.

People were surprised when he made signs to other children. Most people looked around with curiosity. "I lost two children for twelve years. But when I found them, or when they found me, they did not come back alone." Leila and Carol had by then walked up to join Marian and Junior, Leila standing next to Marian and Carol standing next to Junior. "I lost two children for twelve years and found four children, four of the most wonderful children in the whole of Tamale. I am happy to introduce to you the other members of my family, Leila Mahama and Caroline Tigase.

"Please let us put the sad things I have said behind us. I said them to get them out of me into the wind. Let us leave them in the wind and have a pleasant evening. I wish you all health and happiness during the whole Christmas period. And may the coming year see your dreams come true." He lifted his near empty glass of juice, "To the good health of everyone present here and those they are related to."

Carol was the shortest and the fattest of the three girls. Leila was tall but carried a lot of flesh as well.

The other pleasant surprise for the children was the freedom they got from their grandmother, their mother's mother. She came to spend the New Year with them, arriving on the 27th of December. The children were out when she came. She went first to the former house in Moshie Zongo and someone brought her to the new house.

She had her first quarrel with her daughter. She asked how they got such a house and her daughter told her the children's father built it for them.

"Who is the children's father?" she asked with annoyance in her voice and face.

"What sort of question is that? Who is the children's father? My former husband, of course."

The old lady spat at the term former husband.

"Please mother," Matilda pleaded with her mother, "we don't spit like that in this house. Can't you see how the house is like? Look at the floor."

It only made the old lady to spit again and it resulted in a heated exchange between mother and daughter. When they got over the spitting the old lady raised another issue, "Who is your former husband? When did you marry and I did not know? Who did he marry you from?" With each question she made gestures at her daughter.

"How did you think I got the pregnancies and gave birth to the children?" Matilda asked her mother returning the old lady's look. "At the time I was giving birth why didn't you ask me where I got the pregnancies from? Or did you think I got pregnant by drinking water?"

"Why should I have asked?" her mother retorted defiantly. "Would you have been the first to keep a boyfriend and have children with him without marrying him?"

"Well, mother, that boyfriend would be the father of the children," Matilda calmly replied her mother, masking her anger with what the old lady said. "And it is that former boyfriend who built the house."

"He will not be the father of the children if he did not marry you," the old lady said, equally calmly. "And he will not be your former husband. He will only be your former boyfriend."

Matilda stood up. "Mother, you can call him by any title you want. You wanted to know how we got the house. You now know the person. Whatever you call him is left to you."

Matilda walked into her room and left her mother to cut the unproductive argument short. She had just come back to sit by the old lady when Marian came in. She was going to greet when her grandmother said, "Heh! Big Head! Where are you from?"

It made Marian change her mind about the way she was going to greet. Instead she said, "Mama, good afternoon."

Before Matilda could reply the old lady said, "Is it only your mother you saw? How can you greet your mother alone? Big Head, I asked you a question. Why didn't you answer me? I said where are you coming from?"

If looks could kill or melt people the old lady would have been dead or melted. Whatever it was that Marian was contemplating saying she thought better of it and said nothing. She went past them to the fridge to drink water.

"Heh! Big Head, come back here! Look at the stupid girl looking at me like that! Who do you think you are? And you even ignored my question. Come back here!"

Marian stormed back into the sitting room. "Mama, warn grandma…"

Her grandmother cut her short. "Repeat what you just said." She tilted her head. "I did not hear you well."

To the old lady's surprise Marian accepted the challenge. "I will repeat it, Grandma. Mama, warn grandma. She knows my name. My name is not Big Head and I will do what I like in this house. She should not come expecting to order me about. Tell her that."

The old lady rushed up but her daughter prevented her from reaching Marian. Marian walked on to the fridge where she poured water into a glass and came back through the room and went outside the house.

"What! Did I hear that stupid girl right? Did she dare tell you to warn me? Is that how rotten the children have become?"

Marian went round the house to shut the discussion going on inside the room out of her ears. She was still outside when Junior came riding in. She called him and told him all about their grandmother and what had happened between them. Junior grinned and giggled. Marian did that to their grandmother?

When he opened the door the two women were still in the room. He walked past mother and grandmother without saying a word, unlike Marian who greeted their mother.

"Okro Ears! How rude of you! Are you now blind? Didn't you see us when you came in?"

Junior only turned and grinned at them but continued to walk on.

When he was returning from the fridge where he had gone, like his sister, to drink water, he was confronted by his grandmother who got up and blocked his way. He grinned but said nothing. He turned and made for his room and ignored the old lady completely.

The argument with her daughter started again. "Kadua, tell me what you have done to your children. You have spoiled them completely. These are not the children I met when I came here the last time. This is not how I brought you up. I brought up you to respect your elders. What will you do with such rotten eggs?"

Matilda tried a softer tact. She lowered her voice and said, "Mother, look at how you have been treating the children. You never call them by their names. Any time you have to call them it is by an insult…"

The old lady would not hear it. "What are insults? Is your daughter's head not big? Are your son's ears not long? Is it an insult to point out the truth about them?"

"If the big head were normal you would not be pointing it out. They have told you they don't like the names you call them by but you won't stop."

"Who are they to tell me what they like and what they don't like? They have told me they don't like the names, so what? They can't tell me what to call them by. Who are they?"

For the second time Matilda stood up. "These children have changed since they got to know their father. They don't take nonsense. They will tell you what they don't like. I don't know what they will do if you continue to call them by names they have told you they don't like."

It infuriated the old lady and she stood up too. "Look at the nonsense I am hearing from you. Children! These little rats and you say you don't know what they will do. So your children are now stronger than you, is that it? How can children tell me, an elderly person, what they don't like? Who are they?"

Marian was coming in and stood by the door and listened to what was said inside the house. She told herself that her grandmother would not have the best of times this visit. When she came into the room her mother had already left it and her grandmother was alone.

"Look at the big head, as if her useless father just lifted his and put it on her."

Calmly Marian turned on the old lady. "You call our father useless. He built this house you are going to sleep in. He provided the bed you are going to sleep in. He bought the fridge whose cold water I am sure you have drunk already. If he is useless after providing all these things you are going to use, then who is not useless? And how come you are willing to sleep in the house built by the useless man and use things he bought?"

Their grandmother rose in anger but Marian stood her ground. She did not move back. "How dare you talk back to me?" But she did not advance towards the girl. The fact that the girl did not retreat and her daughter not being in the room made her unsure what would happen if she attacked the girl physically.

"Grandma, since our infancy all you do is insult us each time you come here," Marian said looking straight at her grandmother. If the woman needed any convincing that the children had changed this was enough conviction. "We are no more children. If you can only communicate with us by insulting us I am sure you are not going to enjoy your stay here this time…"

Their grandmother took a step forward but stopped when her granddaughter did not retreat or even bat an eyelid. "Look at the stupid daughter of a useless man! Do you dare threaten me? Note that I am not your mother. If the two of you are used to using your mother to wipe the faeces from your anus don't try it on me…"

The old lady could not believe it when the young woman interrupted her. "If you also think we are toilet paper for you to use in wiping your anus, you will learn that we have changed. We are no more toilet paper but human beings deserving to be respected."

The old lady laughed loudly and clapped her hands, raising her face to the sky. When she stopped laughing and made to speak she realised there was no point in speaking. Marian had gone away and left her.

Her ordeal, self inflicted, continued that same evening.

Marian spent a long time in the kitchen preparing palm nut soup, the old lady's favourite soup whenever she came to Tamale. When Matilda told Marian that they were going to prepare palm nut soup to go with *fufu* to welcome her mother, Marian did not protest. She was a better cook than her mother and did most of the cooking when they were on holidays. Matilda did not have patience when cooking. So most often her soups were not well cooked. Sometimes you could feel the raw tastes of some of the condiments that went into the soup. If she cooked groundnut soup, for instance, you could feel the taste of the groundnut paste.

For a while the whole house and the air in and around the compound was filled with the aroma of palm nut soup and goat meat. Junior hovered around and helped her. He blended the garden eggs and tomatoes, pounded the boiled palm nuts and passed items his sister needed on to her. Since their father spoke to them about the need for all children, both girls and boys, to learn how to cook, Junior had offered to help in the kitchen and Marian accepted it. Initially their mother ordered him out of the kitchen whenever she saw him there but when he refused to leave she had to accept his presence there.

The problem came when they had to pound the yam and cassava. Mother normally manned the mortar and turned the yam and cassava while the children pounded. This part of the cooking had to be done outside, behind the kitchen since they could not pound in the house to rock the foundation of the house.

Their grandmother came out and found herself a seat and acted as superintendent of the process. An arm chair critic of a superintendent. She found fault with so many things the children did even before the pounding started. She insulted Junior and even attempted to take back the cassava when he took a piece of cassava from the basin.

"Put it back!" she shouted at the boy. "Are you learning to be a thief?"

As usual Junior only grinned but said nothing, and went on eating his piece. The crisis came when she said of Marian who was pounding,

"Look at her begging the pestle. Why pound as if there are no bones in your hands? You tell me you are no more children but you can't even hold a pestle and pound properly like a grown girl. You are growing to be as useless as your father."

Marian quietly put down the pestle and told her mother, "You and your mother will prepare the *fufu* today. Since Grandma knows so much about how to hold the pestle and how to pound she will pound for you."

"Where is the stupid girl going to?" their grandmother shouted. "Come back here."

Their mother knew that shouting would not help so in a very soft voice she pleaded with Marian who was washing her hands, "Marian, why can't you ignore your grandmother? You should have known your grandmother by now. She just can't keep quiet. She doesn't mean what she says. You know she can't hold the pestle and if you go away that is the end of the preparation of this meal. Please, Marian." Their mother stood up and went to hold Marian but Marian freed herself from her mother's grip.

"Junior and I will find something to eat if the *fufu* is not prepared. I told Grandma she must stop insulting us this trip because we are no more children and won't take her insults. I am not touching the pestle anymore and that is final. Let Grandma demonstrate her knowledge of how to hold the pestle."

Their grandmother was also up. "Kadua, you have really spoiled the children. How do you beg your own daughter? Who is she to say she won't pound? You have to get up and beg her? Beg your own child? My ancestors should come and see how things have changed. Mothers now beg their children."

Matilda was very angry and turned on her mother. "Since you know how to control children without begging go after them and bring them back using your power to make them continue the work."

"I can't bring them back because you have spoiled them already. In my hands the thought of putting down the pestle would never even have gone into their heads." She clapped her hands several times to show her extreme surprise. Then she held her mouth.

Junior joined his sister, all the while wearing the famous smile and never uttering a word. Silently the children moved and left an

457

angry Matilda and her surprised mother stranded in the middle of the cooking.

"At least the soup is ready. You won't have *fufu* but you can eat the yam and cassava with the soup. I have been living with these children for years now and we have our quarrels but they have never walked away from work. You say you won't listen to me. This is what we will be going through if you don't change. You are welcome to change them though, if you think there is a better way to make them do things. I will watch you and learn from you."

It shocked the old woman. "You mean your stupid children are going to get away with this behaviour? You mean you won't sanction them?"

Matilda was putting things together, removing the half paste from the mortar and covering the containers that held the yam and cassava. She went on working as she talked to her mother. "Mother, listen and listen carefully. The house you have come into was built by the children's father. You can see how free we are here compared to the house we lived in in Moshie Zongo. Since the children found their father they have made me realise that I can lose them if I don't handle them with care. If I lose them this house goes too. I want the children. And I want this house. I want the children more than I want the house. They are no more babies. They are grown enough to walk out of me and go to their father. I don't want that to happen. When I think of it, they are not asking that I worship them. So I don't have problems with them. If you cannot accept how we live together I will watch you change things. But don't count on my support if I think you are wrong."

Talk of a shock but the old lady really had it, a big shock. The useless man was influencing her daughter's life. The children were relating to that useless man and even threatening to pack to him? Pack to him? Who was he? Where did he get the children from? He had not married her daughter.

"So are you worried about the children packing to that useless man you are not ashamed to call the children's father? How can you be afraid of that? If they pack to him I will let the police lock him up."

Even her daughter laughed at her. "Do you have a brother or a son who is a police man?"

"What has that got to do with arresting the useless man if he takes my children?"

"You say you don't know Daniel is the children's father." She sent a collection of utensils into the kitchen and came back. "You said Marian told you they are no more children. She is right." She walked round her mother to pick more items. "They are no more children. I don't know what it is that you will tell the police if the children move to their father. But if the police arrive there they will ask why he took the children. If the children are there they will say they were not taken but that they voluntarily left here to go to their father. If you can convince the police to arrest a man whose children have come to him, only you will know how you are going to do that."

The children went out and took a taxi into town and bought food. While Matilda and her mother set table in the sitting room to eat their yam, cassava and soup the children trooped in with their food and set it on the dining table. They all ate in silence, only the children talking to each other. The children occasionally laughed.

For the rest of the evening the children kept to themselves in their rooms and did not even once come into the sitting area. The next morning and for the rest of the day they completely ignored their grandmother. They did not greet her when they met her in the house and would not say anything to her. To the best of their knowledge she did not exist. She did not dare complain to her daughter seeing that her daughter did not see things the way she saw them. The house had changed terribly. The atmosphere was seriously poisoned, as far as she was concerned. She could not stand it. She would lose her sanity if she stayed.

She left for Navrongo before the New Year's Day.

Chapter Thirty

Two rocks were very famous in the Nigerian capital Abuja. One was the Zuma Rock, on the road to the northern states of Kano and Kaduna. It was big, but it was famed not for its size. It was not that huge. But if one looked at it carefully a human face could be seen on the side that faced the road. The Zuma Rock was famous and was mentioned in brochures prepared to inform tourists about attractions in Abuja.

The second was famous because of the villa to which it lent its name. It was Aso Rock. This was an innocuous looking rock, so far as Dan could see. But just below it was the villa that housed the President of the Federal Republic of Nigeria since the capital was moved from Lagos to Abuja, Aso Rock Villa. Visitors to the city were shown the rock just behind the villa, made famous by the villa. It was said that there was a tunnel dug into the rock to provide security to the President in the event of a threat. Dan had never been there and did not meet anybody who knew the history of the Villa well enough to confirm or deny the stories about the tunnel.

The hotel they used for the training derived its name from the phenomenon that gave the Presidential Villa its name. It was called Rock View Hotel. Dan would have preferred Aso Villa View Hotel if he were the one who had to choose a name for the hotel. The rock did face the hotel but one also had a very good view of the Villa as well.

"If you have a good pair of binoculars – not the made in Kenya type, mind – you can see His Excellency the President every morning at his breakfast table," he told Diane.

Diane shook her head; the things this man can say, she said in silence. "I am sure if you have very good binoculars, the made in Ghana type, you can even see His Excellency the President in his bedroom," she said in reply.

Dan shook his head vigorously. "No. No, you can't. As my IT colleagues will say, his bedroom is write protected. To borrow from the vocabulary of my Nigerian comedian friends, what His Excellency the President of the Federal Republic of Nigeria takes for breakfast is 'opendential.' What he does in his bedroom is confidential. So his dining area is accessible to binoculars, good binoculars. His bedroom is pry protected."

He seemed to know and to love the country. Diane knew little about it, was afraid of it and did not like it. She told him.

"The image this country has outside is not a true reflection of the country. It is notorious internationally for two things, domestic violence and crime. It is known outside for religious and inter-ethnic violence and the attacks against foreigners in the Delta area. Its citizens are feared outside the country as fraudsters and tricksters. Nigerians will not deny that some of their countrymen are tricksters and fraudsters. They will not deny that they are themselves not happy with the occurrence of violence. But, Diane, how many Nigerians do you think are practising fraud worldwide?"

"What a question! Dan! How can I know?"

"Diane, let us assume there are 500,000 Nigerian fraudsters all around the globe. That will be a fantastic number, don't you think?"

"There certainly can't be as many as that," she agreed.

"Five hundred thousand Nigerian fraudsters are less than half percent of the population of the country. There are more than one hundred million Nigerians in Nigeria. I don't know how many millions more live outside the country. So the image we have formed about Nigerians collectively is derived from the attributes of less than half percent of the population."

He paused for Diane to digest the information.

"There are thirty-six states in the country," he went on. "Thirty-seven if you include Abuja. Abuja is an independent area called the Federal Capital Territory. If you ask many people outside the country to name only ten of those states they will struggle to mention them. I am sure you have never heard of states like Edo, Abia, Akwa-Ibom, Ebonyi, Gombe, Nassarawa, Kebbi or even Ogun which is next door to Lagos. So the states in which there is conflict are only a small percentage of the number of states in Nigeria. But when one hears of Nigeria outside you will think everywhere people are cutting each other's throats."

Diane studied his face. He knew a lot about the country. Maybe not a lot, she admitted, but he seemed to look at things more holistically than a lot of people did.

"You like the country and the people?" she asked.

"I like the people but not the country."

It perplexed her. "You like the people. But you don't like the country? How is that possible?"

He sighed, one of his famous false sighs. "Nigerians are an interesting people. The country is rich but the number of people who are poor, the percentage actually, is just not acceptable. The income distribution pattern is ridiculous, too few people with too much and too many people with virtually nothing but their empty stomachs. They are assertive, to the extent that they seem aggressive sometimes. You can catch them arguing and you will be afraid they will throw blows in less than a minute. That is their nature. But they are friendly. They joke about every aspect of their lives, no holds, no holds at all, barred. They joke about their ethnic differences, about their corruption, about their presidency, about their security services and about things some other people may consider sacred."

Rock View Hotel, Diane found, provided very good facilities and services and a quiet setting for training. So the five days went very fast. One evening Dan took her out. They hired a taxi. To 'show her something interesting,' as he put it. He took her to a place where women of various shapes, sizes, heights, colours and ages paraded with the invisible for sale sign very clearly on them. Diane knew about prostitution in Nairobi but was surprised to find it on this scale in this country. Even as a woman she was stunned by the beauty of some of the women. When she shared her observation Dan, as usual, had a philosophical response.

"Diane, ugly women can't practise prostitution. They can't survive on it. They can't get customers. Those you say are beautiful probably came into prostitution because of the number of men who were attracted by them."

The women did not hide but stood under streetlights and with people selling things right behind them. Of course as they drove round they found a lot more standing along dark streets. "I am not sure they are afraid to be seen," Dan explained. "I think they are standing in the darkness to catch those customers who don't want to be spotted soliciting the services of prostitutes."

"Like you," she teased.

"Me? I prefer those standing right under the street lights. I want to be sure she doesn't have only one ear, or one eye and that all her teeth are intact and they are not brown."

"How did you know about them? Women don't mean anything to you."

"But you're wrong. Women are one of the continent's most valuable resources. They mean a lot to me."

She hit him jokingly. "I am sure you know what I mean."

"I am sure you know I don't know what you mean because you know I have a three inch thick skull."

It was more than two years since Dan told her about his past and the encounter with the children. It was about two years since she went to Ghana. She knew that Marian had completed and she and her two friends had had very good grades and may realise their dream of becoming doctors. She knew Dan was excited about it and felt very proud of them. Strange man, to adopt his daughter's two friends and take full responsibility for their education at the tertiary level. Pursuing a costly course like Medicine. But whenever he talked about the achievement of the girls he felt only pride. In his mind and in his heart Leila and Carol were his children in the same way that Marian and Junior were.

Diane and Marian wrote each other frequently. Marian acquired an email address and they corresponded via email. She shared a lot of information with Diane, going back many times to her concern about her father's loneliness. She learnt from Marian that the feeling about the relationship between Dan and the other two girls was mutual. Of the three Carol was the closest to Dan. She would change her surname to Apeatu if it would not have been complicated. Leila kept jokingly telling Marian she was going to change her surname. This was especially after Marian successfully changed hers. Marian knew it was said jokingly but she knew Leila would have done it if it were possible. She admired Dan and would have loved to take his surname. They both knew Dan would say no. And they both knew Leila's father would be offended by it. But the truth was that she was closer to Dan than to Mr Mahama. Strange relationship between Dan and the children, Diane thought.

Marian had changed her surname back to Apeatu. She sent her birth certificate to the school and they allowed her to make the change. Dan saw it when he got her terminal report. He asked her about it but did not make an issue out of it. She told her mother later and she remarked that the next thing she was going to do was move to her father's house. Marian hugged her and assured her that she did not have such thoughts. Apparently their mother was changing and the children were warming to her.

From Dan and Marian she knew how much progress they had made in coming back together. She knew Dan's fears about fatherhood had remained only fears. From Marian's email she knew that the children gave him A grade for what Marian called fathercraft.

On the Friday afternoon as he and Diane went round the food stand in the restaurant looking at the variety of foods available for lunch Dan could not help admiring, yet again, the spirit of the Nigerians that made them provide Nigerian food in a hotel of this class. There was *eba*, made from gari. There was no pounded yam that afternoon but they had it about twice in the week. That afternoon there was *tuo,* a maize meal. For the soups there was his favourite *ogbono* or 'draw' soup and another favourite soup, *egusi*. There was no *kuka,* a slimy vegetable soup which went well with the *tuo*. But there was another vegetable soup. He knew that if he chose *eba* he would choose *egusi* to go with it but if he chose *tuo* he would choose the *ogbono* to go with it. It was not all Nigerian dishes but he was always happy to see the amount of local food available. He liked *eba, tuo,* pounded yam and another food that went very well with the *ogbono* soup, *amala*. He chose *tuo* and *ogbono* soup.

Diane was suffering with the amount of spices and had endured a painful one week, choosing only those foods she had been assured had little pepper. But she had questions about the West African concept of little when it came to pepper. Maybe they were taught by different English people, she jokingly told Dan. And got what she knew she should expect from Dan. "You're right. We were taught by those who invented and acted as gatekeepers of the English language. We learnt in history that the students of the students of those who taught us English came to East Africa."

She had known Dan for a long time now but she did not stop being amazed at how easily humour came to him.

This was Dan's sixth trip to Nigeria but this was Diane's first trip there. Unfortunately she would not have the time to see the country. Dan had described the Sultan's courts in the northern states as must see places. He had made her understand that Kano market was the place to shop for a wide variety of things. "You may not have a shopping list," he told her. "All you need to do is roam round it the first day, buying nothing. You will see so many things you want to buy that when you sit down to compose a list you will cut out many items only because of the constraint of your pocket and the fact that there is a limit to the weight of luggage you can carry."

She would not be able to see any place. She was on the plane back to Kenya only a day after the training. That was, tomorrow. So today was the final day in Abuja. Dan had told her he had something to discuss with her but they would discuss it only after the training. So they were going out that evening to a fish joint, something she had been made to understand Abuja was famous for, the fish joints. She would know what he had to discuss with her. She thought it would have to do with her career. Maybe he wanted to wash his hands off Kenya and let her take over all responsibility for training there. She was curious and anxious to find out what it was that he had to discuss that was so mysterious.

The reception called a taxi for them in the evening. They kept the taxi and as she expected of Dan, he invited the driver to have a plate too. The driver took a separate table but the server was told to add the cost of whatever he took to their bill. The fish was nice and since they gave the waitress succinct instructions about the spices she was spared the amount of spice she had been eating in the hotel. She enjoyed it. The topic for discussion was not mentioned till they finished eating and the plates had been cleared.

"Diane, you told me about you and Teddy. At a point we discussed the dilemma of having children if you did not marry. I am going to ask a very personal question. I very strongly hope you will be able to answer it but if you feel strongly that it is something you don't want to discuss with me, I will understand you. Since the last time we talked about you, have you found a fiancé?"

She thought about it, taking a lot of time. Finally she said, "No, I don't have a fiancé."

"Do you have a boyfriend or friendship that you cherish so much you will not want your life to be muddied by someone taking an interest in you?"

She immediately asked herself who it was who could have been interested in her and would not have told her but had told Dan instead. Or how did he get to know about it? She would find out, wouldn't she? But she had to answer his question first.

"I see how easy it is to be a Ghanaian," she said. "Frankly, I have a lot of questions but will can them till you give me the mysterious message. I have a friend but not the type that will make me say someone showing interest in me will only muddy my life. He is a friend, not a boyfriend or lover. I should have gone to the convent after Teddy, don't you think so?" She smiled.

He took her hand in both of his and rubbed it. Strange, thought Diane. "No, I don't think so. Diane, I remember the first time I can say positively I noticed you. It was the second day of the training in Kadoma. I noticed you stood a shade above the rest of the group, even though it was a strong group. I noticed you not as a woman to be desired but a person with a great potential to be a great leader, in a quiet, non-aggressive way. I thought you would go far in understanding leadership and that if you developed that understanding you would make a great facilitator. That was what I noticed about you."

She told herself she had rightly guessed that he wanted to talk about her going completely independent as a trainer.

He released her hand and sat back. "Four, five years later the issue I have to discuss with you has nothing to do with how far you have come since that day and how well you are faring as a trainer of potential leaders. It is something very personal, something I would not have thought possible two years ago."

Diane felt unsure what that meant. She had been sure he meant to discuss her career. He just said no. So what did he want to talk about? She was curious, very, very curious.

466

"The normal order of events in the relationship between men and women is for the man to propose love to the woman. If she accepts they become lovers over a period of time. Then the man proposes marriage. That, I think, is the normal order of things in a normal intimate man-woman relationship. We have been friends for some years now."

She drew in her breath and held it.

"We have been more than partners in training," he went on. "We have been very good friends. But have never discussed love and can't say we have been lovers. But I am not asking you to be my girlfriend. I am going to ask you if you think you will agree to marry me."

The long held breath was now released.

He looked at her for more than thirty seconds before continuing. "We have known each other for five years now? I asked myself why I was falling in love with you now. Was it really love? I have asked myself many questions. Is it love? Yes, I am convinced of that. I must have felt the strength of the feeling about a year ago. I realised a feeling, a strong feeling for you. But I did not think it was love. Just strong like for the woman, I told myself. But I had always liked you so I could not have been noticing like, even strong like, for you only at that time. Over time I thought of love but dismissed it. But the feeling persisted and I had to recognise and accept it for what it was, love. At my age. And with someone whose development I had consciously sought to support.

"I have since accepted the fact and in the last couple of months have entertained the idea of marriage with you. The idea grew till I agreed to let you know how I feel and what I think about our future together."

A minute of silence passed. He leaned forward and took her hand again. "Maybe you don't feel that way. Maybe even if you still entertain thoughts of marriage it is not with me. Maybe to you I am a very good friend and that is what you want us to be, and nothing more. It is okay with me. I shared my feeling and subsequent thoughts with you so that if there is a chance you share some warm feelings about me we can discuss what is possible. If not, we will always remain friends."

When after a long unhealthy silence in which it was clear Dan would not say anything if Diane would not say anything, Diane shrugged and said, "I don't know what to say."

467

After another long silence Dan asked that they returned to the hotel.

He took her hand but it was limp in his. Inside the taxi he noticed that she turned her face away from him and looked out through the window.

Many thoughts went through her mind. Maybe two or three years back she was convinced she loved Dan and loved him deeply. She had thought of the possibility of their marriage but had got rid of the thought because by the time she came to think of that possibility she was sure he would not have any intimate relationship with a woman. He had made that clear in very many ways including saying it. She remembered him telling her he was married to his work and that he would not have any love affair if he could not be sure that he would give the woman how much she needed of him. She knew how many of the female participants had done enough to communicate their interest in him, except say it. If he did not get the message he was certainly not interested in love. She remembered how many people, during her trip to Ghana, had shown how they worried about his single status. Being single and wanting to remain so was a message he quietly shouted to anyone who came close to him.

It had not stopped her from daydreaming. She had, despite deciding to can her feelings, engaged in thoughts of possibilities. Assuming he was ready to marry and to marry her, what would that mean for them, she had asked herself. Would she have to go and live in Ghana? You could entertain yourself indulging in make belief romance, but if it were to turn true in their case, how would she have felt leaving her home, her friends and family to go and live with a husband in another country? It was not that she was against marrying outside one's country. But she contemplated how it would be if it came to that. And how would they live their lives, both engaged in the same work? They were trainers in leadership. Would it be easy for one of them to change careers? Or would they have decided to continue to train? And if they did would they have continued to work together? Would their working together have made the bond of their marriage stronger or would they be multiplying the frequency of conflict between them? Would they carry into the conference halls domestic differences and carry back home professional disagreements?

She had not been naïve enough to propose love to him; she did not want to risk their friendship for an obvious no answer. But she knew one thing for sure at the time; it was that if he were not who he was, certain not to be involved in a love affair, she would not have had any inhibitions proposing to him. She believed he would make a very good partner. He loved people. He was a good listener. He had a very good sense of humour. He was fun to be with. He was kind and very considerate. Even after discovering the extent of his wealth during the visit to Tamale she knew he did not adore matter. Mercy told her how he paid his staff more than any other employer did and how generous he was when he gave them bonuses. She knew how much of his resource fees he gave away through gifts to the people he trained and friends he made. His first love was people and not material things, she knew. He would be the partner who would challenge you to grow and give you the push if you needed one. A wife would be free to share her worries with him knowing he would help her get over them.

She recalled the times he spent with her and her parents and how he and her parents had gotten on well. Her parents liked him, not as her friend or mentor, but as *their* friend.

So if he had not decreed love out of his life she would not have hesitated at all to tell him how she felt.

That was three years back. At the time she knew she felt love, and not only admiration for him. She did admire him, as many people who came into contact with him did. But she was sure she could detect that other feeling that was more than admiration but was so attached to admiration it was sometimes difficult to separate them. Or be detected. She loved him, she was sure.

At that time three years back she sometimes pictured them in a home of their own, with family. She would 'see' him returning home from a trip and being welcome by her and the children. At other times it would be her returning home after being away for weeks and being met at the airport by Dan and the children.

That was three years back. This was three years later. Over the three years she managed to put a lid on the feeling in her heart. She would never have him and it was pointless to cause the ache in her heart to go on and even grow.

Three years later, that evening, out of the blue came a surprising revelation. Was it revelation? She turned to look at the man who made the revelation. His head was tilted backwards, on the backrest of the seat. His eyes stared straight up. She patted him on the shoulder. "What are you looking at so intently?"

He did not answer. What had she expected of him when she clammed up on him like? Since he told her how he felt she had not uttered a word to him. In the taxi she chose to sit far away from him and to look away from him. What did she expect him to do with himself?

She returned to her thoughts and he went back to his.

Among people he had met and interacted with Diane had affected him more than he thought anybody possibly could. He liked her. As he did many of the participants he interacted with but Diane more than any of them. He liked people generally but he more than liked Diane. He liked the friendship with her and so in telling her how he felt about her and what he proposed he had tried to be careful not to threaten the relationship in case she did not want the relationship the way he wanted it.

He was eight years older than her. Even though she had made it known to him that she would have loved to marry she seemed pragmatic about her condition. She was certainly not desperate to marry, he could not say that. She had not shown any desperation to have a man in her life. She would turn a man down unless she had good reasons to accept him. The good reasons did not include her desire to marry. Nor her admitting her recognition of the receding chances of her marrying with each passing year. So she would turn him down if she felt the age difference was a barrier to healthy relationship. Or if she did not feel love for him. What he had not expected was the coldness from her. He went over what he said to see if it was offensive. Even though self-judgement was difficult he believed it was not offensive not because he was lenient on himself but he sincerely thought what he said was not offensive.

In the world of Diane reels of films were running through her mind. He once told her he was married. To his work. He once told her he was sure he would not be able to give a wife as much of himself as she would need. So he would not marry. She knew he liked her and had been impressed with her response to his encouragement for her to hone her skills in leadership development. But he liked other people as well. Like his staff. What made him come to the decision that he would have a girlfriend and even marry? What had changed? Why her? What attracted him to her? And so how was she to respond?

Another interesting thing. It made her smile. She had made up her mind to share with him a decision she had made just before coming to Nigeria. He was the only one she felt confident to share this with. She was able to share it with him because he knew about her problem and when he heard it the first time he did not ridicule her. He had taken her seriously and showed appreciation of her predicament. She knew she could always bring up things she could not mention to others, including her parents. She had very progressive parents who treated her like a sister rather than a child. But there were things she did not feel able to mention to them. There were things she would bring up freely with Dan but feel hesitant to discuss with even Harriet, her closest friend. And this issue was one of them.

She had made up her mind to raise it and discuss it with Dan after the fish meal, before they left to take a taxi back to the hotel. If he had not brought up the issue of his love for her – she sighed saying it that way, his love for her – she would have brought it up. She could not help asking what would have happened if she had told her story first. He would listen. And then when he told of his love for her and the relationship he wanted them to have, how would she feel with what she had told him? But even before then, how would her story have affected what he had to tell her? She thought over that and felt it would very likely not have stopped him telling her his feelings and his thoughts about their relationship. It sure would have made her feel bad but...

She closed her eyes. Thank God she did not tell him first. Tell him what? About Raymond. She met Raymond almost a year back. He had come to work for the NGO Diane worked for before Dan built her to go solo. He came to work for the organisation long after Diane had left but when they met he told her he had heard a lot about her, both from other staff of the NGO and people she had trained.

Like Dan he was eight years older than her, married and had three children. But he was pleasant company and liked his work. They met several times later in meetings, at workshops and in events organised by other organisations. Diane's former organisation invited her frequently – when they had events they thought she could participate in and share her knowledge and experience with staff or when they had a social event. They considered her a part of the family still and invited her to their end of year parties and launch events.

Over the nine months Diane came to like Raymond, like him a lot. And she saw from many small gestures that he would not be averse to a little closer relationship with her. She did not know what his reaction would be if she told him of her plan to have a child. And if he would be willing to make her pregnant. But she decided she would discuss it with him when next they were together. That was what she had wanted to share with Dan

When they got to the hotel Dan got down and quietly waited for her. He did not make any effort to start a conversation. He asked no questions and canned all the jokes he would have cracked about her silence if he were not the cause of that silence.

They did not have to collect their keys from the reception because the 'key' was an electronic card the size of a credit card which they carried on them. They were on the second floor and they had been walking up and down the stairs instead of using the lift. But given her silent mood this evening Dan asked if she would use the lift.

"Why should I?" she asked. "We have not been using the lift."

He said nothing preferring not to tell her why he asked about using the lift.

"You have been very quiet," she observed.

He turned and looked at her. He smiled but said nothing. Hadn't she been quiet too?

She smiled too, her first since he made the proposal to her. "It is my fault we did not talk. That is what your smile said, wasn't it?"

He stopped to say good night to her at her door which was the door just before his but she said she was coming to his room. He looked at her with many unasked questions in his look. He inserted the card into the slot and pulled it out and opened the door and they went in. The curtains were drawn apart. The window opened unto the street which was behind his room. A streetlight was opposite the window and its orange glow came through the window in very fine strands. He went over to the window and drew close the curtains. When he turned

Diane was stretched full length on one of the twin beds, lying face down. He picked the remote control of the AC and switched it on. He then picked the remote control of the TV and switched that too on.

He turned to Diane and asked which channel she would like to watch. She said she wanted to talk so he went and sat on the carpeted floor by her bed.

"Why do you choose to sit on the floor?" She patted the spot next to her on the bed. "You will feel more comfortable stretched beside me."

"I enjoy sitting or lying on the floor," he replied.

They were silent for a full minute.

"Dan, I came in because I had some questions whose answers will help me sort the confusion going on in my mind." She raised herself and supported the upper part of her body with her elbow dug into the mattress.

He leaned against a table behind him, raising his face to look directly at her. "I'll answer your questions."

"Dan, what about me makes you love me?"

This was one of the instances when being Ghanaian helped. Or when one could not help being Ghanaian by posing a question instead of answering the posed question. Sometimes when you knew what lay behind a question you could answer it better. You would know what to say and how to say it. Her face did not tell him anything. He looked at her while he considered the question and composed his thoughts. What made him love her? Hadn't he made that very clear when he told her he loved her?

He sat upright because the back of his head which rested against the edge of the table now hurt. "What about you makes me love you? You don't think you are worth being loved?"

She smiled and shook her head to signify she would not answer the question.

"I am not sure if anybody can put a finger on what it is that makes him or her love the person he or she loves. You wake up one day and recognise a feeling that had been there for a while, initially ignored, maybe later acknowledged and denied but growing. How do you go back and disentangle the web of factors built over time which initiate and feed this feeling?"

She said nothing. She lay there on the bed looking at him and expecting his answer.

"Let us start from the surface," he began. "In any relationship that is not opportunistic, in which a man genuinely loves a woman, I think she must have a minimum amount of beauty. Beauty must feature in the combination of factors that make men sincerely love women, especially to the point where they decide they want to live with the woman forever. A man can say he loves a woman and that he wants her for a life partner when the woman is very ugly. It can happen but that relationship may have an opportunistic foundation. Do you know the song *Good Morning Mr Walker?*"

She shook her head.

"It is a long time ago song. It was sung by a man called Joseph Spence. I am reminded about the song because its lyrics are about this opportunistic foundation in love and marriage. In the song a man says the girl he wanted to marry was ugly but her father was full of money. That after the wedding day he did not care what 'nobody said' because anytime he saw her face he would see a bankbook full of money."

He paused and she smiled. He knows a lot about songs, she told herself silently.

"So if you are proposing a life time commitment to a woman she must have a minimum amount of beauty. It is essential. You won't be proposing to a woman if you feel when you wake up in the morning and find her face next to yours you are likely to mistake it for a man-eating monster. You won't be proposing to a woman if you dread the body you will see when she drops her dress."

She smiled. This man should have been lecturing in a university, she told herself. But then she reminded herself that he was a teacher.

"So one thing about you that attracts me is your beauty. You are beautiful. You have a very shapely body and you have a very beautiful face. But that is the surface. What makes me love you is inside you, felt but not seen." He put his hand on the left side of his chest. "The organ inside here is made of different materials in different people. In some people it is made of clay. In others it is made of rusty iron. In yet others it is made of cheap chrome. I believe yours is made from unalloyed gold."

He paused because she exhaled very loudly. But the concentration of her look on his face did not change. She did not look away nor did the look reduce in intensity. He had an odd feeling that she was looking *through* his head.

"The first time I observed it was when you spoke about the Mathare settlement, who lived there and how precarious their lives were. And what you saw as the reason for their being there when you were where you were. Your father confirmed what you had said when we met him that evening. It is not everybody who is born into easy circumstances who sees things the way you saw them.

"I remember what you told me about you, Teddy and Jane and the fact that you still related with the two. I remember your defending Jane when I condemned her. I remember what you said about continuing to relate with them. I remember what you said about not wishing pain for them. You have a forgiving heart. I see you as a strong woman, capable of very rational thinking and action when others would be emotional. What about you attracts me to you? Many qualities. Your kindness. Your selfless nature. Your concern for others. Your calm disposition even in difficult times.

"Another thing about you which is certainly important in a relationship of the kind I am proposing; you are pleasant to be with. We have spent a lot of time together, in idle conversation. What I mean is, just conversing and not in the planning or facilitation sessions. Sitting over drinks, having meals, the evenings you stayed with me in Tamale when we were not discussing work and so on. We have spent more free time together than I have done with any woman in the last thirteen or fourteen years. And we could spend several hours together and make time go unnoticed. Because the time had been pleasantly spent. You are interesting company. One thing I will very strongly want in a long term companion is the quality of her ideas. The quality of yours is very high. You will challenge me even though you respect me a lot. I can be sure if there is a gap in anything I say or an idea I have, you will point it out or fill it. I will want in my life-long companion someone who will care for me in a positive way. In a positive way in that my interest is her concern but she is not so fanatical in her adoration of me that she will support everything I do, even what is not good. I will want from her love that is positive. You are capable of love, deep love. You admire me in a professional way. But I don't get the sense from you that your love will be blind. I can recall your advice when I told you the fear I had getting re-united with the children.

"Finally, from my perspective we are not only compatible but complementary. Enough factors to make a woman attractive to a man, won't you say?"

She continued to stare at him, saying nothing. She did not move either. He was sure that even though her eyes were fixed on him she did not see him. More than a minute went by without either of them speaking.

She lay flat on her stomach again and bent her legs below the knees backwards, towards the ceiling.

"Now to what I hope will be the final question, Dan," she said as she pushed both ends of the pillow towards the middle and raised her head on it. "The number of times love and marriage came up you were very certain you would not marry. You were already married, to your work. And that is very true. Anybody can see your work is your passion; it is your first love. And it has such a tight grip on you nothing can come between the two of you. You rightly said that if you could not give as much of yourself as possible to a wife you would not marry. You worried that because of work you might not be a good father; you won't be able to give your children as much time as they deserved. Now you have a demanding wife, your work, and children. Something must have changed significantly to make you believe you can juggle work, children and wife. What is it that has changed?"

When she paused he said nothing and they played the game of looks. She could be intense in the way she looked at him. He had never known her to be so intense.

She smiled, a wee smile, but a smile all the same. "What has changed? It is a very long way from that position to falling in love and wanting to marry. What has changed?"

"Diane, let me also ask you a question. You would have preferred that I did not love you, is it? Or would have preferred that I killed the feeling because you think it is wrong, is it? Because you think any relationship more intimate than our current relationship is wrong. Your mood changed from the lively woman I have always known to a dark mood woman since I shared my feelings with you. It was wrong, terribly wrong, wasn't it?"

She smiled, a broader one this time but with it she also conveyed the message that she would not answer his questions. Instead she said, "I asked you a question first."

They played their familiar game of looks again. This time it lasted more than the last one. But this time while he looked intensely and questioningly at her she wore a smile on her face. It was the longest smile since their last minutes together at the fish joint.

"What has changed?" he repeated her question.

"Yes, my dear Dan, what has changed?"

"What I think about life. My attitude to life. That is what has changed."

If he expected any comment from her he got none. Attitude to life was such a loaded statement, she told herself, it could mean a million different things.

When for a full minute she said nothing he got up. She raised her head and followed him with her eyes, unsure what it was that he wanted to do. He walked to the window and drew aside the curtain and stood looking outside for more than a minute.

He closed the curtain and turned to look at Diane but did not return to his place on the floor next to her. Instead he remained standing by the window and spoke. "The children changed the way I see life." His left hand was folded over his chest. The elbow of the right hand rested on the left hand, its clenched fist supporting his chin as he spoke. "You are right about what I thought and said about marriage. You are right about my worry about being available to the children. You are right about my relationship with my work."

He paused and walked towards the bed but stopped at the table on which the TV sat. He put his hands behind him to find the edge of the table and guided his buttocks unto it. He then crossed his hands on his chest. And went on. "Diane, before I found the children, I was like a highly competitive marathon runner. Such a runner is focused on the track and the finishing tape. His mind is on the ultimate prize. He is focussed on winning. He sees only the tracks and not the spectators waving at him. He may run through beautiful country, mountainous and green and very picturesque. He will see none of it. His mind will be on pacing his speed so as to give him the energy he needs to finish and to finish ahead of the others." He paused. "That was me."

Another silence while Diane tilted her head and looked at him. "The children taught me a lot. They taught me life was fuller than work. They taught me life was more than achievement. They made me discover the pleasures outside facilitation and growing people. They did not kill that pleasure, mind. I will always love my job. I will always be thrilled to hear that someone who attended any of the training has achieved something worthy for himself or herself. Has discovered the gold in them and are now appropriately priced. I will always be proud and sleep very soundly learning that an ugly duckling has discovered their true identity as a goose and has flown. My job will always be important and it will always be a source of satisfaction to me."

He jumped and sat fully on the table. "But when the children found me they also brought the world outside my window into my room. They changed me. My work is important. But so are the children. And so am I. I took time off work and went round with the children and discovered what I had been denying myself and what I can have and it won't harm the work. So I have been enjoying myself. And when I took an interest in myself I found I could do with a companion at home. You came and stayed a week with me and left me with a sample of life at home with a companion and I found it desirable. I discovered that it was not as scary as I had always thought it would be. The children and that experience with you changed me. It did not happen overnight. It is something I spent a considerable amount of time thinking about, knowing that you wear a love affair and marriage like your skin, and not like a shirt. You can remove and discard your shirt with no pain. You can't remove your skin without going through extreme pain."

He looked at her contemplatively wondering what she was thinking and wondering what else to tell her. She could see he was not done so she held her peace but he was saying things that were so fundamental she clung on to every word with rapt attention.

"You asked why you. You may now say it was you because you were the one who stayed with me and gave me the pleasure that changed me. It is like making a pass at the first lady you come across, isn't it? But no, I gave you reasons for my being attracted to you. I am sure I may not have felt the joy of having a companion at home if it were some other woman and not you. Don't ask me how I know. I don't know since I don't have the experience of some other woman staying with me. But I am sure I am not just clutching at the first woman who came very close to me.

"I thought for a very long time about a possible closer relationship with you, more intimate than the cherished friendship we have had up to now. I gave it critical thought for many reasons. One is the fact that both of us have scars from past relationships and we should be careful not to add any more." He smiled when she took the deep breath. "I have children so I come to a love affair and a marriage with excess luggage. It can cause pain all round. I had to be sure there would be compatibility all round before taking the step forward as I did this evening after we ate the fish. But that is my one-sided view of the possible relationship between us. You are sitting on the other side and seeing things from a different angle. What you see from that angle is important."

Ever the deep thinking, thorough man, she observed. She wished he would come and sit by her. She wished he would sit by her and stroke her. She wished he would sit by her for her to put her arms round his waist.

After five minutes of silence she stood up. "Can I stay the night here?"

Surprising question, he thought. Of course she could not, she should know that. "Stay the night here? Where is here? You mean sleep in this room?"

"Yes, spend the night with you."

"Where in this room? On these beds?"

"Are the two of us going to put on so much weight in the night that we will overflow one of these giant beds?"

"Of course, Diane, you can't stay the night in here."

She had moved forward and so they now faced each other. "What is wrong with sleeping here?"

"Diane, I ever told you how I felt in the evenings when we sat in the sitting room when you stayed with me in Tamale. Seeing your body covered only in the most private of places by something opaque with the beautiful outline of the rest of the body barely concealed by the gown made me greatly conscious of the woman in you. You are asking to go beyond that and lie next to me, with our bodies rubbing against each other. No, Diane. I know myself. If you sleep in the same room with me, you even say in the same bed with me, I will want to have sex with you."

Another one of those intense looks. She walked towards the door. He thought she was going to use the bathroom but when she went past the bathroom door and tried opening the door, he drew her attention to her purse which she had left on the bed. She came back for it, opened it and took out the electronic card that opened her door, zipped up the purse and dropped it on the bed and went out. At the door Dan said good night but she did not respond.

He sat on the bed she had just got up from, picked the purse and sat thinking for a while. He was in the bathroom brushing his teeth when he heard the knock on the door. He was in a bathrobe and he pulled it tightly round himself before going to look through the peephole. It was Diane. Maybe she was coming back for the purse. Maybe she had left something behind and she was coming back for it. But when he opened the door she brushed past, a lot of things on her hand. He followed her into the room and stood looking as she sorted out a nightgown, toothbrush, some creams and a shower cap. She had come back to spend the night with him, even though he said no. He could only stare at her. But she ignored him. When she started undressing he went to the bathroom, closed the door and went on doing what he had been doing when she knocked.

When he finished bathing and came out she was lying face down on the bed, the only item of clothing on her a white lace pant. He stopped momentarily in his tracks, and then drew the bathrobe even more tightly around him. She got up, smiled at his discomfort and calmly walked past him, toothbrush in hand and went into the bathroom. He had the TV on and was watching Top Cat in one of the cartoon networks when she came out, dressed as she was when she came out of her mother's womb, but for the single string of beads on her waist. His lower lip parted and he did not pretend to be watching the TV even though Top Cat was in one of his bluffing best moods. She ignored his stare and sat on the stool by the table, her back to him. She smeared her body with a cream. Even though she could see him in the mirror she did not look at him.

He was again looking out through the window, his back to the room and the bed when she put on her nightgown and got ready for bed. He turned when she went and stood by him. "It's late, isn't it? It's time to go to bed."

He turned and looked at her. "Go to bed with you dressed this way? Diane, I have been pouring out my heart to you this evening. You know how I feel. You haven't told me anything in reply. Yet you want us to go to bed together with you completely naked, as it were."

She smiled and lifted her face and kissed him on the lips. He parted them briefly and she sucked them but they separated soon. "Dan, what is there to tell you? This is the most beautiful evening we will probably ever share together. I have heard you talk several times and each time I have heard you talk I have stored what you said. I have heard the most musical words from you this evening. What did you want me to say? Oh, I have a lot to say but that will come later. For tonight I think we should merge our feelings by going to bed together. We should merge our bodies into one, what you are asking us to be in future. I thought action, rather than words, will express myself better."

When she lifted her face this time and her lips parted he closed his eyes and parted his lips too. They kissed. Very awkward for him since this was the first time in his life he was having a real kiss. He was not sure he did it right.

When he opened his eyes she was smiling at him. "You are a very process conscious person, aren't you? You made a proposal to me. The next step in the process is a verbal response to you. If the answer is yes, you know you have a girlfriend and you can take her to bed. But if I skip the verbal response and offer to go to bed with you, you don't see the response in that gesture. Why have I never before offered to go to bed with you but am offering to come to bed with you after you propose to me? It doesn't tell you anything."

When she looked into his face and smiled he responded with a small smile of his own. She was right. He was not experienced in that department called love. Maybe he was a process person. No, not maybe. He *was* a process person.

His arms had been folded across his chest. He unclasped them and put them round her and pressed her against him. She looked up. "Dan, we will talk tomorrow. Or some day. This evening I am not emotionally up to a conversation. The most valuable gifts I have received from you so far have been immaterial things. The first was the gift to discover myself and change myself. It is priceless to me. The second most invaluable, to me, was made the day you left me alone in the presence of Mary and Mr Koech, for them to watch me facilitate. I still play back the video of that day many times in my head and each time I still feel overwhelmed by pride. It was another priceless gift. The gift of this evening is equally priced, to me. Why would I accept you so easily and why would I not want to spend time and think about your proposal? We will discuss that later. But if you love me as much as you say you do – and I have no reason to believe you don't mean it – let us go to bed and celebrate it. And talk about other things only later."

He turned off the TV. But before he joined her in bed he opened his bag and hoped he had condoms that were not expired. Luckily he had. When he went to join her in bed, the gown was discarded. She had rolled down the eiderdown that covered the bed and was lying naked in the bed, face downward. He stood by the bed momentarily looking at her, from the back of her head down her back to the mounds just where the legs joined the rest of her body, down her thighs to her feet. She ignored him and did not even stir. When he joined her in bed they put off the lights. She turned and lay half on top of him. They rolled up the sheet and covered themselves.

She was the first to open her eyes in the darkness. It took a while for her to recall where she was and why she was in a tangle. It must have been morning but she could not tell what time. It took a while for the events of the night to come back and for her to agree they did happen. The pressure of another person against her was evidence that it happened. Dan did propose love and marriage to her. She did accept both. And they signed, sealed and delivered each to the other by the surrender of their bodies to each other. Yes, after many years together they did make love to each other. Now she would not have to control her urge to touch him. She owned him. She could do anything to him. Well, not anything. She would not kill him, would she? She would not do anything that would make him cry, would she? No, but she could touch him and not be afraid what he would think about it. She could roll over him right now, couldn't she?

She was aware when he opened his eyes. Like her a confusion went on in his mind which sorted itself out and he recalled what had happened. Diane accepted his proposal and he had a fiancée. Yes, she was no more a friend. She was a fiancée. But she would always be a friend first, even if they married. He was not dreaming. She did not even go back to her room. She was lying next to him. That was the evidence. His future wife was lying next to him. After more than fourteen years he made love to a woman yesterday. It was beautiful. She loved him back. Surprise.

He put a hand on her under the sheets and she responded by drawing closer to him. Her naked body against him aroused him. They made love that morning and got out of bed.

They said little to each other over breakfast and on the way to the Nnamdi Azikwe airport in Abuja. They said little to each other in the plane but they held hands as much as possible. In Diane's mind she had a lot to say but she hoped to say it some day, not that day. She was still recovering from the surprise of the event. Her emotions were still in turmoil and she could be saying things influenced by her emotions. She had communicated her acceptance of his proposal. He understood her. They would marry. There was plenty of time ahead for talking.

Dan had nothing to say. He had said all that there was to say from his end. She had accepted his proposal for them to marry. It was a pleasant surprise. He had expected her to be unsure how she felt. To tell him she liked him but was not sure of love. And to ask for time to think things over and to examine her heart. He closed his eyes and recalled the pleasures of the evening.

Whenever they rolled their heads to look at each other and their eyes met they smiled.

Chapter Thirty-One

Matriculation. There were many milestones of pride in the life of a family. The pregnancy, if the couple wanted children, was one such milestone. The child's first word would be cause for happiness. There were many milestones that gladdened the hearts of every caring parent.

Dan wore a suit, the first time Diane had ever seen him in one. He looked so executive in a suit. It fitted him. It sat on him as if suits were invented for him.

The Administration Block of the University for Development Studies at Choggu in Tamale was busy. It was beginning to fill up. Dan was directed to park his car by a guide. As they walked towards the pavilions that had been erected in the space inside the fence of the Block, Dan looked out for the children. Three of his children were going to be matriculated today. All had been admitted to study medicine. Three girls. Three girls he related with as strongly and warmly as a father could ever relate with children he loved. And who loved him.

He smiled at the different colours that milled about the place.

Diane wore the traditional Ghanaian *kaba* and slit. The dress fitted her well and she felt comfortable in it. She looked at the different styles and colours and thought, these people love colours. And they love fashion, she thought.

It promised to be a warm day. Temperatures could be in the thirties in October.

Dan looked around him for people he knew. He did not immediately see anybody he knew. Then he saw Auntie Gina. She was standing with three other women whom Dan did not know quite well. He approached them and greeted. He joked with Regina who still insisted on calling him his in-law. Her daughter was matriculating too, hence her presence. He introduced Diane, introducing Regina to Diane as his aunt.

"I have told you to stop joking with me this way because you will make death come for me," she joked. "If you keep calling me your aunt, death will think I am old and will come for me without knowing that he is taking away a woman in her twenties."

Dan exclaimed. "Are you that old? I'd always thought you were just sixteen. Your face belies your age."

Diane and the women laughed at the two dramatists.

Regina introduced Dan to her three colleagues.

Now serious, Regina said, "Dan, Marian has made me very proud. I am sure you feel even more proud. Medicine? She has done well. And her two friends making it too! They will continue to be three musketeers at the university."

They talked about children and education, bemoaning the falling standards and rising cost of education.

Dan was still standing with Regina and her friends when he saw Matilda. She was dressed in a Holland made real wax print. She had put on some flesh since the last time Dan saw her. She looked quite nice in her dress and she looked very much respectable, very unlike the Matilda he had been meeting in the past.

He excused himself from the rest of the group and walked over and greeted her. She was with a lady he did not know. She returned his greetings and did not snob him. But she did not introduce him to her colleague. He left them after an exchange or two.

Dan suggested they looked for seats. They were going to look for seats when they ran into Paulina, Carol's aunt. They greeted each other warmly and congratulated each other for their support for the children.

"You must be proud, Dan," Paulina told him.

"Three times as proud as you are, Auntie Polly. I know how much you supported Carol and she very much appreciates it. She keeps saying you did not have to do the things you did for her and you have been very gentle to her. So she could concentrate on her studies at home and at school. She said you would normally go over her results with her and that interest has been motivating to her. Yes, I am proud to see all three of them make it to read Medicine but I know you are proud as well."

"You bet I am. Because of Carol but I am very proud of all three girls."

They made to go and find seats but they were once again stopped, by the matriculating students this time. In their academic gowns they looked very intellectual. There was a lot of hugging and congratulations and patting. Dan showed them where Matilda was when they left the children to go and find seats.

It was a simple ceremony but to the matriculating students and their parents the simple ceremony was another milestone they would be talking to their friends about in future, when they looked through the family picture album. Dan took pictures of each girl as they stood to take their pledge.

Mahama and his wife and Memuna found Dan, Diane and Regina after the ceremony. There were flashes all over the grounds as students posed for pictures, alone, with colleagues, with friends and family. Dan posed with each girl alone and then with all of them. They posed with Dan and Diane and with Diane alone. The whole tribe of Dan, Mahama and his wife and Memuna and Paulina posed with the children. It was a memorable day.

The children all went home with Dan and Diane and crowded the kitchen cooking a celebration meal. They managed to get Dan out of the kitchen complaining that he made the place too crowded and he wasn't needed.

There were broad smiles all around the table. When laughter rang out it was the loud happy type.

Towards the end of the meal Dan told the children that he was going to accompany Diane back to Kenya. When they asked if they were going for a training session he said no he was not going to do work.

Marian stopped eating and looked intently at her father and then at Diane. "Dad, don't tell us that you are going to settle in Kenya."

Diane's loud laughter told the children that Marian was wrong. Diane was not surprised at Marian's reaction.

"If I move to settle in Kenya you will still be able to visit me when you are on holidays. What is your worry?"

"I won't answer you since I know that you are not moving to settle in Kenya."

Diane was surprised that Carol lowered her head and from that position looked from Dan to Diane, no doubt searching their faces for something.

While sipping her soup Carol said quietly, "I think I know what Dad is going to Kenya for."

All heads turned to her but she went on sipping her soup. Till Leila asked, "What is he going to do there? You are always the soothsayer. What is Dad going to do in Kenya this time?"

She went on sipping and looking directly at Diane. "Auntie Diane, should I tell them?"

"Tell them what, Carol?"

"Tell them what Dad is going to accompany you to Kenya for."

"Ask your dad and don't ask me. It is his secret, not mine."

Carol turned to look at Dan but he said nothing. The other children pushed her to tell if she knew.

"I think Dad is going to ask Auntie Diane's parents if he can marry her."

Cutlery were suspended half way to mouths as the girls stopped eating and stared at their father. He only shook his head and smiled. He said nothing even as they continued to stare at him.

Marian got up and walked round the table and stood behind Diane. From behind her she leaned on her and wrapped her arms around the shoulders of the older woman. Diane raised her face to look at Marian who planted a kiss on her forehead. "Welcome to the family, Mama Diane."

Diane could choke with tears. But her ordeal was not over as each of the other girls got up and came over to repeat the gesture. Carol and Leila kissed her on the cheek and each repeated what Marian said. She got up and ran upstairs to cry.

She had been lying on the bed for about two minutes when she heard the door open and someone came in. The person lay on the bed by her and put a hand over her shoulder. Nothing was said. She wept silently for another couple of minutes. Then the tears stopped. Her emotions calmed and she tried collecting herself together.

She did not turn to look at the person lying next to her but she knew who it was, Carol. Carol who had admission to train to become a doctor. She would make a good doctor, no doubt. She was very calm and very composed and in her quiet way very concerned about people. She would be loved by patients because she would give them the care they needed.

Carol. Leila. Marian. Three doctors, daughters of Dan. Her daughters? No, her friends. Her younger sisters. They called her mother but she would not be a mother to them. They did not need a mother. They needed a good friend and that was what she could be, a good friend.

She did not look at the person on the bed when she got up and went into the bathroom. But when she came out it sure was Carol she found sitting on the bed, an eighteen, almost nineteen year old young woman who looked like a twenty-six year old woman. She was short but fleshy, not stocky or plump. But it was not her size that made her look twenty-six. It was the mature look in her face.

She stood up when Diane came out of the bathroom. Diane had to stoop to plant the kiss on her forehead. She smiled. "Mama, children cry for their mothers to comfort them. When a mother cries what will a child do?"

"Exactly what you did, Carol. Just be by her. Children may cry because of pain, anger, sadness or something negative. Mine were of overflowing emotions, positive emotions. Thanks, Carol."

"Don't mention it, Mama."

"And Carol."

"Yes, Mama."

"Drop the Mama, nonsense. I am your sister. I am your friend. I am not your mama."

"Yes, Mama."

"Carol, didn't I say drop the Mama?"

"Yes, Mama, you said that. I have dropped it, Mama."

Diane looked at her. She looked back. But when she began to smile Diane was also forced to smile and even laughed aloud. She did not want to be a mother to Carol. But she expected to instruct her and she would take it. Drop the Mama. Yes, Sister. The defiant Yes Mama was the indication that she was not Mama but a friend and she could be defied.

Carol joined her.

She apologised when they rejoined the others at table. "I did not intend to spoil the mood at the table. But to hear you welcome me and to hear you call me your mother was overwhelming."

Dan leaned back in his chair.

It was Marian who spoke. "Auntie Diane, it does not matter whether I call you Auntie or Mama, I am sure our relationship will be the same. You know how I feel about Dad. When we found him we found a father, a loving father. He found children who worshipped him but you know how I have felt about him being alone. Children don't need their father all the time. They are out in school or in the world and only need him when they come home. Dad is always there for us when we need to come home or need him for anything. I have been worried, and my sisters have been worried like me too, about Dad coming home everyday and living alone without a friend, without a companion, like a buffalo rejected by the herd."

The others all laughed. Diane did not understand the reason for the laughter and so did not join in the laughter but smiled.

"You know I worried about him falling sick in the night. But it is not only about him falling sick in the night. Or at any time. We worried about him coming home and living like an orphan, with nobody to care for him and nobody for him to talk to and laugh with. Nobody to make him feel loved in the house.

"When he said he was going to Kenya with you I did not suspect any relationship with you because you supported Dad's decision to stay alone, saying he did not need a wife. I thought you shared that conviction and that you were two of the same kind, neither of you would marry. Among us we have discussed several times how the two of you would make each other happy. Right from the first time you met us you made us your friends, you loved us. It was easy to love you too. Even if you were not going to marry Dad you would be our friend, our loving aunt.

"I did not understand Dad, for a long time. I remember you told me Dad was right to be concerned about our mother the way he was concerned about her. I am not sure if our mother will ever be as close to us as Dad has been, but we have come to realise she is our mother and we owe her a lot. We have therefore been concerned about Dad, Mama and you. We know even if Mama and Dad come back together they can't be happy together. But you and Dad can be happy together. So if you are going to marry Dad for us it is very good news. A good partner for Dad. He won't be alone in the evenings anymore. We won't have to worry about how lonely he will feel in his old age. You will have a good partner too. Someone who will return your care for him. And for us there will always be a home to come to.

"We are glad first of all for ourselves that the two of you are going to marry. If you are not sure your parents will agree to your marrying Dad we are willing to come along and convince them why they should allow you to marry him."

Laughter all round the table.

Diane bowed her head. Such great words from so young a mouth. "It is a not question of if I am not sure whether my parents will agree to my marrying him. I am very sure they will not agree. I will be happy for you to come along and convince them for us."

Another round of laughter.

"We are also happy for the two of you. I am sure marriage is out of the question now for our mother. Her life has been changing. We hope it continues to change and she finds happiness for the rest of her life."

It made Diane feel guilty and it made her feel like crying. She had taken someone's husband even if they would never come back together. Listening to Marian made her look at all three children. Some moments ago, upstairs, she had considered the golden value of Carol. After listening to Marian she acknowledged that each child was a precious jewel, a jewel made from a different but equally precious gem.

On the Sunday afternoon, that was a day after the matriculation, Dan drove to Matilda's house. Junior met him and confirmed that his mother was in but with one of her friends. He went in and called her. She welcomed him when she came out. It surprised him that she did not start by asking what he wanted.

"I heard you have a friend with you," Dan said. "Can we sit under the summer hut and talk?"

She hesitated but in the end asked Junior to bring them chairs.

"Matilda, when I first thought of building this house, I thought of building it as my house for you and the children to live in. I have been thinking since then, and especially recently. You are my former wife. If the children both suddenly died in an accident would I ask you to pack out of the house? The answer is no. So I asked myself why do I call it my house." He handed her a folder containing papers. "It contains the papers concerning the house, the lease on the plot, the building design, the building permit and all property rate paid on the house to date. It also includes a letter transferring ownership of the house to you. You need to go to the Lands Commission Secretariat and change the ownership of the house from me to you. I have enclosed a cheque for you to cash and use the money for the fees they will require you to pay."

She held the papers in her hand and said nothing.

"Matilda, I have been thinking beyond the house. I could buy a means of transport for you. But if I do and you still drink the way I knew you to do about four years ago, then I am helping you to die earlier or to injure yourself seriously."

He paused, expecting a reaction to the last statement. There was none, even though she looked at him sharply.

When he was sure she would not say anything he continued. "If I buy you means of transport it will be to help you move about faster. As your former husband I owe you a certain standard of living. A higher standard of living than your present one and not a lower standard, not a standard in which you are bedridden and living the life of a vegetable. Think about it and let us talk about it later. We don't have to be married. I owe you and I want to meet my indebtedness to you. But I want to meet it a way that is responsible to you."

With the girls in medical school, Junior much happier at home with his mother and a teacher teaching him privately at home, with a happy Diane breathing rhythmically in sleep beside him and satisfied with the discussion with Matilda about meeting his indebtedness to her, he slept with a relaxed face with traces of a smile on his lips.

Printed in the United States
148682LV00001B/2/P